TALL
TREES
TALL
PEOPLE

Roy Southwell
7-16-05

TALL
TREES
TALL
PEOPLE

A Family's Struggle To Stand While Virgin Timber Falls

REX SOUTHWELL

Pleasant Word

Packaged by Pleasant Word, PO Box 428, Enumclaw, WA 98022. The views expressed or implied in this work do not necessarily reflect those of Pleasant Word. The author(s) is ultimately responsible for the design, content and editorial accuracy of this work.

Unless otherwise noted, all Scriptures are taken from the Holy Bible, New International Version, Copyright © 1973, 1978, 1984 by the International Bible Society. Used by permission of Zondervan Publishing House. The "NIV" and "New International Version" trademarks are registered in the United States Patent and Trademark Office by International Bible Society.

Scripture references marked KJV are taken from the King James Version of the Bible.

Scripture references marked NASB are taken from the New American Standard Bible, © 1960, 1963, 1968, 1971, 1972, 1973, 1975, 1977 by The Lockman Foundation. Used by permission.

ISBN 1-4141-0199-6
Library of Congress Catalog Card Number: 2004103196

Table of Contents

About the Author

R ex Southwell was born and raised in the family home that his father and grandfather built in Kalkaska County, Michigan, which is pictured in this book. He attended the one-room schoolhouse at Davis School, and later graduated from the High School in Mancelona. After serving in World War II, he and his wife, Evelyn, raised their family across the road from Grover and Grace Southwell. During retirement, Rex has kept busy with woodworking, including the building of cedar canoes and grandfather clocks. He resides in Port Charlotte, Florida, and now looks forward to summers in a cottage at Southwell Lake.

Preface

The events in this book take place between the Manistee River and Grand Traverse Bay in Michigan beginning in early summer 1906. This is a historical account of cutting the last virgin forests in Michigan's Lower Peninsula and the transition to an agricultural economy during the first half of the 20th century. This 50 years saw the heyday of the railroad industry, the development of the automobile and the airplane, the tragedy of two world wars, and the Great Depression.

The purpose of the book is neither to support nor to decry the destruction of this great resource, but to record the conditions under which the people at that time lived, their struggles and aspirations.

Early chapters are compiled from conversations I overheard as a youth or as my parents, in their older age, reminisced with neighbors. A very few things that occurred (the incident at the gravel pit for example), I was told by neighbors after my father's death.

Grover and Grace, the main characters, are my parents. This is the story of their lives and of others struggling with them through this period of time. All the stories are true to the best of my knowledge. After the mid-1920's, the narrative is drawn from my own memory. If specific details are not entirely correct, the story does accurately portray the lives of working people in those days. This is not intended to be a literal biography of my parents, but to show the life of a typical family.

Both the area and people described are real. The work they did should be credited to their memories. Where both first and last names are used, the names are correct. Where single names are used, this is not necessarily true.

To avoid confusion, one convention which has changed over the years is perhaps worth mentioning. My family always ate "dinner" at noon and "supper" in the evening. What we called "lunch" is today referred to as a "snack." Throughout the book, dinner is at noon and supper at night.

My respect for the families who struggled without assistance through "the worst of times," is far greater than I can express. The privations of my generation, through the depression of the 1930's, was nothing compared to that of our parents, struggling to provide for their families through those years.

This book is dedicated to my parents, who willingly sacrificed to provide advantages for their children that they themselves never experienced; and to other parents of their generation who had a tough childhood and struggled to give their own children some recreation and opportunities.

Acknowledgements

I wish to express appreciation to those who encouraged me to continue writing this account of the life of early settlers in northern Michigan. I wrote the first draft seven years ago and have struggled consistently since that time. Without considerable help from skilled artisans, it never would have been accomplished.

Some of our children applauded the effort, but not the results of the first writing. What I considered a book, was really a very rough draft. Some of the children and a few grandchildren encouraged me to continue.

Five years ago Fred Beard, professor of journalism in the University of Oklahoma and son of our close friends, Merle and Harriet, was so kind as to read the account. Fred assured me the manuscript contained a book, but the writing of it left much to be desired. He also advised me to introduce the characters. Fred's help was invaluable, and I thank him for it.

After I had rewritten a few chapters, Kristen Stagg kindly edited them, and advised that I change the book from the passive to the active voice. As I rewrote the manuscript it became much more a biography of my parents than was my original intent, nevetheless it does portray family life during that period, as well as the timbering off and settlement of the area. After Miss Stagg edited the entire manuscript again, (a major effort), it became apparent that I would still not be able to present the record in a readable fashion.

I then turned to Jeaneene Nooney, a family friend who had not only edited books in Michigan, but also had an intense interest in the history of the northern part of the state. Jeanne graciously consented to rework the manuscript to make it more reader friendly. Additionally, she was able to research details that filled the voids in my memory. I am extremely grateful for her help. I was ready to give up, in spite of having spent hundreds of hours trying to accomplish my goal.

Finally, this book is important to me because I wanted to represent early northern Michigan life accurately. The generation who experienced those times is quickly fading, and so I've endeavored to faithfully portray life as it was, through the eyes of one family who lived during that exciting era. Perhaps through an observation of those lives, we might truly appreciate the sacrifices that brought a better life for us to enjoy.

—Rex Southwell

Chapter 1

. . . .

Orphan's Home

G. C. was tall for his age, and strong. He had more growing to do, but at fifteen he had a build that showed the promise of the man to come. If he were on his own, he would have left by now, but there was Jack.

Jack was crying again, huddled in the shade, against the big house. G. C. bent over his small, sandy-haired brother. Other boys were tossing a ball around nearby, making the raucous sound of boys at play.

"Look, Jack, we'll get out of here one day soon. Don't cry about it, buddy."

Jack looked up at his brother, his lip quivering. The young boy's expression was enough to make his brother want to cry, too.

"I wanna go back home, G. C."

"I know you do. I do, too, but you're only making it worse by crying like this." He patted Jack's shoulder. "Tell you what, I'll make you a little promise—"

A harsh tone cut through the noise around them. "G. C., what are you doing with these younger kids? You're not allowed here! You get back with the boys your own age!"

They both looked up in surprise at the tall thin man scowling down at them. The older boy said, "Mister, Jack is my brother. He's been pretty scared since they brought us here." He hesitated, wiped the sweat from his upper lip, then burst out, "He ought to stay with me!"

The thin man said, "Go back to your own area—we'll take care of your brother!" He gave G. C. a shove in the direction of the other boys. G. C. thought his nose looked like a hawk's beak. And his eyes were small, dark, and set close together.

There was something different about this guy. He definitely wasn't like Mrs. Evans! She'd met Grover and Jack earlier that week when they were brought to the orphan's home in Coldwater. She gave them a warm welcome, encouraging them to feel "right at home." She saw that they were fed hot vegetable soup and crackers, and then took them to their room, where a straight-backed chair and a bunk bed were provided for each boy.

G. C. gave Jack a conspicuous wink as he turned away, confident that he would find a way to help his brother. He saw a flicker of hope in Jack's eyes.

After having been escorted roughly back to his quarters, G. C. looked around at the older boys. "What happens to us now?"

A friendly smile crossed the sallow face of a boy named George, and he said, "They give us three meals a day until someone who wants a strong boy to work comes to get us."

G. C. said, "Do you think they'll take my brother Jack, too? He needs to stay with me."

George, who had come to the orphan's home two months ago, didn't seem to know or care about Jack. He didn't answer the question. Then he lowered his voice, and said, "Two boys have left since I came. Wish one of 'em would take me. I never did have a real home."

G. C. noted the frail body of his new friend. If someone wanted a boy to work, it didn't look like George would have a home anytime soon. They stopped talking when they saw Mrs. Evans come into the large room. "You boys need to wash up for lunch now," she said.

As G. C. lay awake that night, he thought of Saugatuck and fishing boats. He and Jack had been happy there, free to do what they pleased, even if things weren't good at home. This was a new life, one that was unfamiliar and relied on the mercy of others. He was terribly disappointed in his mother and in his father, too. If only dad had come home when he should have, maybe mom wouldn't have gotten so lonely—and that man wouldn't have come around—but G. C. determined in his heart to move on and not dwell on the past. He didn't like thinking about what brought him here, anyway.

After a breakfast of hot oatmeal the next morning, the boys rode a farm wagon to a field of beans where they pulled weeds until noon. The ride back to the orphanage was noisy and exciting. The team of young black percherons pulling the wagon seemed anxious for their own dinner. Any boy who jumped off the wagon would be able to hurry up and grab a friendly hand to pull him over the tailgate and back into it again.

Mrs. Evans stood by the washbasins, lined up on a bench outside the kitchen door. Shaking her head at the energy of the young teenagers, she smiled. "Get that mud off yourself and your shoes. Dinner's ready."

It was stew and biscuits. The plates were emptied in minutes. When noisy chatter began to fill the room Mrs. Evans appeared again. "You worked hard this morning. Carry your dishes to the kitchen and then you can play baseball this afternoon."

G. C.'s spirits soared. Baseball was his first love, and there were enough boys here to have full teams! Two of the older boys were chosen as captains and they took turns choosing players until all the boys were picked. Each team had eleven players rather than the normal nine, but that was no problem. Everyone could play.

Each captain chose his team. They needed to decide which team would bat first, so they followed tradition. One captain tossed the baseball bat to the other captain who caught it at its center. He held the bat straight up. The first captain placed his hand on the bat just over his opponent's hand and took the bat from him. The second captain then took the bat back, putting his hand directly above the other boy's hand. They continued until there was no place for another hand. The last boy who could get his hand on the bat won the right for his team to bat first.

G. C. was the second one up to bat, and he drove the first runner in ahead of him. He was thoroughly enjoying the afternoon, when from across the fence, he heard Jack's trembling voice. Jack was either hurt or scared. G. C. quickly jumped the fence and knelt beside his younger brother. When Jack felt the warm hand on his shoulder, he peered through tears at G. C.'s smiling face.

"You'll be all right, Jack." G. C. assured him. "I'm just on the other side of this fence. The boys here will be your friends. Go play Kick the Can with them, like you did with me."

There was no time for an answer before they were interrupted by a hard voice from the same thin man who had separated them the day before. His face was as forbidding as his voice, and he carried a braided whip coiled around his arm. "G. C.! I told you before to stay in your own yard! If you come over here again, I'll use this blacksnake on you, you understand me?"

"But Jack needs me! He was with me all the time until we came here." G. C.'s voice was steady but his eyes begged for compassion.

There was no sympathy on the other side.

"Go back where you belong! We'll take care of Jack."

It was another long, hard night for G. C. He lay awake for hours, thinking. Why had he and Jack been brought here, and what could he do to help his brother? It was certain now that he and Jack weren't going to be allowed to remain together. And there didn't seem to be a thing he could do about it. Late into the night he finally fell asleep.

The weeds in the bean fields seemed endless, and the hard man left G. C. alone when he wasn't trying to be with Jack. But the food wasn't bad and afternoon baseball games were fun. If life was not of his choosing, it was at least tolerable. The boys were able to talk through the fence occasionally and after a time, Jack began to accept the separation, in spite of his longings.

One early July day a husky man, sporting new bib overalls, appeared in the dining room at noon with Mrs. Evans. The boys strained their ears in vain to hear Mrs. Evans and the stranger.

George whispered excitedly to G. C., "He wants a boy! I hope he takes me!" George obviously did not have a strong body, but the same was not true of his mind. He had quickly observed and noted more of the operation of the orphanage than anyone else had. George knew Mrs. Evans wanted families to adopt the boys, but was often required to place them in homes as wards of the State.

The man with the new bib overalls, identifying himself as Mr. Hackney, quickly made it clear he had no plans for adoption but would take one of the boys to help him on the farm. Mr. Hackney's eyes inspected the boys seated at the table as Mrs. Evans waited. After several minutes he spoke. "I'll take that blond boy beside the little skinny one. He looks like he could work."

Mrs. Evans delayed her reply as she scrutinized Mr. Hackney. There had been cases where boys had been treated poorly. She wanted a good place for her boys. The state required that she place them in homes whenever possible, but she didn't consider them draft animals and was reluctant to send a boy where they might be treated like that.

After a few moments' hesitation she replied, "They call him G. C. He has a younger brother, Jack. We think it would be best for them to be adopted together."

Mr. Hackney sniffed loudly. He had been told he could have a boy assigned as a ward of the State. Now this lady was trying to send a little child home with him. The husky blond boy looked like he could work, but Mr. Hackney had no intention of taking his little brother. He would only be another mouth to feed.

Several boys in the orphanage were G. C.'s age and didn't have siblings. Mrs. Evans wanted to keep brothers together and had hoped someone would provide a home for both of them. Again she asked Mr. Hackney to consider a different boy. He refused to budge.

Mrs. Evans spoke firmly, "If one of the boys is assigned to you as a ward of the state, you must agree to care for him well, and make sure that he attends school."

After Mr. Hackney promised to give the boy the best of care, Mrs. Evans called G. C. from his baseball game and gave him an encouraging—if forced—smile. "G. C., this is Mr. Hackney. He lives on a farm in Saginaw County and wants to give you a home. It will be a good place for you to live and you can go to school."

G. C.'s eyes brightened as he asked, "Do you have horses, Mr. Hackney?"

"Yeah, boy, I have two teams. You can drive one of 'em. My wife doesn't like horses anyway."

Mrs. Evans desperately wanted to keep G. C. and Jack together, so she urged again, "Mr. Hackney, G. C.'s brother will not be at all happy without him. Jack will soon be able to help with the work."

There was no response from the farmer. He came for one strong boy and one only. G. C. was disappointed that Mr. Hackney didn't want Jack, too, but he'd come to expect that this might happen. He packed the few clothes he owned and left with Mr. Hackney for the railroad depot. They found a seat and settled in for the long train ride. Smoke from the steam engine drifted past the window. G. C. asked Mr. Hackney about his horses but Mr. Hackney didn't feel like talking.

It was an oppressively hot evening when the train stopped at Birch Run, and after drinking their fill of cold water, Mr. Hackney and G. C. began the four-mile walk to the farm, a distance they covered in a little over an hour.

Ruth Hackney looked clearly relieved when the two walked up the driveway. She appeared exhausted. She had milked their dozen cows that morning, fed the newborn calves, and cared for the pigs and chickens, in addition to her household duties. Then she'd milked the cows again. She'd done much of her husband's work while he was away getting the boy. She wiped sweat from her brow. Her dark hair was done up in a knot low on the back of her head.

Mr. Hackney dropped into a chair, stretching his legs, while Ruth hurried to make sandwiches. In spite of her fatigue she smiled at the new arrival. "He called you G. C. What's your real name?"

A grin crossed G. C.'s face. "My name's Grover," he replied. "Grover Cleveland Southwell. They named me after the president and someone just started calling me G. C. I don't mind." He smiled at her.

"I'm not going to call you G. C. Grover's your name and Grover you will be!" Ruth Hackney was adamant. Soon she placed a large plate of sandwiches and a pitcher of milk on the table and told Grover, "There's a wash basin and towel on the cupboard. You clean up and we'll eat."

They were tired but food brought some relief. There was very little conversation as the large plate of sandwiches disappeared. When their stomachs were filled Ruth took Grover to a clean room, near the top of the stairs, furnished with a chair and a sturdy bed. A window looked out over a field of waving grain. A cool breeze lofted the curtain, and in spite of his jumbled thoughts, it lulled him to sleep.

All too soon the summer sun peeked over the horizon and Ruth's voice came in the door. "Time to milk the cows, Grover! We milk before breakfast."

Milking cows was completely new to him. In Saugatuck, when farmers brought a load of grain to town, he had helped unload their wagon and been allowed to drive their horses part of the way back to the farm. Grover loved horses! He had never milked a cow but was sure he could learn quickly.

Mr. Hackney gave him a few instructions. "Front teats first. Left hand on the one nearest you. Squeeze the forefinger first, then the second, the third, the little finger, and do it over again." It looked easy. Mr. and Mrs. Hackney each quickly drained the milk from one udder before moving on to the next stall.

Their cows stood still, while Grover's insisted on putting her foot in the pail! It became a contest between him and the cow. Finally there was no more milk and the teats remained limp in his hand. He noted ruefully that while he had milked one cow, the Hackneys had milked the other eleven. He vowed to do better tomorrow.

They carried the milk to the house in shiny galvanized steel pails where Mr. Hackney cranked it through the new Melotte cream separator. A bell tinkled to indicate the handle was being turned at the proper speed as cream came from the top spout. Grover watched while skimmed milk poured out from the spout below.

The pancakes and sausage links Ruth fixed for breakfast were delicious. An hour and a half in the barn before eating had whetted his appetite to a pitch.

The wheat field had turned from dark green to a beautiful gold and plants drooped from the weight of heavy kernels. Mr. Hackney had purchased a new McCormick reaper to harvest the grain. The machine cut the stalks of grain, packed them in a bundle, and rolled the bundle out on the ground.

Ruth and Grover tied the bundles by taking several pieces of straw, twisting them to resemble a short rope, wrapping the rope around the bundle and tucking the ends between the rope and the bundle. They carried eight or more of these bundles together and stood them up to make a shock at least three bundles long and two wide. Laying other bundles on top of the shock provided protection in case of rain. The shocks remained there until the grain separator, commonly called a threshing machine, made its circuit of the area farms.

It was after twelve when Ruth went to the house to prepare their noon meal.

A little later Mr. Hackney and Grover stopped working to care for the horses and have dinner. The horses were fed and given water. Mr. Hackney finally spoke. "The horses need a half-hour to eat, then we can get back to work."

Through the wheat harvest, every day was the same. Milk the cows, eat breakfast, cut grain, eat dinner, cut grain, eat supper, milk the cows and drag weary bodies to bed.

Although he was happy with the farm work, Grover sorely missed playing baseball. Even when it rained, Mr. Hackney found work for the teenager.

Grover observed that Ruth's workdays were even longer than those of her husband, and so he began washing dishes after the cows were milked in the evening. He marveled that Ruth remained pleasant while Mr. Hackney seemed to grumble constantly.

As autumn brought a gradual end to the summer heat, the oats ripened and the heavy work of reaping grain and standing up shocks returned. The weather had cooled considerably since they harvested wheat in July, also the heads of oats were softer and the straw more flexible than wheat so the work was quite pleasant. As Grover and Ruth gathered bundles of oats into shocks, Grover noticed children with lunch pails walking past the farm. This was now happening each morning. One day when Mr. Hackney stopped the horses for a short rest, Grover asked, "When do I start school?"

"When we get the crops harvested, there will still be plenty of time for you to go to school," he was told. "The crops have to be harvested first." Mr. Hackney shook the reins, indicating an end to the conversation.

Grover recalled Mrs. Evans saying he was to attend school regularly, but it was clearly not in Mr. Hackney's plans so he said no more.

As daylight hours grew shorter and the weather grew considerably cooler, Mr. Hackney and Grover were cutting and shocking corn one morning when a stranger came to the field. Mr. Hackney walked up the row of corn with the visitor while Grover continued to chop the stalks and carry them to the shock. After a short and obviously heated exchange, the stranger walked away. Visitors were rare at the farm. Obviously the stranger had angered Mr. Hackney but nothing was said as they continued working.

That evening after outdoor work was finished, Grover was washing dishes and Ruth was cleaning the kitchen floor when Mr. Hackney suddenly spoke. "You'll start school tomorrow, Grover, but we have to get the milking done before you leave, and we'll cut corn in the evenings."

Obviously Mr. Hackney was not expecting an answer and none was given.

Milking started a half-hour earlier the following morning. After breakfast Ruth told Grover to put on clean overalls and shirt. "Learn all you can; it will help you later," she told him. The brick county school stood just over a mile up the road and Grover walked there quickly.

The young teacher in the one room school appeared to be barely older than some of her students, who ranged from a class of beginners through eighth grade. There were fourteen students in all, with at least one in each grade, all but fifth.

The teacher greeted Grover warmly and inquired which grade he was in. Grover confidently replied that he was in the eighth grade though he hadn't attended school this year.

When it became obvious the eighth grade work was too difficult, Grover reluctantly admitted he had never attended school regularly.

The teacher was not surprised. Boys were often kept at home to help with farm work. Very few of their parents had graduated from the eighth grade, and to many of them, school wasn't that important.

"The sixth grade, Grover," the teacher said. "I'll help you, and soon you'll be able to do eighth grade work." While he was disappointed to be placed with the younger children, Grover felt confident playing baseball with the older ones during recess and lunchtime. He was determined to compete with them in the classroom, too.

Life was more fun now. Working late at night wasn't so bad when he could play baseball at school. He enjoyed the books, too, especially arithmetic. But a lot of Mr. Hackney's corn was still uncut so Grover would have to stay home from school until it was finished.

When at last the corn was all in shocks, Mr. Hackney allowed Grover to return to school. Snow covered the baseball diamond, a huge disappointment. Still, he was back in school and would try to catch up with his studies. Within a few weeks, farm work again took precedence over school and this pattern continued throughout the school year. A few weeks of school, then some urgent work was again required at the farm until Grover simply lost all incentive to catch up in school. He was too far behind.

When spring came, Grover had his long-awaited opportunity to work with the horses. They were a fine team, and there were acres and acres of field to plow. Mr. Hackney went first with his team, followed by Grover and the bays. They plowed round and round the field, day after day.

Mr. Hackney said they should be able to plow four acres each day. On cold days they sometimes reached their goal, but even Grover knew the strength of a horse is limited and four acres was more wishful, than realistic thinking. Even though the horses were stretched to the utmost, they were Grover's friends. He loved them and they responded with a friendly nuzzle when he gave them grain. It was a warm relationship in an otherwise cold atmosphere.

Mr. Hackney was never satisfied with the amount of work he and the boy accomplished. As the summer wore on, Grover began to think of leaving. He was sure there were better places to live than with the Hackneys. At the end of one especially hard day, Mr. Hackney went to the house, leaving him to care for the horses and clean the barn.

Grover finished his evening chores, talked to the team of bays, and gave them a double portion of oats. He walked into the wheat field that extended from the barn to the road. Walking slowly through the wheat, Grover rubbed kernels from the drooping heads, filling his mouth. As the grain turned to a rubbery gum, his decision was final. In the tall grain near the road he lay down and slept fitfully until dawn.

Chapter 2

The Runaway

G rover was hungry and thirsty when he awakened to a bright hot morning. He felt stiff and still tired. He longed for the breakfast he knew Ruth was preparing but he'd made up his mind. He could wash and get a drink of water in a stream several miles to the south.

He already missed the bays; the horses listened to him and gave him affection. Ruth had been kind, too. What a tough life she had. Grover felt sorry for her. Nevertheless, he was resolved not to let the past constrain him, and so he walked on.

It was late in the afternoon when he came to a farm in Genesee County. The house, barns and outbuildings were all painted white, and the rich greenery of the place made a clean contrast. There were blooming shrubs all around the large farmhouse and lace curtains at the windows. These were set off by the neat red trim. A farm like this could certainly use another hand and Grover was sure Mr. Hackney would never find him here.

As a team of horses and three men came in from the field, Grover met them near the white barn with a smile and an offer.

"I'd like to help with the work, if you can use a hand." He spoke to a pleasant middle-aged man, while noticing two other young men about his own age.

The older man hesitated, "We have a lot of work, but these two boys and I have been getting it done," he said. He put out his hand for a shake and said, "I'm Claude French, and these are my sons—Robert and Phillip. Who do I have the pleasure of meeting?"

"My name's Grover. Grover Southwell." He wondered if he should have used his last name.

Mr. French was a man who had prospered on the fertile soil through diligent planning and hard work. He looked carefully at Grover. He noted that the boy looked strong and seemed friendly, although he was dirty. "Come up to the house and get cleaned up. We'll have some supper and think about it," he said.

The girl serving supper was tall and had a winsome smile. About twenty years of age, Grover figured. The family called her Colleen and she sure talked funny. Grover wondered about her. She was obviously not a member of the French family. The meal of chicken and mashed potatoes was so delicious; he ate more than he thought it polite to do. He hadn't eaten for nearly 24 hours. The family seemed happy as they chattered and enjoyed a good-natured laugh now and then. No one asked him why he was looking for work.

After supper the boys picked up a baseball and bat and turned to Grover. "We like to bat the ball around for a while in the evening. "Why don't you come and join us?"

A good meal and now he could enjoy his favorite pastime! Grover responded enthusiastically. "I never miss a chance to play baseball!" One of the boys, Phillip, was quite a clown, and the more the other two laughed, the more things he did to amuse them. Robert was younger and not the comedian his brother was, but still great fun to be with. Grover had missed playing with boys while he'd been at the Hackney's place.

An hour later, when the three returned to the house, they were covered with sweat. They stopped at the pump; each in turn working the handle while another rinsed under the cold water and drank from hands cupped under the spout.

Grover didn't think about having asked for a job all the while he and the others played One Old Cat with the baseball. He hadn't touched a baseball since early spring. Now that the game was through, he was reminded of his situation and wondered if he would be able to get work here. Mr. French hadn't really said.

In the meantime, Mr. and Mrs. French carefully considered what they should do. It would be nice to help this young man, but money was tight. They had paid Colleen's fare from Ireland more in response to an appeal for help than to hire an indentured maid for two years. Still she was a real help. She'd agreed to work for the Frenches for two years to pay for her travel to the United States and she never complained. Now Grover was in the yard playing baseball with their sons and it was obvious that he had no other place to go.

Mr. French walked out as the boys finished cleaning up. Their sons had enjoyed Grover's company and Mrs. French had commented on the laughter as she and her husband made their decision.

French's offer was as abrupt as Grover's request for work had been. "We can use a hand through the fall harvest," he told the boy. "There's room for another bed in the boys room. You can sleep there and we'll give you a little spending money. But after harvest, we'll have to let you go. It's the best we can do."

Grover reached for his hand, and shook it firmly. "Thanks, Mr. French. You won't be sorry."

Not only was he away from the Hackneys but there were other young men who enjoyed playing baseball in the evening. He wasn't going to worry about what might come next until they got through the harvest.

It was a tired but contented young man who dropped off to sleep that night to the snores of the other boys in a large blue bedroom at the top of the stairs, dreaming of the team of bays he'd left behind.

In the morning following a hearty breakfast, Mr. French began cutting wheat. Even with three horses, the reaper was a heavy load in the hot summer sun. White lather stood out on the horses where the harnesses rubbed their backs.

The three young men set up a fierce competition and the bundles of grain were tied and set in shocks nearly as soon as the reaper kicked them to the ground. There was joking and laughter all day. It was impossible to ignore the contrast between work at the Hackneys and work at the French's. Occasionally Mr. French would tactfully inquire about where Grover had worked before coming to his place, but the boy answered evasively and changed the subject.

This arrangement worked well through September. Mr. French was pleased with the progress of the harvest, and his sons enjoyed the companionship of someone their own age. The boys could be extremely tired at suppertime but washing up and eating a good meal brought renewed energy. The baseball and bat soon beckoned them to the open field by the barn. There was Colleen, too. The girl with dark hair and a shy smile, who talked with a strong Irish brogue, was a ray of sunshine to all the family, especially the three teen-aged boys.

When the Frenches began cutting corn Grover began wondering where he would go when the harvest was done. He had nothing definite in mind, and so he resolved not to worry about the future.

Mrs. French took the horse and buggy to town to purchase new overalls and shirts for her sons and the hired hand. Sunday night, when supper was finished, she laid new clothes for the three boys on the table and said, "School starts tomorrow."

Her remark caught Grover completely by surprise. He couldn't let the Frenches know how far behind he was in school. After a short pause and with an acute pang of guilt he said. "I'm 18. I've finished school."

One early October morning, Mr. French and Grover were walking to the cornfield when a man with a new buggy drove into the yard. Grover continued on out to the field and began cutting corn as he heard the stranger and Mr. French discuss the weather and crops. Grover vaguely remembered the stranger's face, but he couldn't remember where he'd seen it before. It didn't matter anyway. Mr. French would soon be back to work.

When he looked up the two men came to the field where he was and Mr. French spoke sharply to Grover. "This gentleman says you're the boy who was assigned to a family named Hackney as a ward of the state. He said you're 17 and should be in school. Did you lie to me?"

Grover looked carefully at the visitor, swallowed hard, then spoke to the farmer whom he had learned to love and respect. "Yes, Mr. French," Grover said quietly, "I lied to you. I didn't see any other way. I'm truly sorry."

Then the months of pent-up anger rose up in Grover as he turned to the other man and spoke fiercely, "You told Mr. Hackney I was to attend school regularly, but the work always had to be finished first! There was never time for school!" He desperately fought back tears. "I want to stay here!"

The depth of Grover's feelings obviously touched the two men. The hostility in Mr. French's eyes disappeared as he and Grover waited for a response from their visitor.

The response was slow. "Mr. French, I'm afraid this happens all too often. We want to provide a good home for every young person in state custody, but it's this way sometimes."

Then, turning to the angry young man, he continued. "We can't let you stay here, Grover. You're a ward of the state until your eighteenth birthday. I'll take you back to the Hackneys, but we'll see that you attend school." The words of the officer were emphatic, but whether they were spoken to convince the young man or himself wasn't clear.

As the men walked to the house, Grover clearly remembered Mr. Hackney's anger when the same officer had informed him just over a year ago that Grover must be allowed to attend school. Grover had no illusions that he would be allowed to attend school now. Eight more months with Mr. Hackney! He would as soon have gone to prison. Turning back to Mr. French, he said, "It's been a good summer, Mr. French. I really am sorry I lied to you."

Mr. French finally understood why his hired hand had appeared suddenly in mid-summer and carefully avoided discussing his past. There was no way he could help Grover out of his circumstances, but he would not let the teen go away empty-handed. For two months, he'd been a companion for Mr. French's sons and a big help with the work. Now he was going to be returned to the Hackney's and there was nothing Claude French could do to prevent it.

"Come in the house and have a piece of pie," Mr. French offered the stranger, "We'll get some water for your horse. He looks like he needs it."

A glass of milk and a piece of pie relieved the tension as Grover struggled to control his hostility. He tried to keep his hands from shaking. He simply could not look at anyone.

The officer, meanwhile, wondered if there wasn't another way to earn a living. Most of his assignments were okay, but he would have nightmares tonight. Leaving the officer and Grover in the kitchen, the hosts went to their living room to consider and talk about what they could do for Grover.

They returned to the kitchen and Mrs. French gave Grover a warm maternal hug while her husband spoke. "You've been a good hand, Grover. There's twenty dollars in the pocket of your new overalls."

There wasn't much that Grover could say; his emotions were so strong. He wanted to express so many things, but nothing formed into coherent sentences. He finally managed to mouth the words, "Thank you," and shook hands all around. Then he forced himself to follow the officer out of the house. Each footstep was an effort. The sun had set, but the brilliant orange edges of the clouds looked like the embers of a dying fire.

The strained silence that prevailed during the buggy ride ended at last at Hackney's well, as the cool water refreshed the horse and the men. As thirsty as Grover was, he'd rather have drunk from any other well in the world.

A tight-lipped, bitter smile crossed Grover's face when he heard the officer and Mr. Hackney arguing heatedly while Grover and Mrs. Hackney were walking to the barn with milk pails. No doubt, the topic was Grover's school attendance, but Grover expected no change.

For a month he attended school regularly and with help and encouragement from the teacher, he began to make progress with his studies.

While school was going well, the harvest wasn't. Mr. Hackney grew anxious. An occasional flock of geese flew by, as the northwest wind became stronger and colder. He complained of the honking sound that they made. Corn still stood in the field awaiting harvest. It was more than the farmer could stand. He paced for half an hour until the boy came home from school one day. "Grover we have got to get the corn cut! Then you can go back to school!"

Grover muttered to himself. "An entire month; that's more than I expected. The officers don't care. They just want us out of the orphans' home."

They worked long days. If snow fell before they finished, the work would be twice as difficult. When the corn stalks dried, the sharp leaves chafed their necks. Grover's hands were rough and hard with the cold and the work. The emotional strain between the man and the boy now added to the physically exhausting field-work. Before he'd walked off, Grover had resented the fact that he was being taken advantage of. Now he was well aware that Hackney was using him as slave labor. Finally, the last shock was tied.

On Thanksgiving Day, Ruth Hackney faced her husband at the breakfast table. "I'm going to stay in the house today. When I was a child, my mother prepared a special meal for Thanksgiving, and I'm going to cook a special meal today." Her tone permitted no argument.

Mr. Hackney looked startled, hesitated momentarily, then simply turned away. The crops were in the barn; he and Grover would care for the livestock.

Although Grover said nothing, Mrs. Hackney's statement brought back childhood memories. On Thanksgiving Day his mother always made a feast! There was usually a goose with stuffing, fresh bread and buttered squash. But the best thing was his mom's pie, made from Cortland apples—no others would do!

Thanksgiving was something close to a happy day at the Hackney's. Ruth sang all morning as she worked in the kitchen, remembering the happy years of her childhood. She was thankful for her home even though life was hard. Mr. Hackney also relaxed. After the special dinner he plodded into the living room, poked the fire in the pot-bellied stove, sat back and actually smiled.

The vacation lasted just the one day. Snow had to be shoveled from in front of the doors, extra straw carried to the animals, and there was corn to shuck.

As Christmas approached, Grover thought more and more of the French's, and made up his mind to pay them a visit. There was no use asking Mr. Hackney's permission; he knew what the answer would be. Nevertheless, Grover resolved to spend Christmas with the French family, no matter what.

December 24th dawned clear. The morning was exceptionally brisk and snow blanketed the ground. When the red sphere of the rising sun broke over the horizon, it looked down on the footprints of a young man plodding steadily south on his journey toward the French's farm. The sharp cold in his nostrils made him bring his hand up to protect his nose from frostbite. The frigid air and exercise intensified Grover's hunger.

He had left Hackney's place well before daybreak and excitement grew as he thought what gift he might give the Frenches.

In the window of a little grocery store at the edge of town, a placard depicted a family holding a box of cookies. "Gingersnaps," Grover read the words aloud. "Everyone Loves Gingersnaps."

The warmth in the store was a relief. The grocer, just donning his apron to start the day, welcomed his first customer. "What can I help you with?" He asked.

"I'd like a quarter's worth of gingersnaps." Grover opened his coat as he answered. A few minutes in the store would feel good.

"A quarter buys a lot of gingersnaps," the grocer said. "They're just five cents a pound."

Grover *wanted* a lot of gingersnaps. There were four members of the French family, plus Colleen. He also wanted something to eat on the road. A grin lit up his face as he answered, "Yes, sir. I really want five pounds of gingersnaps." Grover conjured up a picture of surprised faces when he reached his destination. As he approached the large white house with the red shutters, he could barely contain his excitement.

Mr. and Mrs. French had finished preparations for the holiday, and gathered with the rest of their family in the living room, eating popcorn and eyeing the packages under the brightly decorated Spruce tree, when a loud knocking on the kitchen door interrupted the festivities. Mrs. French opened the door to reveal Grover Southwell standing on the porch. He wore a wide smile, and held what appeared to be a twenty-five pound sack of flour.

"Come in! Come in!" She greeted him in surprise. Turning to the family, she called, "Come see who's here!"

Wondering how he would be received after having been escorted from this farm to his assigned home only months before, Grover noted carefully the expressions on each face.

The teen-age boys instantly appeared, yelping and ruffling Grover enthusiastically, punching his arms and sides and throwing an arm around his neck. Colleen hung back, smiling shyly. Mrs. French gave him a hug.

Mr. French, alone, appeared hesitant.

Handing the bag of gingersnaps to Mrs. French, Grover spoke his first words. "I brought you a little gift for Christmas."

Grover clearly saw moisture in the older man's eyes as Mr. French excused himself and walked into the kitchen.

They all enjoyed a ham dinner with all the trimmings, and then Grover went to the barn to help with the chores. When they had a moment alone, Mr. French finally spoke to him. "Grover, I know you're having a hard time at Hackneys, and I know you were happy helping us here last summer. I can also see you glancing at Colleen." He blew his nose with his red handkerchief. "It's hard for me to tell you this, but you must go back and finish your time with the Hackneys. You can spend the night here, but I'm afraid I can't let you stay."

Mr. French looked Grover keenly in the eye, then turned around and with the currycomb began cleaning the neck of the horse, even though he had just finished doing that chore.

Grover was not surprised. He hadn't planned anything beyond a visit with his friends. He would go back to the Hackneys as Mr. French advised. The farmer was his friend, of that Grover was sure. The man's moist eyes spoke far more than words.

They were a happy group that Christmas Eve, feasting on the special goodies. The table was spread with homemade candy, a brightly decorated Christmas cake, cookies of various kinds, and in a prominent place in the center stood a large bowl filled with Grover's gingersnaps.

When the French boys woke up Christmas morning, Grover had already walked several miles toward the Hackney's place. His heart was heavy, but he had thought a lot about Mr. French's advice: "Swallow your pride, do your work well, even in a hard place. You'll be glad for it later."

His mind wandered as he made his way resolutely north that Christmas day. The previous evening had been great, maybe his best Christmas ever. Grover hadn't thought about his father for some time, but now he wondered about him. Tuden had always given him a gift, and they had even played together on Christmas morning, but later in the day, the saloon had separated his father from the family.

Reaching the Hackney's house late that afternoon, Grover had no fond expectations about his reception, but he didn't really care. Mr. Hackney was always grumbling, let him grumble.

When he got inside the door Mr. Hackney was so mad that he was spitting as he hollered. He had grown accustomed to leaving more and more of the chores to Grover, and now, on the holiday, he and Ruth had been left to do them all!

Grover said nothing until Hackney's fury subsided, then he said, "I took a day off for Christmas. Now I'm back." Mr. Hackney demanded to know where he was but Grover refused to answer. He would not involve his friends in this unpleasant situation.

The life that Grover so desperately tried to escape fell back into the familiar, grinding routine. Again, he wondered at the patience of Ruth, and the quiet way she accepted the long, hard days with no appreciation from her husband. How did she survive? It was the one thing that encouraged Grover to continue. If Ruth could endure and never expect a change in her whole life, he could survive until his eighteenth birthday.

Through the winter, Grover attended school sporadically. Both he and the teacher became frustrated. So much to teach and so little time to learn, and never knowing what days Grover would attend was beyond the teacher's ability to cope.

For Grover, it was something of a relief when the spring plowing brought an end to his schooling. He had tried to learn and appreciated the teacher's help, but he was finished. There was no point in fighting it.

On the Thursday evening before Memorial Day in 1908, Grover had just finished chores when his schoolteacher arrived at the Hackney's door. She politely discussed the weather with Mrs. Hackney and noted how well the field of corn along the driveway was growing. Then she turned to Grover.

"Tomorrow is the day for final tests for the year," she said. You haven't attended school regularly, but I'll let you take the exam anyway. You can do enough of the work to earn your eighth grade diploma."

Just thinking about the test scared Grover nearly witless! What would the others think if he failed? Some had laughed at him when he gave wrong answers in class. It was only four more weeks until his birthday and he had no further need for school.

"Sorry, Miss Allen, I don't want to do it."

The teacher was not easily dissuaded. She'd worked hard to get the young man through eighth grade. There remained only the test, which she was confident he could pass.

She turned from Grover to Mr. Hackney and his wife for support, but found none. They sat watching her. One last time she pleaded, "Grover, the diploma will help you with your future. Please come!"

Grover shook his head. Finally, when she could get no response, the teacher reluctantly turned away in defeat. She had
done all she could.

Each day of his final month at the Hackneys seemed longer
than the one before. At times, Grover felt that he would die of
anxiety or frustration! He counted how many breakfasts, how many
dinners, how many meals he had left at this place. He became consumed with thoughts of what he'd do when he left. Mr. Hackney
grew more agitated as Grover, in turn, was distracted; then would
attack the work almost ferociously.

The one pleasure Grover found was the time with his team of
bays. Grover gave them a double portion of oats most nights and
they seemed to show appreciation. Oh, how he loved those horses!

Chapter 3

. . . .

Tuden

The storm on Lake Superior kept all hands below deck. The crew expected storms as autumn approached, but this one was especially fierce. There wasn't much to do but hunker down and wait it out.

Tuden, the ship's carpenter, had several projects he wanted to finish before making port, but with this storm raging, he was unable to work on deck. He hadn't heard from his wife for some time, and planned to take a train to Saugatuck while the ship docked. Now he might have to fix bulkheads instead.

The ship was in port three days and he was busy every minute. There was still no word from home, which worried him. Of course, he never wrote because his wife knew where he was. She knew Tuden would come home when the layer of ice became too thick for the ships to break through. He missed news from home, though, when his wife didn't write to him.

The ship was ready to sail to Duluth and pick up another load of wheat. Still, Tuden knew he would be home soon; it was the first of November. Probably only two more trips before the ship was laid up for the winter.

The first trip was a breeze. The crew was able to work topside as the ship slipped through gentle swells. The warm autumn sun shining on their backs, together with a soft breeze, lifted their spirits. This was the kind of weather sailors loved. It brought them back year after year to the lake freighters carrying grain, iron ore, coal, and other commodities to the cities on the Great Lakes.

In the evenings, when he wasn't so pressed for time, Tuden wondered about his family. When shipping season ended this year, he determined to buy a train ticket and head straight for Saugatuck. The alcohol problem that bedeviled him in other years wasn't going to stop him this time. His sons were growing up fast. Grover was nearly a man. They could do some things together. Jack, too, was a good kid.

Tuden had never related well to Kate, his oldest child. He loved her, of course, but she was closer to her mother. Tuden would be sure to remember a gift to Kate when he went home this fall.

In mid-November the ship unloaded its cargo in Cleveland and headed for Two Harbors, Minnesota, for one more load of wheat before the ship anchored in port for the winter. Tuden should be home by Thanksgiving.

The trip north was fine, but the return wasn't. A nor'easter was building up on Lake Superior, and the waves grew strong enough to break a freighter in two. When the ship finally turned south into Whitefish Bay, the water wasn't quite so rough.

It took a full day to get through the locks at Sault St. Marie. All the freighters were leaving Lake Superior with a load of grain before ice halted this year's shipping season. Tuden thought the weather surely would improve, but the wind continued to howl. The crew hoped the storm would let up before they sailed into Lake Huron. Some of the ships anchored in the St. Mary's River, but the captain was in a hurry. He wasn't going to let a storm stop him. They would sail on.

Ice built up as waves washed over the deck. It took two days just to reach Port Huron but the captain said, "This is a good ship." They crossed Lake Huron without a problem. The ice-laden ship continued south through the St. Claire and Detroit Rivers, and across Lake Erie to Cleveland. A relieved group of seamen finished the season.

Tuden smiled inwardly as he picked up his final check. Sailing on the lakes could be rough but it paid well. He'd been away from home for eight months. Now he planned to pick up gifts for his wife and children and arrive in Saugatuck for Thanksgiving.

Before parting for the season, the crew stopped in the saloon to have one drink together. No alcohol was allowed on the ship, which made for a long summer.

Tuden went along with the crew, just for one drink.

Two days later, he woke up sorrowful and bitter to realize "just one drink" had cost him a big chunk of his final paycheck. Tuden's head hurt. He felt sick. He had looked forward to spending Thanksgiving at home and Thanksgiving was over.

As he made his way to the train depot Tuden wanted nothing more than to go home. He would think about the planned gifts later.

After the long storm, snowdrifts were piled high along the railroad tracks. The wind made wavelike ripples on the fields; the white snow sparkled like diamonds in the brilliant sunlight. This sight was a tonic to Tuden as the train crossed from Ohio into southern Michigan.

The sun had set and kerosene lamps cast a dim light through the windows as Tuden walked the few blocks from the depot to his home. Wood smoke curled lazily from the chimneys. It was surely a nice time to come home.

He turned the corner to the street where he lived, picturing the kerosene lamp on the kitchen table and another in the living room. The wood stove would shed its warmth throughout the house. He wondered how much wood was left. It was good to have enough dry wood for the entire winter. He'd cut next year's supply of fuel after feeling the warmth of the fire and enjoying the love of his family.

Tuden spotted his house. No light shone in the windows.

He looked for the friendly smoke billowing from the chimney, but saw nothing. Snow piled against the front door. The place was deserted. The last letter from his wife didn't mention any problems but it had been about three months since he received that letter. What had happened to his family?

The door was locked, but through the windows Tuden clearly saw that no one was at home. *Where were they?* His wife had welcomed him in the past, and the boys were always full of excitement when dad came home! It was true, he hadn't told them he was coming. They must have gone somewhere. Still, every indication was that the house appeared to be deserted.

As he tried to piece together what had happened, he thought of the saloon. Just two blocks away, the barkeep usually knew everything that happened in town. He or one of the patrons would know where Tuden's family went. As he walked along the street Tuden could hear the laughter of children coming from inside houses, and see the inviting glow from lamps in the windows. Now that he didn't find that in his own home, it looked even more appealing.

It took a minute for his eyes to adjust to the dim lighting inside the saloon, but Tuden could tell it was full. All his old friends were there, most of them fishermen, a few, sailors like himself. After setting up drinks for the house, Tuden would inquire about his family.

It was a friendly bunch; everyone had something to tell about their work on the lakes this summer. The group listened attentively while Tuden recounted the details of his final voyage of the season. He had been through many storms but had never encountered waves like those on Lake Superior before the ship turned into Whitefish Bay. Then there was the buildup of ice as they moved down Lake Huron. Tuden made his way to the bar.

He knew the bartender well, having spent many evenings on this same stool in previous winters. "What do you know about my family?" he asked. He looked directly at the bartender. "The house is dark and there's no sign of anyone."

The bartender raised an eyebrow as he glanced at Tuden Southwell. Tuden pressed him for an answer. "Do you know where they are?"

The bartender wiped an imaginary spot off the bar surface before answering, "Guess everyone but you knew, Tuden." He looked up. "Your wife and Kate took off. Nobody knows where. Grover and Jack are in the orphan's home in Coldwater. It must be nobody wanted to tell you."

A suddenly sober Tuden made his way out of the bar, and on towards home. When he found a window he could open, he crawled inside. Then he located a lamp half-filled with kerosene and by its dim light kindled a fire in the pot-bellied stove in the living room. After an hour of feeding the stove all the wood it would burn, the house warmed up a little.

Sleep came slowly as Tuden relived the past summer. He was alternately angry with Minerva and then worried about her. Where had she gone, and why? They had gotten along as well as most couples. He resented it when she nagged him about his drinking, but he was never mean to her.

Tuden was away eight or nine months of the year, but he made good money on the Lakes. His family was supported as well as any of the neighbors. His wife had everything she needed. Why did she leave? And where was she? He decided to find his wife and Kate first, and then get the boys. That orphan's home was no place for his sons.

The sheriff was no help. No, he hadn't tried to find Kate and her mother. There had been talk of "another man." Then one day the neighbors complained because Grover and Jack were not be-ing cared for. The sheriff had taken the boys to Coldwater himself.

When the sun rose the next morning the frost on the snow sparkled. How could it be so beautiful outside when Tuden hurt so terribly inside?

He threw himself into cleaning his house. Grover and Jack could live with him. Tuden was a skilled carpenter. He could work in Saugatuck. He didn't have to work on the Lakes, even though his love for the water bordered on obsession.

The train ride to Coldwater was only a few hours, but it seemed much longer. Then there was the walk across town to the orphan's home. *What a big place! Were there that many home-less children in Michigan?*

Tuden found a harried woman in an office and abruptly told her, "I came to get my sons, Grover and Jack Southwell. The sheriff told me he brought them here. They have a home. They're not orphans!"

Mrs. Evans was puzzled. "They were brought here several months ago. Why didn't you come for them then?"

Tuden had trouble controlling his temper. With a slight tremor in his voice, he answered, "I was on a ship on the Great Lakes, and no one told me there was a problem! When I came home, the house was vacant and the boys had been brought here. I've got the house all ready for them. They have a home with me!"

Mrs. Evans paused. The man looked sincere. Sincere or not, there was nothing Mrs. Evans could do for him now. "Your sons have legally been declared wards of the state," she said evenly. "I'm afraid you no longer have a claim to the children. They've been placed in homes where they will stay until their eighteenth birthdays."

Tuden's shock was evident. His wife was gone and now his sons had been taken from him! After a long minute he spoke. "Tell me where they are, I'll go see them. I can at least do that."

Mrs. Evans dropped her voice to a soft tone. "It's been a hard time for the boys, Mr. Southwell. If you go see them, it will be even harder. They're in good homes and they'll be well cared for. If you're really concerned about them, you won't do this."

Tuden felt chastised. He considered Mrs. Evans' words carefully. *He loved his children! How could things have gotten so twisted up? It seemed he'd had a rug pulled out from under him, only somehow, the floor was missing too. Maybe this woman was right. He'd been careless, taken things for granted . . .*

A broken man made his way back home.

There was nothing in Saugatuck of interest to Tuden now. There was work in the winter for ships' carpenters on the ocean. His own father, also a ship's carpenter, had worked on sailing vessels, many of which were still in use. There were also lumber camps in northern Michigan. Tuden had heard of quick fortunes being made from the endless forests.

He decided to head north. Although the pine was long gone from the Saginaw area, there were endless forests further north, near the straits of Mackinaw.

Tuden returned to Cleveland and retrieved his tool chest. In the top of the chest, carefully wrapped in a blanket, was his most prized possession, a fiddle he had purchased several years earlier. He plucked the strings briefly, tuned it to his satisfaction, and fondly replaced it. It had always served him well in the past when he was melancholy, but he couldn't bring it to his chin to play . . . not just now. Perhaps further down the road he'd find the music within again, but not just now.

Tuden's life took on new meaning when the train whistle signaled the start of his trip to the north woods. Whatever the future held, it had to be better than spending the winter in Saugatuck; near to memories—and misery.

Chapter 4

. . . .

Reunion

Tuden bought a ticket to Grayling. He had no specific destination in mind but he'd been thinking about the Deward Lumber Company. He'd heard a rumor that Mr. David E. Ward had acquired the vast tract of pine in a questionable manner, but the big logging camp and huge mill on the Manistee River employed lots of men, and might provide work for him.

A muscular man seated beside Tuden apparently wasn't in the mood for conversation so Tuden's attention turned to the scenery as farmland gave way to forest. When the train moved through Standish, they passed stands of timber that had been left untouched by woodsmen and Tuden's companion, who finally introduced himself as Barney, suddenly grew animated. "Look at that stand of hemlock! Nice timber to work in. A smell all it's own, and not full of pitch like some of the pine," he commented.

Tuden's responded right away. "That's why I'm on the train. I've been a ship's carpenter on the big lakes for years. Now I want to try the woods."

Barney looked at the man beside him, who didn't appear to weigh even 150 pounds. "Unless you're stronger than you look, you'll have a tough time," Barney warned him. "It's a good life, if you can handle it. The food's good, and so is the pay. But the work is hard, and it's sunrise to sunset until the snow's gone!"

Tuden smiled. "I'm quite a bit smaller than you, but well able to do a day's work. I can handle a job as a millwright at the sawmill or fix broken tools."

Barney's interest in the little man quickened, and he gave him a friendly slap on the shoulder. "Well then, come to Blue Lake with me! If you can make a good handle for a cant hook, the company can use you." Barney hesitated and frowned. "They have to be better handles than the last man made, though."

Barney Mitchell was one of the few lumberjacks who handled the logs when they were cut and piled into huge "decks," or loaded onto sleighs to be taken to the sawmill.

Tuden began to give some thought as to how he would make a fine cant hook. The cant hook was an all-around tool that the lumbermen relied on daily. Tuden had not used a cant hook, but he knew that the design was critical. A well-designed cant hook could be depended on to grab the log. If the angle of the hook or the spacing between the hook and toe was not correct, the hook often slipped, and could injure the worker. Then he decided he would think about that later. He wanted to find out all he could from Barney before the train came to a stop.

"Did you ever work for David Ward?"

"I worked at the mill there until Blue Lake Lumber Company was formed." A friend and I hired on at Blue Lake together."

"What made you move to Blue Lake?"

"Listen, you work hard at every camp, but we knew we'd be happier in a smaller camp. Fewer troublemakers there. If you want to come with me, I'll get you set up. If you don't like it, you can move on."

"Sounds good to me," Tuden said.

The cant hook handles that Tuden made fit the hands of the men using them. The hooks and toes grabbed the logs in a way that pleased Barney and his partner, Charlie Howe. "Outstanding!" Charlie had said after trying one out, and Barney said, "Now that's a cant hook!"

Tuden's repair work, commonly called "fixing," made him a welcome presence at the mill. The work was satisfying, and Tuden had a lot of it to keep him busy.

He knew it was good for him, because the busier he was, the less he thought about what happened with Minerva. He'd found out that she was with someone else and that she had a new baby. For Tuden, there was nothing but regret and pain connected with thoughts of her. He had to move on now. This wild area was his new home, and he was determined to make it work. The winters were much harder and longer than they were in Saugatuck, but before he knew it, he'd survived two of them.

The snow was slow to melt in the spring of 1908, or so it seemed to Tuden. In earlier years, he was anxious for the ice to leave the Lakes. Now he was impatient for June. He had learned that Grover lived with a couple named Hackney way down in Birch Run. June 23rd would be Grover's 18th birthday. Long ago Tuden decided that he would go to his son on the date that Grover would legally be on his own. The days crawled by like weeks.

On June 21st, Tuden got on the train from Blue Lake to Birch Run. He was eager to see Grover, yet filled with apprehension. How would he react when he saw his father? Would he understand why Tuden never came to see him? Tuden had heard enough to know Grover's life was hard and he longed to help his son to start a new life. He hoped at the very least to help him become established in some work that might get him on his feet. After a fitful night's sleep, Tuden walked the few miles from Birch Run to Hackney's farm on June 22nd. He wanted to talk to Grover alone.

From the road, Tuden saw a team of sturdy bays pulling the mower around a field of clover. From that distance, he could not identify the teamster. The horses stopped briefly at the farthest corner of the field, then started mowing toward the road. Tuden could see a young man was driving the horses. It must be Grover, he thought. I'll walk out and meet him at the corner.

It had been a long week for Grover. Each day dragged on longer than the one before. Some evenings, he thought about leaving the Hackneys again, but those thoughts were always stifled by his desire to return to the French's. He knew that Mr. French would never allow him to stay with them until he turned 18 and was through with his obligation to the state as his guardian. Grover wanted to go back to the family who had been so kind to him when he came into their yard tired, dirty, and hungry a year earlier. The final week now became the final day. The sun was bright and hot on the morning of June 22, 1908.

Mr. Hackney could hardly wait for Grover to finish breakfast. "We'll mow that field of clover by the road," he told his young ward. "Hitch the bays on the mower. I'll finish the chores. Get as much cut as the horses can stand."

Clover was not the only thing that wilted that day. Sweat stood out on the horses. Grover stopped at the back of the field to kill a horse fly and promised the bays he would get them to the water tank soon.

When they resumed mowing Grover noticed a man at the corner by the road who seemed to be waiting for someone. Farmers did not stand and wait. It must be a stranger. Grover thought, "If he wants anything, he'll come on over."

The stranger moved slowly into the hay field. No one ever came to Hackney's place for a visit; this man must want something. Grover didn't feel like chatting.

When the horses crossed to the end of the field near the road, the stranger moved out to meet them at the corner.

"It looks like my dad!" Grover was incredulous. *"It's been nearly three years! When I needed him, he didn't come. And now that I don't need him—here he is!"* The horses might not know what Grover was saying but the sharpness in his voice made them uneasy.

When they turned the corner, Tuden walked in closer to the team. He wanted to hug his son as he had when Grover was a little boy. Of course, it was not going to be like that this time. It didn't even look like the boy was going to stop the team, although Tuden saw the recognition flash in Grover's blue eyes. After a brief hesitation, Tuden said, "Give the horses their wind, Grover. I've come a long way to see you."

Grover exploded. "You didn't want to see me when I was in the orphan's home or when I was sent here to be a slave! Now, you come!"

Tuden bit his tongue. He, too, wanted to explode, but he had been waiting and planning for this meeting and he wasn't going to blow it now.

"Grover, look, I've wanted to see you all this time. When I came home from work at Thanksgiving, almost three years ago, you were gone. When I found out you'd been taken to Coldwater, I went there to find you, but I was too late; my rights as a father had been taken away! I wanted to get to you then, but Mrs. Evans told me if I really cared about you, I'd leave you alone. She said that seeing you would only make it harder for both of us.

There was stony silence as the wiry little man and his husky son faced one another. Three years had changed them both. The boy became a man and his father was no longer the confident, self-assured person Grover remembered.

Tuden was desperate not to lose this battle. His voice rose. He gripped the edge of the mower and looked up at Grover. Every line in his face testified to the remorse he felt. "I found that you were here, and it looked like a good farm, a decent place. It looked like you'd be well cared for until you came of age, Grover."

Grover stared at the ground.

Tuden looked up at his son's face. He longed to see some faint glimmer of the love that used to be there for him. There was nothing akin to that. He decided to appeal to Grover's practicality. He knew the boy must have been wondering what he would do with himself now that he was free.

"I left the lakes to work in the woods. Grover, It's a great place to earn a living! Why don't you come and see it! The trees are huge, and the air is clear!" After that impassioned outburst, Tuden waited. The silence became almost unbearable. What more could he say?

Grover's mind raced. It was two and a half years since he last saw his father. Tuden had aged considerably. As Grover looked at him, he wanted to see the man who had played with him as a child. Instead, here stood an old stooped man. Why hadn't Mrs. Evans wanted him to live with his father? Grover had so many unanswered questions.

Tuden was beginning to think that he'd made the trip only to shoulder more hurt. He took his hand off the mower seat.

The resignation in Grover's voice was heartbreaking to Tuden's ears. However, the words held a spark of hope. "These horses are my friends. I'll put 'em in the barn. I'd planned to leave tomorrow morning anyway."

Tuden nearly cried with relief. He waited by the road while Grover mowed to the back of the field, unhitched the horses, and stabled them. Grover gave them water and a double portion of oats, then rubbed the nose of each one and turned away. They didn't know this was farewell.

Ruth Hackney was in the garden when Grover stopped to say good-bye. He packed his few clothes and walked down the drive to where his father waited. There was no backward glance for Mr. Hackney, nothing Grover wanted to say to the farmer.

In the town of Birch Run, Tuden bought a solid lunch for them both and they boarded the train for Grayling in mid-afternoon.

Conversation between the father and his son would begin, only to falter. But as the hours passed and the mournful whistle of the steam engine signaled the crossing of a road or the approach of another station, the tension between the two men gradually began to diminish, though Grover was still struggling to sort things out.

The farmland and small settlements eventually gave way to more recently timbered lands. North of Standish stumps and slashings covered vast areas, and, jackpine and young poplar grew everywhere else. At times one could see for miles in all directions. They spent the night at a hotel in Grayling, a rough-and-tumble lumbering town about 15 miles southeast of Deward.

The following morning Tuden and his son boarded the train from Grayling that ran past Blue Lake on its way to Mancelona. Though it was primarily a freight train, there was always a passenger car attached. As the train moved west across the low ground between the Au Sable and Manistee Rivers, Grover got his first look at the virgin pine forest. He felt so moved by the lofty height and incredible beauty of the trees that he made a conscious effort to fix the vision solidly in his mind. The windows were open a little in the car, and it was cool and dark when the train passed under the tall, straight pines. The forest floor was deep with needles from decades of accumulation. The age of this forest was evident, yet these were living things! They saw a hawk dive for a fish in a small lake. The landscape appealed strongly to Grover. He was awed and yet challenged by it.

The land rose visibly from the river valley and the forest changed abruptly from pine to hardwood. The crowns of hardwood trees formed a high plateau with an occasional green hemlock treetop rising above them.

It was closing on evening when the train Grover and his father were on finally reached the terminal at the south end of Blue Lake. Decks of logs lined the shore. A saw carved its way through a large hemlock log in the sawmill. To Tuden, the sound was musical.

He began to relax, a smile crossing his tired face as he spoke. "When you hear that sound, Grover, all's well at the mill. Wait 'til you smell the green lumber."

Grover interrupted. "I'd like to walk back into the pines we came through today."

"A-humph-a-humph-a-humph-a-hmmm." Tuden's drawn out humph Grover remembered well. The familiarity was comforting in some small way. His father had always made that sound when carefully considering any subject. Grover remembered that he used to add a thoughtful twirl to the ends of his mustache when he muttered that sequence.

Tuden ignored Grover's request and said, "The cook will have supper on the table in about fifteen minutes. Let's clean up and eat." He wanted his friends to meet his son.

Tuden was welcomed back by his co-workers at the cook shanty door. He introduced Grover to them. Their response was friendly, but the crew had come to eat. A new man in camp was not a rarity and they could talk later. In camp, there was always food for one more, or even several more. The cook was generous with his provisions and no one left the shanty hungry. Tuden warned Grover that there was no conversation allowed at the table. A customary admonition in camp was to "Eat all you want, then move out so the cook can clean up."

After the hearty meal they walked through the camp, which was built with temporary buildings. A single layer of rough sawn boards was nailed on a framework of 2 x 4's and covered with tarpaper. The material was thin and easily torn but would provide protection from wind and water for several years.

"They call these shanties," Tuden pointed to a very rough, long building. The single men live in the "men-shanty," and eat in the "cook-shanty."

"What about the married men?" asked Grover.

"Up here, these smaller, individual shanties are for men with families. I live in my own shanty because a lot of my work is done at night." Tuden seemed thoughtful. Then, as he and his son walked toward his shanty, he looked straight ahead and said, "I can take another day off. I'd like to walk back to the river with you."

Grover nodded. He had a few thoughts of his own.

The June sun rose early. The red ball shone above the treetops as the men started their trek east. For the first few miles they walked through cutover timber, called slashings by those who saw the desolation. Treetops and broken saplings lay scattered in piles.

Tuden and Grover's spirits lifted when they crossed into uncut hardwood forest. It was magnificent! Maple trees with tall, straight trunks dominated the forest. Often it was forty feet or more to the first limb. Scattered among these were clumps of beech trees, the brilliant gray-white bark glistening in the sun wherever it filtered through the canopy of leaves.

They were grateful for abundant shade. Though the day was hot, the tree cover made their walk comfortable. Rolling hills and valleys dropped sharply to the Manistee River valley. The forest abruptly changed from hardwood to pine there. Now a canopy of needles adorned the crowns above them. Most of the trees were white pine with a charcoal gray bark.

Grover pointed to a cluster of pines with a distinct reddish tint in the bark, and asked his father what kind they were.

"Norway pines. See how they're quite different from the dull gray of the white pine trees?"

Though the Norways were smaller in diameter than the white pines, Grover noticed their tops reached the same lofty height. A breeze gently swayed the tall trees back and forth and the soft sigh of wind sifting through the needles was pleasant music to the men walking below. Grover was fascinated by the exhilarating scent of the pine woods.

When they reached the Manistee River they quenched their thirst with the cold water, then paused to admire the scene. Upstream the gentle ripples indicated submerged rocks. Slightly further the water raced around a fallen tree. No one could be immune to the stately beauty that they witnessed here. Grover would remember the scene of the river winding its way through the majestic pines for years to come.

Next morning Grover found Tuden hard at work. Tuden had to get back to his job, and he felt he'd gotten Grover here, now it was up to him to find work. Tuden desperately hoped Grover could—and would—work at the mill. The job would keep him in the North, and if they were together, Tuden was confident the bonds he so desperately wanted could be re-established.

While eating breakfast with the crew, Grover planned his next step. After being introduced to the boss, he moved confidently to his office. The boss was polite but abrupt. He had "all the crew he needed for the summer. If Grover wanted to come back in autumn when cutting and skidding began, he could probably find work. But not now."

Working at Hackneys had hardened Grover's body. He had the strength to work, and was eager to begin a man's occupation. Though he was willing to do whatever was available, it was obvious he was not going to be offered a job.

As Grover turned to leave, an elderly man, stooped from many years of hard work, rose and in a more friendly tone suggested, "You might get work at Deward. They run a big crew and men come and go all the time. You can take the train back to Grayling and then out to camp, or walk over from here. It's only ten or twelve miles. Just follow the river downstream to their mill."

Grover welcomed the suggestion. His pockets were virtually empty. He'd had absolutely no regrets about leaving the Hackneys, but he did need to earn a living.

Walking along the river, Grover tried not to let himself become discouraged. *It'll be good to stay in the timber for awhile. I can work at Deward until the snow comes, and then come back to Blue Lake.* Then, feeling resentful at the brusque manner in which the foreman at Blue Lake dismissed him, Grover grumbled aloud. "Maybe Deward's a better place to work anyway."

He thought of his father. *Why did Dad come and get me? He didn't care enough to come for more than two years. He said it was because it was better for me.* Grover shook his head in disbelief.

Not able to shake the bitterness towards his father, Grover's thoughts turned to his brother. He wondered where Jack was. He sure hoped he hadn't wound up at a place like Hackney's farm!

Shortly after noon, Grover heard the whine of the big band saw at Deward. He heard logs being rolled, and the exhaust of a big steam engine. Vapor from the engine rose above the broken and twisted trees of the slashings and Grover walked a little faster. The huge decks of pine logs dwarfed those at Blue Lake. He followed the railroad past the mill and lumberyard to the office. It wasn't quiet, but the noise level was much lower than near the mill itself.

No one noticed the young man enter the office. When a large rawboned man rose from behind a work-strewn desk and pitched himself toward the door, Grover stopped him. "I came here to work. Can you use a hand?"

The man showed his displeasure at the interruption with a distinct frown. "You ever worked at a sawmill?"

Grover answered confidently. "Not at a mill, but I can do any job you have."

The man's expression softened, although it was clear he was in a hurry. "We have all the crew we need until snow comes. It's getting towards suppertime. You can eat with the crew and bunk in the men-shanty tonight." In three steps, he was out the door.

With an hour until suppertime, Grover strolled along the riverbank looking at the decks of pine logs. All were large, and some were enormous! The time passed quickly.

While enjoying the bounteous meal prepared for the crew, Grover tried to figure out his next move. He was sure that the Frenches would be glad to see him, but they were more than a hundred miles away and Grover had virtually no money, certainly not enough for a train ticket. Determined not to ask for help from Tuden, he suddenly realized how much he had enjoyed the train trip north and walking through the timber with his father.

In the cook shanty Grover again went unnoticed. Only when the next helping of food was more than an arm's length distant did anyone speak.

With their stomachs well filled, some of the crew moved to a bench against the wall in the shade of the shanty they called home. Leaning against the wall and stretching their legs, conversation came easily as different men recalled years in other lumber camps.

It was nearly dark when an old lumberjack, seated at the end of the bench, looked quizzically at the young man leaning against the corner. "What about you, young feller? You like it in the woods?"

Grover answered slowly. "Well, sir, I need a job. I came here from Blue Lake hoping to find work. They weren't hiring. If I can find something to do, I'll stay until fall."

"Go to Mancelona. Farmers over there are clearing new land. They won't pay much, but you can make it through the summer." There was no shortage of friendly advice, as men who had faced the same problem now became interested in the young stranger.

After a breakfast of fried potatoes and salt pork the next morning, Grover began walking back the way he'd come along the railroad to Mancelona and had walked several miles before the train chugged slowly past him. He was tempted to hitch a ride on a carload of lumber but his better judgment prevailed.

His interest in the trees kept him from boredom on the long walk. He could identify beech trees since there were beech trees in southern Michigan. Maples were not like the maples in the southern part of the state. Their trunks were tall and straight and the leaves were shaped differently. Still, he was sure they were maples.

Tuden had identified evergreens scattered throughout the forest as hemlocks. These evergreens were often massive. Their limbs and needles were entirely different from the pines. Other varieties Grover was not able to identify, but they were all beautiful.

For most of the day Grover walked through timber. He had been able to quench his thirst at little streams, but he was getting hungry.

Abruptly the timber ended and he walked beside a large field of clover. To his right, across the field, stood a big barn and a nice house. A man with a team of horses pulling a mower was coming across the field. Grover smiled as he remembered, *Four days ago that would have been me. I wonder if he's as unhappy as I was at Hackneys?*

It was the first person Grover had seen since leaving Deward. He walked to the field and met the teamster at the corner.

• •

Chapter 5

Lazelles

ice team of horses," Grover spoke sincerely, paused and
then continued, "You've got a good field of hay, here. I'd be
glad to help put it up." Grover made the offer honestly,
though it was an off-hand way to ask for employment.

The teamster appeared to be about forty years old. There was
no way to tell if he was the owner or hired help. Farming was hard
work. Everyone wore the same bib overalls, and in the fields, everyone wore the same coat of dust.

The horses enjoyed a short break as the driver considered the
offer. Warren Lazelle needed help and men who would work for
farm wages were scarce.

Climbing off the mower, Mr. Lazelle walked to the front of the
team and swatted flies off the horses' noses before speaking. "This
team's done enough for today. I'll mow around to the corner by the
barn. Then we'll get some supper. Tomorrow we'll think about putting up hay." He would consult Mrs. Lazelle before anyone was hired,
but passing strangers were always welcome to a meal and a bed.

Mr. Lazelle's wife was not surprised to see an extra person for
supper. Lazelles had no children, but the meal she had prepared

was adequate to serve an extra person. When the men came in the house, the table was set for three.

Mrs. Lazelle's plain face brightened with a welcoming smile when her husband said, "This young man offered to help with the hay." Turning to the stranger, Mr. Lazelle continued. "This is my wife, Mrs. Lazelle. What did you say your name was?"

"Grover, Grover Southwell. I appreciate the invitation to have supper and spend the night. I'd planned to work at Blue Lake but they don't need me through the summer, so I was walking to Mancelona."

Mrs. Lazelle extended a hand, motioning to the wash bench. "If you walked from Blue Lake today, I'm sure you'll want to wash up."

Lazelle's farm afforded a sharp contrast to life at a lumber camp. Mrs. Lazelle's handwork was everywhere, and there were white ruffled curtains. There was friendly conversation at the table, and even coffee and cake to finish the meal!

When supper was over, Mr. Lazelle picked up a stack of pails. "We'll round up the cows." he told Grover. "Mrs. Lazelle will help with the milking when she finishes in the house."

The cattle in a nearby pasture were expecting their evening grain and responded to the farmer's "Ca-boss, ca-boss," by ambling toward the barn. A few cows lingered for one last mouthful of grass.

After waiting in vain for the stragglers, Mr. Lazelle shook his head and remarked. "It's always the same few cows that hang back." The two men walked to the field and brought the strays to the barn.

Grover was entirely at ease balancing himself on the single-legged milk stool, the seat of which was merely one short board nailed across the end of another. As he milked, he couldn't help but compare the Lazelles' place to the Hackney's. The cattle looked the same. Some were ready to calve; others had udders so full the milk leaked, and there were always a few who refused to cooperate. Each cow that entered the barn knew which stanchion was home. So much was similar to the farm he had left; yet the spirit of the place was entirely different. No strain was evident between man and wife. A smile and word of encouragement took the place of Mr. Hackney's demands and Mrs. Hackney's quiet, resigned acceptance. What it really came down to was a difference in attitude.

When the udder on the first cow Grover milked was drained, the twelve-quart pail was nearly filled with foamy white fluid. Grover saw that Mr. Lazelle was also just moving toward his second cow. With a wry smile Grover remembered milking his first cow at Hackneys. The cow had been determined to get her foot in the pail, and it took forever to drain the udder.

"That was the only time Mr. Hackney ever was patient with me." Grover mouthed the words quietly into the flank of a Guernsey cow as he picked up the stool. The cattle munched contentedly on their grain while they were milked. As each stanchion opened, the cow walked out into a small pasture by the barn to enjoy the night air. There were calves to feed and pigs' swill to be mixed before the evening's work was finished. Meanwhile Mrs. Lazelle completed her housework.

Evenings are short on a farm. The sun sets late in June, but when the men finished the evening chores and walked to the house, the large red disc was already dipping below the treetops in the west.

A freshly baked cake graced the center of the kitchen table and when the men had finished using the washbasin, Mrs. Lazelle placed a large wedge-shaped piece before each one.

The cake soon disappeared while the three conversed about nothing of importance, after which Mr. Lazelle told Grover, "Get a good night's sleep. We'll talk about putting up hay in the morning."

The bedroom where they put Grover up was simply furnished with an iron bed, a straight-backed chair by the screened window, and the ever-present slop-jar or "the pot" as it was more commonly referred to. Clean white sheets, a soft pillow and a tan blanket folded neatly across the bottom of the bed provided attractive and comfortable quarters.

Mr. and Mrs. Lazelle were preparing for bed when the tired farmer brought up the subject of the stranger to his wife. "We could use the help. The Lord gave us a good crop of hay, and the sooner it's in the barn the better. I can't pay him much, but we could sure use him through the summer!"

"He's not very old," Mrs. Lazelle commented. "It seems odd that he's out on his own. If we can help him, let's do it. We certainly can use the help! There are always more crops than we can take care of." She wasn't complaining, simply expressing a fact of farm life.

Sun streaming in the window ended Grover's much needed sleep. He rose quickly and went to the barn to help with morning chores. Mrs. Lazelle prepared potatoes, eggs, and a pork chop for breakfast. What a way to start a day!

Mrs. Lazelle poured a second cup of coffee. Her husband took a sip before he made Grover an offer. "We need help with the hay, Grover, but money's scarce. If you want to stay for the summer, we'll give you room and board and find a few dollars for you. It'll get you by until the work starts in the woods this fall. That's really all we can do."

"That's fine. If you give me enough money for winter clothes for the woods, I'll be satisfied. I need a place to stay until fall. And I'm not afraid to work." He was relieved. He hadn't known what to do, and this would give him time to decide whether to stay in northern Michigan or move back south. Lazelles' offer provided a solution, and Grover showed his gratitude.

The men worked together in the fields all day. During the evening Grover's hosts often reminisced about their journey to Mancelona, and how quickly the area had developed from an un-inhabited timber-covered region into the commercial center it had become. On Saturdays they came in from the fields at four in the afternoon. It was the Lazelles weekly break.

For a restless young man of eighteen, the evening off pro-vided an opportunity to walk down the big hill and visit a boom-ing metropolis.

Near the depot east of the railroad sat three hotels bustling with activity. The evening passenger train from the south brought newcomers to the area every day. Some were sightseers, but most arrived in the prosperous new town seeking wealth from the seemingly endless forests.

In a factory along the railroad siding a little further north, three enormous wood lathes turned hardwood logs into wooden bowls. Next to this factory, a plant made square pieces of hardwood of various sizes (handle squares) for shipment to tool companies.

At the north end of the siding, there was Wisler's huge potato warehouse, and a broom factory, which made use of the supply of straight-grained hardwood for sturdy broom handles.

The town, which was established 35 years earlier, was named for the first baby born to a settler in the area. The boom, however, began when the GR&I (Grand Rapids and Indiana) railroad pushed its expansion north to the Straits of Mackinaw. Passenger trains made two round trips daily between Grand Rapids and Mackinaw City, providing fast, dependable transportation for mail, passengers, and express shipments to and from Mancelona. There was also at least one freight train each day, hauling loads of lumber south and bringing industrial products north on the return trip.

Mancelona July 4th parade

Adjoining the hotels was an opera house. Occasionally professional players performed, though local residents provided most of the entertainment. As he walked west down State Street, Grover passed Wisler's Hardware, Schrader's Dry Goods and a drug store on his right. Across the street was Charles' grocery store and McCauley's saloon.

Between the railroad and Wisler's hardware was a small village park, complete with a bandstand. Most Saturday nights through the warm summer months a group of volunteer musicians gave a concert. When the band played a familiar song the audience was invited to sing along and Grover sang lustily. The concert marked the high point of Saturday evening for him. He loved the music and dreamed of owning an instrument.

The streets were filled with people. For most families, Saturday night was a social time as well as an opportunity to buy supplies. Others headed directly to the saloon.

On Sunday mornings, Lazelles took a horse and buggy into town to the newly constructed Methodist church. Twice they suggested that Grover accompany them, but he had never attended church and declined their invitations.

While living at Hackney's place, Grover had never gone to town in the evenings. Here, in a robust young town, excitement abounded. The saloon seemed to be the center of activity. Although Grover went there a few evenings, he knew Lazelles didn't approve. Grover appreciated their kindness and their approval was important to him. He hadn't cared what impression he made on people previously, but Lazelles were different.

Grover had been working on the farm enough to know that one task follows another in quick succession. Haying was finished. It had been a good crop and the mow was full. Now the oats were ready to be cut. Mr. Lazelle purchased the first reaper in the area and other farmers stopped by to see it work. Cyrus McCormick's invention was praised day after day. The art of cradling grain manually would soon be relegated to history. The month between harvesting oats and cutting corn provided the opportunity to clear another field. Farmers always seemed to need one more field.

An area where Mr. Lazelle had cut trees and scattered grass seed among the stumps the year before made excellent pasture for the cattle for a few years. Now the field was ready to plow. Some of the stumps were rotten enough to be pulled or dug out. Mr. Lazelle and Grover piled in heaps and burned the stumps that could be pulled. Those that were not sufficiently decayed would have to be worked around. In a few years they, too, could be removed.

The newly cleared fields were fertile. Tons of leaves from the forest had gradually decayed and formed a layer of humus-rich topsoil. Clearing the land was slow, hard work but a bountiful crop yield was their reward.

As the corn turned from green to golden yellow, Mr. Lazelle reluctantly left stump digging and turned to the year's final harvest. He wanted to cut as much as possible before frost made the leaves on the cornstalks brittle and sharp. The corn knife, with its short handle and curved blade, made easy work of cutting the stalks. Nevertheless, carrying the arms full of corn stalks with ears of corn protruding into their stomachs was heavy, ungainly work for the men.

As Grover carried load after load to the shock, his mind returned to the previous autumn. Harvesting this same crop at Hackneys prevented him from attending school. It was hard not to be bitter about the two years he had worked for Hackneys. Grover mentally erased the past from his thoughts when he suddenly remembered how different it was working for Mr. Lazelle.

In mid-September the weather abruptly changed. A bitter northwest wind brought a gray overcast sky. Low clouds chased one another over the horizon, dropping short bursts of icy rain on the men as they carried the corn to the shocks. Each shock of corn needed to be finished and tied for protection from the wind before the men could stop. It seemed each time a shock was finished, the sun broke through the gloom. So it went throughout the day.

In the evening, the wind died and the sky cleared. As the men carried milk from the barn to the house, a brilliant full moon crept above the horizon. Morning dawned clear and cold on a frosty pasture, as white as if it had snowed. The grass crunched under their feet as the men walked to the barn. This was a preview of snows to come.

The corn stalks were quickly turning brittle Leaves cut sharper and sharper into the necks of those carrying their loads to the shock. They turned their shirt collars up for protection, but despite every effort, their flesh grew raw as the days wore on. Both men were delighted on the day, one week later, when the last shock was tied.

When the corn shocks were stacked in the empty haymow on the ground floor of the big barn, autumn's harvest was completed. Mr. Lazelle said, "You've been a fine hand, Grover, a good worker. Thanks, son. I wish you all the best." He gave Grover an extra twenty dollars for clothing and he and Mrs. Lazelle bade him goodbye. Grover was free to leave and look for work, once again, in the logging camp. He hoped he'd get hired this time.

Cover Picture, Grover is standing 5th from the right

Chapter 6

Blue Lake

B risk mornings brought a flow of adrenaline, and the faint odor of dying leaves forecast winter snow, as geese gathered in flocks to fly south and lumberjacks returned to logging camps. Both the logging companies and lumberjacks were counting the days until logging began.

Waiting for snow to fall is something akin to waiting for the first pitch in a baseball game. The thrill of felling a tree more than 100 feet tall precisely in a small opening has many of the same characteristics as a ball game. This game, however, is played with axe and crosscut saw. To be able to look at the tree, decide which direction it leans, determine how near 90 degrees each way from this direction they can "pull it," then fell it where there is no log or hump of earth large enough to break it, is an acute skill. All this is done quickly, and the proficiency with which it is accomplished is a testimony to the expertise of the sawyers. This ability also determines how many logs they cut each day, which in turn determines the size of their paycheck, since sawyers are paid by the number of logs they cut.

Most of the men returned to the camp where they worked the winter before. Some, who were not happy with their previous employer, looked for greener pastures in another camp.

Grover now eagerly anticipated his first winter of working in the timber. He had confidence in his ability with horses, and he'd learned that teamsters were in great demand in the logging camps, where horses provided the strength to move logs from the forest to the sawmill. Grover was confident he would have a job at Blue Lake.

He noted the contrast between walking this November day and when he'd covered the same route in June with his dad. It was remarkable. When Grover arrived in Mancelona in June the weather had been extremely hot. The sun had beat down mercilessly and any cooling breeze was noticeably absent. Now the trees were bare. The northwest wind blowing on his back hurried him on his way and the cold wind was biting his ears. He looked down at his leather boots and the laced legs of his new wool pants. He mentally thanked Mr. Lazelle for the extra—though unexpected—money. Now he was properly dressed for work in the woods. Grover really appreciated the comfort they provided. He also believed that his telltale farm clothing had contributed to his being denied work at camp the summer before.

His excitement mounted when he crossed the summit of the last ridge and looked down on Blue Lake. The large decks of logs that had lain along the south shore of the lake when Grover walked away from the camp almost four months earlier were nearly gone. They had given way to piles of lumber, which now lined the railroad track. He descended the hill and approached camp, looking for horses. The camp needed a teamster for every two horses, and Grover desperately wanted to be a teamster.

Suddenly Grover's thoughts turned to his father. Tuden had brought him here, obviously, he'd wanted to be with his son. Grover hadn't thought about his father very often through the summer. He still felt a strong resentment, and at the same time, an attachment to the man he had known as a child. His father had aged. He would be almost 50 years old. *He looks much older than that.*

Grover ducked his head as he entered the cramped lumber camp office. Several men stood around inside the rough board building. Grover wondered if he would be remembered. More importantly, he wondered if the boss would recall advising him to return in the fall. When Grover approached them the previous summer, they had appeared too busy with other matters and barely noticed him.

This time he was greeted with a smile. "You look like you're ready to start work." This remark was more than Grover expected.

"I'm ready!" Grover responded quickly. "If you have a team of horses available, I'd like to work with them."

"We just bought a young team of Percherons that are only partially broke," The boss responded. "They're good horses but they need to work in the yard a few days before going to the woods." A frown crossed the brow of the busy man. He hesitated slightly as he looked Grover over carefully before continuing. "If you want to tackle them, you're hired."

"What's your name, son?"

"Grover Southwell."

The foreman called to one of the others just inside the door. "Pete! Got a job for you."

A strapping young blond man who didn't look to be much older than Grover walked over and stuck out his hand. Grover gave it a shake as the foreman said, "This here's Pete. He'll show you to the horses."

Pete said, "Sure ting, Boss."

Pete led the way out of the tiny office toward the barns. He had an accent, which Grover took to be Swedish or possibly Norwegian, though he didn't know for sure. Grover bent over to snatch a clump of sweet clover as they walked. They were a fine-looking team. Well-bred and well conformed. Obviously, the company spared no expense on the animals they purchased. Grover fed them each some of the clover, and rubbed their necks. They seemed fine with that. Pete didn't know of any names that the horses might have had previously, so Grover named them Jim and George.

The young horses and their novice teamster were well matched. Grover's love for horses was rewarded by the willing response from his team.

As they left the barn, Pete offered to show Grover around camp. Blue Lake was typical of logging camps at the time. It consisted of a barn for the horses, a blacksmith shop for repairing tongs, cant hooks, chains and other materials. A men-shanty provided sleeping quarters for the single men. Beside the men-shanty was the cook shanty, the center of all activity. The cook shanty contained a kitchen, dining room, and living quarters for the cook. There the crew ate three meals each day and relaxed on cold winter evenings. Across the railroad tracks stood a row of tarpaper shacks for the married men and their families. At the end of this group of buildings, and hardly distinguishable from them, stood the camp office.

The cook was a vital part of the crew. He was expected to provide good food, and lots of it, for the men. Word of the quality of the food was discussed, not only in the camp where he worked, but also throughout the area.

The shacks for married men were about twenty feet square and built over a frame of rough two by fours. Single boards were nailed on this frame and covered with asphalted felt, or tarpaper. Once securely fastened to the wall with large washers over the heads of the nails, it provided a good, cheap protection from the wind, rain, and snow. Nothing covered the open framework on the inside of these buildings. The only partitions separated the combined kitchen and living room from two small bedrooms.

A cook stove was provided in the kitchen. A heating stove, made of sheet iron warmed the living room. This stove turned cherry red each morning when it was filled with wood to warm the cold house. With nothing to insulate the building, ice often covered the water pail on cold winter mornings.

For the six months of winter, these cramped quarters were home for the married lumberjack and his family. The lumbermen and their families endured these small shacks because they were close to the work. With long hours put in, being close to home gave the men more time with their families.

To provide their fuel, the men cut and the horses skidded the dead tree trunks to their living quarters when they returned from work in the evening. Then they cut and split their stove wood each night by the light of a kerosene lantern.

The "two holer" behind each shack provided bathroom facilities. A well next to the cook shanty was the only source of water. Grover and Pete took the opportunity to get a cold drink from the well.

"What do folks do for supplies out here," Grover asked.

"Nobody needs to leave camp all vinter," Pete said. "Supplies come in on da train. Camp cook, he orders supplies every week. Wives, too, dey order supplies, but not too many choices—dey complain dey don't get the same ting they order. Dey learn how to be happy, anyways." He grinned. "Dis camp have small store in da office. Not too much dere, but plenty stuff." Pete then told Grover he had to go, and left him to his own devices.

As the days wore on, the unfamiliarity faded into routine, and Grover made some observations of camp life. Many times the legs of the men's pants were wet when they came in from work. The pants were hung around the stove to dry overnight. When weather was extremely cold and the stove in the men-shanty was fired to a dull red all the men's pants dried by morning. When the weather was milder, there was less fire through the night to dry them. In the men-shanty, since there were many more pairs of pants to dry than there were stoves to hang them around, some of the men were forced to go to the woods the next morning wearing pants that were damp.

A married man with his own stove could be assured of dry pants each day.

Most men were largely happy with their work. It was strenuous but clean labor. The smell of freshly cut wood was stimulating. Pine, of course, smelled like turpentine. Hemlock had an odor like no other. Many considered it the most pleasant of all.

Since there was nowhere to spend money in the winter, men were able to save almost all they earned for worthwhile purposes. Usually their dream was to buy land, which was normally sold for a reasonable price after the timber had been removed.

A different group of lumberjacks saved their stake until spring when they went to the saloon and "lived it up" until the money was gone. One man said, "It sure lasted quick!"

Year after year most sawyers returned to camp with the same partner. If they weren't compatible, the end of the work year was the end of the relationship. Only rarely did friction cause them to part before the winter's work was finished. Personalities—as well as physical strength—kept men together. Nowhere was compatibility more important than between two men on opposite ends of a crosscut saw.

Even as the farmers' goal was to cut a hundred shocks of corn in a day, the sawyers constantly counted toward the hundredth log. Only a few strong, skillful men ever made this quota. Most merely worked toward that end.

The teamster fed and harnessed his horses in the morning before going to his own breakfast. When the other men began work, his horses were also ready. In the evening the teamster fed and watered the horses, cleaned the animals and their harnesses, and added fresh straw to their stalls.

The long awaited snowfall came in mid November. Sawyers had already begun work. Now the fresh clean snow made it possible for the men to skid the logs.

Grover was emotionally drawn to this work. He liked the constant challenge and variety and learned quickly. Some "tricks of the trade" he learned from watching; others he was taught as the need arose.

When a tree fell, a limb on the bottom of the log could be driven into the ground and make the log impossible to skid. The skidding tongs, however, could be hooked in a way so the log would roll enough to chop off the limb, "hooking a roll." Every teamster needed a sharp axe.

The work was hard, but the pay was good. Now Grover was able to begin saving money.

On an occasional Sunday, Grover spent time with Tuden. Since Grover worked days and his father made repairs to the mill at night, there was little time for the father and son to be together. This separation grieved Tuden, although Grover really didn't miss his father much. Tuden had worked on the lakes during all the summers of Grover's boyhood, returning only a few months each winter. Grover still had trouble accepting his and Jack's placement in the orphans' home and spending those hard years with the Hackneys.

The winter passed quickly and when logging was done for the year Grover followed the other single men to Mancelona. He had money to spend, and his new friends spent theirs freely. Grover, now accepted among the lumberjacks, shared his time and money with the others until one spring morning he awoke with a start to realize he was nearly broke!

Events of the past year flooded Grover's mind. He had left the Hackneys, worked through the summer on Lazelles' farm, and then moved to the logging camp, which he had thoroughly enjoyed. Jim and George, his constant companions, were good horses and he enjoyed working with them. Some days had been extremely cold, but hard work and woolen clothes kept him warm. Most of all, his work was appreciated. His heart sunk as he considered working on a farm for another summer. Farm work could be interesting, but it would cost almost an entire summer's income just to buy wool clothes for the next winter.

Once more discouraged, Grover trudged up the hill to Lazelles' in the spring of 1909. If Mr. Lazelle needed a hand for the summer, Grover would be glad to help him while he made some decisions about his own future.

Mr. Lazelle was pleasantly surprised to see Grover again. Yes, he needed a hand for the summer and, yes he was willing to hire the young man again.

Grover didn't find the work as enjoyable as he did the previous year. Both Mr. and Mrs. Lazelle were nice, but after logging wages the previous winter, it seemed he was wasting his time. Lying awake on hot summer nights, he resolved next spring would be different.

Through the long summer, Grover was a frequent visitor to the bandstand in the little park in Mancelona on Saturday nights. He loved the music, and occasionally someone recited a poem. Poetry intrigued him, especially "The Village Blacksmith" by Longfellow. Grover memorized most of the poem the first time he heard it.

It was said "Potatoes were king," since potatoes provided most of the agricultural income in the area. Mr. Lazelle had a large field of potatoes. Many hot days found Grover walking up and down the long rows carrying a three-gallon sprayer, looking for hills of potatoes covered with bugs. He sprayed the bugs, pumped up the sprayer, and continued along the row. Bugs multiplied fast, but Grover kept them under control.

In September the potato vines ripened. Mr. Lazelle hired several men to help dig the smooth white tubers. With six-tined pitchforks, the men rooted out the potatoes. Moving backward, they each dug two rows, shook the sand from the potatoes, separated them from the tops, and left them for children to pick up. Children were given a two-week potato vacation from school in order to help harvest the crop. Gathering the potatoes into bushel crates was back breaking work, but the children usually earned enough to buy their winter clothes.

Each evening Mr. Lazelle and Grover loaded the crates on the wagon and took them to Wisler's potato warehouse in town. Mr. Lazelle wanted to clear more land for potatoes the next year and Grover agreed to help dig stumps until Blue Lake hired their crew for the winter.

The tall trees, the odor of the freshly cut wood, the friendly competition among the crews, all worked like a magnet pulling the crews back to camp year after year. Grover was no exception; he was anxious to begin work in the timber again.

In early November, snow again blanketed fields and forests. The green of summer had given way to autumn's color, which in turn, changed to a dull brown. The frost on the snow sparkled like diamonds in the sunlight, as Grover walked the dozen miles back to Blue Lake.

In camp the excitement built as crews drifted in. The camp boss was expecting Grover, and he welcomed his young teamster by mentioning the horses. "Jim and George are restless after an easy summer, but a few days' skidding will take the edge off. See if they remember you."

Grover took the horses some oats, curried their manes, and rubbed their necks. Soft muzzles against his shoulder assured him he was not forgotten.

When he went to the forest with Jim and George the first morning, three other teams were already working in a small area. The voices of all the teamsters were audible. Grover was extremely pleased—and surprised—that the horses remembered his voice and ignored the commands of the other teamsters. It was almost as though he and the horses had never been separated.

The "Gee," "Haw," "Giddyap" and "Whoa" was obeyed more according to the tone of the teamster's voice than his pronunciation of the word. When Grover spoke a soft, "Easy now" his team cautiously eased into the load. A sharp command of any kind caused their ears to prick up, and they treaded nervously. Grover loved the high-spirited Percherons, and preferred them to Belgians or Clydesdales, though all were common in the woods.

When loading logs on the sleigh, a skid (a pole approximately six inches in diameter and 12 feet long) was placed at each end of the sleigh. This was adequate to hold the weight of the log. A notch was then chopped in one end of the skid to keep it from slipping, and the notch placed on the bunk (side of the sleigh). The other end sloped down to the ground, and the logs were rolled up the skids and onto the sleigh.

To roll the logs up the skids, a long chain (decking line) with a large hook (swamp hook), made especially for this purpose, was hooked to the bunk of the sleigh. The chain was pulled under the log, then over the log and across the sleigh. The team of horses, pulling the chain, rolled the log up the skids and onto the sleigh. This process was called, "cross hauling."

At other times the logs were skidded to a central area and placed in large piles or decks, hence the name "decking line."

Often the log did not go up the skids evenly. Grabbing, and holding its leading end with a cant hook held it until the log rolled evenly up the skids.

Use of a cant hook called for men who were both quick and strong. The log needed to be kept nearly straight as it rolled up skids. If either end was allowed to get very far ahead of the other, it could not be straightened and the log had to be allowed to roll back to the ground, re-hooked, and the process repeated.

Several days passed with one team of horses not being used. A man who was new to the area was hired as the final teamster. He was a muscular man, who talked loud and long into the evening about his experience with horses and the amount of work he could accomplish.

The next morning he carried a long blacksnake whip to the woods. All went well until mid-morning. The old horses, which had not yet become hardened to the work, grew very tired. When they reached the skidway, the teamster brutally flogged them with his blacksnake.

He stood his whip in the snow while he unhooked the log, then turned the horses toward the standing timber and looked for his black snake.

Not at all impressed with such treatment of the horses was Barney Mitchell's partner, Charley Howe, who had picked up the whip and stood it in the snow next to him.

When he didn't find his whip where he had placed it, the teamster bellowed, "Where's my blacksnake?"

Charlie calmly replied, "It's standing right here." He said it as a challenge.

The teamster took two steps toward Charlie. For a long minute, the two men faced each other, until the new teamster turned and left. The whip and horses were forgotten. Stopping briefly at the men-shanty for his belongings, he left the camp.

Men were usually left to defend themselves, but many a lumberjack, though not a teamster himself, would not condone harsh treatment of a horse.

Often in the evenings a group of men gathered at the cook shanty where they played various musical instruments. Charlie Howe played a violin and Tuden brought his fiddle when work allowed. There were two banjos in the group, a guitar and, much to Grover's delight, a mandolin. The mandolin called a "potato bug" captured Grover's attention. He loved that potato bug! This was the instrument he wanted to play.

When the month ended, Grover received his first paycheck and immediately ordered a mandolin from the Sears and Roebuck

Grover at Blue Lake Lumber Yard.

catalog. Two weeks later his package arrived. Grover's first thought was of his father. Tuden played the fiddle so possibly he could help Grover with the mandolin.

Tuden hid his surprise the evening Grover came over to excitedly show off his new "potato bug." It tickled him that Grover seemed to have caught or inherited his fascination with music.

Tuden had been disappointed the previous winter to have almost no contact with his son. Although he was glad Grover was getting along well, Tuden had been alone for a long time and yearned for a closer relationship. Perhaps this little potato bug would be a way for that to happen.

Grover listened carefully, mentally recording the notes and repeating them on his mandolin. In a few weeks he brought his prized mandolin to the mess hall and began playing with the others in the evening, softly at first, then with growing confidence.

During these evenings of relaxation, the tension between Tuden and his son gradually eased. Music began to narrow the gulf between them. Often Grover brought his mandolin to Tuden's shanty in the evening for help as he picked his way through an unfamiliar song. Grover especially loved the soft music in three-quarter time. "Over the Waves" was his favorite song.

It was an enjoyable winter for Grover. He had a team of Percherons, his mandolin, and music in the evening, and an opportunity to work in the beautiful forest. He was in no hurry for the spring thaw, but when March snow squalls gave way to bright April days, Grover was glad to see an end to winter.

The following summer Grover worked at Blue Lake piling lumber.

Boards from the sawmill were loaded on horse-drawn carts and pulled down the tram (an elevated road made from rough lumber) to be "stickered up" (put in piles) along the tram.

To provide air for the lumber to dry, narrow strips or stickers were laid across each layer of boards at two-foot intervals before covering them with the next layer of boards. This was continued until the piles reached a height of twelve feet.

Two men handed the boards to two others who carefully placed them on the pile and arranged the stickers. Leather aprons were necessary to protect clothing from the rough lumber. The work was hard, but the boards were clean, and the smell of the fresh-cut lumber was pleasing.

Grover lay alone in his bunk looking out the small window at the stars after a particularly good evening of music and laughter. He suddenly realized that he was happy. He was steadily employed and developing a strong body. He had a good relationship with the other men in the crew, and was even beginning to grow fond of Tuden.

Grover's desire for music seemed insatiable. Tuden had a vast repertoire of songs he could play on his violin and was pleased his son had an ear for music and accompanied Tuden with his mandolin. Occasionally they played cards with the other men. A few books were available, but for Tuden and Grover, the music provided both recreation and an outlet for the soul.

Chapter 7

Fire!

On a hot August morning in 1910, the crew at Blue Lake awoke to hear a grave tone in the conversation between the cook and his wife. When they arose, they could see a dull red glow hovering over the entire eastern skyline. The normally quiet breakfast time buzzed with conversation. The men knew the strangely colored sky could only be caused by a fire. Because of slashings that were left after the timber was cut, fire was a constant threat. The fine twigs from the treetops were as dry as kindling. Once a fire started in the slashings, it could move with amazing speed into the standing timber. The unanswered questions were "Where is the fire, and how close is it to Blue Lake Camp?"

Before the crew had finished breakfast, those questions were answered. A lathered black horse careened into camp. The exhausted rider threw himself off the heaving animal, tossed the reigns to a boy, then aimed for the door of the mess hall. Three men got up to make a place for him to sit and catch his wind. "I just came from Deward . . .," he said. He took several gasping breaths, then in a hoarse voice started again, "A fire started in the slashings near the river—now it's in the standing timber—and it's headed this way!" It was painful to watch him attempt to speak; yet they hung on every word. Two men steadied him from toppling over. He struggled to regain enough breath to speak. "Our crew has been working straight through the night trying to put it out—but the dead treetops are powder dry—and the wind carried firebrands over our heads. Now the crowns of the trees are on fire!"

The men looked at each other. The fire was out of control. The only possible way to stop it was to start a backfire where the timber had been cut between Blue Lake and the fire. Grover took a quick look at the boss. The man drew himself up, ready to leap into action. If enough men could get there and burn a controlled area before the raging fire arrived, they just might be able to stop it.

The strained rider found enough breath to speak once more. "The men from Deward are coming—if the crew from Blue Lake helps, we might be able to get this thing stopped!" There was no need for discussion. Grover jumped up and in three steps was out of the cook shanty. He bounded to the barn and threw the harnesses on Jim and George while other men loaded shovels, axes, and saws in the wagon. He made the horses run at full speed the entire mile to the slashings.

Each man quickly decided where to start as the wagon came out of the standing timber into the cutover area. They leapt off the wagon, and went to work starting fires. They lit them in the dry limbs of trees that had been harvested. The limbs caught easily. The small fires gained momentum over the area, slowly at first, licking and crackling. There was plenty of fuel to feed the hungry flames. Soon, though, there was popping, as combustible natural materials began to take. As these fires burned east, they joined together and continued into the slashings. Then, armed with shovels and axes, the men struggled to prevent fire from moving backward into the tall standing timber. A wide area must be consumed before the huge fire from Deward arrived or it would jump the backfired area and burn into the forest.

The day that started with a half-eaten breakfast would be the longest, hardest day in the lives of the lumbermen. All morning they shoveled sand to direct the fires they had started. Even late in the afternoon small fires continued to break out behind them. These had to be quickly covered with sand. Fortunately, the soft sand was easy to dig, but it was heavy work.

They needed water. Tuden had set two big cans of water in the wagon, but every bit was required for the men and the horses; there was none available to fight fire.

Even though the fire in the pines was still a half-mile away, the heat was fierce. The exhausted, overheated men drank more and more from their precious supply. The water was lukewarm but still a great relief to the men. All through the daylight hours they worked, hoping and praying that the burned over area would be wide enough to stop the inferno.

Long before the backfires had burned far enough to provide security, the dazed group of men watched the raging fire sweep down on the burned-over area. By now, the heat was nearly unbearable. The horses whinnied and whirled as they attempted to break loose. Grover could hardly hold them! They were not accustomed to such abuse. They were hungry and thirsty. Where was the teamster they had learned to trust? Why didn't he lead them to safety?

The men from Deward fought equally hard on the south end of the fire line. All day they worked harder than they ever had to set up this burned-over piece of land that might save their property, their homes, their families, and livestock.

The sun finally set that day on a weak and exhausted group of men, who watched as the inferno roared up to the burned-over area and then, ever so gradually, died out. They had fought a tremendous battle, one that required stamina above what they thought themselves capable of, and finally now the fire was diminishing!

A crew of men watched over dead trees and old stumps that continued to burn for days. These fires required unrelenting vigilance. It was impossible to tell when the wind might scatter more firebrands. No one wanted a repeat of the last few days. Already more than a thousand acres of choice pine had burned—a devastating loss! There were still vast areas of hardwood and hemlock, but those great pine forests that were so majestic were gone. A ghostly scene covered miles and miles of formerly prime forestland. The tallest pines were still standing, but blackened and charred, with no hope for life left in them. There was too much damage.

As the smoldering fires continued, no one relaxed at either Deward or Blue Lake. The imminent possibility of a strong wind spreading the fire again was a nagging worry. There were so many smoldering fires that would just have to burn themselves out. The hot, dry days continued for a week before the dreaded wind came. The smoldering fires were fewer but still a definite danger. The southeast wind grew stronger by the hour.

At noon, black clouds suddenly rolled in. Lightning blazed across the sky, thunder began to rumble, then build to a roar that did not cease. The rain nearly burst out of the clouds, and quickly became torrential. Waves and waves of it poured across the scorched countryside. The sound of pounding rain was beautiful music to the men's ears. There would be no more nights of fitful sleep and nightmares about flames roaring through the treetops. They could rest now.

The huge fire had changed not only the forest but the men as well. They had saved their homes and all that was dear to them, but the prospect of a future with wage-paying work was gone. There was no music in the evenings. The men were irritable. The boss was no longer cheerful and friendly.

The desolate, blackened landscape that had once been lush green forest now presented a challenge to Mr. George Root, a son-in-law of the deceased David E. Ward. Root managed the great tract of timber acquired by his father-in-law, which stretched across four counties and spanned fifty miles in either direction. The dead pines would soon be infested with worms. Any logs cut into lumber during the following winter would be as valuable as ever, but after another summer the boards would be damaged by wormholes.

Soon after the rain, George Root[1] came to Blue Lake one morning, where he stayed in the office nearly two hours. The men wondered what could keep Mr. Root in one place for such a long time. He was known as a man of few words, efficient and harsh.

In mid-morning, while a freshly sharpened band saw was being put on the mill, the boss came out where the crew was enjoying some cool water. A freshly sharpened saw was installed every few hours, the only break for the crew throughout the day. A huge smile spread over the face of the normally somber manager. He said, "Mr. Root from Deward Mill wants to cut the pine killed by the fire as soon as possible. We will work next winter salvaging those pine trees. It's good work for us, and we'll save all we can for him."

At one time majestic pines had covered nearly all the eastern part of Michigan's Lower Peninsula. Now all that remained was this burned-over area and some parkland near Grayling, which Major Hartwick's widow fortunately, had donated to the State.

Grover thought of the day that he and his father had walked through the now devastated area when he first came to Blue Lake. The beauty and the awesome height of the trees were firmly fixed in his memory. He was sure that for the rest of his life, he would only have to close his eyes and see those tall, straight trunks and hear the whisper of the wind through the needles on the crowns

---

[1] Research leads us to believe that George Root was in charge of Deward Mill in 1910, and probably was the man who came to Blue Lake Camp to strike a deal. He is listed as postmaster in 1901. From Frederic Times 1903: "In charge of this enormous industry is Mr. Root, a son-in-law of the late Mr. Ward and one of the executors of the [David E. Ward] estate." The Postmaster does not change until 1917.

far above his head. He grieved the loss of this beautiful forest, but there was gratification in knowing that he would have an opportunity to work in those trees again.

Gradually with the prospect of work to come, the men's spirits lifted. Music once more drifted from the cook shanty when the sun cast its shadows across camp. The chatter of conversation moved to the coming winter's work in the charred pine forest.

Through the autumn, huge decks of logs piled at the end of the lake gradually changed into piles of stickered lumber beside the railroad track. The hours of daylight grew shorter, and frost began painting pictures on the shanty windows each morning. The leaves turned from a soft green to beautiful autumn colors, then faded. The rains pelted the leaves before wind swept them to their resting-place on the ground. In November, Grover couldn't ignore the loud honking of migrating geese. On dark cloudy days, the long V's of the flocks skimmed above the treetops. The seemingly endless flocks of geese never ceased to amaze him, and the lumberman's eyes turned often to admire their majesty.

Everyone expected an exceptionally prosperous year both for Blue Lake Lumber Company and the men. Mr. Root wanted to salvage as much pine lumber this year as possible. The logs were cut in sixteen-foot lengths and many of the trees would yield six logs.

Lumberjacks, knowing of the fire and fully expecting a profitable winter's work, gathered from across the state to work in Michigan's last pine forest.[2] Among the new sawyers was a young man named Lee Williams, who stood almost a head taller than most of the others. Reports of the fire had reached the wild, uncut areas of the Upper Peninsula where he worked. The lure of a winter's work in the tall pines proved irresistible; Lee and his partner left the hardwood forest, and were among the first arrivals at Blue Lake.

---

[2] Michigan Ghost Towns Vol. I, Dodge, 1970, Glendon Pub. p 78, "This and one stand in U.P., was the last big stand of virgin pine in the state."

Grover was intrigued by the strength of this good-natured sawyer. Lee was ready to use his strength whenever it was of help, yet in no way did he indicate that he thought himself superior.

One day when a tree fell, Grover was attempting to roll over a log that was pinned by a huge limb that had been driven into the ground. Lee chopped off the limb while Grover and the horses kept the log slightly rolled. The brief interlude of cooperation was the first contact between the two and they forged a friendship that was destined to continue.

Lee had left home to work in logging camps when he was very young. Being blessed with an exceptionally strong body and an eagerness to learn, he was already numbered among the most capable of sawyers. Now Lee and his partner were eager to get their crosscut saw into some of those big pine trees.

Bruce and Lee Felling Tree

This winter Lee and Grover were making a killing because of the fire—there were no limbs to cut off except on the very top log of the tree. Most days Lee and his partner cut more than a hundred trees!

The work was not without problems. Norway pine trees contained large quantities of pitch. Even before the pitch was visible to the eye, the saw would become sticky. A crosscut saw was hard enough to pull without the added drag from the pitch. Grover soon learned that a quick swab with a rag soaked in turpentine cleaned the pitch and the saw again slipped smoothly through the saw-kerfs. A can of turpentine was a must that had to be added to his stash of tools.

The sleigh road had to be kept smooth and hard or the heavy logs would break it up quickly, so the road was kept covered with a layer of ice. A large water tank, specially equipped with a boom, spread water on the sleigh road. Each night one man with his team of horses sprinkled as much of the road as possible. The nights were cold, and within a few hours, the newly sprinkled road was frozen solid. Ice on the road enabled the sleighs to be pulled quite easily, even with the heaviest of loads.

At the same time, the ice made it difficult to gain traction. The horses were sharp-shod. The blacksmith sharpened the horses' shoes so they cut into the road. As soon as they needed it, the horses were shod with freshly sharpened shoes so they could work on the slippery roads.

It was three miles from the standing timber to Blue Lake and before long more horses were needed to haul logs to the mill than were needed for skidding. Grover and his beloved Jim and George left the skidding crew to work the sleigh haul. Grover felt that no team could compare to his, and with every new task, he appreciated them more and more. He often found them an apple or carrot after work was done.

Each team of horses worked the cross haul to load the logs on the sleigh they took to the mill. It was critical when the log rolled onto the sleighs that the horses stop. Jim and George soon learned when their tugs became slack the pull was finished, and they stopped without even being told.

The fastest way to the mill was across the lake, and time was money, so as soon as the ice became thick enough to hold the weight of the load, the teams walked across the lake. Before the lake froze solid it was necessary to follow the shoreline.

The possibility of an air hole was always a hazard when crossing the lake. Although the layer of lake ice was adequate, the air hole might not be visible from above. The ice over an air hole was dangerously thin, even though its area might be small.

The second weekend in December was frigid for several nights in a row; the stars shone brightly and a brilliant display of Northern lights danced across the sky. Temperatures dropped well below zero at night and the days warmed only slightly.

The cold snap hastened the boss's decision to take the shorter sleigh route across Blue Lake with the logs. A hole chopped to determine the thickness of the ice proved it was more than adequate to support the horses and their loads.

After breakfast, the foreman met the teamsters at the barn. "There's plenty of ice now," he said. "You can drive the teams across the lake."

Grover was the first one to cross the lake with his loaded sleigh. An occasional patch of snow blotted the blue surface of the ice. The sleigh glided easily as the horses made their way to the mill. Jim and George walked at a brisk pace as the heavy load almost coasted across this new section of road. When they were nearly in the middle of the lake the ice gave a resounding "crack" and the right front runner of the sleigh dropped into the water. Almost immediately, as the horses struggled with their load, the ice gave way under them.

Grover jumped from the sleigh and began to cut the tugs to free Jim and George from their load, when the sleigh dropped through the ice. An old teamster veteran of many years in the woods was not far behind with his load of logs. He cupped his hands and shouted, "Get away from that hole, Grover! No use you going in the lake with 'em!"

Grover gave one last quick attempt to free them, but he felt the ice sloping away from him. He scrambled away as fast as he could and dove for the shelf of lake ice. He went into the icy water up to his hips, but was just able to slide onto the firm ledge.

The logs would have floated, but the iron shoes on the sleigh runners as well as the chains binding the logs to the bunks were so heavy that the entire load settled quickly from view. Grover watched in horror as his beloved horses went down.

Someone helped him onto a sleigh and covered him with a horse blanket. The uncontrollable shivering did not stop his mind from working. His devastation was evident beyond question. He vaguely acknowledged the concerned sympathy of the other men. Everyone knew that Grover had a real attachment to those horses. The lake was deep and neither horses or sleighs were ever found.

It was a devastating blow to Grover. He now realized how much he had loved those horses. He lay awake that entire night, trying to work it all out, reliving the experience, trying to make sense of it. For a long time after, he would wake suddenly, wondering how he might have saved them. The realization that there was nothing he could have done did not ease the pain. Nor did the compassion of others.

The old teamster who had been following Grover explained that with soaked wool clothing and heavy boots weighing on him, he surely would have gone down with the sleigh and the team, had he kept trying to free them. There would have been no saving the horses, and they would have lost him, too, if he had not gotten out when he did. You had to look at it logically.

Logic didn't make sense to Grover. His beloved Jim and George were gone—in less than a minute's time! Here, then gone. He felt like he'd been gutted alive.

Good horses simply were not for sale in the north woods that winter. Perhaps it was a good thing for Grover that none were available. The days seemed to stand still, and he began to turn frequently to his "potato bug." Music became his sole companion. In the evening when he was emotionally drained, he picked up the mandolin. There was no desire for company; Grover just wanted to be alone with his music.

The boss gave him a job using a cant hook to build big decks of logs. It was hard physical labor. Grover began to realize that the fatigue actually brought a measure of relaxation to his body and his mind. He realized it was better this way. No team of horses could ever replace Jim and George.

Grover's first partner in building decks was Charlie Howe. Grover marveled that Charlie could take one quick look at a log and place the decking line properly so the log rolled smoothly up the skids. They seldom had to touch the log until it landed squarely on the deck. The challenge made the work interesting to most men, but it was vital to Grover in his present state of mind.

When the warm sun destroyed the iced sleigh road in late March, the men from Blue Lake had fulfilled their contract and huge decks of pine logs lined the shore of Blue Lake.

With help from the crew of the Blue Lake Lumber Company, Deward Mill salvaged all the burned pine in one winter, and Mr. George Root, notoriously hard to satisfy, expressed appreciation for a job well done.

As Grover looked back, he realized he had been through a lot that year. He had witnessed one of the most devastating fires in the region and helped to stop it. He had lost two horses that he was deeply fond of and proud of. Nothing could replace what had been lost.

Still, some good things came out of the year. For both the
Blue Lake Lumber Company and their employees, the winter of
1910–11 had been a hugely profitable season, and the men were
glad to have had the chance to work in the virgin pine. Nevertheless, Grover learned to take nothing for granted. Not even a horse.
Not even a tree.

One warm Sunday morning, while most of the crew took advantage of the time off to catch some extra rest, Grover and his
father seized the opportunity to walk together through the woods.
The fresh spring air was rich with the faintly sweet aroma of wild
flowers and moist earth. Tuden began to tell Grover about a choice
piece of property he had found. The place was especially attractive
to him and he had been waiting to bring up the subject. "Son,
there's a piece of land south of Mancelona that I've been looking
at." He glanced at a chickadee flitting in the branches overhead.
"A road runs along the south side, and there's a spring-fed lake
near the southwest corner covering three or four acres. It's about
30 feet deep and the water's clear and cold." He looked at his son's
face to see if he were catching his meaning. "It's a nice place."

After a lengthy pause with virtually no response from Grover,
Tuden continued. "The timber's been cut on it, but trees are growing around the lake. He waited. "It would have been nicer before
the fire went through . . . but it's coming back."

Although he was disappointed that there was no response from
Grover, Tuden forged ahead. "The place was covered with hardwood, and any soil that can produce a good hardwood forest is
certainly good farm land."

Grover understood his father's interest in the property and that
he wanted him to work it with him, but he just was not ready to

take up farming again. Farming was a lonely occupation, fraught with problems, which rested solely on the farmer. Working in the timber excited him. The pay was good; he could work with horses, and he liked the pace, the action. He was not ready to resign himself to working a homestead. Grover didn't want to hurt his father's feelings, but he couldn't make himself choose what Tuden wanted. Finally, he spoke.

"I'm sure it's a nice place Dad, but I'm really happy with the work in the timber and I guess I'm just not ready to leave it."

Tuden was quiet for some time before continuing. "I plan to stay on the job as long as Blue Lake's working, but I'll try to buy that piece of land anyway. The work I'm doing at Blue Lake is all right, but working out in the timber's more than I can handle. I'm getting too old to go to another camp and start over again."

The two men walked for some time, each lost in his own thoughts. When they turned back toward camp, Tuden said. "I'll need a team. Logging camps sell their horses cheap when they're past their prime. An old team can do my work. I'll grow most of my food. And I can shoot a few rabbits through the winter. This way I can take life a little easier."

It saddened Grover that his dad was getting older. It saddened him that he couldn't do this just to please him, but he couldn't see himself there with him. Not yet.

Grover enjoyed the summer. He had left piling lumber and was driving a team of horses that brought logs from the decks to the sawmill. The skidway by the saw held about a dozen large logs, more if they were smaller. As these rolled down the skids to be put on the sawmill carriage, Grover and his team replenished them from the large decks of logs by the lakeshore.

These horses could never replace Jim and George, but they were not a bad team. All horses used in the camps were of necessity good ones, and as they became familiar with Grover, the team and teamster's mutual respect made the work flow.

In the warm summer evenings the late sun slanted horizontally in the small windows of the dining hall. Tuden was always the leader with his violin when music drifted from the cook shanty. Another man played the banjo and Grover was making great strides with his mandolin. No one owned printed sheet music. It wouldn't have been useful to these musicians anyway, since none of them could read music. They played "by ear", or from memory.

As the warm summer days shortened and were replaced by the cool of autumn, the huge decks of pine logs dwindled. The logs had all been cut into lumber when the crews began drifting in to begin the next winter's logging.

Men in the lumberyard welcomed the arrival of the sawyers. Work at the mill was good, but the cutting of the big trees never lost its thrill. The cry of "T-I-M-B-E-R-R-R!" as a tree began to lean, the crash as it came down, splintering any sapling unfortunate enough to be in its path, was exciting. This was the peak of life for the lumberjack. It was it's own form of intoxication, and its addiction brought the men to camp as soon as plummeting temperatures announced the arrival of winter.

The logging crew was much smaller in the winter of 1911–12. Blue Lake Lumber Company was cutting the last of its timberland. It was better to hire fewer men to work all winter than to hire a bunch of men for just a few months. It was a melancholy crew who realized that what had been their winter's work for a number of years was coming to an end. Some began to comprehend that the seemingly unlimited forests stretching across the region of the Great Lakes was being depleted. And it was happening sooner than anyone had seemed to expect.

One evening in the mess hall, while the cook scrubbed pots and her children played underfoot, the group of musicians reminisced about long forgotten old tunes. One of the older men, scratching his head and mumbling to himself, recalled parts of a song that had been common at a time when horses were replacing oxen.

The words of the song, "The Little Brown Bulls," brought to mind the size of the logs as well as the strength of the oxen.

The old sawyer sang the words he remembered.

"It's three to the thousand our contract does call."

The hauling is good, and the timber is tall."

The group sat silently while the old man continued to strum his musical instrument.

"Too small, said McGlosky, to handle our pine . . ."

With furrowed brow, the old lumberjack picked slowly on his banjo. He shook his head and laid his instrument aside, saying. "I guess that's as far as I can go." As was often the case, he had no idea where he had heard the song or the rest of the lyrics. It was another bit of lost lore, the end of an era.

"What do the words mean, Mr. Svenson?" asked the cook's boy. "Well, sonny, 'three to the thousand' is talking about three logs that would put out a thousand board feet of lumber. That's the big trees! Lots of 'em in the early days contained three hundert and thirty board feet in just one log! But if ya think that's somethin, some were even bigger than that!"

The sun crept higher in the sky as March storms gave way to April showers and the last of the choice maple trees owned by the Blue Lake Lumber Co. were cut and brought to the mill. All that was left were a few scraggly maples and some decent beech trees; nothing the company felt valuable enough to bring to the mill on bare ground. Blue Lake Lumber Company was no more.

The end came as no surprise. Tuden had been emotionally preparing for many months and had selected a team of horses he planned to buy. Both animals were well past their prime. However, Mike and Nell were still strong enough to do farm work for several years. Tuden purchased the team and determined to buy some land. He invited Grover to join him in purchasing the property. "Son, that 120 acres is still for sale. You'll want to settle down some day. It's a good place," Tuden reminded him.

Grover, young, strong, and loving the work in the timber, had no interest in buying property, and he still declined to invest with his father.

Tuden drove away from Blue Lake in the spring of 1912 with his new team and an old but serviceable wagon. He was sorry to leave his son, but pleased that the years in camp had enabled him to provide for himself. He bought the little lake and the 120 acres of land that accompanied it.

Young poplars were starting all around the land. Near the lake was a cool clean spring. Tuden had searched for a good water supply when he first looked at the property. Fresh water was essential. It would be good to have the house near the spring, and he definitely wanted to live by the lake, where it's pristine water reflected the surrounding scene in a small valley. About twenty yards from the lake, and even nearer the spring, the land was high and dry. It was the ideal location for his home and Tuden chose a spot for a temporary shelter. A natural inlet from another small spring provided a perfect place for a boat, and Tuden determined to build one as soon as he found time.

Choosing an opening between stumps, near where he planned to build a barn, Tuden took time to grub up some loose dirt and plant a few potatoes and rutabagas to provide food for the coming winter.

Tuden's well-stocked tool chest and the trees around the shore of the lake were all he would need to build a good house. With his broadax and adz,[3] Tuden hewed beams from the pine trees near the lake. From the abundance of dead cedar logs on the ground Tuden laboriously cut blocks and made a foundation for his pine beams.

He completed the shell of the house and covered the sides of it with tarpaper before the autumn chill came. Rolled roofing gave shelter overhead and a little sheet iron stove in the middle of the kitchen heated the house and cooked his meals.

By winter, Tuden was well pleased with what he'd accomplished. He'd planned well. His small basement contained plenty of potatoes and rutabagas. He had purchased enough hay to keep his horses until spring, and with Mike and Nell to provide the horsepower, he could drag home wood for his fuel as needed.

The tired, but content old man now considered his need for furniture. Through the summer, he had slept on a pile of straw in the corner. He now made a straw tick, by making and filling a heavy cloth bag with straw. This he stitched up and basted with a large X to keep the straw from bunching up in one part of the tick.

Tuden needed at least a table and a chair, but he was getting by with a plank laid across two blocks. He wanted his furniture to be worthy of his carpentry skills. During the winter, he would have time to make a presentable table and a comfortable chair.

Now he was finally able to relax and read a few books. He had always enjoyed reading and not since he left the lakes had he really been able to relax and read. This winter, his only serious obligations were feeding and watering Mike and Nell, and keeping an adequate supply of stove wood.

The house, covered only with single boards, required a lot of fire in the little stove to keep the room warm. Still, it was a major

[3] similar to a broadax, but with the cutting edge perpendicular to the handle rather than parallel to it

victory just to have shelter for the winter. Tuden enjoyed the evenings, sitting by a warm fire playing his fiddle, or reading by his
kerosene lamp. Life was good.

On a bright morning in early December, he hitched Mike and
Nell to the little sleigh he had made and drove to Mancelona. He
needed flour and a few other groceries, but Tuden's mind was on
a shotgun.

Snowshoe rabbits abounded around the lake and he was ready
to put one in the cooking pot. He had planned for some time to get
a double-barreled 10 gauge. He wanted a good shotgun and Wisler's
hardware stocked quality merchandise. Jesse Wisler, a hunter himself, showed Tuden an L. C. Smith with Damascus barrels. It was
exactly the shotgun Tuden wanted. He hefted it, looked down the
barrels, turned it over and over, and then wondered if he should
buy something a little less expensive.

The temptation was too great. Tuden bought the shotgun and a
box of number 4 shot. He had strong opinions about ammunition.
Number 4 shot was big enough to kill a rabbit a long way off, and
the meat wouldn't be full of pellets. He went home a happy man.
"Tomorrow," Tuden resolved, "There'll be rabbit for dinner."

Chapter 8

Railroad

G rover shared his father's love for water. He had walked with Tuden around the 120-acre parcel and looked carefully at the little lake. The lake was somewhat hidden by the sloping hills around it. As it came into view, it was a lovely surprise, quiet and serene, nestled in the hollow like a diamond on a green velvet pillow. One had the feeling of being just out of touch with the busyness and worry of the world beyond. The lake was small but pristine, and springs bubbled up through the white sand bottom in a small bay at the Southeast corner. These springs provided abundant, clear water. A continual flow out of the lake at the opposite corner carried the overflow in a small stream to a neighbor's pond. Grover was happy for his father. This would make a fine place for Tuden to live.

The years at Blue Lake had lowered the emotional barriers between father and son. While Tuden was settling into his new home, Grover was looking for work elsewhere. He wasn't willing to leave the life of the lumberjack. After putting in two winters at the Blue Lake Camp, he was confident he would be welcomed to any lumber camp. He boarded the train for Mancelona to seek work.

He'd heard about the Antrim Iron Company, just a mile south of Mancelona. The owners had purchased large tracts of hardwood forests from the Grand Rapids and Indiana Railroad. They were setting up a sawmill designed with the latest technology. The company was building its own railroad from Antrim to their forests in Coldsprings Township. They planned to bring the logs from the forest and roll them directly from the railway cars into a "hot pond" heated by waste steam from the engine providing power to the mill. This would wash the logs before the conveyor brought them to the saw. Not only would this make the operation a clean one, the performance of the saw would be much better, and the blades would last longer. As the train neared the site of the company, Grover was amazed at the size of the place. This was going to be a huge enterprise!

He descended from the train and strode across the yard to the office. It was a much larger office than either Blue Lake or Deward. Grover waited until a tall man rose from behind his desk. He was obviously in charge.

"I'd like to work for you," Grover said. "I worked at Blue Lake Lumber Company until they closed. Horses work well for me."

"We won't be using any teamsters this summer, the owner replied, but you can check at camp when snow comes." The conversation was over as the tall man walked out the door.

He shouldn't have been surprised. Still, after working at Blue Lake, and having more than satisfied his employer, Grover had convinced himself that he'd receive a welcome at Antrim.

He thought of his friend, Lee. Lee always had work in the Upper Peninsula through the summer. But how could he find him? He was determined not to spend another summer on a farm.

As Grover turned to leave, he glanced at another man behind a desk. The sign on his desk said, Ray Nothstein, Bookkeeper. He looked at Grover, then said, "They're building a railroad to the new camp this summer, you might find work there."

"Where is it?"

"About five miles southeast of here. It's near where Blue Lake harvested the past year, in some virgin hardwoods and hemlocks. They're calling it Gorham Camp." He returned to his work.

The railroad was being built to the same camp where Grover planned to spend the next winter! Walking along the newly laid railroad tracks, he soon reached the work place. It looked like a mass of confusion! When Grover asked to see the foreman, he was answered in a foreign language and waved on up the track.

Grover's legs were taking him briskly along the railroad grade in search of the foreman, but his mind was moving even faster. Life had certainly taken some unexpected turns since he left the Hackney farm. Only a few years had passed, but in that time he had been reunited with his father, moved to the north country, worked on a farm, skidded logs, fought a terrible fire in the pines, piled lumber, and lost a team of horses through the ice. Now, here he was along the railroad, searching for any form of work that would keep him busy until the next logging season.

When Grover approached the next group of workers, one man was pointing at something, which obviously did not meet his approval. His appearance was striking. The face appeared to be that of a man in early middle age but his hair was already gray. His eyes, a steely blue, glistened under dark eyebrows. There was no question; this man was the foreman.

Grover approached the obviously harried individual and started to speak, but was interrupted.

"If you're looking for work, young man, you came to the right place. Building a railroad bed is work—all work."

Grover grinned. The abrupt speech was familiar from his days at Blue Lake. "Where do I start?" He asked.

The foreman's response was as steely as his gaze. "I need your name." The words weren't unfriendly, but they invited no idle chatter.

When Grover's name was duly recorded on the book that went back in the foreman's pocket, he continued. "Come meet your partner." Abruptly, he turned and walked a short distance into the woods where another young man was cutting railroad ties with a two-man crosscut saw. "Ollie, here's your new partner. I hope he holds out longer than the last one."

Before leaving, he turned again to Grover. "Ollie's been here long enough to know what we want. You can work with him." With that introduction, the foreman returned to the railroad grade.

Ollie turned out to be a good partner. In a crew made up of mostly immigrants, Ollie found an instant friend in the young lumberjack. Though his English was limited, Ollie had a quick and easy humor which greatly shortened what might have been long, hard days.

This partner's speech intrigued Grover. "Ollie, once I understand what you're saying, we'll get along fine," he told him. Ollie nodded, but Grover couldn't be sure he'd been understood.

Ollie showed him how to select smaller trees; and then they'd cut them down and hew the edges to make a flat surface four-inches wide on one side. These were crossties, usually just referred to as ties, which would support the rails. Those who cut the ties carried them to their place on the railroad grade. Cut from green trees, and about six inches thick, they were heavy, but could comfortably be carried by two men.

The big Norwegians were known for their strength. Later that night in the cook shanty Grover heard an older man tell a story of a big Norwegian who was carrying a tie alone when the foreman stopped him. "Hey," the foreman said, "we double up on those." A little later the Norwegian struggled back with a tie on each shoulder!

The crew building the railroad was entirely different from the men Grover worked with in the woods. Most had recently immigrated. Their relatives had mailed letters telling of the great opportunities awaiting them in Michigan's timber. Since there were limited opportunities in home countries, they had ventured across the Atlantic. The crew was an eager, hard working group, seeking a fortune in the raw north. Grover began to learn about his new job.

At the forefront, was a group of Swedes. They were digging out stumps and shoveling sand to build the roadbed up to the required height before the rails were laid. The fair complexion and light hair clearly indicated their Nordic ancestry. They were a cheerful group; they spoke almost no English, but communicated enthusiastically amongst themselves.

The grade, or roadbed, had to be built a few feet higher than the land it crossed so snow plowing wouldn't become an insurmountable problem in the winter. Where the ground was relatively level, the men merely dug holes along the track and shoveled the dirt onto the grade until they achieved the desired height. These were known as "Swede holes," after the men who dug them, and can still be found along the old railroad grades built by lumber companies.

Using just their shovels and a wooden tamping block, which made a firm base for each tie, the men leveled both the tie and its flat face in preparation for the rails.

Hard on the heels of the men placing the ties came another crew laying rails. The rails, carried on flat cars, were kept as near as possible to the crew using them. As soon as new rails were laid and spiked into place, the engineer in the steam locomotive inched closer.

The men laying rails came from Italy. Like the men from Sweden, they were recent arrivals to the United States and eagerly seized the opportunities available to them. Though their knowledge of English was limited, they worked well together. The foreman learned early the importance of communication and congeniality, and placed his employees accordingly.

Railroad spikes were driven into the ties so the head of the spike, which extended from only one side, held the rails firmly in place. There was a small head on the sledgehammers that drove the spikes so the head could clear the round top of the rails as spikes were driven into the ties. It was a skillful man who could consistently hit the spike with those sledgehammers! Four spikes were driven in each tie, one inside and outside each rail, more than 10,500 spikes per mile. It was hard work and the hours were long.

The job was completed by the beginning of November. As soon as the last rail was laid, the locomotive attached a few cars and made several trial runs. The speed was increased each time, until it moved about 20 miles an hour. There was some swaying, but not bad. Considering that it was a logging railroad, it was really quite satisfactory.

When the railroad crew drew their last paycheck the next step was not easy for most of the men. The largest percentage were immigrants. Some went to live with relatives; others wandered through the area, seeking any job they could find.

The rail line terminated at Gorham Camp, Grover's destination since he left Blue Lake. He welcomed the cool autumn weather, which foretold of the approach of the clean white snow. Snow meant cutting and skidding logs. This had been his goal throughout the summer. He appreciated the work on the railroad, and especially the companionship of the young Swede, but his first love was horses. Surely this time he'd find a welcome at the Gorham logging camp.

Grover approved of the newly constructed buildings in the camp. Once again, it was a confident, almost brash, young man who spoke to Cash Phelps, the logging foreman. "I'd like to drive a team of horses for you this winter. I was a teamster at Blue Lake until they ran out of timber."

Cash briefly scanned the young man with his eyes. He assessed his capabilities: *clean cut and well built. His youthful age is against him, but then, age can be deceiving.* Cash decided to give him a chance. "We'll need teamsters. My name is Cash Phelps. What's yours?"

Grover introduced himself, followed Cash into the office, saw his name entered on the payroll then moved his few belongings to the men-shanty. The shanty smelled of freshly cut hemlock. It was a pleasant change from the odor that had gradually developed in the railroad car through the summer. The car had served as a men-shanty.

The cook shanty, also newly built, was well fitted out with tables and benches. It was obvious to Grover that a sizable crew had built the living quarters while he had been working on the railroad. Briefly he thought about his father. Tuden could have been a great help in building the camp. He wondered if he'd managed to build a place for himself and his horses. He hadn't often thought about either Tuden or his fiddle during the summer. But now that he was in the logging camp, he missed the presence of both. He didn't realize how much he'd appreciated Tuden when he was there at the camp with him. That evening, though, Grover and his mandolin were enthusiastically welcomed as the men gathered in the cook shanty with their instruments

The cook at Blue Lake had put on a better spread, but Gorham's offered good solid food. It didn't take long for Grover to realize that there's nothing like a hard day's work in the woods to turn plain fare into a delicious feast.

Horses arrived at camp, carried in boxcars on the new railroad. Grover was impressed. All were big, young, healthy animals. A team of high-strung black Percherons caught his eye. How well they were broken he didn't care; he asked for them. Older teamsters, who could have first choice, showed no special interest. Grover was delighted to receive the team.

Virgin timber lined the railroad tracks. It looked like there would be work at Gorham for many years. Suddenly, Grover found his heart was filled with gratitude for his father's care for him.

Though similar to Blue Lake in some respects this camp had it's own characteristics. Grover began to get a feel for how things progressed here.

A steam locomotive equipped with a crane, known as a jammer in the lumber woods, moved along the rails picking up logs and loading them on the railroad cars. A cable, which the locomotive engine wound on a drum, picked up the logs and placed them on railroad cars. Two chains were attached to the end of the cable. At the opposite end of each chain was what the men called a "swamp hook." One hook was placed on each end of the log to be loaded. When the cable was pulled the chains were drawn together holding the log securely. After the log was loaded two men, each with a rope attached to one of the hooks, pulled the cable back to the deck and hooked the next log. The logs were taken to the mill each day.

The timber was excellent. The skidding was good. After just a few days, Grover and his new team understood each other well. He missed some of the men who had been his friends at Blue Lake, but he already loved his horses and was developing friendships with other men.

He missed Charlie, the cant hook man. Charlie and his violin had been a mainstay among the musicians in the winter of 1912–13 and the quality of the music suffered without Charlie or Tuden.

One of Grover's new friends was Barney. Barney's new partner at the log deck was young and strong, but not particularly industrious. One morning when they were decking logs along the tracks, the swamp hook on the decking line slipped. The log began to roll back on Barney and his partner.

Barney quickly stabbed the log with his cant hook. The log was heavy and Barney dared not let it go or he might not be able to get out of the way as it rolled down the skids. It was almost more than he could hold, even though he was a strong lumberjack. Barney shouted to his partner, "Grab the log!"

The new hand had jumped back out of the way when Barney grabbed the log, and now casually asked, "What for?"

"Grab it! I'll show you what for," Barney shouted as he strained to hold the log. Slowly the other man walked back and hooked his cant hook on the log.

When Barney was sure the man's cant hook held it solidly, he released his hold and left the young man alone holding it. It was a severe strain for the newcomer while Barney slowly pulled the chain back under and then over the log, hooking the swamp hook securely to one of the logs on the deck.

When the horses had pulled the log up the skids and onto the deck, the new cant hook man was trembling with fatigue.

Barney shook his head in disgust. "What for—*what for*? Now you *know* what for!"

Although Gorham was a new camp, men had gathered from camps throughout both of Michigan's peninsulas. All agreed there would be work for many years and morale soared.

The following year, on a brisk November evening of 1914, the newly formed group of musicians gathered in the mess hall to tune their instruments. The lead violinist "sounded his A" and the others began tuning up. The strains were starting to become somewhat similar, and all were ready for the first tune of the evening, when a stranger interrupted them.

"I'm getting a group together for a dance in the new Coldsprings Town Hall Saturday night," the newcomer announced. "The hall is finished and the dance will be a dedication."

Excitement greeted the news of the first get-together in the area. Obviously the dance would be well attended.

When the buzz of conversation slowed, the stranger said. "Every one in camp is invited. The township is buying a piano and Tuden will be there with his violin. If you bring your instruments, we'll have a good orchestra."

Grover grinned with pleasure. He really wanted to see his father, and to learn that the old man's talent with the violin was somewhat famous gave him a great feeling.

The stranger offered a glowing description of the new facility.

"The Coldsprings Township Hall was finished just before snowfall and they went all out. It's seven miles south from Mancelona on the Darragh road. The meeting hall's on the ground floor and the entire second floor's a dance hall. There are two wood stoves and several spittoons, for those with a wad of tobacco. There are toilets in back. The lady's is on the left side and the men's on the right. They're big enough to take care of a crowd."

The visitor assured the men that the occasion was well planned.

"The ladies will provide food. It'll be a real social time. A lot of new families have moved in, and this is the time to get acquainted." This rare occurrence caused quite a stir. Most accepted the invitation with enthusiasm and Grover was no exception. Music anywhere attracted him.

The hall was only a mile and a half from Tuden's new home. Grover had been concerned about his father's preparations for winter. He would be able to see Tuden at the dance and find out first hand how he was getting along.

When Grover arrived with his friends from camp, it was clear that lots of folks were as excited about this as the men from the camp were. Social occasions away from town were few and far between, so the dance was well attended. Almost all those in Gorham camp, married and single alike, traveled the four miles to the Coldsprings Town Hall. The group filled the second floor dance hall. Some people came to dance; others came to hear the music. Everyone wanted to share the excitement of meeting new residents in this growing area.

It was nearly midnight when a table was carried up from the first floor and filled with refreshments. Many young children were already asleep on their mother's laps and the families soon returned home but the single people continued their revelry on through the night.

A few of the men had gathered in the corner where one of them opened a bottle of whisky. Conversation centered on prohibition. A fast growing segment of the population favored outlawing alcohol as a beverage. Its consumption among the younger men was increasing. Women and men with families were increasingly being vocal about shutting down the saloons. Most men agreed that voters would never approve such a restriction. One of the men pointed out that someone usually brought a bottle whenever a group gathered. It added to the excitement. Another laughed. "Yeah, quite often there are two or three bottles, and some of us don't know how to get home!" When the laughter subsided, Tuden, who had indulged rather freely in alcohol, spoke vehemently.

"Boys, listen to me! I've made lots of mistakes in my life and nothing's been as big a mistake as the time and money I spent on booze!"

Suddenly the room grew very quiet, as the crowd looked on in surprise.

"When I was young working on the Great Lakes, I made some pretty good money. When winter came, I started home to see my family. I had a big check and big plans for the family and was eager to get home. But when we passed the saloon, I stopped for a drink with the other men."

"When I sobered up, a lot of my money was gone. I didn't remember to take anything to my children. I just hurried on home."

After a short pause, it was a broken old man who looked at Grover and continued. "One year when I arrived home, the house was empty and Grover here was in the orphanage."

The old man trembled. "After that, I vowed never to take a drink again. But if I pass a saloon or you hand me a bottle, I can't leave it alone. Look at me now! Some of you are no better off. If prohibition gets on the ballot, I'll be one who votes for it!"[4]

Excitement from the big get-together at the Coldsprings Town Hall lasted for days, but gradually died as the men returned to work in the forest.

The snow fell softly on an early December morning. Grover was hooking the tongs on a big maple log to roll it up and chop a broken limb off the bottom when a friendly, familiar voice boomed from behind him.

"How's it going Grove? It's been a while since we cut that pine over by the river." The voice belonged to Lee, Grover's closest friend during the winter they had worked together at Blue Lake. Lee loved the timber, and he loved working in a new location. He was a top-notch sawyer, and could hire on almost anywhere.

---

[4] Tuden's chance to vote for the 18th amendment came a few years later and he kept his word. Alcohol had caused him serious problems, but when prohibition removed saloons from Main Street, the temptation to drink was removed from his life.

Grover quickly crossed the short distance to where Lee and his partner were notching a tree. "Hi, you oversized runt! I didn't see you in the cook shanty this morning. When did you come?"

"We came in yesterday. I've gained a wife and a son and you didn't see me at the cook shanty because I have my own private cook." Lee retorted with a smile as he and Grover exchanged a warm greeting. Acquaintances were numerous, but friendships were not so common in lumber camps. Both men were happy to be reunited.

Lee didn't come to the cook shanty in the evenings now. None of the wives attended the evening music sessions, and Lee preferred to spend the time with his family. Occasionally Grover walked across the track and enjoyed a relaxing evening with his friends. Lee and Ruth's contentment was markedly different from the constant restlessness and competition among the single men.

The winter passed quickly. Snow consistently covered the trails where logs had dug their way into the earth the day before, yet the weather was not severe. The snow seldom grew too deep for horses to work efficiently. It seemed only a short time until delicate spring beauties and violets began to appear in open areas, while snow still covered the ground in the more dense forest.

Many of the men at camp returned to their plots of land and spent their summer digging stumps. It was an annual struggle for those who dreamed of owning their own farm. For those who wished to stay at camp there was work through the summer, cutting and skidding the trees near the railroad. Both Grover and Lee chose to stay.

Six months after the dance at Coldsprings Town Hall, the man who had sponsored it welcomed the spring of 1915 with the announcement of a repeat event. Personal invitations were delivered to Gorham Camp, to the few farmers earning a living from the soil, and the two families who now lived on the shore of Manistee Lake.

Once again, there was excitement in the air as the shanty boys headed to the Town Hall. From the looks of it, there were just as many others there to socialize. Lee, who towered almost head and shoulders above the other men and with stamina to match, danced the entire night.

Grover played his mandolin, and he enjoyed the music and conversation. This time, however, he began to take note of the young ladies whirling across the floor. Grover considered asking one to dance, but decided against it. He hadn't been introduced to them and had never danced. This was an area that he hadn't had a chance to polish himself on.

A few weeks later, when the trilliums (locally known as lilies) dotted the forest, Grover picked a large bouquet and brought them to Ruth when he walked across the track to spend the evening with his friends.

When the conversation turned to the recent social activity, Lee looked seriously at his friend. "I have a sister you should meet, Grover. She's a quiet girl. It would be good for you and her to get acquainted. The next time there's a dance, I'll bring her."

Grace, the sister Lee referred to, was two years younger than Grover's friend. Lee and Grace had been close friends throughout their childhood. Although he hadn't been home for some time, Lee knew his sister had continued attending school and lived in Rapid River Township, which adjoined Coldsprings on the west.

Grover smiled. "I'm doing fine. I'm not really looking."

Lee was his friend and Grover wanted to remain friends with him, but being friendly with Lee's sister was something else again. He was happy with his horses, his mandolin, and the occasional social night.

There was no more discussion about this meeting, but when the next dance took place in late July, Lee brought his sister, Grace. He told her she needed to get out and meet some people.

The evening seemed like a continuation of the previous dances. There had been no other community activity. Neighbors seldom strayed from home; all their time and efforts were directed toward providing for their families.

After the first bubble of conversation ended and many had moved to the dance floor, Lee made his way to where Grace was seated. He casually drew her attention to the orchestra. "That young man with the mandolin is a good friend of mine, I think you should meet him." Grace glanced toward the young man. His curly blond hair seemed to want to choose its own direction. She noticed he was dressed neatly, and that his attention seemed to be centered on the old bald man beside him. She wondered what the two men might have in common. The older man was stooped. A ring of white hair covered the back and sides of his head.

Lee waited for a response, but Grace wasn't sure of her own response to this proposition. She turned her attention to the lady beside her without answering.

Not easily dissuaded, Lee waited until "The Irish Washer Woman," finally ended and appeared at Grover's side. "Grover, I brought my sister tonight I'd like you to meet her." Lee was smiling; sure the introduction would meet with the approval of both. Since they were both his friends, surely they would become friends too.

Grover frowned. His mandolin was tuned, and he was ready to play the next waltz. Still he didn't want to disappoint Lee. Carefully laying his treasured "potato bug" on the chair, Grover walked to the back of the hall where a row of young ladies sat.

Lee stopped in front of a tall girl with carefully combed long dark hair. "Grace, this is the young man I told you about. His first love seems to be horses. You should teach him to dance." This was his introduction.

Grace was obviously surprised. She had indicated no interest in meeting Lee's friend but her good manners dictated that she behave politely. The smile that lighted her face was forced as she rose and extended her hand. "I've danced very little, but we're not among professionals." Grace said to Grover.

Music again filled the hall. Grover and Lee's sister moved slowly across the floor, following the movements of those leading. Tension gradually disappeared as topics of mutual interest found their way into the light conversation.

For most of the group, dancing was more of a learning experience than a demonstration of skill, so no one felt ill at ease as they moved—whether it be shuffling, hopping or dancing.

Square dancing was popular and the caller often called, "Change your partners." So it was that Grover and Grace enjoyed the companionship of several partners before the evening ended.

Grover had really enjoyed himself, forgetting his mandolin for the time. He and Grace danced together several times, but when the evening ended neither was interested in seeing the other again.

Chapter 9

Grace

E lias Williams kissed his bride, carried her from the home of her parents and seated her on his sleigh. He was proud of the team of horses that were hitched to the sleigh. He'd worked long and hard to purchase them. He was even more proud of the beautiful girl who had consented to become his bride, Mary Hubble, whom he called Polly. They'd been married two years previously in a small town in Ontario, in the New Castle District, near the north shore of Lake Ontario.

The year was 1844. The young couple had decided that the United States provided more opportunity for them than their homeland, and they were already packed to make the journey to Michigan.

The Williams's endured considerable hardship, traveling for weeks across the province of Ontario with all their possessions loaded on the sleigh. They finally reached the shore of Lake St. Clair on the second day of March.

The weather was unseasonably warm for so early in the year. Elias knew crossing the ice would be hazardous but he was young and energetic—and quite probably foolish—and they drove across the lake. The United States government had opened the thumb area of Michigan for homesteading. 160 acres of land, a quarter section, was available free to anyone who built a residence and improved the property. The Williams's were eager to choose their homestead while the choicest parcels were still available.

Elias and Polly claimed a quarter section of fertile land in St. Clair County, Michigan, and built a small cabin and planted seeds between the stumps where trees had been cleared. As the years passed, the family grew to nine children and the farm prospered.

Other homesteaders weren't as fortunate. For various reasons, including hardship, after doing the work of improvement and receiving a deed for their homestead, many people moved on. Elias was able to purchase an adjoining quarter section, and he and Polly cleared it of stumps. With his profits, Elias had opportunity to get into the lumbering business, and the family became quite well off, if not wealthy.

The backbreaking years of pioneer life took their toll. At the age of 43, Elias was forced to retire at his farm due to poor health, and he died twenty years later. Upon his death the farmland was divided among the children. Charlie and Wilmar, older than the others, each inherited forty acres with a comfortable house.

Charlie was restless. Soon after the turn of the twentieth century, he moved his family to the rapidly developing Mancelona area of northern Michigan, where opportunity abounded. He bought forty acres near the headwaters of the Rapid River, which was a spring fed stream. It supplied water for the family and livestock throughout the year

Wilmar's forty acres was a sizeable inheritance, but it was not enough land to enable another generation to prosper in the manner of his parents. He sold his place in early spring, 1906, and followed his brother Charlie to Mancelona. The newly cutover land was reasonably priced and Wilmar bought 160 acres of land with a small house, located less than a mile from Charlie. The house was small, but there was space for him and his family, which included three sons; Lee, Albert and Louis; and two daughters; Grace and Emma.

Wilmar rented a boxcar and accompanied by a team of horses, two cows, and a sow about to pig, rode by rail to Westwood with other freight cars. From Westwood, Wilmar drove his livestock to their new residence. His family had the luxury of making the same trip on the passenger train. Westwood was a small settlement consisting of a railroad depot, a store, a church, and several houses, and was just four miles southwest of Mancelona. Their new home was three more miles southeast.

Grace, who would be fourteen years old on September 13, was excited to meet young people from different backgrounds. Many were from Indiana, and like Grace, had moved with their parents to the developing area. On Sunday mornings, she walked with her mother and sister three miles to Westwood to attend church. After church, a group of young people often walked to Rainbow Lake, carrying food from home for a picnic. For Grace and her sister, Emma, life was sweet. This bit of utopia, however, was not to continue.

After a mediocre yield the first summer and a complete crop failure the following year Grace's father, Wilmar, told his brother, "You'd have to have two showers of rain and one of manure every week to raise anything here!"

Wilmar grew despondent because of the poor harvest, and went to look for a more productive area, leaving his wife and children to fend for themselves. Lee, the oldest child, was sixteen, mature, exceptionally big and strong, and for a period of time supported the family.

Grace soon developed a serious health problem, in which she became very weak, enough that she was unable to attend school. Her ailment was never properly diagnosed. The doctor prescribed various medications trying to find a cure. Nothing brought any improvement and for a time Grace was bedridden. Her mother, Anna, did what she could to support the family after Lee left but was unable to meet the doctor bills. The doctor, who had not been paid for months and had exhausted the medicine available to him, refused to continue Grace's treatment. With her medication now ended, surprisingly, Grace began to improve. The next year she returned to school. She had fallen far behind her classmates, but studied diligently, finished eighth grade, and was awarded her diploma.

Grace worried that her mother was unable to support the family. So she walked to Mancelona, found employment as a housemaid in the home of Mr. and Mrs. Thompson, and slowly paid the overdue doctor bill. She had given up all thoughts of continuing school, but as bright summer days gave way to autumn, she looked longingly across the street, where other children were enrolling for classes in the new school building.

**Louis, Emma, Wilmar, Lee, Anna,
Grace and Albert Williams**

On the last Monday morning in August 1910, shortly before her 18th birthday, Grace was busy helping her employer prepare the young children to start classes. Unable to contain herself any longer, Grace blurted out, "Oh, how I wish I could attend high school!" The instant the exclamation escaped her lips Grace's face turned deep pink. She was ashamed. Her employer had provided well for her and Grace didn't want to show a lack of appreciation.

Grace with colt

"Why don't you start high school now?" Mrs. Thompson asked. "You can stay here and work for your board. If you do the ironing too, I'll give you fifty cents a week to pay for incidentals." Whether the lady of the house was being helpful or whether she was just trying to keep her housekeeper didn't matter to Grace. She was so excited she hurried across the street and enrolled in high school. Being much older than her classmates embarrassed her at first, but her teachers encouraged her to continue. Older students who came to learn were good examples for the younger pupils.

In addition to keeping house for Mrs. Thompson, Grace completed three years of high school in two years and, with continued cooperation from her employer, attended County Normal[5]

---

[5] County Normal was an instructional school designed to certify rural teachers quickly.

the following year. That year in County Normal earned her a teaching certificate.

A few weeks before her 21st birthday, Grace began her career as a teacher. After her long struggle, at last she was teaching children. All the rural families sent their children to one-room country schools. The students attended the same school through eighth grade. For most, the end of eighth grade marked the end of formal education. For too many, even completing eight grades was impossible because their help was needed to provide for their families.

Grace began her work as a teacher in the "Day" school, named after an early resident in the area. The school building was two miles away from where Grace's mother still lived with her younger children.

The years had been very difficult for Anna. Her eldest son, Lee, after taking his fathers place as the provider for the family, had left home years earlier. The younger boys did what they could, but there was almost no financial income.

Grace was pleased to be able to help. She moved home with her mother, sister and two younger brothers. The two-mile walk, night and morning, was no greater distance than some of her young students traveled each day. It was a pleasant winter for both Grace and her overburdened mother.

Meanwhile, Wilmar finally found a farm, which met with his approval across the state near Alpena. He prepared a log house for his family. When spring crops were planted, the long missing husband returned and took Anna, Emma, Albert and Louis to live in their new home.

Grace was on her own and so she moved to a farm near the school, in which the owners had an empty room. The money she paid for board was a welcome addition to the family's income.

Twin brothers, about Grace's age, lived a mile and a half north from where Grace had lived with her parents. Grace had attended church and shared an occasional picnic at Rainbow Lake with these boys when they were children. It was not surprising when one of the brothers, Jerry, began to call on Grace more and more often.

The dances held at Coldsprings Town Hall, the only community activity, were well attended by the younger generation. They allowed Jerry to become better acquainted with the young teacher.

On Halloween, the dance featured a costume party. As usual, Jerry escorted Grace to the social. The smell of cider and pumpkin pie was in the air. Costumes were nothing fancy but they added a sense of fun for the participants.

Late in the evening, Grover Southwell laid aside his mandolin and moved onto the dance floor. More relaxed now, he enjoyed the company of several of the young ladies briefly. When the orchestra began to play "Over the Waves," Grover's favorite piece of music, he asked Grace for the pleasure of her company during the waltz.

Shortly before the music stopped, Grace asked about the little old bald man with the violin. It had intrigued her as to what could be the common bond between them.

Grover smiled as he answered. "That's my dad. He brought me to Blue Lake from southern Michigan. When the Blue Lake Lumber Company closed, he bought a piece of land a mile and a half from here. He's built himself a house and barn and is very content. I wanted to keep working in the timber, so we only see one another at occasions like this."

Grover and Grace continued to talk through the break in the music. The couple, still together when the orchestra began the next selection, moved onto the floor together for one more dance.

Jerry had been watching Grace especially closely this night, because he had in mind to ask her to marry him when he took her home that evening. But as he watched her dance with the lumberjack named Grover, he thought she looked especially lovely in her blue dress and satin hair ribbon, and he wanted to be the one with her. Then, when he expected her to find him for the next dance, she danced with Grover again! What in the world was wrong with Grace? Why, she was making a fool of him!

Before the music stopped again, Jerry had let jealousy completely overtake him. He abruptly stomped out of the building. Ruth, who was occupied near the entrance with getting her daughter a drink, looked up in time to see him untie his horse from the hitching rail, and ride towards home in his buggy—alone! She knew he would later regret his fit of temper.

When the dancing ended, costumes were removed and the women set out the food they had carefully prepared. Grace set out a place for two, including fried chicken, and apple pie. She looked around expectantly for Jerry to join her.

Grover, who came to the dance on the camp wagon with his friends Lee and Ruth, noticed the empty space next to Grace and wondered why she was alone.

Ruth found her husband. "Lee, you'd better take your sister home. Her escort left, and she shouldn't go home by herself."

Lee frowned. Some of the men had been drinking rather freely from the bottles that had appeared throughout the evening. Lee was reluctant to send his wife home on the wagon without him, but he couldn't leave Grace alone either. Lee looked questioningly at Grover, and hoped for some help.

Grover, somewhat embarrassed, said, "Look, I'll be happy to walk your sister home, Lee, but I don't want to come between a lady and her escort."

Ruth said, "Grover, on this occasion, we could really use your help."

Lee moved to the table where Grace was seated. "Grace, I don't want you to go home alone. I'd take you home but I need to stay with my wife and son." She glanced at him, her head tilted. Lee continued, "I talked to Grover. He's my closest friend and I'd like him to walk you home. I'm not trying to get you to associate with him if you don't care to, but you shouldn't walk home alone. I know I can trust him to get you home safely."

Grace was embarrassed and quiet as she started the journey home with a different escort than she'd set out with. After a strained silence in which neither could think of a comfortable topic Grover blurted out, "I wonder what was eating Jerry. It couldn't have been the short time you and I danced—but something sure put a burr under his saddle!"

Grace frowned and brushed a strand of hair behind her ear. "No doubt it bothered him when I danced two sets with you."

"But that seems so unreasonable."

"I know. He's seemed jealous before this, but we have no commitment. Grover, I'm sorry that he was upset, but it's kind of you to walk me home."

She didn't know what else to say, then, "I'd have been all right alone, but Lee still thinks I'm his little sister." With the ice broken by their brief exchange, conversation came easier as the pair walked the four miles to Grace's lodging.

"Lee told me you were sick for two years, then went back to school," Grover said. "I missed a lot of school, then quit in the eighth grade. Didn't it bother you being older than the other students?"

"It was hard at first, I never really was one of the group, but it didn't matter," Grace said. "With the school work and house work, my day was full."

The autumn evening was exceptional for late October with warmer than normal temperatures. The conversation turned to Grover and Grace's childhood as they walked the last mile. The similarity of their carefree childhood and the problems of their teenage years were vastly different, yet each one's struggle had left its mark.

Grover paused at her door for some time. The southwest wind was gentle and warm. The autumn sky was brilliantly lighted with a full moon, and filled with twinkling stars.

Grover suddenly noted Grace's long brown hair, as the breeze blew it across her face. She wore a blue satin ribbon in it, and the contrast between it and the darkness of her hair charmed him. The conversation had been good. Grace loved children, so did Grover. His mind was filled with new thoughts when he greeted the rising sun while walking back to Gorham Camp.

Grace also saw her companion in a different light. He had a strong, sure stance. His manners were above reproach, and once he relaxed, his conversation had actually been interesting. She liked his curly blond hair. She couldn't see his eyes on the walk home, but she remembered their clear blue color when Lee had first introduced them.

It was daylight by the time Grover reached camp, wide-awake. It was good that he'd had that hour and a half alone. He needed to put the evening's events in perspective.

Until now Grover had been content caring for his horses, working strenuously during the day, and frequently playing his mandolin in the cook shanty in the evenings. Now everything changed. "What happened to Jerry?" Grover asked his team of horses as he cleaned and fed them before going to the cook shanty for his own breakfast. Surely nothing he and Grace had done could have made her escort jealous. They had discussed Grover's father, and when the music started they danced through a second set. Why had Jerry left so abruptly? Maybe he had gotten sick. If so, he should have told his date.

In some ways, she reminds me of the Irish girl at French's. The same long brown hair and graceful walk. He hadn't remembered Colleen for a long time, but the memory brought a warm feeling that Grover couldn't quite understand.

He'd liked Colleen. Thoughts flitted through his mind like butterflies. *She was nice. She was earning every penny of her debt to the French's. She was always pleasant no matter what she did. She prided herself on good work.*

"I sure would like to see her again," he said to his horse. He looked around to make sure that no one else had heard him.

He began to be lost in that sweet reverie of living at the French's house and feeling part of a family there. When his thoughts returned to the present he had to admit that Grace was different. *She's more a friend, or a companion, than a girl.* The walk was special somehow . . . so different from a friendship with a man.

Soon Grover was back at work skidding logs. The horses often got wet from the falling snow. Each evening Grover carefully dried them, smoothing their manes and tails with the currycomb. The harnesses required extra care, now, too. Grover and the other teamsters, carrying a kerosene lantern, went to the barn and wiped the harnesses with oil. They needed to be kept pliable for the comfort of the horses.

While Grover worked at the lumber camp, Grace kept just as busy with her teaching. Along with the children's regular studies, preparations were underway for the Christmas program.

On a mid-December evening when Grace finished grading her student's papers, she looked at the rows of empty desks. *It's Friday evening and the floor has to be swept and mopped for Monday morning. This janitor work may pay an extra five dollars a month, but tonight it looks overwhelming!*" Then, as she realized how much she and the children looked forward to the Christmas program, she gained more energy. She thought of how little Roy's parents would be so pleased with his recitation. And there was Emma's poetry reading.

"We'll just see that those parents aren't disappointed!" she said aloud, as she rose from her chair to head for the broom. In no time the room was tidied and clean.

Grace pulled the scarf tightly around her mouth and nose and thought of the coming holiday, as the raw northwest wind chilled her face on the walk home. She thought of the walk home on Halloween night. The air had been fresh then, but the breeze was soft.

Grover was friendly, the stress of the circumstances had diminished quickly, and they found much of common interest. Grace realized she would like to see him again. Thoughts of the young lumberjack occupied Grace as she continued home.

She remembered how Lee had talked of his friend. He'd said, "Grover's a good teamster. He loves his horses, and he gets along well with the crew." *And what else was it?* Oh, yes. "Grover's had some rough years but he doesn't seem to have any bitterness."

Then, as she remembered the October evening, a smile played across her face. He hadn't known how to dance, but he was game to try it. *And he does love music.* She'd heard him sing, and she thought he was a fine singer. There was always a smile on his face when he played. It was fun to try to extract bits of information about him from their short time together.

The Christmas program at the Day school was on the last Friday evening before the holiday. Two older students welcomed the parents as they came in the door. Soon the little school building was packed. Even the horseshoe shaped room was full, including the bench at the back between the hallway entrances.

A young man sitting quietly, alone in the back of the school, caught the glances of the parents. Questions were whispered, but no one had answers.

Grace was busy. The children were introduced. Those in the younger grades gave their recitations first. Interspersed with songs, and a one-act play, the various presentations continued until the oldest had finished. When the program was over, Santa Claus shuffled in the back door with a bag over his shoulder and presented each child with a gift. Grace could now mingle with the parents. One by one, the families came and expressed appreciation for her efforts.

As the crowd thinned, Grace suddenly noticed Grover, sitting quietly in back. Her heart jumped! She knew she couldn't be rude to the parents, but Grace hoped he would wait.

Gradually, she worked her way to the back of the school. She forced herself to be calm when she spoke. "Good evening, Grover. Did you like the program?"

Grover smiled. "The program was great! "I wondered how you'd control all those kids.

"I love them." Grace replied. "They're good children. I've always wanted to be a teacher, from back when I entered my first year of school." Grover was impressed. He'd observed Grace's competence. Throughout the evening he kept wondering whether she would approve of his coming there. Her greeting gave him confidence.

Grover motioned toward the litter covering the floor. "I can help you clean this place up." The tired teacher gratefully accepted his offer. The room was quickly cleaned and Grace's work was completed until school would begin again after the New Year. It seemed the walk from school ended all too quickly. In his pocket, Grover was carrying what he hoped would be a welcome Christmas gift.

They arrived at Grace's residence before Grover mentioned his real reason for coming. Abruptly, he opened his coat and handed Grace a small book of poems by Sir Walter Scott. "I wanted to get you a little something for Christmas. Do you like poetry?"

The gift came as a shock. Grace hesitated while her mind raced. Could she accept it? She hardly knew this young man, but to refuse would be insulting. Grace had been pleased to see him at the program. "I love poetry," Grace's response was sincere. "Scott is one of my favorite authors. I'll treasure the book." Grover felt he could now mention his real objective. "I'd like to escort you to the New Year's ball, if you aren't committed."

Grace's face betrayed her joy. Occasionally she had wondered if the conversation at Halloween would ever be continued. "I'd be pleased to attend the ball with you, Grover. I'll fix something for the lunch." Grover hated to say goodnight, but it was late. He pulled his hat down. "Well then, it's a date."

The dance at Coldsprings was almost the only social occasion available for the young people of the area. The Opera House in Mancelona provided entertainment, but very few would travel so far.

Through the week, Grace thought about the coming event. She hoped Jerry would not visit. Grace had enjoyed being with Jerry earlier, but she neither wanted to continue their relationship nor to offend him.

Jerry, his self-esteem injured, had waited for several weeks, sure that Grace would contact him. Now, unbowed, he determined to look elsewhere. After all, he had his pride.

The afternoon of December 31, Grover polished the brass ornaments on the horse's harnesses. He then picked out the cleanest of the horse blankets to keep his team warm during the ball and, with some scrap boards, made a seat for the logging sleigh. When he arrived to pick Grace up, Grover was well prepared. He had purchased a dark, reddish-brown horsehide robe. It was attractive and was also very warm. The robe insured their comfort even though this last evening of the year was much colder than normal. Grover tied the horses to the hitching rail and covered each of them carefully with the relatively clean horse blankets. Then, somewhat ill at ease, Grover entered the hall with his date.

Tuden was leading the music with his violin. The local musicians were happy to be playing with the stooped old man but for the first time since the local dances began, Grover's mandolin was missing.

In spite of the cold night the celebration was well attended. Younger couples danced while the older couples talked. Mothers with young children gathered in the hall below the dance floor. The New Year was greeted with a joyous song. The food the women had so carefully prepared was quickly dispatched, and the revelers began the cold ride home.

Grover's horses, uncomfortably cold even with the blankets, were happy to begin moving. Traveling at a brisk trot, their flying heels kicked snowballs in the faces of both Grover and Grace. They laughed as they tried to dodge them, and Grover realized that Grace was becoming much more than simply the sister of his friend Lee.

It would be several weeks before Grover and Grace saw each other again, but both entertained thoughts of their next meeting.

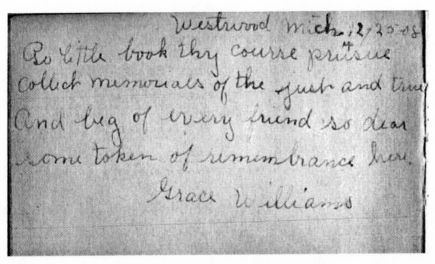

Grace's entry in her autograph book

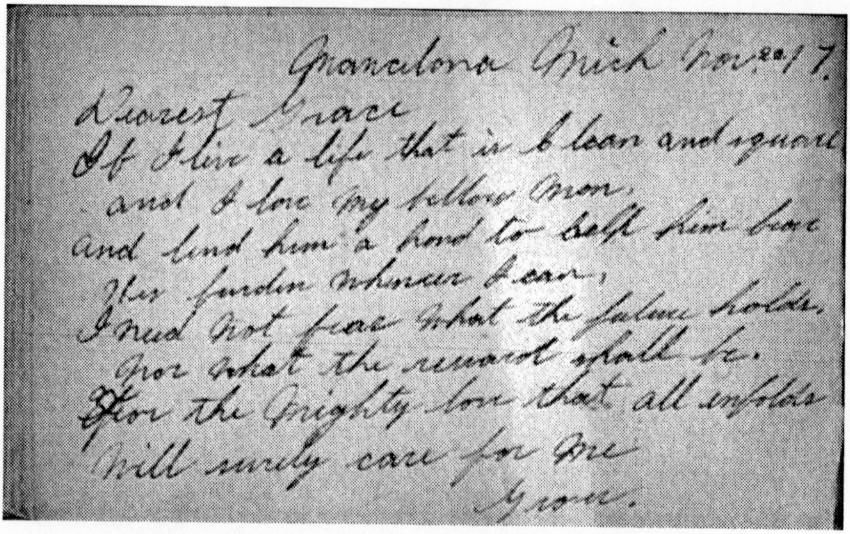

Mancelona Mich Nov. 20 17.

Dearest Grace

If I live a life that is clean and square

and I love my fellow man,

And lend him a hand to help him bear

His burden whenever I can,

I need not fear what the future holds,

Nor what the reward shall be.

For the mighty love that all unfolds

Will surely care for me

Grover.

Grover's entry in Grace's autograph book

Chapter 10

Two Questions

The friendship that began when Grover walked Grace home from the Halloween dance began to grow. They attended every social function at the Town Hall throughout the winter. One Sunday morning in early spring Grover walked to Grace's. Snow still covered much of the landscape; old, tired snow. Everyone seemed anxious for the winter to be over, though they were forced to admit that in this North Country, it could be a long way off. Every chore was doubled by the effort it took to deal with the snow and ice.

As he neared her house, Grover was excited. Today would be a happy day. He had no qualms about what he was about to do. He was confident that Grace had enjoyed their time together as much as he had, and he was not a man who wasted time. He patted his front pocket to make sure it was still there. A ring set with a large star sapphire was nestled inside. It was a beautiful stone. He hoped she wouldn't mind that it wasn't a diamond. But he knew she was a practical girl. That was part of her appeal.

Feeling the small packet in his front pocket, Grover smiled. He stood before the door ready to knock, but his confidence began to waver. He stared at the frost patterns on the door glass. He took a breath, and rehearsed again the words he intended to say.

Grace hummed to herself as she prepared to go to church in Westwood. She wondered if her friend, Josephine, would be over the virus she'd had last week.

Her thoughts were abruptly derailed by a knock at the door.

It was Grover! He'd never come to her house before! She hid her surprise and greeted him. "Come in, Grover!"

Grover was not tactful, but he always expressed himself clearly.

"The snow's going fast," he said. "The school year will be over soon."

"Yes. . ." She paused. ". . .the children are quite distracted by the warmer weather." Grace wondered why Grover walked six miles from camp to see her early on a Sunday morning. He had never shown an interest in going to church. And something put that wide grin on his face.

He appeared to be trying to think of some other topic to discuss, and then, he abruptly reached in his pocket and pulled out a small parcel.

"I've brought a little gift for you."

Grover handed her the little packet. The shape of it clearly indicated a ring box.

"Wh—why, Grover!" She gasped. She held the box at arm's length. Her mind raced like the time Grover handed her the book of Scott's poetry. He was impetuous but sincere. There were always surprises. . . but he had been considerate of her each time she had accompanied him.

"Go ahead, open it." Grover watched her intently. He gave her a penetrating gaze. "Look, Grace, this isn't a diamond, but I hope you'll accept it as such," he urged.

Grace couldn't speak. It seemed everything she thought of to say would be wrong.

Seconds passed like hours. Grover's enthusiasm seemed to wain. He seemed to have difficulty now making eye contact. It appeared he expected to be turned down. He said softly. "We've had some good times together. I'd be a good husband to you."

Grace's eyes seemed to be frozen to the white box. She had drawn it cautiously towards her, and now she opened it. She made another little gasp.

Grover forced himself to wait for her response. He wanted her companionship; he wanted to build a life with her, raise a family. He'd hoped that she felt the same. Why doesn't she say something? He'd expressed himself as well as he knew how. He would say no more.

After what seemed like an eternity, the corners of Grace's mouth lifted slightly, then her lips curved into the most beautiful smile he'd ever seen. It was like seeing the sun rise after spending the night in the forest. She held out her hand. "See if it fits!" she said. Grover breathed a sigh of relief as he took out the ring and slipped it on the third finger of her left hand.

Now she found the words to say to him. "I've thought about marriage . . . but I really can't say I expected a proposal so soon, Grover!"

"Do you like it?" he said.

"It's beautiful! And, Grover, whether it's a diamond or not doesn't matter in the least. It's more than I could have hoped for!"

At this, he surprised her again by pulling her toward him and squeezing her tightly around the waist. Grace caught her breath, just before he kissed her. She thought that maybe she could get used to surprises!

Once a decision was made, Grover saw no need for delay and on April 14, 1916, when the trilliums were beginning to bloom, a pastor from Mancelona married the brunette teacher to the blonde teamster at the Methodist Church. Bruce Williams and Edna Catlin were the attendants.

The day of the wedding dawned bright and sparkling.

Several of Grace's friends and a few men from Grover's camp were guests. In turns the guests congratulated and teased the groom, who, in a brand new suitcoat looked as though he might be a tad uncomfortable. His broad grin, however, let everyone know he was more than comfortable with his decision.

The bride was lovely in a stylish black dress with a bunch of Venice lace at the throat and a rose corsage. Her dark hair was luxuriously drawn up and caught with a small noisette of flowers.

When the ceremony was over, Edna held a luncheon at her home for the wedding party. The house was polished and decorated with the finest family linens. The large spatterware coffeepot was brewing and made the air rich with the aroma. There were little meat sandwiches and deviled eggs in neat rows on a large platter bor-

Grace and Grover's wedding photograph
April 21, 1916

rowed from the church. In the middle of the table was a two-tier wedding cake that the local bakery had turned out in grand style. It was small, but elegant.

Tuden, who had driven to the wedding with his faithful team, Mike and Nell, presented the newly married couple with an envelope.

"I have a little gift for you. You might want a place of your own."

Grover lifted the flap of the plain white envelope, and pulled out a deed for forty acres of land! It was the eastern third of the 120 acres that his dad had struggled so hard to buy.

Grover was unable to speak. He blinked back the water that seemed to be getting in his sight.

The fact that his father would give them part of his property moved him deeply. Who was this little old man? Though his thoughts were focused on his new bride, he suddenly realized that he and his father hardly knew one another. At times they had seemed so close, at others they'd disagreed to the point of angry words. Grover swallowed hard and tried to choke back the tears. As their friends exclaimed over the wonderful gift, he felt somehow removed, and just a little weak in the knees. In a flood, the memories of the years at the Coldwater orphanage and at Hackney's came rushing over him. He had felt deserted during those years, even betrayed. Then his dad had tracked him down, and brought him to Blue Lake. Since then, their relationship had been building slowly. Grover had only remembered his father sporadically after Tuden left camp and bought his own place. Now this grand present!

Grace broke the silence. "What a magnificent gift!" Should she address him as "Dad"? Tuden's eyes shimmered and he gave her a fatherly kiss from under a tobacco stained mustache. He stepped back, took out his handkerchief and wiped his nose rather loudly.

Certainly he was different from her own father. Wilmar Williams was a strong, domineering man; Tuden seemed old and frail. She wanted to get to know him. There was more depth to this little man than it appeared. His gift touched her and she was grateful for what it meant to Grover. She would always be grateful for that.

A week before the wedding Grover had inquired about the Engmark place, a mile from their new property. Louie Engmark had built a house and barn and cleared about fifteen acres of land. Then he had moved to Detroit with his wife Beatrice, and the place stood vacant. The location was ideal for Grover and Grace. Grace wanted to continue teaching, and she could walk from their new home to school. Grover found a job with a homesteader who was cutting and selling logs from his property.

By autumn, though, plans to teach were put off by a new development in their lives. Grace was becoming heavy with their first child. Now teamsters were in demand at Gorham camp, and across the railroad track from the cook shanty an empty house was available for Grover and his budding family. He skidded logs that winter with a good team of horses which was absorbing work, and Grace was content to live in the tar paper shanty that the company provided.

In February, a tiny baby came, and they called her Edna. Grover could hardly contain his excitement! He wanted to be the best father he could be! And Grace seemed so serene and motherly after her labor. It looked like everything was going to be perfect. Dr. Walton seemed withdrawn, however. He took a long time washing his hands. Ruth had come to help, and she placed the freshly bathed infant into her mother's arms. Then Dr. Walton asked Grover to sit down. "I know you both want this baby, Grover, but her breathing is so weak that I'm afraid she has no chance to survive. There's nothing we can do for her."

Little Edna died ten days later.

The blow was devastating to the young couple; but Grace was shattered. Her arms ached for her little one who had been taken. She rose each morning with a wounded heart, tired before she had begun her day's work. Grover felt the pain keenly, too, but he was more worried about Grace. He was busy all day and he worked to the point of weariness. Blissful sleep came quickly for him, but not for Grace. She moved through the motions of each day in heartbreak and sorrow, and could not sleep at night. The summer dragged by.

The hot summer days finally ended and trees brightened with autumn colors. The yellow-gold of the beech trees made the woods look golden and the maples were all hues of scarlet. The colors of the leaves and the chill in the air were bittersweet; almost symbolic of the sense of passage they would come through.

In October, they received the news that Grace was expecting another child. The discovery filled them with hopeful gratitude; no news could have been more welcome! Dr. Walton said the pregnancy appeared to be normal; the prospect looked good. Grace prayed fervently for a healthy child.

Lee and Ruth lived just two houses up the railroad track from the Southwells. Grace and her sister-in-law became close confidants, working and sewing together while Ruth's two children played underfoot. Both families were comfortable in their little houses. In the evenings, Lee and Grover worked together, cutting and splitting wood for the next day's fuel. Their financial needs were being adequately met and life was sweet throughout the winter.

When the huge snowdrifts next to the railroad track vanished and the trout lilies bloomed, Grover and Lee had to tell their wives that there would be no work at the camp this summer. Families could stay in the company houses if they wished, but there would be no employment until the next season's snowfall.

They heard from Jack, Grover's brother. He was working, and would come to visit when he could. Grover was grateful that they had not lost contact, and although he liked to see Jack, he brought back a part of Grover's life that he'd have preferred to forget.

Grover and Grace were growing impatient for their child to be born, but Grace was feeling well and they expected to have a strong child. Grover stayed close to his wife through May and June. The child's birth was imminent, and they were both longing for that day and for the child. Finally, on June 23, 1918, Dr. Walton announced, "It's a boy!" Ruth was with them again, and she cheerily handed the little boy to his mother. Grover saw that the hair covering the head of their newborn son was dark just like Grace's. He had a son who resembled the woman he loved!

Grace was overjoyed with the warm little baby to hold and to love. They named him Harold Freemont Southwell. Freemont was in honor of Tuden, whose given name was Oren Freemont Southwell.

Grace always addressed her son as Harold. However, Grover took one look at the long dark hair and immediately dubbed his son, "Brown," the name by which he called him until "Brown" was a grown man.

Grover was determined that his son would have all the love and opportunities he had been denied as a youth. He was willing to do anything necessary to provide for his wife and child.

The sawmill in Antrim was the most modern in the area and the lumberyard was constantly filled with quality lumber that was being loaded on railroad cars and shipped to various cities.

There was no work in Gorham camp for several more months, but in Antrim, they were hiring men to load the lumber onto the railroad cars. Grover began to walk the six miles up the railroad track to Antrim each morning, work ten hours, and walk home again in the evening. He was able to do the journey in an hour and a half. Three hours a day walking to work and back, plus 10 hours a day loading lumber, (including a half-hour for lunch), kept Grover away from his wife and son from 5:30 in the morning until 7:00 in the evening, six days a week. The long days were tiring for Grover, but being away from his wife and baby distressed him more than anything else.

It was lonely for Grace, too. Her brother and Ruth had gone to the Upper Peninsula to find work there. Grace was busy caring for Harold, pumping and carrying water from the well by the cook shanty, and carrying wood from the woodpile that Grover cut each Sunday to cook their meals. She prepared an early breakfast for her husband, packed him a big lunch, then waited to eat supper with him late each evening. She was concerned that her husband was working too hard. He didn't complain, however, and just seemed to be thankful to be healthy and able to do the work.

The long daily grind throughout the summer was broken up by one of the men in Grover's crew. In the evenings, Grover would relate the latest antics of John. John never took work seriously. He usually worked hard, but sometimes became more interested in storytelling than in the work. Though it was disrupting, John's stories were funny and the crew liked him.

One morning, Claude McGill, the lumberyard foreman, stood impatiently waiting for John to complete one of his stories. When the story dragged on, Claude spoke sharply. "Come on John, let's go!"

John took off his leather apron, climbed down from the railroad car, put his hand on the foreman's shoulder and said. "Where we going, Claude?" Mr. McGill opened his mouth to speak, looked at the crew, who were all laughing, shook the hand off his shoulder and walked away.

A few days later Claude came by and again John had stopped work to tell a story.

Claude stopped him in mid-sentence. "John, you're holding up the crew. I'll have to send you home."

John resumed working immediately and said, "I can't go home, Claude. My wife will just send me back." Once more his wit had saved his job but it was the last time. He was fired a few days later. Times were lean, and foremen wanted their money's worth from the crew.

The summer wore on slowly for Grover and Grace. The green forest gradually changed to autumn gold but Grover hardly noticed the beautiful walk along the railroad. This year he wanted the leaves to fall. Remembering how impatiently he had waited for snow at the end of his first summer in the north, Grover thought of the similarity. That year he was waiting to begin work at Blue Lake. This year he was anticipating evenings with his wife and son.

The long awaited snow—and return of lumberjacks to camp— came in early November. The men-shanty was filling with single men; housing for married men was at a premium. Lee, who always seemed to be at the right place at the right time, now came to occupy the house beside his sister and her husband.

Grover and Brown were always together when he was home from work. Grace was overjoyed at the delight they found in one another. She thought about it a lot: *Life doesn't get any better than this.*

In January of 1919, a young minister who held church services in lumber camps during winter months asked to hold meetings in the cook shanty each evening for a week. Word of the meetings spread quickly. Most people in camp were interested. Some had attended similar meetings at other camps; while others had never attended any kind of church service. The young minister asked for someone to help the cook clean up after evening meals so meetings could start by seven o'clock. Grover, Grace, Lee, and Ruth were happy to help.

Grace had always attended church as a girl. She had followed her mother's example until her marriage to Grover. She missed singing hymns, the social times, and even listening to the sermons. She was eager for the meetings to begin.

Grover had never attended a church service in his life. His parents had not been interested in church. At the orphanage in Coldwater, although he had the opportunity to attend a service, Grover preferred to play baseball with the other boys. Of

Jack, Tuden, Grover, and Harold Southwell

course at Hackneys, there was time for nothing but work.

Lee wasn't interested in church, but he and Ruth went to the meetings with Grover and Grace. All the other families in camp attended, so did most of the single men. Some wanted to hear the minister. For most, it was a break in the monotony of the winter evenings.

Small songbooks were distributed. The minister played an accordion and the group joined in the energetic, if untrained singing.

The message following the music was short but emphatic. "Hell is a real place and it's the destination of everyone who refuses to accept Christ as savior. The fire of Hell burns forever! The forest fires some of you have seen are nothing compared to burning in Hell!" The preacher had the lumberjacks' attention.

The following evening was similar. A number of songs, followed by the young minister telling of God's love for all people, and His desire to save them from eternal punishment.

The third night the message was longer.

"Folks, some of you think you can please God by doing the best you can. The best you can do isn't good enough," the evangelist said. His demeanor, curiously, was not condemnation, but explanation. "We've all done wrong and God calls it sin. Sin is just another word for rebellion towards God. But he sacrificed Jesus Christ, His own Son, to pay for my sins and yours. My friend, God will forgive you if you accept Christ's payment. It's the only way to escape the fires of hell."

Grover and Grace lay awake for a long time before sleep came. All this preaching was new to Grover. Grace had attended church regularly growing up. Her mother had told her of God's love and Christ's sacrifice, but Grace had never really listened. She had continued to attend church after moving away from home. It seemed to be enough, but now she wasn't sure.

Grover skidded logs as usual the next day. His mind returned to the preacher's description of hell. The fire he had witnessed in the pines along the Manistee River vividly depicted what hell was like. *I've done the best I could, Grover thought. I work hard and try to make a good life for Grace and Brown. I haven't had a drink since we were married, but I'm a long way from being perfect.*

As the day wore on, Grover tried to remember what the minister had said. Two things stood out in his mind. "Hell is a real place," and, "God sacrificed His Son to pay for your sins."

Grover could not imagine sacrificing his own son. It was more than he could fathom. By the time mid-afternoon came, he had made his decision.

When the minister finished his message that evening, Grover and Grace were the first to express a desire for Christ's forgiveness. It was a new experience. Both felt confident that their futures were secure, and they resolved to teach their son what they had learned this week.

Grace looked for her brother. She loved big, rugged Lee, who had been a like a father to her for so many years. Grace wanted her brother to join her and Grover in this new life. But Lee and Ruth didn't seem to understand.

Chapter 11

The Farm

When the evangelist moved on to take his message to another logging camp, Grover, Grace, and little Brown settled into a comfortable routine.

It was an excellent winter for the timber harvest. Snow came early and yet was never deep enough to seriously interfere with

Stacked haycocks at the farm

the horses ability to work at skidding logs. The new railroad jammer, moving by its own power along the rails, provided a fast, reliable way to load the logs onto railway cars.

Grover confided to his horses. "Just a few more years of work in the woods," he told Polly as he brushed her mane. She brought her head back to him for a stroke. "These forests won't last forever." He could see that there would only be a few years left of lumbering.

It was time to plan for his family's future.

That evening, when supper was finished, Grover played peek-a-boo with Brown until Grace finished washing dishes. When his wife picked up her knitting, Grover said, "Ma, I think we should plan to move to the farm. The timber will not last through our lifetime and we can begin clearing land this summer. It'll be a better place for Brown to grow up anyway."

Grace stopped knitting, looked directly at her husband and waited for him to continue.

"Louie's decided to stay in Detroit. He makes more money working for Ford than he could on the farm. We could rent the Engmark place until we get a house built on the land Dad gave us."

Grace nodded her head in agreement. "The farm is a better place for children." For several minutes, both were lost with their own thoughts.

Grace said, "We have some money saved. But do you think we can make it on our own?"

"We can buy a cow this spring. She'll furnish our milk and butter." Grover began to warm to the idea. "We can plant a garden and that'll furnish most of our food."

"Yes."

"Louie built a pretty nice place. There's a well by the house, and a good stream runs across the farm. There's plenty of timber for fuel and enough cleared land to provide feed for a team of horses and a couple of cows. I think we'll be able to live there until we get a place of our own."

Grace began to knit again. "I can see that the move is needed; but I'm still not sure if we'll be able to get along."

Her natural reserve was well-known to her husband by now. "If Dad will let us use Mike and Nell part of the time this summer," Grover said, "I can plant crops and haul the material to build a house. I don't think he uses the horses very much. Back when he bought the land, he had wanted me to go in on it with him. I wasn't all that keen on it when he asked. Then he gave us the forty acres for our wedding present."

Brown was trying to get his daddy's attention by pulling on his hand. Grover tousled his hair, and grabbed him into a bear hug.

"I know dad'll be pleased if we move there. It would be good for Mike and Nell, and for him, too. A little smile played across Grover's face. He's a great carpenter, but that's about all you can say for him as a teamster."

The following Sunday Grover walked the seven miles to see Tuden, who was stumbling across his roughly plowed garden, mumbling about a team of horses that didn't know where they were going and wouldn't pay attention to anything they were told.

Surprised to see Grover, Tuden walked to the spring where a tin cup hung conveniently on a branch. He handed Grover the cup and said, "Have a drink and cool off," then wiping his brow with a blue bandana, Tuden sat down on an old pine stump.

Grover filled the cup and drank deeply of the fine, pure water. "That's a good spring, Dad." He drank a second cup, then hung the cup back on the branch and turned to face Tuden. "Grace and I've decided to start building a house up here this summer. We'll need horses to do it. I'll need to plant a garden, skid up some wood, and make a few trips to town for building material. We wondered if you would let us use Mike and Nell part of the time."

Tuden twisted his mustache and mumbled his usual long hmmm, before answering. "I'll need the team for a few weeks this summer to work on the road." He said. "That's pretty well my year's income." Soon, however, he nodded his head and added, "The horses don't do much else but stand by the barn and fight flies. It'll be good for 'em to work a while."

That night at the supper table, Grover said, "Well, Brown, Granddad's going to let us use Mike and Nell." Grace looked up from mashing Brown's potatoes. She understood the message was for her. She held her husband's gaze, and smiled. They began to talk about how to move various items so that they wouldn't be broken when they arrived at the house. Their excitement resulted in lots of chatter in the following days about working toward building a place of their own.

The next Saturday, Grover sent a letter to Louie:

Dear Louie,

If you're not coming back north this summer, Grace and I would like to rent your farm again. We've decided to build a place of our own and we'd like to rent yours until our house is ready to occupy.

Best Regards,
Grover Southwell

Time dragged as Grover and Grace waited for Louie's answer. If Grover was to continue working in Gorham camp the following summer, he had to decide soon. There was no empty house, other than Louie's, near enough to their property for Grover and Grace to live in while building their own place. Since they had decided to move to the farm, work at camp had grown less appealing to Grover. He was anxious to begin work at the forty.

Nearly two weeks later, a letter from Louie finally came on the logging train.

"I'm going to stay in Detroit, Grover," Louie wrote. *"You're welcome to live on the farm for at least a year."*

When winter's logging ended, Grover got up early, walked to Tuden's place, borrowed Mike and Nell and the wagon, and was back at Gorham camp shortly after noon. Grace had their belongings already packed, awaiting his return.

When they ate their dinner, Grover loaded the bed and the crib he'd made for Brown on Tuden's wagon. Dishes and clothing were added and the little family was on the way to their future home.

Grover fed the horses old hay left in the barn, wiped them down with a cloth, and vowed to buy a currycomb at his first opportunity. Mike and Nell were a good team. Grover would see they were well cared for.

When Brown was asleep in his crib, the wagon unloaded, and their own bed put back together, Grover and Grace were more than ready for a night's sleep. It had been a long day, but a good one.

Their immediate concern was a cow to provide their milk and butter.

It was only a half-mile from Louie's house to Grace's Uncle Charlie's home. Unlike Wilmar, his brother, Charlie had stayed in Coldsprings Township. With several sons, Charlie had combined a little farming and a little logging with his income from holding township office to provide financially for his family.

Uncle Charlie had several cows. Possibly, he would sell one.

The next evening Grover and Grace walked across the field to Uncle Charlie's place. Sitting straight on his dad's shoulders, Brown twined his fingers firmly in Grover's curly hair. The discomfort from his hair being pulled was more than offset by the joy of having those little legs on his shoulders and small heels bouncing off his chest.

Uncle Charlie and Hattie, his wife, were surprised to see their visitors. They had assumed their niece and her husband would stay in camp. Now they welcomed them as neighbors. "Sure, we can let you have a cow. We have two heifers freshening this spring," said Uncle Charlie, apparently pleased to have a ready sale. "We have a Holstein and a Guernsey to sell; take your pick."

Charlie found a halter he could loan Grover and, with help from one of Charlie's sons, they led their newly acquired possession home. In the morning there would be warm milk for Brown.

The cow provided more than enough milk for the family to drink. Cream rose to the top of what remained and was churned for butter. When Grover and Grace lived in camp, these commodities were luxuries. Now they were in abundance every day.

The next task was preparing a garden. Grover covered an area near the house with decomposed manure from a pile behind the barn, then used a plow and spring tooth drag borrowed from Tuden to prepare the plot. Before returning Mike and Nell to his father, Grover also plowed and dragged a small field for corn.

Grass was already growing in other fields. Grover was confident that hay cut from those fields and the little patch of corn would provide enough food for their cow through the winter.

Grover and Grace were eager to begin building their own house, so as soon as the spring planting was finished, they walked across the swamp to their property. The site Grover had tentatively chosen for a house was on a hill near the northeast corner of their forty acres, bordering a wagon trail running past their place. They were confident the Township would build a road once their house was occupied. Grover wanted his wife's input.

Grace was delighted. "There'll be a cool breeze across the high ground on hot summer days," she said as she looked around thoughtfully. "Some of these trees are big enough for shade already."

Timber had been cut from the area some years earlier. A few remaining maple trees had reached a diameter of about four inches. These trees would provide shade for the couple in the brief periods when they allowed themselves a break from their heavy work preparing a home site.

Because cedar was almost impervious to rot, it was Grover's choice for the foundation of the house. There were large cedar trees in Louie's swamp that the wind had uprooted. With the help of Mike and Nell, Grover skidded the large cedar logs to their new home, hewed a flat top, and set them in place for a foundation.

Their garden was growing. They were already able to pick peas and green beans for the table. Soon there would be potatoes. The cow was furnishing an abundance of milk and butter. The foundation for the new house was in place.

Grace asked her husband. "Have you thought about a cellar? We need a cool place for potatoes and the other vegetables."

Grover admitted with a frown he hadn't thought of a cellar. "It's a good thing you thought of it now." He said. "It has to be dug before we build the house."

A cellar was a virtual necessity for food preservation. As Grace said, they needed a cool place to keep a winter's supply of potatoes, as well as canned fruit and other vegetables.

The house was to be 24 feet square. Grover dug a 10 by 16-foot cellar under the south side, and made a stairway. This space would be more than adequate for their little family.

When the annual work on the roads began, Grover shoveled sand for the township while Tuden was busy with his horses. "Dump boxes" on the wagons were used to haul sand. These boxes were nine feet long, three feet wide, and one foot deep, and held a cubic yard of sand. The crewmen shoveled sand into these boxes until they were level. After horses pulled the wagon to the desired location, other men pulled out the ends of the box, lifted the sides, and one by one tipped over the bottom planks, dumping the sand.

All the men living in the township who had horses were offered the opportunity to work on the road. A man with a team of horses was paid seven dollars for a ten-hour day, and a man without horses received half as much. This was considered good pay. The township also needed many men without horses to shovel sand on the wagons and level the sand where it was dumped.

In mid-August, the township's road money for the year was depleted. They made progress each summer toward developing a satisfactory wagon road for all the residents. Every year new homes were built, and each summer as many roads as tax money allowed were finished.

While Grover and Tuden were busy at work on the township road, Grace was equally busy in her garden. Weeds were pulled and vegetables were picked (or dug up) and canned. Between Grover's pay from the township road and the food Grace had prepared and processed for winter, they were as financially well off as they would have been staying in camp.

Now Grover was able to buy building material, so he drove Mike and Nell to the lumberyard at Antrim. He remembered that when the hemlock boards had been sorted, any board containing too many knots was rejected when the lumber was loaded on railroad cars. These knotty boards were sold at low cost to local residents. If handled carefully and used discriminately, Grover was confident the knotty hemlock would build them a good house.

Remembering the foreman at Antrim, Grover went to him while in town one day and said, "I need material to build a house, Claude. What do you have that I can afford?"

Glancing at the horses and wagon, Claude replied. "Take what you can use out of that pile of hemlock. It's ten dollars a load. Get as much as you want."

The price was better than Grover expected. Claude allowed him to choose what he wanted and Grover took only what he considered satisfactory. He and Grace would have a good sturdy house.

Tuden had made a list of construction materials. They would need 2 x 8 planks for joists, 2 x 4s for studs, and one-inch boards for sheeting. Grover and the faithful old horses made five trips from Antrim with material.

Tuden came each morning to help with the building. The years of toil showed clearly on his slender frame. What Tuden lacked in physical strength, though, he more than made up for with his knowledge of building and working with wood. The tool chest that he carried from ship to lumber camp and on to his little house had all the necessary tools. From broadax and adz for hewing timbers, to saws, hammers, levels, and the heavy plumb bob, they didn't need to purchase any tools. Grover had never seen such a heavy plumb bob. He lifted it and asked his father. "Where'd you get that?"

Tuden grinned. "I wanted one that will hang straight when the wind's blowing so we'll know which way is straight up." He was ready to start work.

The cedar logs that Grover had so carefully placed for the foundation were not as level as they looked. With Tuden's help, a level line was soon placed around the house, just outside the base. A little careful swinging of the adz to remove the high spots satisfied the old ship's carpenter. Now the joist could be laid.

The men were confident they could complete the shell of the building before bad weather set in. Grover's physical strength and Tuden's years of experience were a good combination. As the walls of the house went steadily up, the walls between father and son went down.

The framework for the walls was complete by mid-September. Tuden was cutting rafters and Grover was spiking them together when an ominous column of smoke appeared in the sky. The smoke was blowing almost directly toward them, and both men were well aware how quickly fire could travel through slashings that were left from the cut over timber.

The smoke quickly became a dark cloud and billowed closer. Looking toward the rising smoke, Grover voiced both men's thoughts. "That wind's blowing straight north. We'd better forget these rafters and see about Grace and Brown!"

Mike and Nell stood in the warm autumn sun hitched to the wagon. Grover untied the lines and encouraged the horses as only he could, to reach Grace and little Brown while there was still time.

It was none too soon! When the men arrived at Louie's farm, Grace and Brown stood in the yard watching the fire move into the swamp. When the fire reached the evergreen tops, it jumped from crown to crown. Firebrands (burning twigs) began falling in the yard and on the house.

Dry cedar shingles covered the roofs of all the farm buildings. Suddenly, a small fire appeared on the roof of the house. Grover put a ladder against the house as Tuden pumped water.

Grace's cousin, Clare, ran across the field from Uncle Charlie's house to help.

Clare and Tuden pumped and carried water. Grover extinguished ember after ember on the house roof. No sooner did he put out one fire than another started! The wind was searing! The larger fire, after burning the remains of the forest, was now only 100 yards away. The bare field, with nothing to burn, prevented it from coming closer.

When the fire slowly subsided a few hours later, three fatigued men and a greatly relieved woman, holding her son tightly, collapsed by the well. Grace had stayed in the field with Brown, where the heat was less intense. Even there, the smoke and heat had been hard to endure.

The fire had started by Rainbow Lake and cut a narrow swath across the intervening mile and a half to Louie's farm. Fortunately, the road passing on the opposite side of Louie's farm and the field beyond it provided a barrier to the spreading fire, which burned itself out. After a short break, the men poured water on the firebrands that still smoldered in the yard.

Once they were able to relax, Grace and the men expressed amazement that the barn had been spared. Was it a quirk of the wind, or an act of God? No one knew for sure, but whatever the reason, the family was grateful they still had a place to live.

Long after the sun had dropped beyond the horizon, Grace and Brown finally drifted off to sleep. Grover still lay wide-awake. The memory of the Blue Lake Fire and now the fire here caused him to marvel at the vast energy of an uncontrolled blaze and the helplessness of men as they faced its monstrous wall of heat.

He thought about how close they had come to losing it all. The fierceness of the wind driving the blaze north may also have been what prevented it from spreading either east or west. The area that burned was devoid of plant life. It was apparent that the wind, which had seemed so much an enemy, had actually prevented damage to Tuden's, Uncle Charlie's, and Grover and Grace's properties. It was a thought that impacted them with a deep, unspeakable humility.

Tuden needed a day off. Grover certainly understood. Although he was in the prime of life, he too felt extremely fatigued after the tension of the previous day.

The following evening he walked across the swamp and looked at the burned over land before going on to his father's house. How well had the old man snapped back from the physical and mental strain of fighting the fire? The question troubled Grover as he walked. He realized now how much his father meant to him, and that the old wound caused by his father's error had scarred over and healed.

He found his father reading a small, well-worn book. He got up and made a cup of tea for Grover. They made small talk, mostly about the fire. Grover didn't directly inquire about his dad's well being, and he didn't stay long. However, as Tuden watched him return home across the field, he indulged himself in a small pleasure. His son hadn't wanted to borrow anything, hadn't brought

Grover and Grace's home partly built

anything. There could only be one reason he walked over. Tuden knew that he'd come to see how he was, and the warmth and concern of the gesture was not lost on him.

The normal time for the first frost in autumn had already passed and it was time to get the crops harvested. Both men had a field of corn to cut, potatoes to dig and carry into their cellars, and for Tuden, there were rutabagas, his most prized vegetable. Grover's house could be finished in cold weather, but the temperatures dictated harvest time.

Father and son worked together. By early October, the corn was in shocks and the vegetables were in the cellars. Their attention returned to building.

The sparkling air of October in northern Michigan was bright and crisp. The bracing air and periodic morning frosts energized the men as they prepared for the long winter that would soon be upon them. Grover had separated the building materials back when he'd unloaded them from the wagon. Each dimension of lumber had been piled in its place. His effort was rewarded as he and his father struggled to finish building before snowfall. Tuden, too, had prepared well. The saws, planes, and drawknives were sharp and ready for use.

The house progressed daily. The rafters went up, the roof boards were nailed on, and the roof was covered with tarpaper.

In early November, they nailed sheeting on the walls and window, and then nailed in the doorframes. Temporary boards and tarpaper were placed across these openings to keep out the snow, and the project was brought to a halt.

The temperature was dropping with each day, it seemed, and they'd already seen snow. Grover and Tuden cut dead trees from where the fire had burned and skidded them to their houses to provide fuel for the winter. It was much easier to cut the logs, skid them to the house and cut them up there, than to cut the stove wood in the forest and then handle individual logs or sticks.

Brown was playing happily on the floor and Grace was preparing dinner when Grover came in from cutting stove-wood. He pulled off his gloves and hat. "Ma," he said, "I think we should go back to camp for the winter. It would be more profitable than anything else I can do here."

"What will we do with the cow?" Grace asked. "And there's a winter's supply of food in the cellar, too."

"Maybe Dad or your Uncle Charlie will keep the cow." Grover replied. "We could take the food to camp with us."

Well, if that's what you think, than we'll get ready for the move." She was not eager to pull up and pack up and relocate, but there wasn't much choice, if it was the wisest decision.

Grover walked to Gorham camp the next morning. There was plenty of snow for skidding logs. *Has the winter's crew already been hired?* Grover wondered as he walked the four miles to camp. *No smoke's coming from the stovepipe where we lived last winter, I might not be too late.*

Entering the office, Grover asked. "Can you use another teamster?"

Mr. Phelps looked up in surprise. "I thought you were a farmer," he said. "But there's an empty house and a team in the barn. When can you start?"

"It'll take a couple days to get moved," Grover replied. "Can I use your horses and sleighs?"

Permission granted, Grover drove home with the team, tied them to the sleigh so they could eat the hay he had brought for them and ate his own dinner. Then with a grinning son comfortably snuggled on his lap, he drove down the hill to his father's house.

He found his dad washing potatoes. "Dad, we're going back to Gorham for the winter." Grover said. "Do you want to keep the cow? She'll furnish all the milk you want, and you can have the calf in the spring."

Tuden carefully considered the care that would be required. "Water's no problem, I can take the horses and cow to the lake to drink, but I don't have enough hay for Mike and Nell and a cow, too."

"I put up more than enough hay for the cow. We'll bring it over before we leave," Grover promised.

Tuden decided he had room in his barn. The cow could stay with his horses. "I guess I could do that. I can use the milk and butter."

Together, Grover and Tuden moved the hay and corn shocks to Tuden's barn, and led the unwilling cow across the field to her new winter home.

The next morning he and Grace got up early, loaded their belongings on the logging sleigh and by mid-afternoon they were unpacking once again at Gorham camp.

When they got to the shanty that was waiting for them, Lee and Ruth were there to greet them, with tea, cookies, and good-natured chatter. Grace had not been looking forward to the time at camp, but now she realized that she would enjoy the winter with Lee and Ruth next door. Grover would enjoy his team of horses, and they would all enjoy the comical antics of little Brown.

The vegetables Grace had canned were stored in boxes in the corner of the kitchen and the potatoes placed in the coolest corner of the little house. They provided a major part of the family's food and enabled the young family to save more money than they had been able to in previous winters.

The winter was uneventful. There was enough snow to move the logs but not too much for the horses. Most of the lumberjacks from the previous year returned. The quantity of harvested timber was enough to please the company owners.

Grace, Grover, and Harold at Gorham Camp

When lack of snow brought the logging season to an end in the spring of 1920, Mr. Phelps asked Grover. "You coming back next winter?"

Surprised but pleased, Grover answered with a wink. "Keep the same house for us. Grace has it fixed up the way she wants it."

When the winter's work was finished, Grover borrowed a team and wagon from his employer to bring doors and windows from Mancelona to their new home, then helped store the equipment in preparation for the next winter.

The sun was high in the sky the day Tuden arrived at camp with Mike and Nell to move his son and his family to their new home. Grover was anxious to get things done!

He looked at the sun. "It's going to be late when we get to bed tonight," he told Grace.

Tuden heard the comment, but was unruffled. He had gone over and hung doors the day before. It was true the windows still had not been placed in their openings, but that wouldn't take long.

Grover's irritation was not lost on his father, but Tuden said nothing about what he had done the day before. It was character-istic of the old man. He would let his son chafe. Grover could see for himself when they arrived at the house.

As they arrived with the wagon, Grover could see that the doors were already hung, and he smiled broadly at his dad. The old man still had a few surprises left in him!

"Well now, aren't you something?"

Tuden had the last laugh. He'd been waiting to see Grover's face when they got there.

The spring sun was setting when the windows were finally in place and the wagon unloaded. Grover hugged his wife. They were home!

The abundant lunch that Grace had carefully packed filled the stomachs of the foursome. Tuden drove home with his team. Grace tucked Brown into his crib and covered him with quilts. It was going to be a cold night in the house, still open at the top of the walls. Grover had to close around the eaves as soon as he could.

They cooked breakfast the following morning outside on an open fire before Grover left for town with Mike and Nell to buy a range. Since they didn't plan to spend winters in their new home for a few years, the range would allow Grace to provide meals while warming the house on cold mornings.

Grover and Grace discussed stoves, and determined that a good stove was worth the price. They bought a Kalamazoo range with a warming oven above the cooking surface and a reservoir on the end opposite the firebox to provide large quantities of warm water. As soon as Grover finished installing the range in the kitchen, he sealed the remaining opening along the eaves.

Grover and Grace had no well of their own but the spring at Tuden's place was a source of fresh water. Grover carried two pails the quarter-mile to his father's house for water with Brown riding happily on his shoulders, but the two-bucket supply of water was meager. Carrying it from Tuden's spring was not only tiring but also time consuming. The couple agreed that a well was a necessity.

They hadn't planned on the additional expense. Reluctantly, they agreed they would have to borrow money to pay for the well, but where to borrow it? Who had a hundred dollars to loan?

Grover emptied the last pail of water into the reservoir of the range. Holding the pails in one hand and Brown's foot with the other, he began his twice-daily walk to Tuden's spring. Brown tried to wiggle his foot free. He had no need for his father to hold his leg with his hands firmly entwined in his daddy's hair; he was in no danger of falling.

Walking down the hill to the spring, Grover knew he must find money for a well. His wife was expecting another child in October. After giving Brown a drink and drinking deeply of the cool spring water himself, Grover discussed his predicament with his father.

Tuden knew what to do. "The bank will lend you the money and I'll sign your note."

Reluctant to accept more help from his father but never having borrowed money, Grover hesitated before agreeing Tuden's signature probably was necessary.

The president of the Mancelona bank, Mr. Mills, was only too happy to oblige. Tuden had borrowed when he bought his property, and had made payments faithfully. Grover was another customer, and the bank had money to lend.

With one hundred dollars in his pocket, Grover immediately went to see Mr. Berg, in Bellaire, the man who drilled all the wells in the immediate vicinity.

"I have two wells to drill first, then I can do yours," a tired Mr. Berg answered Grover's question. "I charge a dollar a foot. The well point and pump cost extra."

The well was 96 feet deep, Mr. Berg had to drill 96 feet to find water, and the pump and well point added still more to the cost. But the good news was Grover had his own well! The water was cold and clear, and tasted good. The gravel and sand at the bottom of the well pipe would purify all the water they needed.

Grover and Grace squeezed the extra dollars for the pump from their sparse savings. Grace especially appreciated the fresh water. The drinking water that had been so cold when Grover dipped it from Tuden's spring was anything but fresh and cold after sitting for hours in the water pail.

Grover continued to pull stumps and help his wife care for the garden and can vegetables for the winter. Brown dug in the sand. The little family was thankful for their own home.

On a brisk morning in early October another son was born. Unlike his brother, whose brown hair had so delighted his father, this boy's blue eyes and snow-white hair, (what there was of it), pleased his mother, who told her husband, "That's exactly as I picture you when you were born."

Grover responded quickly, "First we got Brown. Now we have White." Grace's protests that Brown had a real name fell on deaf ears. To Grover the boys would always be Brown and White.

The actual name given to Grover and Grace's second child, and duly entered in Dr. Walton's records, was Rex Wilmar. The name Rex was chosen after a friend in Grover's youth, and Wilmar, in honor of Grace's father.

Doctor Walton insisted that Grace stay in bed for ten days to allow her body to return to normal, as the custom of the time dictated. Rex was born on October 5, 1920. Grace restlessly stayed in bed and looked from her window as the leaves fell from the trees across the road. When the doctor allowed her to get up from her bed, the leaves were gone. It was nearly time for the annual trek back to Gorham camp.

Weak after the enforced inactivity, Grace struggled as she packed for the return to camp. "The little shanty will be full this winter," she said to her husband.

It was a raw November day when they moved to camp. Brown was a rugged boy and seemed to enjoy the brisk wind in his face. Grace was concerned about baby Rex on such a cold day but there was no reason to believe that another November day would be any better. The little family, with their possessions loaded in Tuden's wagon, left their new home for another winter in Gorham camp.

Grover wrapped the horse blanket, which he had purchased for his first date with the tall schoolteacher, around his wife. Grace was comfortably warm, and holding Rex close to her breast, the baby was well cared for. Brown was happy to be seated between Grover's legs, intermittently grasping the lines to the horses as they moved to Gorham for another winter.

When his family was safely settled in their winter home, Grover went to find what horses he would use for the winter.

"We have another young team of Percherons we'd like you to take this year, Grover. They're good horses but aren't very well broke." Mr. Phelps looked questioningly at his teamster.

Hiding the surge of joy that he felt at the challenge, Grover replied, "Let's take a look at them."

The men walked together to the horse barn. The boss, although familiar with horses, did not share Grover's love for the animals. When they entered the barn the boss walked well behind the restless young team. The horses were obviously not happy to be idle.

Grover walked slowly up beside each one, turned their faces toward him, rubbed their noses slightly and grinned when one horse reared back. He said. "I think we can get along together."

Walking back to his house, Grover picked up Brown and said to his wife. "That's the team I'd like to have for the farm."

Chapter 12

Transition

Since Grover preferred being home with his family in the evenings, he no longer went to the cook shanty with his mandolin. One evening, an older violinist came to the house.

Grace welcomed the visitor. A visit was unusual in the logging camp. When the day's work was finished, the men were ready to relax and were not interested in venturing out in the neighborhood.

After discussing the weather and the work, the visitor posed a question to Grace. "Now that Grover has a family, he doesn't come to the cook shanty. Would you mind if a few of us brought our instruments over some evening?"

"I think that would be real nice," Grace responded quickly. "Our boys don't have to go to sleep early every night. Grover and I will enjoy the music, and I suspect the boys will, too."

The little house rang with music on one night nearly every week. Grover and his wife served tea and brown sugar cookies. The men came across the track together, each carrying a chair in one hand and an instrument in the other. Grover nailed spikes in the exposed two by four studs, and soon two violins, a banjo and a guitar adorned the wall.

Grover and Grace agreed that life was good.

One morning shortly before Christmas, when Grover was chopping a limb off a log, the axe glanced off the limb and cut a deep gash in his kneecap. Reluctantly leaving his horses to the care of another teamster, Grover wrapped his jacket tightly around his leg and walked the quarter mile back to camp. Grace carefully removed the jacket from Grover's wound to reveal the long gash. "Grover, I can't take care of this—you need a doctor!"

Having walked a quarter mile with blood gushing from the wound, Grover agreed. It was customary to care for your own wounds, but if Grace said he needed a doctor, one would have to be called.

Hurrying across the railroad track to the office, Grace said frantically, "Grover cut his knee pretty badly. Please call the doctor." Once the doctor was convinced the cut was serious, he agreed to ride to camp on the logging train that afternoon.

Grace bandaged Grover's wound tightly and they waited impatiently until the logging train chugged its way to camp three hours later, carrying Dr. Walton with his ubiquitous medical bag.

"Grover, you're fortunate the cut wasn't any deeper. You came close to losing the fluid from under the kneecap! You'll have to stay off that leg until it heals. I'll send you a crutch on the train tomorrow. If you give it a chance to heal, the knee'll be all right."

Dr. Walton was well aware that his patients often forgot his advice the minute he was out of sight. Before leaving for Antrim and his home in Mancelona a short time later, Dr. Walton again warned Grace. "Keep your husband off that leg!"

The family now faced a financial crisis. Not only did they have an unexpected doctor bill, but also there would be no income for at least a month while Grover's leg healed. Grace was determined to earn what she could.

Men living in a men-shanty always needed to have their clothing washed. Providing this service was often the only available income for widows or wives whose husbands were unable to fully support them. This was the job Grace took on. She carried two pails of water from the pump by the cook shanty, heated the water on their range, and scrubbed clothing on her washboard. The work was hard and it provided very little income. Grace recalled her mother's struggle when her father went away to look for a better farm. Life was hard for a woman with a family to care for and no husband providing for them.

After hobbling around the house for a week on his crutch, Grover could wait no longer. "Ma, I can't stand having you scrubbing clothes to keep us eating. I'm going to talk to Mr. Phelps. He'll advance us money until I go back to work."

Grace reluctantly agreed, but insisted, "Grover I'm going to earn what I can."

Antrim Iron Company's policy was to advance scrip (coins manufactured for use only in the company store—not legal tender elsewhere). Grover could borrow what he needed. Grace continued to wash clothes for three more weeks, while Grover hobbled around on his crutch.

Late in January, Grover threw away his crutch and reported to the office for work. He could walk, barely. It was obvious he would never keep up with the young team of horses he'd been driving, but he could swamp (cut brush) for some other teamster. By this time Grover was ready to support his family and was sure this kind of work was available for him.

Fortunately Mr. Phelps had already given the situation some thought and made Grover an offer. "I need another man to scale. The scalers are getting behind and the men want their pay. I'll pay a dollar a day more than you got driving horses, and it'll give you the rest of the winter to get that leg limbered up." Scaling meant counting the logs for the sawyers and measuring wood for the woodchoppers. This was a great solution to Grover's problem! The extra money would help make up for the time he had lost.

Each crew of sawyers was assigned a strip of timber. Behind them came the woodchoppers cutting the remaining treetops and small trees into four-foot lengths, splitting any stick more than six inches in diameter and stacking them into piles to be measured. One half cord, 4 x 4 x 4 feet or more, was to be in each pile. The woodchoppers were to cut from the same strip that had been assigned to the sawyers ahead of them.

Grover was not only responsible to count the logs and scale the piles of wood, but to see that the men followed their assigned boundaries. It was always a temptation to jump across the line for some choice trees or to leave a tree at the edge of the line. Some trees were extremely hard to split and the woodchoppers could usually identify them by sight.

The scaler was responsible to prevent cheating. He was given a hammer with a stamp on one side. With this he marked the end of each log he counted and a few sticks in each pile of wood he scaled.

Occasionally someone was tempted to saw a thin piece off the end of a marked log, or the marked sticks of four-foot wood that they had already been paid to cut. These had the appearance of new work and it was quicker than cutting logs from standing trees, or cutting and stacking a new pile of wood.

Additionally the woodchoppers, who were to pile the wood in a reasonably square pile, learned to "lay up" the piles. That is, pile the sticks of wood around holes. They could "lay up" a porous pile much more easily than cutting the extra wood to fill the gaps. If the holes were not too apparent, the scaler didn't question the size of the pile. But if the holes were unreasonably large, the scaler was required to "dock" the woodchopper by scaling it for less than its apparent size. Naturally, this caused friction between the scalers and those cutting wood. A scaler's ready response to such an objection was, "I touched the pile and it settled a quarter of a cord."

Walking daily through the snow was therapy for Grover's stiff knee. Initially the pain was hard to bear, but each week he saw an improvement. Long before the snow was gone, Grover yearned to be working with horses. Still, the extra money was important and his work with the scaling rule was proving satisfactory to both workers and management.

Brown was three and White only seven months old when Grover and Grace moved from Gorham Camp to their home in mid-April 1921. Each time they moved, the wagon became heavier.

This year, they had several projects in mind for the homestead.

When spring planting was finished Grace asked her husband to build a better "privy." The lean-to they had used the previous year was hardly acceptable for the children. Grover made a four by six-foot outhouse with three seats, two for adults and a lower one for the boys. After digging a hole some fifty feet from the house big enough to last two or three years, Grover carefully moved the new building in place over the hole. It was top-notch, equal to any in the neighborhood.

The next project was a chicken coop. Grover built the coop on cedar logs so he could skid it from place to place. Inside, some poles across the back provided a place for chickens to roost, and boxes separated by partitions, gave the hens privacy to lay their eggs. A dozen hens supplied eggs for the family, and the rooster faithfully fulfilled his role as an alarm clock each morning.

Soon the inborn desire to reproduce became apparent among the hens. When Grace went to gather eggs, one of the hens pecked fiercely at the hand feeling under her for eggs. Grace smiled as she placed twelve eggs in a special nest she had already prepared and put the ferocious hen on them. Placing a potato crate over the hen to encourage faithfulness to her task, Grace said to her, "Take good care of your eggs." For three weeks the dedicated hen stayed on the job. When the restraining crate was removed, the proud hen led her little chicks across the floor.

In mid-July, Frank Cunningham, an early resident of the township, walked over one afternoon. Although he lived two miles east of the Southwells, he was considered a neighbor. Neighbors rarely had time to visit each other. Frank had come to northern Michigan from southern Ohio years earlier. He was an ardent trout fisherman, and he occasionally walked several miles to the Manistee River during the warm summer months and fished throughout the afternoon. He cooked his catch in the evening, and then slept under the open sky. Early in the morning, he returned to his fishing, and then walked home with his catch. Fish were plentiful and Frank was a skilled fisherman so he consistently took home an enviable catch of trout.

Frank was animated. "Grover, I was fishing in the Manistee yesterday and when I walked through the slashings where the pines used to be, there were blueberries like I never imagined! The ground was blue with them! We're going to go pick some. Do you want to go with us?"

Grace responded instantly. "If there are that many berries, we could can some for winter." She looked at her husband for confirmation.

Frank said, "Myra would like to go, too, but we don't have horses. We wondered if you'd want to make the trip with a wagon?"

"It would be good to get some berries, but with Brown and White, that would be a long hard trip." Grover looked questioningly at his wife. "What do you think?"

Frank was normally a quiet man, but it was amusing to see how excited he was about the exceptional crop of blueberries. "Our son, Jean, is Rex's age. Myra thought she and Grace could take turns caring for the boys while the other picks berries." Grover and Grace were delighted with the idea. It would be fun to break up the routine of daily chores with a little excursion.

"Let's get ready tomorrow and go the day after. Tuden may want to go, too. They're his horses and it's his wagon." Grover greatly appreciated the use of Mike and Nell, but did not take them for granted.

"Oh, of course, get Tuden to come!"

Early Tuesday morning, the Southwells, with Tuden contentedly sitting in the back of the wagon with Harold, picked up Frank and Myra at their home and continued eastward to pick blueberries.

Grace had packed lunch for both families and Myra had done the same.

Frank said the berries were big and covered the ground. Since they would probably go only once, each family brought a washtub.[6]

"I can't imagine filling that with berries, but it will hold whatever we pick." Grover expressed the thoughts of everyone except Frank. Frank just grinned.

The sun was high in the sky and becoming oppressively hot, when they rode down the last hill to what was now a blueberry plain. The scent of the ripe fruit was wonderful. Even though Frank had described the abundance of the wild fruit, the others were amazed! Where the forest fire had burned, blueberry brush covered the ground. The entire area was literally blue with ripe berries. Some were as big as the end of a man's thumb. Everyone started right in picking the luscious berries. Brown's face and hands turned purple with the juice from the berries he ate. The babies also shared, as their mothers carefully gave them the very best and biggest berries, one at a time.

Frank had a blueberry picker. A scoop with long wooden fingers, it plucked ripe and green berries alike. It also picked some leaves and twigs but by using the picker they could pick a lot of berries in a few hours. Grover and Frank kept the berry-picker

---

[6] a galvanized steel tub about 12 inches deep and 30 inches in diameter

busy. It was tough on the back but each in turn swept the picker under ankle-high bushes, separating as best they could the berries from sticks and leaves.

Brown followed Tuden as his grandfather strolled through the berry bushes, picking only the biggest and best, until the pail he brought was filled with beautiful fruit.

At lunch the berry pickers were able to rest their backs. Blueberry bushes are low to the ground, and picking them is notoriously hard on one's back. The families gathered under a maple tree, which had somehow escaped the loggers' attention. Since both ladies had prepared abundantly there was food remaining to munch on during the ride home.

Tuden was accustomed to being alone, although he never felt lonely. But he thoroughly enjoyed Brown tagging on his heels all day. After lunch, Tuden had contentedly leaned against the tree and nodded off from time to time with Brown sleeping beside him. In mid-afternoon, while others picked berries, Tuden drove the horses to the river for a drink. When the families were ready to go home, the horses would be ready too.

By late afternoon, both washtubs were filled with berries.

The tired, but happy group gathered by the wagon as Tuden, with Brown at his heels, hitched his horses to the wagon for the trip home. When Tuden climbed to the seat to drive Mike and Nell home, Brown was beside him reaching for the lines. Taking her son by the hand, Grace said. "Come sit by me, Harold. You can drive horses when you're a little older."

Tuden, who had been both surprised and pleased at the attention he received throughout the day from his little grandson, said, "Let him drive 'em, Grace. All they want to do is go home."

Grover was pleased to see Brown's interest, and he nudged his wife. "He likes horses as well as I do!" Then he said, "I don't think Mike and Nell will cause their young teamster any problems. They just want to go home, like dad said."

It was not a fast trip, but the old team plodded along and everyone was grateful to allow the horses to do the work. The sun had set and the three boys, including Brown (still seated between his grandfather's legs), were sound asleep when Frank and Myra climbed down from the wagon with their washtub full of berries.

"We sure appreciate the ride to the river," Frank extended a thankful hand to the wizened old man as he spoke. In turn, Grover and Grace expressed their thanks for an opportunity to pick the berries. If Frank hadn't gone trout fishing, none of them would have known the berries were there.

Tuden was obviously worn out. Grover quietly mentioned this to his wife.

"We'll unload, then I'll help with the horses, Dad," Grover set out the tub of berries and carried Brown into the house. Tuden started to speak, then quietly waited.

Grace asked her father-in-law if he wanted more berries than were in the pail he had picked. When Tuden replied negatively, she hurried to put the boys in bed.

After Tuden walked stiff-legged into his house, Grover unhitched Mike and Nell, took off their harness, gave them water and hay, cleaned them off with a currycomb, then returned home to a well-deserved night's sleep.

Sorting the stems and leaves from the tub of blueberries was a lot of work, but work Grace was happy to perform. Most of the stem and leaf trash floated when they put the berries into the water. Even though they all ate fresh berries and Grace made several blueberry pies, she still canned thirty quarts from their tub. The sense of accomplishment and having prepared well for the snowy season ahead was fulfilling. She smiled broadly. "These will taste so good this winter."

The crops were harvested and the family moved back once more to camp for the winter. When they stacked all their provisions in the kitchen, Grace observed, "This place is sure small after living in our house all summer! The vegetables and berries fill one whole corner."

Grover looked at the space his wife had left in the kitchen. There was a bench for the washbasin and soap dish. The towel hung on a nail above them. The water pail sat beside the washbasin filling the space that remained in the corner of the kitchen. When Grace washed dishes she had to move the water pail and basin to make space for the dishpans. "It'll be tough, Ma. I hope you can manage for the six months of winter."

"I wasn't complaining," Grace replied. "I was just thinking how much I enjoy our own house."

Grover agreed. "Yes, it's been real nice there. Some day maybe we'll do well enough to make it without having to work here at the camp."

"That will be a happy time," Grace said.

Due to the slowing of available work in the woods, some of the sawyers and woodchoppers from previous years didn't return and life became difficult for those in the men- shanty through the winter. Though alcohol was illegal, bottles periodically appeared and fights broke out. Several of the older men left and those who replaced them were not congenial.

Grover had been asked to scale logs and wood again. He needed as much money as he could save, so he abandoned his precious horses and worked his way through the newly cut areas with his scaling rule.

The atmosphere at camp was entirely different now. No one came to Grover and Grace's place with musical instruments for an evening of music. In addition, there was frequently trouble in the men-shanty.

Grover and Grace had their boys and were content to be alone with them. In the evening Grover tuned up his "potato bug" and he and Grace sang. Again, the music was soothing for Brown. Oddly, White showed no interest.

Grace's thoughts returned to her and Grover's commitment to Christ and His teachings. When they had heard the evangelist so passionately tell them of God's love, Grace had dug their Bible out from among her books of poetry and began reading a portion to the family each evening. Shortly after beginning to read Scripture, Grace remembered the prayer her mother had taught her as a child. When nightdresses had been placed on her sons, she began to teach them the same prayer:

Now I lay me down to sleep.
I pray the Lord my soul to keep.
If I should die before I wake,
I pray the Lord, my soul to take.
God bless Daddy and Mama,
Granddad and Grandpa, my brother and me.
In Jesus name, amen.

Grover hadn't thought much about the commitment he made. But it touched his heart as one of his sons knelt by his knee each evening and recited the simple prayer.

In the spring when the Southwells returned home Grover walked over their south forty acres, and realized that they could never be farmed.

"I'm afraid that we're going to need more land." Grover told his wife and sons over a meal of potatoes, carrots and canned chicken. "The south half of our forty is a swamp with a steep hill on each side." After a brief pause he continued. "There's still two acres east of the barn I can clear but the South twenty is just too hilly to farm."

Grace cast a questioning look at her husband, then returned to the unending effort of getting food in Rex's mouth, instead of around it. She pondered how they might acquire more land without much in the way of cash.

When his own mouth was empty, Grover continued. "Dad has eighty acres right behind us. It's more than he'll ever use. I'd like to buy the north forty from him."

"Are you sure your dad won't need the land?" Tuden had been extremely generous when he gave them the forty acres they now owned and Grace didn't want to take advantage of him. Grover had pondered, too. His father wasn't strong. Tuden had enough cleared land for his horses without his north forty. His real treasure was the lake. Thinking Tuden might be happy to be relieved of the burden of paying taxes on that forty, Grover and Grace decided to make him an offer.

Grover walked down the hill to his father's house. The setting was so picturesque. The lake was sheltered in a small valley, with a field and a garden plot and the small, well-built house. Tuden had just returned from his little lake with three bass strung on a willow crotch. The old man was relaxed and happy.

"What do you think of my boat?" Tuden pointed to his prize. He had built a twelve-foot boat, pointed on both ends and made paddles from a dead pine tree. He kept the boat between two spreading white cedar trees in a little opening beside a spring on the edge of the lake. It was a beautiful spot. The narrow opening was just wide enough for the boat. Tuden could step out one side of the boat and onto dry land.

He seemed to be in a good mood and for a few minutes he exulted about the delights of living on his own lake and how happy he was that he'd been able to buy the place. After a short pause, the old man picked up his fish and asked. "Does Grace like it here?"

"She does. She's very content," Grover answered. "Grace loves her children and she loves her garden. I never thought anyone could be so happy pulling weeds!" After a short pause, Grover approached the subject he'd come to discuss. "Dad, we really need more farm land to be able to make a living. And I've been doing some thinking. If you want to sell your north forty, we'd like to buy it. It would help us and you'd get rid of some taxes."

Tuden's brow wrinkled. "Hmmp-a-hmmp-a-hmmp-a-hmmp-a-hmmm."

Grover was careful not to change expression, although he smiled to himself.

Tuden needed time to think. Laying his string of bass in the cold water, the old man sat down on the exposed root of a big pine stump. Grover waited quietly. The next move was his father's. Several minutes passed before Tuden broke the silence.

"I'll never use that land." He nodded his gray head as he spoke. "If you want to buy that north forty, you can have it for what I paid for it. I'll still have the lake and what land I need."

Grover tried to contain his excitement. With his mission accomplished, he waited until his father picked up the string of fish and the two men walked to the house together.

Not until Tuden began scraping the scales from the fish did Grover take his leave and stride rapidly over the hill to his waiting wife. "We have another forty! Dad only asked the two hundred dollars that he paid for it!" "Most of that land is level and some of it has very little brush. We'll need it when we come home to stay." Sleep came slowly that night as each began to excitedly plan for the future.

Chapter 13

. . . .

High Points

B y today's standards, the bright moments of the next few years seem very tame. But the daily struggle to put food on the table required a responsibility to routine, just for a family to survive. A break in that routine, no matter how trifling, brought a welcome relief from all the hard work. Several events highlighted the next few years while the Southwell family divided their time between Gorham camp and their home on the farm.

In the spring of 1923, Grace sat at the kitchen table looking at one of several seed catalogs. It was a quiet scene as the late afternoon sun slanted through the windows, bathing her in soft light. The boys were on the floor playing. She suddenly looked up and gushed, "We need apple trees!" The boys, in unison, stopped in their tracks, and looked up at their mother to see why she was so upset. She sighed and looked at Grover. "There are so many things that would be nice."

Grover had been clearing the last small field north of their house. It was the last of the dead brush left from the timbering that concerned him. If another forest fire should occur, those would go up like a box of wooden matches. He answered Grace with the wide grin that often brightened his face.

"I got a place ready for apple trees this morning—you can go ahead and make out the order!"

"Oh, Grover!"

Grace excitedly pored over the catalog again, this time with a definite purpose. After a few minutes, she gave the boys a sugar cookie with milk, and then she and Grover carefully planned their orchard together. It would be years before the trees would bear, but they wanted each variety for a special use. They decided on one Yellow Transparent tree, the earliest; one juicy and early-ripening Wealthy; one Wagner for winter; and a Russet for storage in a pit and so they could have apples even when the snow was gone. They added four apple trees to the annual seed order. Grace was thrilled! Something about apple trees called up a vision for the future, a permanence that she longed for, a settled life. One in which they could invest themselves and raise their family.

She calculated and planned, and saved every penny to use it in the wisest place. She completed the order and put it on the small table by the door to be mailed. That took care of the fruits and vegetables, and they had fresh milk and fresh eggs. Things were shaping up for the little family.

Grover began to clear a six-acre field adjoining his father's property. Across the fence, between Grover and Tuden's buildings lay a small field that was lush with pasture for Mike and Nell. Beyond the house and to the right, the little lake nestled below dark green cedars. The scene was one of tranquil beauty.

The following day when Grover came to the house for his noon dinner, Grace met him at the door with a worried expression.

"Rex is sick. He has a terrible fever!"

Grover went to see his son, who was lying on the bed. White's breathing was labored. Grover put his hand on his son's forehead.

"I'll go see Dr. Walton." Grover would take no chances with his boy's health.

The family ate a hurried meal before Grover grabbed his hat and walked to Mancelona. Mike and Nell would not be able to make the trip any quicker than he could, so there was no point in taking time to hitch them up.

Grover walked the eight miles briskly. Two hours later, he was speaking to the doctor. "Our little boy is really sick, Doctor. Can you come right away?"

Dr. Walton asked a couple of questions, then headed to his stable with Grover.

This was the first time Dr. Walton had seen Grover since the injury to his knee a year and a half earlier. Clearly, Grover was much more anxious about his son than he had been about himself. House calls were a way of life for rural doctors and Dr. Walton kept a young, fast thoroughbred and a light buggy for just such occasions. Even with the doctor's lively little horse, it was late afternoon before Grover returned to the house with the man.

Dr. Walton's examination of Rex was brief. "The boy has diphtheria." He told the anxious parents. "You'll have to keep his fever down. Keep cold, damp, cloths on his head all night. I'll come back in the morning."

Digging into his black bag, Dr. Walton brought out a small bottle. "Give him a teaspoon of this every two hours and keep a spoon between his teeth so his jaw doesn't set. If we can get him through the next 24 hours, he has a chance."

All night Grover and Grace kept the teaspoon in Rex's mouth. Their arms ached and they got little sleep. Rex drew shallow breaths and lay very still. His fever remained high. Grover and Grace replaced the cold cloths frequently. "I'm sure thankful for the well," Grover told his tired wife as he brought in another pail of fresh water.

After what seemed like days rather than hours, the sun came over the horizon. Grace leaned her head on her husband's shoul-

der. "I hope the doctor comes soon." She felt sure Rex was growing weaker, but did not want to say it aloud. His breathing had
become so faint.

Much earlier than Grover and Grace expected, Dr. Walton
appeared at their door. He carefully listened to Rex's breathing,
felt the boy's forehead, and then used his thermometer to check
his temperature.

"His fever's a little lower. His jaw will not set now, so you won't
need to keep the spoon in his mouth. Keep the cool cloths on his
head, though, until the temperature drops. It looks like he'll pull
through. You were lucky!"

Grace boiled a pot of coffee while Dr. Walton sat on the end of
Rex's bed. Looking at Grover, he said, "The baby's heart will be
weak, but in time he should outgrow it."

Listening in the kitchen, Grace's encouragement from the doctor had been short-lived. She was relieved to hear that their son
would probably live yet her weary body slumped at the warning of
a weak heart in her little boy. She prayed a quick prayer and put on
a courageous face.

"Coffee's ready."

The call from the kitchen raised the two men from the edge of
the bed. "I'm afraid the bread's dry, but it's all I have this morning."
Grace wished she had much more to offer the doctor.

"I'm just glad for the coffee, the bread is a bonus! I was up half
the night helping with a childbirth." Dr. Walton's shoulders sagged
as he soaked the bread in his cup. He was glad he didn't have to
give these folks bad news. After eating the large slab of bread and
finishing the coffee, the doctor straightened in his chair and spoke
again. "I've done all I can do for your boy. His fever's going down.
He should be up and running around in a couple of days. As he
took up his hat and headed for the door, he said, "If you need me
again, let me know and I'll come."

Grace swept a tear away as she thought of how close they had come to losing their little Rex. She managed to compose herself enough to say, "Thank you, Doctor. We are so grateful you came."

Frank and Myra Cunningham came to Gorham as cooks in the winter of 1924–25. The previous cook had moved away and Myra's brother told Ford Munn, the new camp boss, that Frank and Myra had cooked for a crew in Ohio.

When Mr. Munn asked the Cunningham's to work, they agreed to come for one year and see how it went. Their son Jean, now four years old became the friend of all the men who came to eat. Jean was well behaved and carried the lighter dishes for his parents as well as relaying any request from one of the lumberjacks to his father in the kitchen.

One bright sunny day after the noon meal, little Jean was missing. He had been in the cook shanty when the food was placed on the table. Suddenly he was gone. His parents called, but received no answer. There were frozen skidding trails in every direction. Jean could have walked to the woods on any one of them. *Why did he leave? Which trail did he take?* Mr. Munn, the camp boss, directed a search for the boy. When the crew started out on the different trails, Fred Williams turned back toward camp and glanced at the cook shanty. "Well, bigosh! There's Jean! He's sitting on the roof!"

Jean was seated with his back against the warm chimney, watching the crew and wondering what all the excitement was about. A ladder that Frank used to shovel snow from the roof was left against the end of the building and Jean had used it to "get up in the world." The relief was evident, not only in Frank and Myra, but also in the entire crew. The winter weather would have been brutal to a little guy like him.

Grover and Grace's completed home

Rex, Harold and Jean at Gorham Camp

Harold, Rex and Jean developed a bond which strengthened throughout their lives. When Jean was not at the Southwell's, Harold and Rex were at the cook shanty with their friend.

Sun had melted much of the snow, and the days were warming, when the last big storm of the winter struck. It proved the old saying about the month of March: "In like a lamb, out like a lion." Whatever the reason, the storm was a doozey. The extra snow extended logging season through most of April. When spring finally arrived, it came in a rush. Pools of water lay along the railroad tracks where the ground had frozen solidly through the winter.

Jean had a new pair of rubber boots. Wading in the puddles sure was fun! Water above his ankles was no problem. He was having a ball!

Jean's two friends, Brown, age six, and White, four years old had new boots like Jean, but their boots (more commonly called overshoes) had rubber soles and canvas tops. If Jean could wade in the puddles, Harold and Rex decided they could wade in the puddles too. Their overshoes, however, kept out snow but were not impervious to water. The three boys had a joyful afternoon as the wind blew their wood chip sailboats of various sizes and shapes, across their makeshift "lakes."

When Brown and White returned home, their legs were soaked to their knees. Grace, who was always fearful for her sons' health was horrified at her boys shivering. The temperature had fallen close to freezing. Grace scolded them as she dragged off the boy's wet clothes.

"You'll catch your death of cold. Don't you ever wade in those puddles again!"

Though Brown and White had enjoyed the afternoon immensely, they agreed to sail their little boats from the shoreline. For a time, compliance with Mother's rule was easy. The temperature stayed below the freezing point for several days and the three young friends ran and slid across their temporary ice rink.

When the bright sun came out again, the ice rapidly disappeared from the boy's skating-rink and Jean again stood in the puddle with his rubber boots, guiding his wood chip "steamboat" across "Lake Michigan." Brown and White obediently launched their boats from shore and waited patiently for them to cross to the other side but the wind was not cooperative. Brown and White could wait no longer and the water was not very deep.

"I'll push 'em across," Brown volunteered.

"Me too," White chimed in.

The water grew deeper and deeper and the boys' feet got wetter and wetter.

Grace put potatoes on the hottest part of their wood range to cook for supper and went outside to call her sons. Looking down the track, she could see that their lake had returned. Happily bent over their wood chip boats, the three boys stood ankle deep in water, oblivious both to wet feet and to their anxious mother's approach. For Grace, this was a moral crisis. She spoke sharply to her normally obedient boys.

"Come out of that puddle! What did I tell you?"

Surprised at her tone of voice and suddenly noticing where they were standing, the boys hurried to their mother. Jean stood innocently in his rubber boots, wondering what the problem was.

Hurrying back to the house to get the wet clothing off her sons, Grace was alternately scolding them and wondering what action she would take. Once the wet shoes were removed and dry pants replaced the soaked ones, she made her decision.

Pointing at Grover's razor strop, which always hung by the washbasin, she spoke emphatically. "I told you boys to stay out of the puddles. I'm afraid you're going to get sick. If you wade in those puddles again, I'll spank you with that. Do you understand?"

They understood!

The next afternoon, Brown and White stood obediently on the bare shore while Jean sailed his tall boat across the water. Jean had found a wide chip with an unusual extension up from one side. It was the only such chip to be found. The wind carried it across the water while the flat chips hardly moved. It was a genuine treasure!

All three boys admired this special boat. When a gust of wind tipped it over they all rushed to its rescue. The water was above their ankles. Brown felt the icy water creep through his pant legs. He hadn't intended to disobey, but the precious boat had capsized! Now that he was wet anyway, he might as well enjoy the afternoon.

Anything Brown could do, White could do, too. It was always that way. The three of them had a marvelous afternoon until Grace came to the door. "Harold! Rex! You boys get home this instant!" There was no mistaking the tone of her voice or the situation. The boys hurried home.

Grace's mind raced. The last thing she wanted to do was to spank them with that razor strop, but she had promised. The boys must learn that a promise had to be kept. "I'll be careful." She spoke the words aloud convincing herself she was doing the right thing.

Grace met her sons at the door, the razor-strop hanging from her right hand. Harold, the oldest, was first. Swinging the strop back over her shoulder, Grace felt the sting. It was about right. She would hit herself each time to know how much it stung. "If only I hadn't made that promise," she thought.

Both boys had felt the palm of a parent's hand across their rear ends from time to time, but the razor strop was a terrifying new experience. Actually, it didn't hurt that much. The real pain was that their mother would actually hit them with such a thing.

Fortunately, the water was drying up. The temptation eased, the Razor Strop Lesson was remembered, and another moral crisis was behind them.

Frank and Myra honored their commitment to cook in Gorham camp for one winter. The lumberjacks enjoyed both the food and the Cunningham family but when Mr. Munn asked them to stay one more year, Frank turned it down.

"I was elected township road commissioner," Frank said, "With that income and what we can raise on the farm, we'll be all right. You'd better find yourself another cook."

For Grover, Grace, and their sons, the winter of 1925–26 seemed much longer than usual. Lee and his family had not returned, and Jean no longer lived just across the railroad tracks. Both Brown and White missed his companionship.

The new cook was quickly nicknamed "Greasy Killarney" by the crew, not in a derogatory or demeaning way, but in friendly needling. The food was good and Killarney's specialty was pie. He was careful to see that no one could complain about a lack of it. There was always pie remaining after the noon meal. This was probably by design. Killarney had no children of his own and enjoyed the little folks in camp. Each day when the noon meal was finished and the crew returned to work Killarney set what remained of the pie on the step of the cook shanty and called. "Come and get it!"

After a few such calls, all the camp children were waiting in front of their respective houses, prepared to race with the neighbors. It was first come first served. Sometimes there was a complete pie. There was at least one piece of pie available for everyone. Brown and White had an enviable location directly across the track from the cook shanty. There were bigger children who could run faster, but the shorter distance gave the Southwell boys an advantage.

Soon Grace began to notice that her sons had no appetite when Grover came to supper. This would not do. Grace could understand the camp cook's love for children and did not want to interfere, but some restriction was necessary.

"If Mr. Killarney gives you one piece of pie you can eat it." The boys were told, "but if Mr. Killarney gives you a full pie, bring it home and we'll have it for supper."

It seemed like a terrible hardship to boys aged seven and five, but they remembered the razor strop. There was no need to have that lesson repeated.

There was no school in the logging camp, and because Grace wanted Harold to be prepared for school the following year, she began giving him school lessons. Harold loved to be outside, regardless of weather, and had not the least interest in how many fingers two on each hand might total. Neither did he care if B followed A. In spite of Grace's patient guidance, Harold's answers usually reflected more about the depth of the snow, or what the boys were doing two houses down the track.

Rex, however, was very intrigued by the numbers of fingers he had, and found the recitation of the ABC's of great interest. He was more than willing to answer for his brother. Harold liked this arrangement. If he hesitated, Rex would give the answer. That should satisfy his mother. Harold looked wistfully out the window, waiting for his mother to let him go play in the snow.

Grace patiently explained that Harold needed to learn what she was teaching so he could enter the second grade when he attended the Davis school the following year. However, Harold was not interested.

The only room with a door in the little shanty was Grover and Grace's bedroom. Soon that room was turned into a schoolroom for Harold. This was effective as long as Grace was careful to keep her voice low. Rex was always at the door, his ear pressed to the crack. He usually knew the answer and was always ready to supply it for his big brother.

Once Harold realized he had to complete his daily lesson before he could enjoy the snowflakes in his face, he had no trouble learning.

As Grace washed up the dinner dishes, she sometimes drifted off in thought. She mused that this would be the last time they had to leave the farm and move back and forth between the camp and home. It had been a time of trial, but a good time, too. She thought of people that they'd come to know so well through living and working at the camp. The good times they'd had with Lee and Ruth, the Cunningham's, the cooks and the musicians, the other lumberjacks, even the horses brought a smile.

What had been thousands of acres of choice hardwood and hemlock timber remained now as slashings, waiting for decay or a forest fire. The memories of tough, but interesting times were all that was left of it. It was the last year for Gorham Camp.

Chapter 14

Home to Stay

On April 14, 1926 Grover and Grace came home to their little house to stay. It was ten years to the day since they were married. They had lived frugally and saved as much as possible. Now they needed to buy a team of horses and some more cows. A good team of horses came first, and Grover was excited as he brought home the local paper. "There's an auction sale in Elmira," he said, "and they're selling a young team of Percherons."

Grover appeared at the door of the Mancelona bank when Mr. Mills opened for business the following day. "Mr. Mills, Grace and I have moved to the farm to stay. We'll have to buy a team of horses and some cows. We've saved some money, but we'll need a little more."

Mr. Mills seemed surprised by the frank request. "Have you borrowed from us before?"

Grover was surprised. He had expected Mr. Mills to recall him, but realized it had been four years since he'd gotten his previous loan. "I borrowed a hundred dollars from you when we needed a well, and we paid off the loan the next winter. I'd like to borrow five hundred dollars. We'll pay it back with income from the farm."

As soon as Mr. Mills checked the record of Grover's prior loan, he approved the request for five hundred.

Two days later, Grover got up early, walked to Westwood, and caught the train to Elmira to attend the auction. His mind was focused on that team of horses. A young team would enable him to make good use of his time. *How many men are going to want those horses?* Grover was alternately confident and worried. A good team was expensive. He hoped to buy them for three hundred dollars. Of course, they might not be as good a team as the advertisement indicated.

"If they aren't good, I don't want 'em at any price," he decided. "If I don't buy that team though, I don't know where else to look." Realizing he spoke aloud, Grover bit his lip. He didn't want the other passengers to hear him talking to himself.

Arriving at Elmira, he walked two miles from the station to the farm. He passed large, newly cleared farms, one with a collie that followed him, barking. *Why is this guy having the auction? With new farms being cleared, why is this man quitting?* Finally he concluded that it didn't really matter why the man was having the sale; Grover's only concern was getting a team of horses.

He didn't want to appear too eager so he gradually worked his way to the barn where the horses were stabled. A group of about fifteen men stood around the stalls. Grover moved up as close as he could without being rude. He still could not see anything. A tall man with a hat was on the left, blocking the far stall. Then, to his right, he saw a large head rise from his oats. What Grover saw excited him.

The horse had a keen, intelligent look in his eyes, which were set off by the white blaze. The neck was gleaming, the color of a deer in summer coat. Grover nudged closer. The body was well muscled and trim. Grover began to move right up to the stable boards, then casually to the left. When he looked up, he saw the other horse. He was a perfect match to the first horse, with more white. He looked to be calmer than the first one, but every bit as sharp. The team was alert, extremely fit and well cared for. *Looks like it's the team I want.* He wondered how many other men were going to bid on them.

He inspected the harnesses hanging behind them. They were good harnesses, probably more quality than Grover would have bought, but good harnesses weren't so easy to come by.

The auctioneer was typical of most, and he kept the valuable items until last. Grover looked carefully at what he and Grace would need on their farm. Small tools were selling for more than they were worth. He would wait. *I have to have a spring tooth drag. If the price isn't too bad on the team, I'll buy that and the wagon. The only thing is, If I don't get the horses, I'll wish I hadn't bought the drag and the wagon. It'd be a long trip with Mike and Nell to get anything home from Elmira,"* Grover mumbled. He wished Grace were here. They had always made big decisions together. Today, he was on his own.

It was mid-afternoon before they put the livestock up for sale. Many of those at the sale had already made their purchases and left. Grover took note of the ones bidding on the tools. More specifically, he noted those who were not bidding. Apparently, Grover wasn't the only person wanting that young team of Percherons.

Finally, the owner led the horses out. Walking around the nervous team, the auctioneer noted that they held their heads high. He called attention to the alertness of their eyes, their clean legs, and especially their stature. The more nervous one, the one with the most white, stamped and snorted. The calmer one held his head still, but his ears were forward and his long tail swished constantly. He shifted his weight uneasily. The movement of the horses only showcased their strength. They were beautiful.

When he'd noted all the desirable characteristics, the auctioneer asked for a bid.

No one wanted to bid first. Finally Grover spoke, "I'll give two hundred-fifty for the team and harness." Although he would gladly pay three hundred dollars, he hoped the team wouldn't cost that much.

Grover said no more as others gradually upped the ante. The price was now just above three hundred dollars. Grover wanted the team, but so did two other men.

The bidding stopped at three hundred-fifty, as one of the men turned away.

Grover said, "I'll give three-sixty."

Surprised at the bid from one that had been quiet since his initial bid, the other man quickly raised him by ten dollars. Grover agonized. He wished Grace were here. *We need that team, but that's an awful lot of money.* Thoughts came quickly as his heightened senses tried to search every angle of the decision. *It's a good harness, too.*

The bidding continued slowly. Both men wanted the horses. Their brows furrowed as Grover and his competitor added ten dollars per bid. Grover knew he had to stop. He hesitated, then made one last bid. "I'll give four hundred dollars," he said with finality. The buzz of voices around him stopped.

His competitor shook his head and walked away. It seemed the young man he was bidding against would never quit!

As he stepped up to the cashier to deal with his purchase, it began to sink in. He had the team—they were his horses! He fluctuated between jubilation at having the team to show Grace when he got home, and disbelief at the price he had paid.

He got his new team harnessed. Cap and Jack were not names Grover would have chosen for his horses, but he let them keep the names they'd been given. He loaded the spring-tooth drag on the wagon, then began the twenty-mile drive home. He would not reach his destination until long after dark, and he knew Grace would be worried. He thought about what he'd just done. *I paid too much but I won't look back.* He refused to struggle with what could not be changed.

The yellow light of a kerosene lamp glowed in the window as Grover approached the house. *What would Gracie say?* He decided to put the best light on it.

Grace had been listening intently for some time. *Will I hear horse hooves or not?* She looked down at two young boys who had long since closed their eyes for the night.

"Whoa." Grace heard Grover's voice and hurried outside.

"It's kind of dark, Ma, but you'll like these. They're alive!" He was beaming. "Come look in their faces."

Grace brought the lamp out to see what Grover had bought. She saw the bright blaze, and the keen eyes.

"I spent almost five hundred, Ma, but we have what we need. I'll put the horses in the barn, then tell you all about it."

It was a good thing Grace had time to control her reeling emotions while her husband stabled the horses. Grover never seemed to comprehend that he might not be able to buy the things he wanted. The horses looked fine—very fine. She guessed that her horse-loving husband could not resist such quality stock. By the time he returned to the house, Grace resigned herself to the expense. *What's done is done,* she reasoned.

The Southwells needed four more dairy cows. Cream would be the main source of income to repay the loan from the Mancelona bank and provide the needs of the family.

Both Grover and Grace wanted Guernsey cattle, if possible. The milk from Holsteins didn't contain enough butterfat, and Jersey's were a delicate breed, not sturdy enough for these winters.

Rex, Bryce, Harold at newly built home

Uncle Charlie was willing to sell two cows and Ot Stoddard supplied the other two. Another hundred and sixty dollars of their precious funds were gone. Grover and Grace realized they were almost out of money but by skimping, they would be able to manage.

Grace washed the dishes and the boys were comfortably in their beds when Grace said to her husband, "Grover we're almost broke but we'll *have* to buy a few things for the house."

Grover thought he saw a tear. He wrapped a muscled arm around his wife and pulled her close. "Don't you worry, Ma. I know it's hard to see the money go so fast, but we had to have the horses and cows. This year, I can use Cap and Jack when the township does the roadwork and each year our income from the farm will be better," Grover promised. "The more land I can clear, the more cattle we can feed. The more cattle we can feed, the more cream we can sell."

Grace couldn't help but be encouraged by her husband's rise to the challenge. He seemed to thrive on formidable tasks.

Each week Grover took a five or ten gallon can of cream to the railway depot in Mancelona and shipped it to the Blue Valley Creamery, in Grand Rapids. Each week the empty can from the previous week was returned to the railway dock with those of the other farmers, waiting to be picked up by their owners.

The Southwells used skim milk to make Dutch (cottage) cheese. However, a family can only eat so much Dutch cheese. Grace allowed the extra skim milk to curdle and fed the curds to her chickens.

Grace was not a waster. After throwing a half pail of whey on the garden, she could tolerate it no longer. "Grover, we're throwing away a lot of skim milk and whey. We could feed more chickens or get pigs, but we can't just waste it!"

While Grace was concerned with the waste, Grover's mind and interest was on the field he was clearing to plant corn. "It's the middle of May, Ma! The corn has to be planted or it won't get ripe."

Grover knew they shouldn't be wasting the skim milk. Skim milk was great pig feed, but he couldn't let skim milk interfere with planting corn. Once more, pulling his troubled wife close to his chest, Grover pleaded, "Let me get the corn in and next week I'll build a pigpen."

It was a hard workweek, shortened by a day's long hard rain. The pasture was beginning to get dry so the rain was welcome, but pressure was building to get the corn planted. There was such a short growing season. Moreover, there was still the pigpen to build.

Saturday evening the corn planting was finished. When supper was over Grover sat on the floor playing blocks with his sons while Grace finished cleaning the kitchen. Soon she joined them, and together the four constructed a building according to the design laid out by the children.

Grover placed a block where Brown indicated it should go, arose, stretched his legs and placed his hand on his wife's shoulder. "I'll get a pigpen ready and build the pigs something that will pass for a house."

Grace placed one more block on their children's construction project and gave her husband a pleased smile when Grover added, "We need a sow that's ready to pig. She'll eat the extra skim milk and the little pigs will be meat for us next winter. If she has a decent litter, there'll even be little pigs for us to sell."

With a hundred-foot roll of woven wire, cedar posts from Louie's Swamp, and scraps of boards left from building the barn, Grover quickly constructed a good pen for a sow and her future litter.

Ot Stoddard had a sow he wanted to sell. She was three years old and a far bigger sow than Ot wanted to keep. "Come look at "Old Suz," Ot urged Grover. "She gave me two good litters but I'm keeping a younger sow."

"Old Suz" became the Southwells' prized possession. A large, exceptionally docile, expectant sow, Suz was well able to take care of any skim milk the family could spare.

Grover found a fifty-gallon drum to use for a swill barrel. Each day he poured the excess skim milk in this container. To the milk, he added table scraps, potato peelings, and vegetable cuttings. Every few days he added enough bran to maintain a reasonably thick consistency. The concoction soured and gave off a terrible odor, but Suz welcomed the portion twice a day as Grover poured it in her trough.

Early on the morning of June 1st Grover came to the house after milking the cows and announced. "Come see what Suz gave us!"

Brown and White, still in their nightdresses, were carried by their parents to the pigpen. There they saw old Suz stretched to her limit, with 12 healthy piglets each fighting for a nipple. Grover carefully entered the pen, scratched old Suz on the back, and handed a piglet to Grace. The sow trusted them for she gave no indication of disapproval. After both boys had a turn feeling the smooth white skin the little wiggling piglet was returned to resume nursing.

For three weeks Grover worked long days with his newly acquired team of horses, pulling stumps in preparation for a much larger field of corn he would plant the following year. Each day Grover's pleasure with his purchase increased. The bond between horses and teamster grew stronger. He felt that, after all, he'd made a wise investment.

Cutting and hauling his own hay, then helping his father get his own hay to the barn kept Grover busy until township road-work began. For six weeks Grover and his new team of horses worked to build roads for the township.

Grace, with reluctant assistance from her young sons, kept the garden weeded and carried the weeds to the pigpen, where old Suz wolfed them down gratefully.

On a hot sultry day in mid August, when the day's work was finished, the milking done, and supper over, the family virtually gasped from the heat. Although the day was hot, food had to be cooked on a wood stove. Cooking in late afternoon added to the discomfort of the already warm house, but there was no alternative. Grace endured the heat.

With supper over, the family went to sit under the maple tree in the front yard. It seemed a nice place to spend the evening. Grover brought chairs from the house for Grace and himself. The children preferred to play on the mat of cool grass.

On this night, however, the family had hardly been seated when mosquitoes descended in clouds. It was far too hot to return to the house, so Grover made a smudge. He cleaned the last of the smoking embers from the kitchen stove and placed them in a pail. Carefully carrying the hot embers, Grover covered the burning coals with grass. A thick smoke quickly emerged from this combination. Mosquitoes would not come into the smoke.

Now the family had a choice. They could sit in the smoke and be free from the biting insects, or move out of the choking smoke and swat insects. It was possible to be just at the edge of the smoke and the mosquitoes would stay away, but the margin between smoke and mosquitoes was narrow. As the direction of the gentle breeze changed, so did the location of the smoke. There was little rest as the family tried to escape the buzzing insects.

Brown and White competed for the nearest spot to the smoke without actually choking. Their parents allowed the smoke to drift past them and alternately brushed away mosquitoes, then leaned to one side to escape the smoke.

Twilight was fading when an unusual sound approached from the north. Listening intently, Grover spoke in surprise, "It's an automobile!" All members of the family instantly rose to their feet to see who was coming. This was unexpected to say the least.

A shiny, black "model T" Ford chugged slowly up the driveway from the narrow, rutted, road and Ot Stoddard stepped from the running board to greet his neighbors.

Mosquitoes forgotten, the new car was examined and admired. A few merchants living in town owned automobiles, but it seemed a luxury no farmer could afford.

"I didn't expect to see a neighbor with one of these!" Grover walked admiringly around Ot's new contraption.

"It's a great time saver, Grover. I can go to town and back in less than an hour." Ot was obviously pleased at the admiration, not only from Grover, but also from Grace, who was holding the hands of Brown and White to keep them from climbing on the running boards.

When the excitement eased, Ot came to the purpose of his visit, which had plainly influenced him to invest in this modern form of transportation. "A couple of friends and I are planning to put telephone lines through Rapid River and Coldsprings Townships. There are a lot of people living here now, and more are moving in all the time." Ot waved his hand in a wide circle, indicating the area to be included. "If enough families want the phones, we'll put the lines in."

He went on, "We'll connect to the main lines in Mancelona. You'll be able to talk to anyone in the United States who has a phone."

The offer was a complete surprise to Grover and Grace. Gorham Camp had a telephone but that was a business. They couldn't conceive of having this convenience in their own home!

Grace spoke first. "It would cost a lot of money and we're just getting started. I don't see how we could possibly pay for it."

Ot persisted. "We've figured what it will cost to buy the phones and put up the lines, and how many people live here. If most of the families take a telephone, it will only cost you five dollars a month. It'll take several years for us to get our money back, but after that, we should show a profit. We're willing to take the gamble."

Grover thought he would like to have a telephone, but said nothing. He was always willing to spend more money than his wife thought they should. Grace had already said, "No." He would leave it at that. He gave Ot his regards.

When Ot turned to leave, Grace surprised them both. "It would be a real help if someone gets sick," she suddenly said. "Remember how long it took to get the doctor when Rex had diphtheria?"

Grover had been thinking of the time it could save him making trips to town, and told their neighbor, "We'll take a telephone, Ot.

After again mentioning how much time the automobile saved him, Ot adjusted the gas and spark levers and left for home. Grover and Grace smiled at one another as each picked a boy up from under the cloud of smoke and hurried inside the house, now cooler than it had been. The hungry mosquitoes would have to find another source of food.

The next day when Grover was harrowing a field to plant rye, a root caught the spring tooth drag and broke the frame. The drag frame could be repaired in Mancelona. Earl Robb had a reputation for quality welding, and at a reasonable price. Though money was tight, paying for the weld didn't bother Grover as much as the time it would cost.

During the two hours he sat restlessly on the wagon driving to town, he thought more and more about Ot and how much time an automobile saved. Grover always wanted to get more done than he could possibly accomplish and now he was spending four hours making the round trip to Mancelona. It would take another four hours to go and get the drag and that was just too much wasted time.

Grover stopped at Harry William's garage. A shiny new black Ford, just like Ot's, sat in front of the garage to be admired by anyone passing by. Grover walked to the back of the garage where Harry was adjusting the rod bearings on an older car.

"How much is that Ford?" Grover asked, knowing he wouldn't buy it without talking to Grace.

"Beauty, isn't she?" Harry wiped the grease from his hands and walked with Grover to where the car was parked. She starts on a dime, too." He turned the ignition key to battery, pushed up the spark lever, pulled the gas lever down a half-inch, engaged the crank and turned it a quarter turn. The new four-cylinder engine responded immediately. "You want to go for a ride?" Harry finally asked.

"Not today. I was in town and wondered about the cost." Grover said. Harry was well aware that the yearning for a car grew on anyone who took a ride. More and more people were buying automobiles.

"I can sell you this car for three hundred and eighty dollars." Then Harry made his sales pitch. "I don't know when I can get another one."

"That's a lot of money. I'll have to talk to Grace." Grover was grateful for his fine team, but would much prefer to spend the time plowing, or pulling stumps, with his horses than driving to town. A car sure would be nice.

It was noon when Grover, growing more impatient by the hour, arrived home. He watered the horses, put them in the barn and fed them before going to the house where his own dinner sat on the table. Grover hardly tasted the meal and heard little of what his sons said.

The preoccupation was not lost on Grace. "What's bothering you Grover?" she asked, "You aren't with us today."

Grover looked steadily at Grace. "It took all forenoon to go to town and back. I've been thinking about what Ot said. A car would save us a lot of time."

"Grover, we *never* could afford a car!"

Grover dropped the subject for the time being. "I'll think about it some more." He asked himself, *am I thinking straight or do I just want the car?*

One evening when the family gathered in the living room, the boys were playing on the floor, Grover was strumming his mandolin and Grace was contentedly watching and listening.

When Grover stopped playing to re-tune a string, Grace looked up from the children and told her husband. "We'll need to go to town soon, Grover. We're out of flour and the boys need overalls."

The next morning Grover helped Grace climb up on the wagon. There was a spring seat for the two of them and the boys sat comfortably on a blanket in the wagon box behind them. Although the horses walked briskly, it was two hours before Grover tied them beside Charles' Grocery store. Across the street, at Medalie's dry goods, Grace found overalls for their sons before returning to purchase the needed groceries.

When their shopping was finished the family started home. At the corner, the shiny black Ford still sat in front of Harry William's garage.

Grover stopped the horses. "Sit in the front seat of that Ford, Ma," he urged. Grover could not suppress a grin at the dismay evident on his wife's face.

Climbing down from the wagon, Grace followed her husband to the car, where Grover opened the front door and invited her to "Step up and have a seat." Grover wanted his wife to feel the soft cushioned seat. There was really no reason to refuse, but Grace, who had forgotten all about purchasing an automobile, saw the intent quite clearly.

Now Grover made his best sales pitch. "Ma, we're going to have another child this fall. That wagon is pretty rough. This car will be easier for you and save us a lot of time. We can drive to town, buy groceries, and be back home in time for you to cook dinner. And you won't be all worn out when you get there."

Harry Williams suggested the Southwell family take a test ride.

Two excited boys were already in the back seat, so Grace moved between them, holding each child firmly. After cranking the engine to life, Harry climbed into the driver's seat and invited Grover to sit beside him.

Before beginning the drive, Harry explained. "On the left of the steering column is the spark lever. It needs to be at the top when you crank the engine. As the engine picks up speed, you pull down the spark lever accordingly. The gas lever is on the right, pull it down until you're going as fast as you want to drive. Between your feet, the low gear pedal is on the left, the reverse pedal in the middle and the brake pedal on the right."

"The lever from the floor on my left is the emergency brake when it's all the way back. It keeps the car from rolling when it's parked. Ahead a little is neutral. You put it in neutral to use low or reverse and push it all the way ahead for high gear."

When Harry pulled the gas lever down to the speed of a gallop, Grover admonished him. 'That's fast enough!" The wind in his face felt exhilarating, but Grace was holding the boys tightly in the back. If she got frightened, the ride would end in a disaster.

Back at the garage, Harry played his trump card. "You can pay a little now and the rest by the month if it's easier that way."

Grace told her husband. "We can't afford to buy a car, Grover, we haven't even finished paying for the horses yet."

Not a bit dissuaded, Grover thanked Harry for the ride, and promised to "think it over."

Convinced the purchase of an automobile would have to be postponed, Grover returned to caring for his crops.

When Grace again needed flour, sugar, and more canning jars, the family again made the slow trip to Mancelona with the horses. Grover chafed at the time being wasted as the horses plodded along. A car would pay for itself with the time he could save.

"Ma, let's see if we can buy a used car. I can't be wasting all this time and it will be better for you." Grover was confident it was the right decision.

Not at all convinced, Grace was nevertheless resigned. She could see Grover had already made up his mind.

The shiny black Ford was still parked. Although Harry had hinted the Ford would soon be gone, if it were, another exactly like it had replaced it.

While the grocer filled Grace's order, Grover walked the hundred yards to Harry's garage.

Now convinced Grace would never approve of buying a new car, Grover told the salesman, "Harry, we don't feel that we can buy a new car. Do you have a used one?"

"I just finished tightening the bearings on this 1923 model, Grover. I took it on a trade last week." Harry measured his customer with his eyes as he spoke. "It's only three years old. The seats are good and tires still have plenty of tread. You can have it for half price."

Grover closed the deal. Grace was not as excited as her husband was, when he explained their good fortune to find a barely used car they could afford. Grace reassured herself. *We owe an awful lot of money, but the convenience will be nice.*

The next morning found the family again riding to town in the farm wagon. Excitement abounded, "next trip to town will be with the car!" Grover told his sons as the team broke into a slow trot.

Harry had cleaned the seats and washed the windshield. The paint had faded but the car really did look good.

Brown and White climbed quickly into the front seat, where Brown took over the steering wheel.

Grace was having trouble getting the boys from the car back into the wagon. "Grover, you've never driven a car. I want the boys to go home with me." Grace was adamant. No amount of coaxing would sway her.

Grover remembered his boyhood. Oh, how he loved to drive the horses when farmers came to Saugatuck. He knew how much his sons wanted to ride in the car and he knew it would be safe, but he also knew his wife.

"You better go home in the wagon," Grover told Brown. "Your mother needs you to drive the horses." Grover's eyes pleaded with his wife. He wasn't sure Grace would understand, but he wanted to soften their sons' disappointment at not being allowed to ride in the car.

Grace nodded. The horses were well trained, letting Harold drive them would not be a problem.

After one last yearning grasp on the seat of the Ford, White slowly climbed into the wagon.

Grace seated between her sons on the wagon seat, cautioned, "Be careful, Grover. Don't drive as fast as Harry did."

Grover's first drive was more difficult than he had anticipated. Getting from low gear to high without the car jerking took a little practice. Grover wanted Grace to be at ease when he took the family for a ride. The car would go lots faster than Grace would want to travel.

Coming up the hill by Catland marshes, Grover had to use low gear. *Maybe if I was going a little faster it could make the hill in high. I'll try that next time.* Grover was learning fast.

Arriving home in time to carry in the groceries, Grover was smiling and confident. Now he promised the children. "We'll go for a little ride after dinner." Grace surely understood that he could handle the car now.

Rubbing the noses of Cap and Jack when he put them in the barn, Grover told them. "The car's fast, but it won't ever replace you."

All the family was excited on the Saturday before Labor Day when they first drove to Mancelona for groceries in their Model T Ford. It was a bright hot, morning. The wind coming in the side of the touring car felt fresh on their faces.

Even Grace was beginning to appreciate the car. The wind in her face *did* feel refreshing and the seat was more comfortable than the wagon. She also realized that it would save considerable time. Really Grace enjoyed the ride, but would have enjoyed it more had she been able to forget the money they owed.

When they stopped at Charles' Grocery store, black clouds were beginning to fill the western sky. "It's going to rain, Grover." Grace was concerned.

Grover reassured his wife as he took side curtains from under the rear seat. Harry had held one up beside the car and showed him how they snapped on. Grover told Grace, "You buy the groceries while I snap on the side curtains."

They placed the groceries in the back of the car with the boys, then Grover started the car and the family was out of town when the storm hit. It was a typical summer thunderstorm and the rain came in torrents. Grover pushed the single windshield wiper back and forth with his left hand while steering with the other. Grace could see nothing. Grover was kept busy! Each swipe of the wiper gave him a view of the road. He pushed the gas lever up until he felt a slight jerk, then pulled it down a little bit. It was no time to kill the engine.

"I can't see a thing, Grover. Can you tell where you're going?" Grace was clearly shaken. "Don't drive so fast! How can you see?"

"I can see, Ma. If you had a wiper, you could see, too. I can't go any slower without putting it in low gear and we don't want to do that."

Now the boys stood on the rear seat, trying to see out the flexible windows in the side curtains. Grace was afraid they would fall out. She became as busy with the boys as Grover was with the windshield wiper. "Don't stand on the groceries! You'll make holes in the bags."

Grover was relieved she had something to keep her mind off the road.

The sky cleared and the hot sun was again beating down when the family drove safely up to their back door. It had been a strenuous trip for both Grover and his wife.

After the car was unloaded, Grover put both arms around his wife and hugged her tightly. Turning Grace's tense face toward him, he said. "Ma, it really was a tough drive home, but the car made it and we're dry. If we'd been in the wagon, we would have been soaked. This 'tin Lizzy' is worth everything it's cost us."

Chapter 15

Davis School

The following Tuesday Brown and White started school. The Davis School, a mile south, bore the family name of Myron and Ella Davis, early homesteaders. The schoolhouse was built on an acre of land purchased from the Davis homestead and was near their farm buildings.

The first half-mile from the Southwell's house to the school was called the "Mountain Road." It was named because of a steep hill where the road descended sharply before winding around a little swamp.

Virgin hardwood timber covered the land east of this part of the road except for an area near the swamp. A large group of hemlock trees covered the low land. In autumn, the hemlocks seemed unattractive in the midst of the multi-colored maples, but in winter, they were a beautiful green island in the midst of the otherwise bare forest. On the west side of this road was the forty acres that Tuden had given Grover and Grace when they married.

The second half-mile on the walk to school lay between virgin hardwood forest on the west and the Davis farm on the east. The first morning Grace walked to school with Harold and Rex. Releasing her sons to the custody of someone other than herself for the first time was not easy. "I'll feel better when I see who's teaching them," Grace said.

Grace was more relaxed after meeting their teacher, Edith Fudge. Miss Fudge was confident that she would enjoy working with her nine students, and felt well prepared to teach the basic three subjects of reading, writing and arithmetic, plus geography and history. High school and County normal had prepared the young woman and she seemed competent to begin teaching, although she had only just celebrated her nineteenth birthday.

After returning home, Grace was busy all day with laundry and ironing. She couldn't help but think about the boys, though— often. She was somewhat anxious and wondered how they were doing. When Harold and Rex came home happily swinging their lunch pails, she was relieved. She could never forget the doctor's warning about Rex's weak heart, but he appeared none the worse for the day's walk.

She put a sandwich, a dish of fruit, and a sugar cookie in their lunch pails each day. At school, small hallways at the entrance provided shelves for the lunch pails. Boys entered through the hallway on the left and girls on the right.

Harold and Rex did well in school. Harold especially liked playing baseball with the older children at recess and noon. The books were not interesting, but he did what Miss Fudge asked. Rex had always been fascinated with books, and there were lots of them. He would gladly sit at his desk through recess looking at a book if Miss Fudge did not gently urge him to go out with the other children.

Baseball grew to be an obsession for Harold, as it had for his father. Since Harold played with the older boys at school, he constantly urged Rex to play catch in the evening. Gradually, his younger brother became intrigued with the sport, too.

Grover loved to see his sons playing in the autumn evenings. On his next trip to town, he purchased a bat. *I'll get gloves for them next spring*. Each evening, when he could spare even a short time, Grover played ball with his sons. On those evenings, with his Gracie crocheting on the porch, he felt as if he simply could not want for anything more.

This was the first winter Grover and his family stayed in their new home. It was going to be much more comfortable than living in the tarpaper shack at Gorham Camp. The walls were boarded inside and out, and there was much more room. All the canned vegetables and potatoes were stored safely in the cellar. Grace could get them as they were needed. They were no longer piled together in one corner of their living room.

In October, Ot Stoddard and his partners began setting telephone poles every 50 yards up the half-mile road to the Southwells. Behind them came the horses and wagon, unrolling wire. A man with climbers fastened to his feet, nailed insulators on the poles and fastened the wire to them. In two days, the poles were set and the wire was strung.

The next day Ot came with their telephone, fastened it to the wall in their kitchen, and attached the wire. "Your ring will be three longs." Ot assigned various combinations of shorts and longs for each telephone. "Here's a list of the rings for others on the line. One long ring calls the operator in Mancelona. She'll connect you to anywhere in the country. Any calls you make through the operator cost extra."

Grace first called Uncle Charlie and his wife, Hattie, answered. It sure didn't sound like Aunt Hattie, but Grace could understand every word. Harold and Rex each had a turn, wondering at the sound coming from the handle they held to their ear. Grace retrieved the receiver and hung it back on the telephone. "It's not a toy. We have it so we can talk to someone when it's necessary."

Grover's next project was to get wood for their winter's fuel. At Gorham camp, they had skidded dead trees to the house when coming from their daily work.

Just across the road from the Southwell home was a square mile of the same choice timber that had provided work at Gorham Camp. This timber was also dotted with dead beech trees.

"If I can get permission to cut those dead beeches, we'll have good wood," Grover told his wife. "The old tree tops are starting to rot. They've been on the ground too long."

Grover was casually acquainted with Tom Nelson, who had lost one arm while working at the Antrim Iron Company sawmill. Now Tom was employed by the company to constantly cruise (drive his horse around) their various stands of timber to prevent potential theft. Grover thought Tom might give him permission to cut the dead trees and waited for Tom to drive by.

Anyone traveling by their house was welcome to a cup of coffee and one of Grace's sugar cookies, and Tom drove past at a most opportune time.

Grover hailed the timber cruiser. "Come have a cup of coffee, Tom. It'll take the chill out of you."

Over the cup of coffee, and the welcome cookie, with a bug (a raisin), Grover broached the subject of fuel. "Tom, the company doesn't use any dead timber. I'd like to cut some dry beech trees for our winter's wood."

"I know the company doesn't use them," Tom replied, "but my orders are to report anyone that I see taking something from their forests. I'll stop at the office and see Ray and let you know about it when I come by next week."

It seemed like a long week. Grover helped Tuden gather some of the best of the remaining treetops on his property to provide his father's fuel for the winter, and then waited impatiently for Tom. Surely the company wouldn't prevent him from cutting trees from which the bark had already fallen. The bare wood was visible for a hundred yards through the green timber.

True to his word, Tom returned a week later. "You can have the wood, Grover, but there's other timber going to waste and they'd like you to cut it for them."

He was seated at the kitchen table with a warm cup of coffee in his hand. He looked at the plate of cookies forming a centerpiece, then said, "Ray said the company wouldn't be cutting the timber on section 17 for some time. The wind blows down good hardwood, and more of the hemlocks die each year. They'd like to get the fallen maples and the hemlocks that are dying, cut and skidded to a road where they can pick 'em up. It could make you a good job."

Grover looked at his wife. This sounded like a great opportunity. There was no other work available unless he drove to Antrim and piled lumber. This was a great idea! He could work all winter right near home. Inwardly elated, Grover asked, "How much will they pay to get those trees salvaged?"

Tom shook his head. "They don't let me in on the details. You'll need to talk to Ray."

The next morning, Grover cranked the "Model T" and drove to town.

Waiting impatiently while Ray seemed to have an unnecessarily long conversation on the telephone, Grover eventually caught the man's attention. However badly the company wanted to salvage the timber being wasted, Grover did not expect a lucrative offer.

He said, "Tom told me you were interested in salvaging the down stuff on section 17. What are you willing to pay?"

Ray had prepared an offer. "We can pay you three dollars a thousand board feet for the logs and two dollars a cord for the 4-foot wood. The logs are to be decked, and the wood piled for scaling, along the roads that are there. Cut the logs and wood the same as we did at Gorham."

Grover had been doing some calculations on the drive to town. He would have to hire men to cut the logs and wood while he did the skidding and hauling. He had expected a better offer. It was, however, the right time and the right place for Grover to work. He could live at home, farm in the summer, and work across the road during the winter.

Grover slowly shook his head positively. "All right. I'll save all I can for you this winter. I'll start as soon as there's enough snow. How often will you pay?"

"Tom will scale whatever you have on the roads once a week. You can stop and get your check, or Tom will bring it the next week." The deal was completed without the customary seal of a handshake, but both men knew that once an agreement was made it would be honored.

Three unkempt bachelor brothers, Charlie, Frank, and Dick Bowring had moved—uninvited—into an empty shell of an abandoned house just west of Louie's farm. Grover was confident he could hire them to cut the logs and 4-foot wood. Everyone has to eat, and it certainly did not appear they were prosperous enough to sit out the winter without work.

As he returned from Antrim, Grover stopped to make an offer to the brothers, a motley looking group who had earned the nickname of "The Fuzzy Brothers" from their neighbors. Judging by appearances, they shaved intermittently and hadn't bothered with a barber to have their hair cut.

Charlie's hair had turned gray, Frank and Dick were not as old, and Dick obviously was the youngest.

Grover drove into what used to be a driveway as the three men filed out to greet him. In his customary direct manner, Grover said, "I took a job on section 17 cutting the hardwood that blew down and hemlock trees that are dying. If you want to do the work, I'll give you a dollar a thousand to cut the logs, and a dollar-thirty cents a cord to cut and split the four-foot wood. I'll skid the logs and haul the wood; Tom Nelson will scale it for the company, and you'll get paid once a week."

Dick answered quickly, "It's up to "Churley.""

Charley, or "Churley," depending on who was doing the talking, took a fresh chew of tobacco and squinted at his neighbor. When his mouth was filled, and the remaining tobacco was back safely in his pocket, Charlie answered, "I'll go look at it tomorrow." The conversation ended, Charlie returned to the house with Frank and Dick following.

Grover grinned. They don't make snap decisions.

The next morning the Fuzzy Brothers appeared on Grover and Grace's doorstep. "Let's look at the timber," Charlie spoke for the group.

Grover walked the men across the road where a group of freshly fallen maple trees lay together. He stated, "This is some of the hardwood." The three men inspected the jam pile of hardwood trees carefully.

"See that big hemlock covered with red bark?" Grover asked. "We cut those too. They'll begin to rot in a few years. Both you and I can make wages this winter, maybe even for several winters."

Ignoring his brothers, Charlie took another chew of tobacco. "When do we start?" He asked.

"You can start on these maples now," Grover answered. "I don't want to cut the hemlocks until there's snow."

Again, Charlie answered. "I'll sharpen tools tomorrow and start the day after." Charlie turned away and his brothers fell in behind him as they returned to their home, walking in single file.

On the appointed morning, the sound of axes rang from the Jam pile across the road from the Southwell farm.

While the Fuzzy Brothers cut logs and 4-foot wood from the uprooted maple trees, Grover cut and hauled bone-dry beech trees for his winter fuel. The dead wood was extremely hard. Cutting it was also hard, but it made great stove wood. The first week of November drew to a close as Grover's new crew finished cutting the first group of fallen trees.

Grover wanted snow so he could use knee-high sleighs to haul the 4-foot wood. A wagon was above his waist. It was much easier to load the wood on sleighs, but the ground was still dry.

The following Monday morning, Grover spoke reluctantly as he finished his pancakes. "I'll have to start hauling 4-foot on the wagon, Ma. The woodcutters are going to need money and we don't get paid until the wood's piled on the road."

Later that same morning Charlie said, "We need some money; we've worked a week."

"I don't get paid until the wood's on the road," Grover admitted. Looking at the gaunt faces of his crew Grover offered, "I can give you $10. Will that get you by until Tom scales some wood?"

Charlie again pulled the tobacco from his pocket, filled the side of his mouth from its contents while his brothers waited, and spoke as he turned away, "That'll be all right." In single file, the men returned to their work.

For three weeks, Grover hauled wood with the wagon. The logs would have to remain where they were until snow fell. For skidding, Grover had made a "crazy dray."[7]

---

[7] The name derived from the way the dray followed the horses. The purpose of its unusual construction was to facilitate moving between stumps or over uneven ground. Rather than being rigid, it was made of a single cross piece (a bunk) attached near the front of two runners. Chains to pull the dray were connected to the ends of the runners and joined together some six feet ahead, where the horses were hitched to pull the load. The front of the log, or logs, to

On Thanksgiving weekend the snow finally came. Softly at first, then a northwest wind brought much colder weather and the white blanket of snow. They sat at the table as Grace laid out the bounteous Thanksgiving dinner, and Grover fervently thanked God for the gift of the snow as well as the food.

Grace was carrying a baby through the summer and Grover was concerned for Grace's comfort. At the same time, it was the excuse he needed to buy a new automobile.

The baby was born on December 16th. Both dad and mother were glad to have the phone. The memory of the delay when Rex was sick was still fresh in their minds. This time they just picked up the phone and contacted Dr. Walton right away. In spite of having the comfort of a new REO, the depth of the snow required the doctor to go back to his trusty horse and cutter. In little over an hour he was there, however, and in a few hours Grace delivered her third son, Bryce. Grover was satisfied to call this son by his given name.

Jeff and Zony Garrison had moved into the Engmark house, and the two families had become close friends. When they were phoned and told of Bryce's birth, Zony immediately offered to care for Grace for the ten-day period the doctor said she must stay in bed.

The day before the tenth day, Grace insisted she was strong enough to help with Christmas dinner. Grace told her, "Zony, you've done enough. Go home and cook Christmas dinner for your family."

When the warm spring sun began shining through the windows, Grace was getting cabin fever. So Grover took a ham from

---

be skidded, were loaded on this bunk and the back ends of the logs dragged on the ground. This prevented the dray sliding ahead and hitting the horses when going down a hill. If one runner hit a stump as the dray was being pulled, the ends of the bunk could pivot and the runner would slide around the stump. On a level trail the runners came ahead evenly. When in the woods, often one runner was ahead of or behind the other. Thus, it acquired the name, "crazy dray."

their pork barrel and they drove over to Jeff and Zony's to show off their infant son and take the Garrisons a token of appreciation.

All winter long the Fuzzy Brothers cut logs and wood while Grover hauled them to the roads. The winter's income was as good as Grover had received the previous year in camp.

When Brown and White picked the first wild flowers as they walked home from school, Grover paid his crew their last check. It was time to turn his attention to his farm. Grover and his crew discussed working together again the coming winter. Charlie reckoned, around a mouthful of tobacco that they would pick a few cherries and maybe some apples to get through until fall.

Chapter 16

Work and Play

In 1927, the fields of alfalfa planted in prior years began to ripple in the June breeze. Bumblebees, the only bees to work in alfalfa blossoms, welcomed the beginning of the blooms, indicating haying time.

Cap and Jack did the mowing and raking, but after the hay was raked into endless windrows, Grover used a three-tined pitchfork to pile the alfalfa into neat haycocks. When the hay was stacked in these piles the haycocks would shed most of the water, if it rained before they could be hauled into the barn. These haycocks could quickly, though not easily, be pitched onto the hay wagon.

One Saturday evening in midsummer, when the chores were finished and Grace was feeding Bryce, Grover spoke up. "Ma, let's take a little ride over to Deward tomorrow. It's been a while since we picked the blueberries and I wonder if the trees are beginning to grow back. We can ride over there in a couple hours, now that we have a car."

"I'll make a lunch we can eat by the river." Grace responded enthusiastically. "We have cookies and I'll make egg sandwiches."

Sunday dawned bright and still. Grover cranked the milk through the separator. He told the family, "It'll be warm today, just right for our ride."

By the time Grover mixed bran in the swill for "Old Suz" and fed her, Grace was ready with lunch in the picnic basket and Harold and Rex were each munching a cookie.

Grover knew there were no roads where he planned to go. Since the pines were gone there was little to attract anyone to the area around Deward.

"We won't have a problem, Ma." Grover, always confident, re-assured Grace, who, true to her nature, had begun to worry. "We'll drive on the old logging roads. I'll take the ax, in case there's anything lying across the road."

Grover cranked the engine and their Model T came to life. They drove up to the Darragh Road, and filled the gas tank at the Darragh store. He didn't want to run out of gas when he ventured into the unknown. From Darragh, they drove east, crossed the Red Bridge on the Manistee River, and headed toward Frederic. It was a reasonably good road, gravel as far as Manistee Lake.

As soon as they crossed the Manistee River, Grover looked for a road north. He felt sure there had been a road following the river, but if there was one, he sure couldn't find it. Once again Grover reassured his wife, "There'll be a road from Frederic to Deward, Ma." They drove the extra six miles to the little town of Frederic. This time Grover was right. The old road from Frederic to Deward had been cut deeply by wagon wheels. The road was easy to see, but not so easy to navigate. The soft sand road slowed the narrow tires. The drive to Deward was largely uneventful, although it took longer than Grover expected. The sight of the river and the bridge was encouraging but Grover stopped to examine the bridge's old construction carefully.

The timbers supporting the bridge seemed solid, but many of the top planks had been removed. There were solid planks to carry the left wheel, but there was a gaping hole where the right wheel must go. Always optimistic, Grover was sure there would be a way to get across.

Planks spiked on the side of the bridge's supporting timbers provided an answer. "I can knock some planks off the side of the bridge for the right wheel," he said.

With pants and shoes off, Grover picked up his ax and stepped into the cold river. "It's a good thing it's not early spring! The water's deep enough now." Swings against the planks with the side of the ax pulled the spikes from one end of a wide plank. Carrying the loose end back and forth, Grover gradually worked the spikes loose from the end of the plank that was over the deep water. He repeated the operation from the other side of the bridge. Two planks were enough.

The water proved too enticing for Harold to resist. His legs were wet to the knees when Grace dragged him from the river. Brown's efforts to help his father had been to no avail.

Grover didn't show that he was faced with a difficult challenge. *If we can get across this bridge without a problem, Ma will quit worrying.* His concern for his wife's state of mind was as great as getting across the bridge. With the two planks laid end-to-end, he covered the gap. The rest of the bridge was solid. There was no question in Grover's mind about driving his car across the bridge. Still, he left his family on the bank while he drove across. The large planks lay where he placed them and the crossing was made without mishap.

A second crossing was made on foot with White on his shoulders and a steadying hand for Brown. One more time Grover crossed the river. This time he carried Bryce, with a now more confident Grace walking by his side.

While their father kept Brown and White from venturing too far into the swift stream, Grace placed a blanket under a tree and opened the basket of food. They filled their cups from the rapidly flowing river and wolfed down their sandwiches.

Brown and White, cookies in hand, waded into the water while their mother repacked the basket. Even after their father had cranked the "Model T" to life, the boys were more attracted to the river than to their ride. Small boys love water and these boys were no exception.

"The road to Blue Lake is a few miles north from here. We can drive along the river till we find it," Grover assured Grace. He forcibly dragged his sons from the water.

He was relaxed now. They were returning to the area where he had worked for the Blue Lake Lumber Company. The road along the river was easy to follow, but the strain of the drive through soft sand wreaked havoc on the car. The radiator boiled over and the jug of water that had not been used at lunch was poured into the radiator. Grover knew the car would need more water soon if the road didn't improve, so he refilled the jug from the river.

"This is where I walked when I first came to Northern Michigan," Grover wistfully recalled, thinking of that first walk in the big timber with Tuden. "The trees were more than a hundred feet tall with limbs only at the top." Suddenly, he realized that his two young sons could never sense the awe that he'd felt that day as he walked through the virgin forest. His expression changed to disgust. "Now look at it! Skingarians!" Grover coined his own word to describe the self-serving lumber barons' desolation, the "skinning" of the land. The ferocity of his feelings was difficult to control.

In that moment, the joy of the excursion was over for Grover. Suddenly he felt melancholy, tired. He was anxious to get back to the farm where there was life, not just stumps and sparse shrubs. What the loggers had not taken, the subsequent fires had.

Grace felt sadness at her husband's deep sense of loss. She remembered the big trees too, and loved them, but she felt helpless to express any encouragement to Grover. No one could give their children back their rightful legacy.

One good thing emerged from their trip. Grover and Grace gained confidence with their automobile. They now had no doubt that it would carry them up the big hill from the river plains and on to their home.

The loose sand trail on the river plain gave way to deep ruts as they followed the old wagon road up the long hill to where hardwood forests had replaced the pine. The faithful Ford ground its way slowly to the top of the hill, but steam once more spouted from the radiator. Grover poured in the jug of water and the boiling stopped.

Grover's years at Blue Lake Lumber Company had been the first "real life" he'd enjoyed since his childhood. Not only did he enjoy the work, but he also gained from the experience. The short drive to Blue Lake was filled with memories, of characters and events and everyday challenges.

The remnants of the old Blue Lake Sawmill were scattered along the south shore. Clear blue water had washed away much of the debris. What had been a large pile of sawdust was decaying and plants emerged through the shallow pile. Grover led his family through the jumble of rotting boards and past the rusting boiler, that had once fed the steam engine. "This is where Tuden's shanty stood." Grover looked at what had been the floor, then continued. "Over here was the barn."

Rotting railroad ties led through what had been the lumber-yard. Grover called Brown and White back from the old roadbed, then smiled broadly as he told the family about the big pike some men from Saugatuck had caught. The fish were so big and tough to land that Doc had to shoot them with his 25–20 before they brought them into the boat.

The drive home took them past Squaw, Papoose, and Indian Lakes. As they continued west, the road was still a rutted two track but soft sand gradually gave way to firmer soil, and traveling was much easier after they passed between Big and Little Twin Lakes on a road almost level with the water.

The sun was dropping below the horizon when the Southwell family reached their own yard. Grover attempted to awaken the boys but gave up and carried them into the house. Although he, too, was tired, there were still cows to milk, livestock to feed and water and, for Grace, supper to prepare.

The next morning Grover was glad to get back to work with his horses. Cap and Jack gave him a good pull on a stump each time he asked. On rare occasions, the stump stood fast but the horses always gave their best effort. Grover was careful not to hitch them to something they couldn't pull, because horses, like people, can become discouraged.

Summer had ended and Grover was busily loading shocks of corn on the wagon when Grace's cousins, Bruce and Fred, stopped him with excited voices.

"The trout are running in Rainbow Creek! "They're hard to spear but they're sure good eating," Fred said.

"Put the horses in the barn and come with us," Bruce looked at Grover with pleading eyes.

Grover shook his head. "Grace is looking for me for supper, and the cows still have to be milked." With the exception of baseball, Grover had never taken time for relaxation. The invitation to spear trout with Bruce and Fred was tempting, but he just couldn't do it.

"There are some big trout in that creek, Grover, and the run won't last long. How about tomorrow night?" Bruce couldn't stand it. He and Fred loved fishing and hunting and thought Grover needed some time off. They were both single men.

Grover thought about it. Fish would taste good. Then he said. "I'll go with you tomorrow night. I've never given Grace a mess of fish."

Bruce waved his spear in farewell as he and Fred continued on to the little river.

Grover stabled the horses and walked to the house with mixed feelings. There was so much he needed to do before snow came. He knew Grace would be pleased that her cousins asked him to go fishing with them. While only a mile separated the families, they rarely did anything together.

A gusty wind from the northwest and occasional raindrops foretold a cold, wet night when Grace's cousins stopped the next evening, carrying two-short handled spears.

A canvas bag tied at the corners was draped over Fred's shoulder. It was hardly a fit day to work or fish, but excitement tightened Fred's throat. "We took home six good trout last night, but you should have seen the one we missed! He won't get away tonight!"

"It'll get dark early," Bruce eyed the dark sky as they hurried to the creek. "We should have a half hour. That's enough."

Submerged logs lay across the creek. Deep holes formed under many of the logs where the disturbed current forced its way through the narrow passage. Under these logs, the trout lay, waiting for a worm or insect as it washed down the stream. It seemed that each hiding place was home to a trout.

Bruce handed Grover a spear and picked up a dead tree limb. "I'll poke a trout out for you. Get ready, they're quick."

Grover expected to see a fish come out of the hole, but saw nothing more than a dark streak flash past him. It disappeared under a log a few yards upstream.

Bruce laughed at the shock on Grover's face. "Quick, aren't they? We miss most of them, but you'll get the hang of it."

The three men moved to a hole where they thought the fish had stopped. Fred was upstream and Grover downstream, holding their spears expectantly when Bruce worked his tree limb along the bottom of the log.

The trout flashed upstream where Fred was poised. A quick jab of his spear found its mark. "That's one!" Fred was jubilant. "Now let's find that big one."

The men worked their way upstream toward Davis Lake. Fred missed two trout, but got another. Grover had yet to make a successful stab. Each time, the fish was just too quick.

Grover offered the spear to Bruce. "I'll poke them out. I can't hit one anyway."

"You'll get the knack of it; we miss most of 'em too," said Fred. "I'll poke them out. Bruce can use my spear."

"They sure are quick! One flash and they're under the next log." Grover shook his head in frustration as he pulled the spear back from the sandy bottom. "I'm spearing just behind the tail."

The big trout that Fred was eagerly expecting to see again had either left for one of the lakes or stayed hidden. Nevertheless, the men speared some trout, and missed a lot more, before darkness brought an end to their evening's activity.

Grover was satisfied. After missing repeatedly, he finally managed to anticipate the fleeting shadows and speared two trout. The men all walked home in animated conversation. Each of the men had a story about the fish that got away.

The yellow glow of kerosene lamps in the kitchen and living room penetrated the pitch-blackness and greeted the three bedraggled fishermen who stumbled home from Rainbow Creek. It was familiarity with their surroundings rather than eyesight that enabled them to find their way.

Grace welcomed them and immediately put on the coffeepot. "You must be chilled to the bone!" She shook her head at their appearance, adding two sticks of dry wood to the kitchen range.

The three fishermen were more eager to show off their catch than they were concerned about their appearance.

Grover took the cutting board from where it hung on the wall and laid it on the table. Fred began pulling trout from the canvas bag. One by one, he laid them across the board. There were eight brook trout, all measuring more than twelve inches in length and two of them nearly eighteen, their heads and tails overlapping the sides of the board.

The beautiful colored specks on the "brookies" intrigued Grace. "They're beautiful fish! How do they taste?" Grace asked Bruce, who, though still unmarried, was her own age.

"You can find out tomorrow," speaking in unison, Bruce and Fred grinned broadly. From the time they had first invited Grover to accompany them, they had no intention of keeping any of the fish they caught, but gladly gave them to Grover's family. Grover needed recreation and this might push him into taking time off to hunt in the winter. In any event, Bruce and Fred kept their own family well supplied with fish.

The next evening found the Southwells relishing the excellent fish, which they'd rolled in flour, and fried in hot fat until golden brown and crispy on the outside, while white and firm on the inside. There was nothing quite like it. No delicacy could compare.

Thanksgiving morning was accompanied by the first significant snowfall of the winter. While Grace finished preparations for the family's annual feast, Grover took the horses and dray across the road for stove wood.

Grover selected one of the dry beech trees, received permission from Antrim Iron Company, and cut it into two logs about thirty feet long. Cutting a short piece from the treetop to use as a skid, Grover turned a short chain into a decking line, and rolled the biggest end of each log on the dray. Using the same chain to bind the logs to the dray, Grover told Cap and Jack, "Let's go eat Thanksgiving dinner. This'll keep Mama warm for a few weeks."

The Thanksgiving feast was nearly ready when Grover came into the house. He had fed and watered the horses and cows, adding a little grain for a festive treat. The livestock might not know what day it was, but Grover did.

Grace had stuffed a big rooster and there was squash from the garden as well as cranberries from the marsh on section 17. The berries were scarce this year, but Grover had dug through the bushes until he found enough for this special day.

For dessert Grace made Carrot Pudding. Her mother, Anna, had always made suet pudding for Thanksgiving but Grace had found a recipe using carrots to replace the suet. She said the suet was just "too rich." The pudding was covered generously with a sauce called "Sour Daddy." This was a slightly tart, creamy icing, which took its name from the small quantity of vinegar in it.

Bryce was content to sit on his mother's lap and give her unneeded assistance while she and his father played Flinch with Harold and Rex in the afternoon. Grace was delighted. A farmer's wife had little time for relaxation but this afternoon, she was not only relaxed, she had the entire family together for a few hours. On most days, their only time together was at meals and bedtime.

Grover looked across the table at his sons when the game ended and offered them a different activity. "Let's go out and get the stink off us." Grover smiled as he used the expression.

Grover decided it was time for the boys to learn the use of a crosscut saw. Cutting wood with Harold and Rex's help would take longer than doing it by himself, but the boys had to learn to work. Grover worked with one of the boys at a time, patiently pulling the saw as far as their little arms allowed then pushing it as his son pulled it back. When a half dozen blocks were sawed, Grover split them and the boys carried the pieces to the wood box in the house.

Cutting wood together became a nightly chore. Grover and Brown sawed off a block of wood, and Grover split it. Then while Grover and White cut the next block, Brown carried in the pieces from the previous block. The process continued, with each boy carrying in the pieces from the block he had cut, until there was plenty of fuel to feed the stoves the next day.

Occasionally Grover required the boys to work together, sawing off a block. Neither Brown nor White liked the arrangement. It was much easier to work with their father. Even when Grover was exceptionally tired from a long day's work, he was patient with his sons and they learned to "pull their weight."

Through the winter, Grover's patience began to be rewarded. More and more often Brown, who always wanted to be active, dragged his younger brother away from a book. "Let's cut the wood before Dad gets home." Whether his intention was to help or to relieve boredom, the result was the same. It was a grateful father who only had to split the blocks of wood, and he helped the boys carry them into the house.

Winter's work cutting and skidding logs and four-foot wood for Antrim Iron Company started well. In early November, the Fuzzy Brothers began cutting four-foot wood. Choice maple trees had blown down in an area north of the cranberry marsh. The maples had to be cut before they were covered with snow. The dead and dying hemlocks could be cut later.

For more than a month, Grover hauled four-foot wood six days a week. The wood was easy to split, and the Fuzzy Brothers seldom needed a splitting wedge. Both they and Grover were making good money. The area where the trees had blown over was nearly all cut and hauled to the roads.

Dying hemlocks, their red bark visible for a hundred yards through the open hardwood forest, attracted Grover and his crew. They had made reasonable wages cutting and hauling the four-foot, but their income would improve when they began work on the big hemlock trees.

"After Christmas, we'll cut the hemlocks." Charlie said the words they all were thinking.

Breaking the layer of ice that covered his drinking water, Grover handed the jug to Charlie. One by one, the crew drank deeply. Charlie first, then Frank, and Dick, all in turn. Everything the brothers did was in that order. Returning the jug to Grover, they loaded their saw, axes, splitting sledge and wedges on the sleigh and rode toward home and the long holiday weekend that beckoned.

The night before Christmas, Grover and his two oldest sons cut extra wood for the next day. Christmas was a day for celebrating. The livestock would need their customary care and, of course, the work Grace did in the house would go on as usual.

"It's going to be a white Christmas, Dad!" White excitedly announced as snowflakes coated the wood he was carrying into the house.

Grover hoped the snow wouldn't fall too heavily. A thin layer of snow was best for skidding logs.

Grace woke in the night to the howl of a strong northwest wind. Snow beat against the bedroom window. Cold wind and fine snow seeped through each tiny crack around the window frames. She was happy the family was all home.

Grover awoke to an exceptionally cold house. Ice covered the water pail. He took live coals from the big stove in the living room to start a fire in the kitchen range. He put more wood than usual in both stoves and soon the stove in the living room glowed a dull red.

Grover looked at the packages in and under the Christmas tree and smiled as he anticipated the children's excitement. Gifts were a major part of Grover's life. Generous to a fault, he loved to give things to his family. He was also delighted with whatever he received. He liked the surprise.

The temperature was becoming reasonably comfortable and Grover, who had quietly built the morning fires, banged the griddles noisily on the kitchen stove as he crammed in one more piece of wood.

He grinned as Brown and White emerged from their bedroom rubbing their eyes. They raced to the Christmas tree. The gifts from Santa Claus lay conspicuously to one side: six-foot ash skis! The boys had often dreamed of owning skis but never expected such a great gift. The biggest gift they received each Christmas came from Santa Claus. There would be something else from their parents. Santa was a tradition, whether he came from the North Pole or emerged from Dad and Mother's bedroom. He was a welcome guest!

Grace emerged to enjoy the smiling faces and excitement. She shut her bedroom door, hoping Bryce would sleep a little longer. There was no use attempting to keep the rest of the family quiet. There was high excitement as the boys opened their few presents.

Grace got the water into the pot for coffee. As daylight began to peek in, Grover and Grace became aware of what was happening outside. The snow was falling fast and the wind blew it in an almost horizontal direction! The black silhouette of the barn appeared in ghostly outline, then was hidden by the blowing snow.

"It looks like quite a storm, Ma," Grover said. He frowned, then sipped his coffee. After eating his breakfast, Grover carried pail after pail of water to the livestock in the barn. "It's not a fit day for them to be out," he told the family. "Anyway, it's easier to carry water than to get cows to the pump house on a day like this."

For three solid days, the cold northwest wind battered the house and barn! The wind howled and snow blew through cracks in the haymow, forming a thin layer over the hay and cornstalks. Drifts surrounded the buildings.

On the third day, Grover said, "It'll break tomorrow. We usually get a three-day storm about the first of January, but I think this is the worst I've ever seen."

Grover's prediction was correct. The following morning the sun shone and frost sparkled everywhere. The thermometer read –20° F. Frost covered Grover's mustache when he carried pails of milk into the house.

Always the optimist, Grover said, "We can wade through the drifts." He felt it was the best thing he could say about the snow. "Today we'll get the stock out and bring them to the pump house. Cap and Jack can break a path for the cows and they can drink from a washtub."

Although the livestock was able to get out a little now, the storm ended Grover's work in the woods. Horses cannot work in snow more than belly-deep. Now there were fully three feet of snow in the woods. There was no need for Grover to discuss work with his crew. They knew. Logging was finished for the year.

When snowfall was extreme, the township used snow-rollers—hollow steel drums approximately eight feet wide and four feet in diameter, pulled by four horses to pack the snow on all the main roads. This made the roads passable for horses and sleighs throughout the winter. The telephone enabled Frank Cunningham, the road commissioner, to contact all the farmers and summon them with their horses to help. Grover was busy logging the winter before and hadn't used his horses on the snow-roller. Now he was able to use his team to help pack the roads so farmers could get to town.

After the big Christmas storm, the load was just too much for four horses. It was a struggle for the horses to walk through the snow even without the roller. Each roller now had three teams of horses. The front pair was primarily for breaking a trail. It was a struggle for all the animals, but especially the lead team.

Snowfall continued intermittently for weeks; horses and men struggled to keep the roads packed. Farmers rolled snow through the day and cared for their livestock morning and evening.

When February brought clear, biting cold temperatures, the snow stopped falling and the crisis was over. Mr. Cunningham thanked each farmer personally for his help through the emergency. He checked to see that each had received the same wage as was paid for building roads in the summer. Then he warned, "We won't be able to build any roads next summer, not even the mile from Twin Lakes to Pickerel Lake, like I'd hoped to do. The money's all gone."

When school re-opened soon after the New Year began, Brown and White joyously slid on their skis through the snow. The big hill that went around the swamp was known as "The Mountain Hill," even as that half-mile was called "The Mountain Road." The hill was far too steep for Brown and White with their limited experience on their new skis.

Always ahead, Brown was the first to try turning the corner. Dropping his dinner-pail, he swerved to avoid a head-on collision with a big maple tree and fell in the soft snow. White, already part way down the hill, sat down between his skis before he reached the sharp turn.

At lunchtime, Brown and White joined the other boys who owned skis on the hill just south of the school. Henry Davis, who had enjoyed skis for the past several winters, had no trouble staying upright as he rode down the hill and even turned corners. The other boys were sure they could soon do likewise. Each time they fell in the soft snow, they carried their skis to the top of the hill and started down the same slope, determined to follow Henry around the sharp corner.

While Brown and White were enjoying the winter snow Grover was struggling to get water to the livestock. Since the heavy Christmas snowstorm, their cattle and horses could no longer reach the creek by Tuden's lake for water as they had in the past. Carrying water to the livestock was a long, hard job and a washtub was not an ideal solution. Grover figured that if he installed a big water tank and a stove in the pump house he could bring the cattle and horses to the water.

"Ma, I need to buy a water tank and a stove for the pump house," Grover said. If you need groceries, we can get those, too."

Wisler's hardware could be depended upon to stock what their customers wanted. Prices sometimes seemed high, but Grover didn't linger in thought about purchasing a 100-gallon water tank, the little sheet metal stove he needed, and a few lengths of stovepipe.

Two days later, he had built a small addition on the front of the pump house to house the new water tank. The tank was covered by a trap door, which could be lifted and hooked to the building while the horses and cattle drank. Two narrow boards, nailed together to make a V, formed a trough to carry the water from the pump to the tank.

The little sheet metal stove stood near the tank. From the stovepipe, Grace could now see a curl of smoke drifting upward. The water still needed to be pumped, but the livestock could carry the water to the barn in their stomachs instead of Grover carrying it in two 16-quart pails.

Grover also used the pump house as a small repair shop. In logging camps, a man in the blacksmith shop made cant hook handles and the whipple-trees and eveners with which the horses were attached to their load. Tuden had made these at Blue Lake

Lumber Company and until now had supplied them for Grover. But Tuden was struggling just to care for himself. With a workbench, Grover could make his own replacements.

When he needed to make repairs, Grover built a fire in the little stove before going to milk the cows in the evening. By the time chores were finished, his little workshop was warm enough for him to work as long as necessary by the light of a kerosene lantern hanging from a nail.

Once the repair was finished, Grover had to find or cut a large chunk of wood to keep the fire burning throughout the night. Grover finally could retire; knowing the water would not freeze in the water tank before morning. That is, at least not freeze hard enough to cause damage.

The wood from which Grover made the handles, whipple-trees, and eveners had to be free from knots and the wood grain must be straight. He also preferred that the wood not be too heavy. The horses might not notice a few extra pounds, but the teamster who dragged the whipple-trees and evener back to hook up the load felt every extra pound, especially when a day drew to a close.

Grover looked carefully for an ash tree. Ash was the lightest wood available with sufficient strength for his needs. He thought ash must surely grow among the other hardwoods, but there was not an ash to be found.

There was plenty of ironwood, trees aptly named! The wood was also very strong, and is what Grover used to make his whipple-trees and eveners. While the wood was green, he split the pieces to the approximate size he needed, and then finished shaping them with a drawknife, often called a drawshave, and a wood-rasp. Ironwood was much heavier than ash but was less likely to break.

When the snow was nearly gone in the fields Grover used horses and sleigh to haul the pile of manure that had accumulated through the winter, and spread it on the garden and future cornfield.

Harold, Rex, Grover and Bryce with Cap and Jack

In the four-acre field Grover had cleared the previous year, he had heaped together a large pile of stumps. Once the snow was nearly gone from the field, Grover shoveled most of the snow from the top of the pile. He gathered pine roots filled with pitch, worked them under one corner of the pile of stumps and kindled them. The fire started slowly but soon the smoke and steam from the melting snow created a large billowing cloud.

When the pile had burned, a huge pile of charcoal remained. Grover decided to host a party. "Grace likes a bonfire and the boys will love it," he told himself.

"Ma, lets have a little weenie roast." Grover suggested. "We have a pile of charcoal like you wouldn't believe! I'll drive to town and get some hot dogs and we'll celebrate spring."

Brown and White jumped for joy. Grover took his jackknife from his pocket and handed it to Brown. "Go cut some roasting sticks while I'm gone. Make long sticks; that fire's still hot." He cautioned, "Be careful with that knife. It's sharp!"

White took full advantage of the opportunity to ride to town with his father. Brown was older and went with his father quite often. When White was able to go, he usually was the third member. Today he could ride in the front seat!

Grace hugged Bryce as she planned their meal. "We have enough cooked potatoes to make a salad, and I baked bread today. We'll get a can of pickles from the cellar, and be ready when your dad gets back."

In less than an hour Grover and White had driven fourteen miles and purchased hot dogs for the party. Grover even splurged for a bottle of catsup and a jar of mustard.

Brown and White liked getting as close to the fire as the heat would allow so they could poke the still-flaming embers with their roasting sticks. Each person roasted his or her own hot dog. Whether roasted or burned, they were eaten with great delight.

The fire was warm, even though the evening was becoming cold. Grace sat contentedly on a blanket with Bryce asleep on her lap.

The sun had dropped from sight and a full moon shone brightly when Brown and White finally threw their roasting sticks in the fire and were willing to go home. The evening of family fun wouldn't be repeated for some time but it would be relived for months (and years) afterward.

The last day of school was a time for celebration! All of the children, some with the help of their teacher, wrote invitations to their parents to rejoice with them. Mothers prepared sandwiches, salads, and even lemonade for this special occasion.

Miss Anderson, the teacher, brought a small treat for each of the students and any little brothers or sisters who might share the day.

At noon, eleven students from four families gathered with their parents at the Davis school. The bountiful meal was spread on the teacher's desk and the desks in the front row. Some children ate at their desks but most carried their food outside and ate under a big maple tree.

After dinner, there was a softball game. There was always a softball game when families came together. All of the fathers, some of the mothers, and even Miss Anderson joined the game.

Mr. Brown

On the Saturday after Memorial Day in 1928, Grace was calling the family to supper when an automobile drove up and a man in a suit emerged. The suit itself proclaimed that the man was not local, since suits were reserved for weddings or funerals among those fortunate enough to own one.

Grover was careful not to act surprised and welcomed the visitor. "We're just sitting down to supper. Come in and we'll see what Grace has for us tonight."

After protesting just enough to be considered mannerly, the rather thin man introduced himself as Mr. Brown, a missionary with The American Sunday School Union. He apologized for appearing at mealtime, but Grace protested that, humble though it was, it was no inconvenience; and he joined the family for the evening meal.

After supper, Mr. Brown straightened up in his chair and cleared his throat. He explained his mission. His intent was to help people in Michigan conduct Sunday Schools in the rural areas for three months each summer. "We must teach boys and girls that God loves them!" His voice was nothing special, but when he spoke about the children his inflection and emphasis demonstrated the depth of his concern. "Most of the children in these rural areas have never attended church."

"In every township there's a schoolhouse or town hall where the Sunday school could be held," Mr. Brown said. "The American Sunday School Union provides all the lesson material and song books, but we need adults to teach the lessons." He looked intently into first Grover's, then Grace's eyes.

If Grover and Grace were willing to conduct Sunday school for the summer, it would benefit their own boys as well as other children in the area, Mr. Brown urged.

Grace turned and looked questioningly at Grover, who glanced at the clock. It was time for him to milk the cows.

Grace slowly replied, "There surely is a need, but we've never considered ourselves any kind of leaders. We'll need to think about it." She wanted to talk with Grover privately about it. Then she said, "If you would care to spend the night here, there's a cot in the living room where you can sleep."

Mr. Brown, who depended upon invitations like this for a night's lodging, gladly accepted.

Grover, meanwhile, went through the motions of his evening chores, deep in thought. His thoughts returned to Gorham camp, the revival meetings, and the commitment to Christ he and Grace had made. Grover milked the cows, put them out to pasture with the horses, cranked the milk through the cream separator, gave most of the skim milk to the pigs, and returned to the house.

Mr. Brown had used the time to tell Bible stories to the Southwell children. Bryce, shy at first, was sitting on Mr. Brown's knee when Grover came in from his chores.

Mr. Brown laid sample packets of the Sunday school lessons on the table beside the lamp in the living room for his hosts to examine; now he waited while they considered his request.

Grace waited for Grover to make a decision. When none was forthcoming, she spoke for them both. "Well, Mr. Brown, it's past our bedtime. I'm afraid we start our day quite early around here. We'll talk it over and let you know in the morning."

Grover remembered the evangelist in Gorham camp and their commitment to Christ, but leading a Sunday school had never entered his mind. "Do you think we can handle it Ma?" He asked.

Grace spoke with passion. "It's really important for our children. "I've taught regular school classes, and I can teach them about Jesus. I'll teach the children if you lead the singing."

Grover laughed softly. His wife seldom got carried away. "I sing to the horses, Ma. I'll do the best I can." Over a breakfast of pancakes and homemade sausage the next morning the details were arranged. Grover offered to contact the township supervisor to get permission to use the town hall.

Mr. Brown said he would survey other families during the week and see how many children would attend. He'd come back the following Sunday with lesson material, open the service, and preach a short message.

Although the children had been happy to be dismissed from school for the summer, they missed the contact with other children and began to happily attend Sunday school.

The Township hall had adequate facilities to hold Sunday school but it was not designed for children. There were steel posts on the ground floor of the town hall to support the floor above. Rex found these posts vastly entertaining. While Grover led a song, Rex slipped away from his mother to swing around and around the post—that is until his mother caught hold of his hands and jerked him back to his seat.

There were also spittoons strategically located throughout the building. These often contained tobacco juice leftover from board meetings. Even though Grover and Grace carefully emptied the spittoons before services began, there was sufficient residue for the children to cover their hands and wipe brown goo on their mothers' legs.

The boys and girls who lived near enough to walk to the town hall came regularly. A few parents who brought their children stayed to listen and help. Most of the parents thought Sunday school was a good idea for their children, but their own lukewarm interest soon waned and they no longer bothered to make sure their children attended either.

Mr. Brown attended one of the Sunday schools each week to encourage the untrained leaders. In late August, he arranged a social gathering for all the Sunday schools in the area. These became known as "group gatherings." These get-togethers were well attended. Women brought their favorite dishes and there was an abundance of food. Men, even those who only brought their children to Sunday school, found time to gather with other farmers to discuss the crops, the weather, and their common problems.

The Sunday school group conducted by Grover and Grace was invited to attend the gathering in Evergreen Township, where they had met for several summers.

It was Mr. Brown's opportunity to speak to the adults. His neatly combed hair glistened as he spoke passionately. He emphasized that everyone had sinned and was bound for hell. He then explained that God, because of His great love for mankind, had sent His son, Jesus Christ, to die on a cross, thus paying the penalty for the sin of everyone who would accept Him as their own Savior. This was the only "church" many of the adults would ever attend.

Each spring when the regular school year ended, Mr. Brown went faithfully through the area, opening Sunday schools wherever adults could be found to provide leadership. Thus, each spring, Grover and Grace could expect to find Mr. Brown on their doorstep in late May. And each year, Mr. Brown found a warm welcome, a meal, a place to sleep, and volunteers to conduct Sunday school for the summer.

The location was changed from the town hall to the Hardy School, where there were no spittoons. The schoolhouse was also a more central location for children who attended. With that single change, the Sunday school continued for seven years. As roads and transportation then became more adequate, regular church attendance gradually replaced the summer Sunday school.

One summer on a day in mid-July, Mr. Brown stopped at Grover and Grace's home with unexpected news. "Two girls from Grand Rapids have offered to teach Bible schools this summer," he announced enthusiastically. "The girls will be able to conduct two-week schools in four different locations. The church where the girls are members will furnish the lesson material. All they need is a place to stay. It's a great addition to the summer Sunday school. I thought you might consider allowing them to stay here."

Grace was very busy, canning peas and Swiss chard. Beside her regular housework, there were Sunday school lessons to prepare, chickens to tend to, and the garden to weed. All these weighed on her mind as she mentally digested what Mr. Brown was saying.

Grover, too, was busy cultivating corn, and clearing brush and stumps from next year's cornfield.

The Southwells' hesitation surprised Mr. Brown. The girls' generous offer to provide a two-week Bible-study for the children was surely an opportunity no one would refuse. Twice Mr. Brown began to speak, and twice Mr. Brown bit his lip and waited.

"I doubt that anyone who has children attending Sunday school has a spare bedroom. We'd love to have them teach Bible school, but we don't have a spare bedroom either," Grace said.

Mr. Brown was well acquainted with the frugality of life in the rural areas. He assured Grace, "The girls aren't expecting to be treated as guests. They only ask a place to sleep and simple food. I won't press you, but they'd be content with the same provisions you've given me."

Once again, Mr. Brown was invited to spend the night while Grover and Grace pondered their answer to his request. The next morning, a rather weary Grace said, "I suppose if the girls aren't expecting too much, I can't very well refuse."

Mr. Brown was pleased to have a home for the girls and set a starting date for the school. As he turned to leave, Mr. Brown added one more bit of information. "I'm not sure if I told you, but Miss La Sore is blind. It's not a problem though. She and Miss Duffy work well together."

Grace was dumbfounded! *What have I gotten myself into?*

When Mr. Brown brought the two girls, Grace was instantly relieved of her worries. Tall and dark-haired, Miss La Sore gave no indication of her handicap. A winsome smile brightened an already attractive face and when Miss La Sore moved, Miss Duffy was always with her.

Miss Duffy provided handiwork for the children and gave them Bible verses printed on cards. These were to be learned at home and recited the next day. Miss La Sore, with her beautiful soprano voice, taught them chorus after chorus. Besides singing simple songs the children learned Bible verses. In the evening while Miss Duffy helped in the kitchen, Bryce sat on Miss La Sore's knee and was soon able to join his brothers as they sang "Jesus Loves Me."

When the two weeks of Bible school were completed the love and energy of the two ladies had deeply impressed Grace. She was now slightly embarrassed by her original apprehension of how to care for a blind lady and her companion for two weeks. She felt that they had ministered to her, rather than she serving them.

Chapter 18

. . . .

Luxuries

s the summer of 1928 drew to a close, Jack Frost ripened
all the plants that had not yet matured, and when Grover
stepped into the autumn air on these crisp days, the sharp
aroma of frozen witch-hazel delighted his senses. All that remained of harvesting was moving the remaining corn shocks into
the haymow.

On October 14 one of Grover's childhood friends drove up in
mid-afternoon. Harry Allett was undeniably Irish, irrepressible,
and was always fun company. Harry called his wife Nellie,
"Squaw," which bothered her not a bit. Harry had heard that ruffed
grouse (which the locals called partridge or "pats") were plentiful in northern Michigan and hunting season opened the next
morning. He was hoping that Grover could take a few days off
and hunt with him.

Harry was shocked to learn that Grover did not own any kind
of firearm. "Grover, I brought this little 410-gauge shotgun and I
hardly ever use it. Take a day off, show me where to hunt, and try
it out. You can't be without a shotgun!" Harry spoke confidently as
he handed the little single-barrel shotgun to his friend.

Grover came close to laughing as he looked at the little opening in the end of the barrel. His dad had always wanted the biggest shotgun. The 410 appeared to be something of a joke.

He tried to conceal his opinion of the little weapon out of consideration for his friend. "I haven't done any hunting, but Frank Cunningham said there's a ridge of high land along the northeast corner of Manistee Lake that runs between the lake and a small swamp and it's a nesting area for the birds. It should be a great place on the first day of the season."

Harry helped Grover feed the livestock and milk the cows while the friends reminisced about their childhood days at the fishing dock in Saugatuck. Once his chores were finished, Grover agreed to spend the next day hunting. "We'll go in the morning. I haven't taken a day off all summer. Almost no one stops work to hunt, so we might hit the jackpot."

The following morning found the two childhood friends driving along the rutted sand road at dawn toward Manistee Lake. The three-inch wide tires followed deep ruts. The swaying of the car seemed to exaggerate the sudden bends. There was nothing Harry could do to avoid following the ruts, which forced him to drive much more slowly than he wanted to. He was used to better roads.

It's always darkest just before daybreak, and the magneto lights of the Model "T" Ford depended on engine speed to provide illumination. Harry apologized to his host. "If we could get up to 25 mph these lights would be a lot brighter!"

Grover, who was fighting to stay erect as the car followed the crooked ruts, grinned. "You're doing okay Harry. If we took the horses, we'd still be only a mile from home."

The men reached their destination at sunrise. They parked the car nearly a half-mile from where they planned to hunt, and walked from the high land down to the lake. Grover led Harry through a small bog to a place where the ridge of high land lay along the lakeshore.

Harry paused to admire the scene. "What a beautiful sight, Grove. If this was in southern Michigan, there'd be a house here."

Grover smiled. He wondered about his friend's sanity. Who would want to live here? It was certainly no place to plant a crop of corn or even pasture cattle. It was, however, an ideal place for birds. Partridge had nested there the previous spring, and the hatch had been good. As the men walked slowly along the lakeshore, many of the birds flushed from almost beneath their feet, the stillness of the morning shattered with the thunder of their wings. Occasionally Harry was able to drop one of the vanishing partridge.

Grover watched carefully. He was sure he could never hit a bird. They disappeared before he recovered from the startling thunder of their wings. Grover also looked at the little single barreled 410-gauge, and wondered what it could really do. After watching some of the birds run several feet before flying, Grover was ready. He found that if he was quick enough to shoot the birds before they took wing, his little 410 was very effective.

Grover and Harry returned to the farm at mid-day with ten plump birds. Watching the men skin the birds and listening to their excited rehashing of the morning's hunt, the ladies' minds turned to the use of the meat. "We pin bacon on the breasts and roast them," Nellie said. "They're a little dry otherwise."

Grace was pleased with the suggestion. "We don't have bacon, but there's fresh side pork in the crock."

It seemed ages to Harry and Grover since they had played on the dock at Saugatuck. Tales of the intervening years tumbled out as they were enjoying potatoes, bread and blackberry pie.

Soon Grover noticed the lengthening shadows, looked at the clock, and suddenly remembered his dad. "Let's walk down and see Tuden, He'll be tickled to death! No one from Saugatuck has come all this way before."

Tuden sat patiently in his double-ended boat, his fishing line dangled loosely in the direction of a wooden bobber. Whether Tuden had been sleeping or just nodding, a sudden call from shore made him jump. The voice sounded familiar, but Tuden couldn't place where he last heard it. Pulling in his line, Tuden picked up the paddle he had carved from the remains of an old pine log, and paddled for shore. He was glad to see someone, but at the same time, he was unhappy to come ashore without fish for supper.

Harry greeted the old man. "I knew I'd never find an old sailor on shore! Let's see your fish."

Tuden inspected the speaker, spit out his tobacco, and reached in his pocket for a fresh plug. "If I didn't know better, I'd think I knew you in Saugatuck. It's been a long time." He said no more. Cutting a piece of tobacco from the plug of "Brown Mule," Tuden waited for a response.

Grover and Harry walked out on the cedar plank and carefully dragged the skiff up on the bank.

Flashing his quick Irish smile, Harry shook the old man's hand. "I sat on your lap when I was a baby and I used the baseball bats you made for us kids. You called me lots of things, but my name's Harry."

Tuden's winters in Saugatuck had been pleasant. When he was sober, the young boys flocked to him and it was the great joy of his life. Tears came to Tuden's eyes and he held Harry's proffered hand with both his own. "I never thought I'd see you again." He sat on the old pine stump and drifted off in thought.

Grover broke the silence, saying, "Harry came up for partridge season. There were a lot of birds by Manistee Lake and we brought home enough for a good mess."

Early the next morning Grover and Harry drove to Manistee Lake again, hoping for a repeat of the previous day's hunting. Grace and Nellie found their newly established acquaintance developing into relaxed friendship. After getting Harold and Rex off to school, Grace cut slices from the side pork. The ladies covered the partridge breasts carefully with the salted, fatty, meat

and put them in the oven with half of a large Hubbard squash
and a few large potatoes.

The October day was exceptionally brisk. The fire in the kitchen
range, which provided heat for the oven, spread its welcome warmth
throughout the house. Grace added sticks of hard red beech to the
glowing coals and spoke to her newfound friend. "The men will
appreciate the warm house today." Throughout the summer cooking meals made it uncomfortably warm in the house. The heat
would be welcome today.

When Harold and Rex returned from school that afternoon, it
sure "smelled hungry"! The combined aroma of side pork and partridge filled the kitchen.

"I'm hungry!" The cry came in unison as and Harold and Rex
set their lunch pails on the kitchen table. Nellie looked at Grace.
"It sounds like home. An hour after a meal, if a boy smells food,
he's hungry." The Allet's had left their own teen-aged son home so
he could go to school.

The hunters returned much later than the day before, but the
game bag was filled with birds. After retracing their steps of the
previous day with limited success, Grover and Harry found more
partridges as they continued along the edge of the swamp. Grateful for the cool day—and a much colder night—which would keep
the game from spoiling, Grover and Harry cleaned the carcasses,
and hung their prizes in the corncrib.

Grace and Nellie, alternately carrying Bryce, had walked down
to Tuden's and invited him to eat supper with them. Grace tried to
invite him regularly, but opportunities were scarce.

Rex, who always wanted a drumstick from a chicken, was disappointed. "There's not much to eat on these legs!" Most of the
meat on this game was in the breast. Moistened with fat from the
side pork, they were delicious.

Everyone left the table stuffed. Rex always ate as much meat as
he was allowed. Whether or not he ate anything else depended on

how closely he was watched. Even Tuden had to express appreciation. The legs of his chair creaked as he pushed it back from the table. His eyes sparkled as he said, "That was a good feed!"

The little 410-gauge shotgun intrigued Tuden. He always used his trusty 10-gauge and would have used an 8-gauge if it had not been outlawed. Tuden looked the little 410 over carefully, picked up one of the little shells, gave an abbreviated "Hmph," and promptly dubbed it "the mouse gun." Grover laughed aloud at the contempt in his father's voice, "I'd have said the same thing yesterday morning, Dad, but it'll kill a bird just as dead as your cannon will."

After a much more leisurely meal than any of them were accustomed to eating, Grover did the evening chores while Harry walked home with their guest. In a life of hard work upon hard work, this was a memorable day.

The following morning, when Harry and Nellie prepared to leave, a cold Northwest wind brought clouds sweeping low across the sky. It was too early for a snowstorm, yet an occasional white flake portended what was to come.

Grover helped Harry snap the side curtains on the Model T. Grace was concerned that Nellie would freeze on the long ride home.

"I'll take Harry's coat off his back if I have to, Grace!" Nellie promised. "We'll be all right. The sun will probably come out before we go very far."

Grover returned from the corncrib with the partridges, almost frozen solid, in a burlap bag. "Take these with you, Harry. Thanks for coming. It's been great seeing you again." He added, "Are you sure you want to part with that little shotgun?"

"You need that shotgun, Grove!" Harry spoke with some vehemence. "Chuck used it when he was learning to hunt, and your boys are about that age." Then looking at the burlap bag Grover had placed on the floor behind the seat, Harry hefted it and looked inside. "I'm not taking all these birds! We'll take one for Chuck, one for Squaw, and one for me. The rest are yours; they'll remind you to go shoot some more."

Brown and White stood with their lunch pails, hesitating before leaving for school. Harry's remark about them soon using the little shotgun had not fallen upon deaf ears.

Harry shook Grover's hand, and then turned to the boys. "You help your dad. And keep your nose clean. Someday you'll be just like him."

After cranking the Model T several times before it coughed and began to run, Harry said, "She don't like cold mornings, Grove, but once she gets started, she don't know the difference." With that Harry stepped past his wife to his seat behind the steering wheel, settled in, gave a quick wave, and they were gone.

Soon the cold winter weather returned. Occasionally in the evening, after the chores at the barn were finished, the wood boxes filled, and water was carried in for the night, Grover took his old "potato bug" from its case. Then he and Grace sang some of the songs they had so loved before their marriage. "Daises Don't Tell" was their favorite.

Daises won't tell dear, come kiss me, do,
Sweetheart I love you, say you'll be true,
And I will promise always to be,
Tender and faithful, Sweetheart, to thee.

In my dreams I fancied you were by my side.
While I gathered Daisies, one long chain you twined.
'Round us both you twined them, you have heard it o'er.
Daises never tell, dear, make that dream come true.

Brown was fascinated by the mandolin. Grover was pleased to have a son following in his footsteps and taught Brown to play a few cords. Brown soon learned to play the songs also. Often in the evening, while White read a book, Brown carefully picked his way through some new song.

One night, just after the family finished supper, Tuden came through the kitchen door. The door slammed shut. Grover quickly slid a chair behind the old man. He seemed very upset. After Tuden was seated, Grover asked, "What's wrong, Dad?"

Tuden exploded. "If the boys want to learn to play the fiddle, I'll teach 'em!" After catching his breath, Tuden continued. "I noticed someone's been using my fiddle. I'm pretty sure it was your sons."

Grover frowned at his oldest son and waited for an explanation.

Brown said nothing, but looked straight into his father's eyes and nodded. The story gradually unfolded. When the boys came home from school, it was no farther home going past their grandfather's house than to walk up the mountain road. When Tuden was away, they would stop at his house. The boys knew Tuden kept his fiddle in his bedroom. It was a golden opportunity to practice. Surely it did no damage. They were careful to put it back just as they found it.

The boys knew that they were not allowed to use anything that belonged to someone else without asking, even if it belonged to their granddad. They never dreamed they'd be discovered. They were reminded of the proverb that says, "Your sin will find you out."

After Grover and Grace assured Tuden that this would not happen again, a pacified Tuden left for home. Grover quickly convinced the boys with old-fashioned discipline that it was not in their best interests to stop in at Tuden's house when he was not there!

In late March 1929, the harsh winter weather gave way to bright sunny days. The snow melted quickly and everyone started to get spring fever. A neighbor who bought a radio invited Grover, Grace and their children to come over for the evening and listen with them. What a remarkable invention! "How could the music come from that wire on the roof, down into the box, and then out the speaker?" All wondered, but no one had an answer.

Grover and Grace discussed this marvel for some time. Both of them really wanted a radio. On the next trip to Mancelona they looked longingly at the radio playing in Schroeder's furniture store. New radios were terribly expensive, but Mr. Schroeder offered to sell them a used Atwater Kent. Grover and Grace agreed it was within their means.

The price of batteries had not been discussed. When this was added to the price of the radio, the cost was considerably more than Grover and Grace had expected to pay, but their desire was so strong, they relented, and now they had a radio of their own. The family could hear Bradley Kincade sing ballads, and there was a comedy program called "Amos 'n Andy" broadcast every Saturday night. This was a weekly highlight for many years.

Grover and Grace were distressed to find that "B" batteries for the radio were expensive and short-lived. They would have to ration the use of the radio to save the batteries for the important programs. The children reluctantly got used to limitations on the use of the radio.

Snow disappeared from the timbered areas. Spring Beauties, interspersed with the ever-present leeks, transformed the forest floor from the pressed-down leaves that showed every contour of the land, to one of smidgens of green dotting the woods. The delightful pink striped flowers of the Spring Beauties were cherished harbingers of the lush green season ahead.

Farmers were eager to prepare the fields for planting, but first there was a semi-annual spring ritual at the township hall vying for their attention. Township officers were elected on odd-numbered years. In many ways, these elections affected the lives of local people much more than the state or national elections, which took place in the autumn.

Frank Cunningham paid a surprise visit one afternoon. Grover wiped his hands on a rag as he took time out from sharpening tools in the shed and shook Frank's hand. "I'm not going to run for re-election as Coldsprings Township Road Commissioner, this year, Grover." He wiped his mouth with the back of his hand. "I came over to tell you, because I think you should run for the office. It's an important job and it pays pretty well." He wasn't sure if the frown on Grover's face expressed shock or consternation, but decided he'd say what he'd come for.

"More and more of our people are getting automobiles. We should work on roads that will help the most people each year. I believe you're the best man for the job."

At that time, road commissioner was by far the most important office in the township. Most of the annual tax money was spent building roads, and everyone wanted roads built in their own area. It was critical to elect a commissioner who fairly distributed the resources and location of each new road. It was also crucial to allow each man in the township an opportunity to share in the work and the payment for services rendered. A fair and wise man was required for the job.

Grover's first reaction was surprise that Frank no longer wanted to be Commissioner. The residents were satisfied with his work. There was no question that Frank could have the election if he chose to run. Frank had walked almost three miles to be sure Grover was the first to know of his decision. That, the obviously sincere statement, and Frank's concern for the continuation of a sound road building program had the desired effect on Grover.

He considered Frank's recommendation as he stood facing him. "You're doing a good job, Frank. Why don't you keep the office?"

Frank would have preferred not to answer, but he said, "There are some headaches that go with the job, Grover. I'm just not willing to put up with them any more. You're younger than I am. You'll be all right."

"I hadn't even considered running for office, Frank, but since you really don't want to be commissioner, I'll talk it over with Grace."

When chores were done for the evening, Grover thoughtfully picked up his old "potato bug" and tuned the strings. The family sang a few of Grover's simple "ditties." These evenings seemed to be a rarity now.

Grover waited until Grace finished tucking the boys in bed for the night before broaching the subject. "Ma, Frank Cunningham stopped today. He doesn't want to be the road commissioner again." He scratched a place behind his ear. "He thinks I should take the job. I've never considered holding an office. What do you think? Should I should run?"

"My!" She was impressed that Frank wanted to pass the torch to her husband. Then she nodded and said. "You can do it, Dad. You scaled for Antrim Iron Company. Everyone was pleased with your work, there. Go ahead and run. You can handle the job."

Grover respected his wife's opinion. She had a good sense of direction.

Once he made the decision, Grover put forth his best effort. Following long established custom, he stood in the town hall the day of election, handing a Dutch Master cigar to the men as they came to vote, then casually mentioning that his name was on the ballot for road commissioner.

The room was filled with tobacco smoke, and the spittoons got a lot of use as neighbors waited for the results of the balloting.

It was well past midnight when they finished counting the ballots. Grover won by a good margin. He walked the two miles home contemplating his new responsibilities. It was a warm April night and his mind shifted between his new duties as road commissioner and the need to get crops planted.

Grace awoke from a fitful sleep when her husband entered the house. She and Grover lay for a short time discussing where the need for roads was most critical.

The sound of a nighthawk swooping for a mosquito intruded on their conversation.

"Let the nighthawk work now," Grover smiled as he noted the familiar sound. "Let's get some sleep. Then we'll be ready for tomorrow's work.

The Darragh Road was by far the most heavily traveled in the township. The first two miles north of the town hall were quite hilly. Sand ruts on the hills were especially bad. Nearly at the center of those two miles was a conveniently located gravel pit. Grover decided the township could afford to gravel those two miles.

"We'll start spreading gravel when most of the farmers finish haying," Grover told Grace.

Almost all the farmers brought their horses and wagons to help build the road. Other men and even some of the older boys shoveled gravel or dumped the gravel from the dump boxes.

Grace's brother, Lee, unexpectedly asked to help with his shovel. Lee possessed a degree of wanderlust, apparently inherited from his father and grandfather. An occasional change of scenery cured any dissatisfaction Lee might have with his employer.

Until now, Lee worked as a sawyer or woodchopper. He loved the clean hard work, and was able to use his strong body to provide for his family. No matter whether Lee was felling trees and cutting them into logs, or cutting the remaining tops and small trees into four-foot wood, he was happy. Farming held no attraction for Lee. Others could work with horses and cattle if they wished. He preferred to work in the woods.

Lee had been out of lumber work a couple of weeks so he welcomed an opportunity to renew old acquaintances. He would shovel gravel for a couple of months and then move on to some new logging camp.

Grover was pleased with his crew. The men were glad to earn some much-needed cash. Shoveling gravel is hard work but the men put their heart into their work as well as their bodies. Nevertheless, Grover was soon to learn first-hand of the headaches that caused Frank to give up the office.

On one particularly hot July day the crewmembers gathered as usual and were visiting amiably while the horses were eating the hay and oats their owners provided. Horses took about 30 minutes for their meal, ample time for the men to eat their own food and relax. Maybe it was the heat, but suddenly tempers flared. An argument erupted among the men.

Grover reluctantly went to quiet the uproar. One man stood alone. Several others were demanding that he leave the jobsite.

"What's the problem?" Grover asked, "I thought the job was going well."

Jim spoke for the group. "His wagon's shorter than the others, and he's drawing the same wages we are. That just ain't right. He should either get a bigger box or go home!"

All grew quiet as Grover walked to the toolbox, picked up a ruler and measured the box in question. The box measured 36 inches wide inside, 12 inches high, and nine feet long.

"Jim," Grover said, "his box holds a yard of gravel. That's what the job calls for."

Seeing that his response obviously had not defused the tension, Grover measured one of the other dump boxes. "You men apparently want to give a little extra or you wouldn't have made your boxes a foot longer. That's good, as long as your horses can handle the load, but his wagon's legal." He looked directly at the man who spoke up. "He'll stay on the job."

Jim looked at the other men and, convinced he had their support, spoke sharply. "You might be the commissioner, but there's a half dozen of us. We say he goes!"

Lee observed this exchange from a distance, and heard that last remark. Quietly he knocked the ashes from his pipe and stood beside Grover and the besieged teamster. Lee was over six feet tall and his physique was extremely fit and well-proportioned. His muscular superiority was, at the very least, intimidating.

Jim's support quickly faded. Still filled with anger, he spoke one last time. "Grover, it just ain't right that he draws the same wages we do." When there was no reply, Jim joined the others now hitching their horses to their wagons. The conversation ended and no more was said about dump boxes.

Gravel was a great improvement on the hilly road, especially because most families now owned an automobile. Their cars no longer swayed from side to side as the narrow tires followed deep ruts. Gravel roads were well worth the cost.

When two miles of road was completed, the road crew drew their last check and returned home to harvest their crops. Even after paying the men, there was money left in the township treasury to pay for snow rolling.

In late August, when Sunday dinner was finished and the family lingered at the table before washing dishes, Grace suddenly asked. "Grover, do you think we could drive over and see Jeff and Zony? I know it's a long way, but we have four hours until time to milk. We haven't gone for a ride this summer."

Harold and Rex voiced their approval. "Let's go, Dad!"

Jeff and Zony had moved from Louie's place to a farm near Chestonia, a small community between Mancelona and East Jordan.

Grover was surprised by Grace's request, but readily agreed to the outing. "Brown, you and White help your mother and I'll get the car ready."

The ride to Chestonia was pleasant in the "tin Lizzie." A cool breeze flowed through the touring car. Brown and White reached their arms outside, first allowing the wind to push their hands up, then tipping their hands and letting the wind push them down.

After passing through Mancelona, the Southwells drove down a long, steep hill and across Cedar River. Leaving the river valley, their faithful "Model T" crawled up the hill on the other side, slowly weaving from side to side, tires never leaving the ruts cut into the sandy road.

At Chestonia, wild land suddenly gave way to prosperous farms, as Grover and the family approached their destination.

"That's why Jeff moved here," Grover said admiringly. "Look at the height of that corn!"

Jeff and Zony were obviously surprised to see visitors. Not many people made a trip unless they needed something. Concern gave way to a warm welcome when Grover nodded toward his wife. "Grace couldn't wait any longer to talk to Zony."

Jeff laughed, and gave Grover a hearty handshake while his wife and Grace excitedly drew one another into an embrace. After exchanging greetings and news, Grover walked through the newly tasseled corn. "The land's heavier here." Jeff picked up some clay as he spoke. "This soil holds moisture longer. At Louie's place, we never did get enough rain."

While the men sat in the shade watching their sons play baseball, Jeff said, "Farming's better here, Grover, but we want to get a place of our own. Zony and I've talked it over. I think we'll go back to Detroit when the crops are in."

Grover's face clearly showed his disappointment, but he waited for Jeff to continue.

"Ford's paying good wages." Jeff answered his friend's unspoken question. "He's selling all the cars he can build. We think we'll be able to save enough money to buy a farm somewhere if we work downstate for a while."

"Well, I can't say that I blame you, Jeff. If I could get Grace to leave, we'd find something else, too." Grover thoughtfully chewed on a blade of grass as he looked out over the farm.

On the way home, the faithful Ford was crawling slowly up the hill from Cedar River when the engine suddenly sputtered and died. It sounded like it was out of gas. Grover removed the front seat and placed the gasoline measuring stick in the tank. The wet gasoline on the wooden measure showed the tank to be a quarter full.

Grover pushed up the spark lever, adjusted the gas, and spun the crank twice as he prodded his memory to figure out the problem. It sure sounded like it quit because it was out of gas. Still, the measuring stick showed a quarter tank.

Grace could see they were in big trouble! She never should have suggested going all the way to Chestonia. How in the world would they get home? "It's about ten miles home." Grace spoke the words more to herself than to her husband. They would have to carry Bryce.

Grover kept at it and figured out the problem. Harry, the Ford dealer in Mancelona, had warned him to keep the tank nearly full if he was going up any steep hills.

The gas, from the tank under the front seat, flowed to the engine by gravity. "If the tank's full, Grover, gas will get to the engine. If the tank gets too low, well, gas won't run uphill!" Harry had said.

"Ma, we have to turn the car around. You steer and the boys and I'll push. When we get the car turned around it'll start." Grover spoke with more confidence than he felt.

Grover smoothed sand away from the front wheels and helped Grace get the wheels turned. She held the steering wheel while Grover and the boys pushed the front end around to face down the hill.

"She'll run now, Ma." Grover's confidence returned as he spun the crank. Two spins, three spins, Grover's confidence was fading. One more spin. The responding put-put-put brought new life, not only to the engine of the Ford, but also to the hearts of Grover and Grace.

One question remained. Could Grover back his car up the sandy hill?

"The sand's really soft where we turned the car around," Grover observed aloud. He turned to Brown and White. "You boys are strong, push with all your might until we get past this messed-up stretch of road, then you can get in."

With strength they might not otherwise have found, Brown and White struggled. The "Model T" slowly worked its way through the soft sand and into harder ruts.

Grover relaxed as the car continued its slow backward climb. Before they reached the top of the hill steam billowed from around the radiator cap. "Only a little bit farther." Grover pleaded with the faithful automobile. "Just go around this corner, then we'll get you a drink."

After a couple more tense minutes backing through deep ruts, the car slowly crept around the corner, and over the crown of the hill. Grover turned the car around toward home, and shut off the ignition.

Turning to his worried wife, he said, "We're going to make it Ma, but we'll have to let the engine cool before we put water in the radiator."

Once steam ceased blowing, Grover slowly unscrewed the brass cap and poured water from the gallon jug into the still hot radiator.

Now that they were on a level road, gasoline flowed readily to the engine as the family returned home. Grover quietly promised himself. "I'll remember that lesson."

The sun had almost set. Grover pushed the "tin-Lizzie" faster than ever before. They whizzed on home, possibly exceeding 30 miles an hour. There was no speedometer, but Grace was sure they were going too fast!

It was well past bedtime when Grover finished milking the cows, feeding the pigs, and giving his team of blacks their expected box of oats. Finally he was able to relax at the kitchen table while he and Grace rehashed the events of the day and ate their late supper.

Chapter 19

Recreation

Harvest is the most satisfying season in a farmer's life, the culmination of the year's endeavors. The September days of harvest were over now. Vegetables from the garden were all canned or stored in the cellar. Grover had finished cutting and shocking the corn.

Only one crop remained to be gathered; the winter's potatoes. In a life dependent upon the seasons, the repetition of tasks brought memories of previous years. The briskness of the days and thoughts of special harvests flooded Grover's mind. He remembered the spearfishing they'd done in Rainbow Creek, and the trout they'd caught.

Grace's cousins, Bruce and Fred, had moved to Elk Rapids where they opened an "Indian Trail" gas station and were developing a wholesale oil and gasoline business. Uncle Charlie and Aunt Hattie had followed. Possibly, no one was taking advantage of the annual trout run up Rainbow Creek, which flowed from Davis Lake to Rainbow Lake. Grover decided it was a great opportunity to share an exciting evening with his sons. All through the afternoon, he'd husked corn and thought of the deep holes where trout would surely be hiding. Bruce had given him a spear when he moved away.

When Brown and White came home from school, their father asked if they remembered the trout from Rainbow Creek, and wondered if the boys would like to try to get some more. Brown's enthusiasm was no surprise to their dad, but White's yelp of excitement tickled Grover.

The Southwells were not disappointed. There were plenty of trout in the creek—big beautiful, speckled trout! Grover thought the fish were bigger than last time. Apparently, no one else was harvesting them.

Trees had fallen across the stream, and over the years, the obstructed current had washed sand from under the dead logs. The result created quiet dark holes where trout lurked, watching for worms or insects carried downstream by the current. With two sons eager to poke sticks into the holes under the logs, Grover quickly speared all the trout he thought he could use at one time. The brief experience a few years earlier had taught him to anticipate the fleeting shadows.

"Think you can hit one, Brown?" Grover handed the spear to his elder son as he asked the question.

"I can hit 'em, Dad!" Brown exclaimed confidently. While poking sticks under the logs, he had watched the dark streaks emerge, and seen his dad successful at getting the fish. Now it was his turn.

Some things are more difficult than they appear. Several times a big trout passed under Brown's waiting spear. Each time the dark shadow was just a fraction of a second quicker than his spear. Brown handed the spear back to his father. Grover smiled at his son. "They're quick, aren't they? I was ready to give up before I hit the first one." Pretending not to see the proffered spear, Grover led the way upstream to a partially submerged log. "Let's see if we can find another one."

Carefully positioning Brown where a trout was most likely to pass within reach, Grover prodded more fish from their hiding places. Davis Lake, the inlet to Rainbow Creek, was in sight when Brown finally, and with great delight, pulled his spear from the water with a large, brightly speckled trout at the end. Time after time they'd wait, mostly without breathing, until Brown had made his stab with the spear. Then a torrent of exclamations and squeals would spill out of the two boys, who were glorying in the hunt!

Daylight was fading fast, so White's turn would have to wait for a future evening.

Grover watched the big pie moon rise that night with rich satisfaction. He was thrilled to be able to live through his sons what he missed in his own childhood. The father-son connection with his own offspring would be a different relationship than he'd had with his father. Grover could never give them all the things he wanted to, but joining his sons in pursuit of exciting game fish in the golden evenings of September 1929 was a priceless memory that he would cherish for many years to come.

Grover filled the potato bin in the cellar while Grace lined the shelves with canned vegetables. The 6-gallon crock was filled with sauerkraut. The 20-gallon crock awaited pork later, after butchering in October. Carrots and beets filled a small bin beside the potatoes. A few fresh cabbages were piled on top of the other vegetables. This finished preparations for the Southwell's winter.

When Grover had hauled the last shock of corn to the barn, he asked Cap and Jack to pull stumps with him, until snowfall, in preparation for next years planting.

The Fuzzy Brothers—Charlie, Frank, and Dick—appeared single file at the barn one evening when Grover was milking the cows. Without any preliminary social chitchat, Charley announced, "We're ready to start cutting logs."

"There's plenty of trees," Grover agreed, "but I'll have to talk to Ray before we start. I'll go see him tomorrow."

The discussion being over, Charlie turned and retraced his steps, with Frank and Dick quietly following in single file.

True to his word, Grover drove to Antrim the following morning.

"Yes, the company wants to salvage all the dead hemlock," Ray answered without hesitation. "They want the maple and beech the wind's broken off or uprooted, too. You can start cutting any time."

The allure of the timber that infected Grover when he first came to Blue Lake would never leave him. Grover could easily understand why Lee and so many others returned to logging camps year after year. Now he felt he had the best of both worlds. He, Grace, and their three boys lived in their own home. He worked in the woods each winter and expanded their farm through the summer. Grover had everything he could ask for.

"Into every life a little rain must fall," an old saying warns. In Grover's case, the little rain was "little squirrels." Red squirrels were eating the corn intended for their livestock. These frisky little creatures became more than just a nuisance. Each morning when Grover walked out of the barn carrying pails filled with milk, more and more squirrels ran from the corncrib. His frustration was apparent on his face as he saw how his hard work was being stolen piecemeal. Much more of this and he'd be cleaned out before the hard part of winter set in. He poured the milk into the cream separator.

"We have to do something to get rid of the red squirrels, Grace," he told his wife.

He carefully maintained proper speed as he cranked the fresh milk through the cream separator, shaking his head as he continued. "There's no way to keep them out of the crib. Every morning when I come out of the barn there are more." He stopped momentarily. "I'll see if Brown wants to get up early and shoot a few. That might scare the others away."

Grace gasped. "You wouldn't let our son use that shotgun, would you? Harold is only eleven years old! Please don't do that, Dad."

At the fear in Grace's voice, Grover abandoned the idea. He was sure that Brown would be perfectly safe, but Grace was too scared even to consider it. Something had to be done, though. Grover could not take time from his work to chase squirrels.

Sitting at the breakfast table, Grover focused on his oldest son. Brown was a strong and dependable boy. Weighing his words carefully, Grover said. "Brown, red squirrels are coming to the corn crib at the crack of dawn every morning. They're ruining a lot of corn. I'd like you to get up early and sneak down to the corncrib just as soon as it's light enough to see. When the squirrels run out of the crib, see if you can chase them up a tree. When you get one treed, I'll get the mouse gun and you can shoot it."

White was small for his age and, not being strong, often stayed behind when Grover called on Brown for help. White was usually content to stay in the house. Today, however, White was first to answer. "I'll do it, Dad!" With the excitement of spearing trout fresh in his mind, the possibility of shooting a squirrel instantly changed the boy from a tag-a-long to an active participant.

Brown, surprised at his brother's sudden interest, added, "Maybe we can catch one."

The first gray streaks of dawn in the eastern sky touched the uneven treetops across the road when Grace woke her sons. She had only to say, "squirrels" and both Brown and White were wide-awake.

With new-fallen snow muffling their footsteps, the boys had nearly reached the corncrib when several squirrels jumped from the crib and raced for the woods, with two young boys in hot pursuit! One chose an elm tree to escape. On a long limb extending over the field, the squirrel stopped.

Brown stayed to watch the squirrel while White called their father. Grover, smiling at the obviously excited boy, left his milking and hurried to the house for the little 410-gauge shotgun.

"White, you can have the first shot," Grover decided. Since he had responded first, he would go first. "If you don't hit him, Brown can try." Grover expected to have to kill the squirrel himself, but he would give both boys an opportunity.

White stood almost directly under the squirrel, which had scurried to the very end of the limb. White aimed and aimed, and aimed once more. The more he aimed, the more the barrel of the gun wobbled back and forth. Just when Grover had decided he was never going to shoot, the little shotgun gave a sharp report, and wonder of wonders, the squirrel fell dead! White was ecstatic, while Brown was just a bit envious.

The two brothers continued to chase squirrels from the corn-crib but no other squirrel ever went up a tree. It was a great disappointment for Brown. He still had not fired a gun, but, as Grover reminded him, he *had* speared a trout!

The squirrels must have tired of being chased from their breakfast or found another source of food. When several mornings passed with no squirrels at the crib, Brown and White gave up the chase and slept in the extra half-hour. Grover was happy with the results of his sons' efforts, and he told them, "There should be enough corn to last "Old Suz" through the winter."

Snow limited the food supply not only for red squirrels but also for mice, which found their way into the farmhouse in large numbers. Every night Grace set mousetraps and every morning one or more of the traps contained a mouse. She lamented to her husband. "I cannot find a way to keep the mice from our food! I don't know what to do."

All the following day, Grover mechanically skidded logs with his faithful horses. The mice were a problem. Not only were they destroying the Southwell's food, they were a source of consternation to his wife. Grover had to find a solution.

Preoccupied with the problem, Grover walked to the kitchen range where Grace was busily stirring supper. "Ma," Grover told her as he wrapped a strong arm around her waist, "I think we can lick that mouse problem. I'll make a cupboard and hang it from the ceiling with wires."

Grover built a solid cupboard with a large screened front door and suspended it from the roof of the cellar with heavy 9-gauge wire. The hanging cupboard outsmarted the mice. Grace kept all the perishables in what she dubbed "The Swing Shelf." Mice persisted and Grace made every effort to eliminate them, but they could no longer destroy her precious food supply.

Grover and his three-man crew of lumberjacks spent a profitable winter cutting hemlock and uprooted maple and beech trees. A March blizzard that cancelled school for a week also kept most children cooped up indoors. Once school resumed, Brown and White were glad they had their skis! That first half-mile on the mountain road would have been tough to wade through without skis.

Henry Davis, who lived on a farm next to the school, built a ski jump with an old barn door on the hill behind his house. At lunchtime all the boys with skis took turns on the jump. Henry usually made the jump without falling, but for the others, it was a learning experience!

The first day on the jump was so much fun, in fact, that they lost track of time. When the boys returned to school, Miss Anderson told the erstwhile skiers, "For each minute you were late coming back to class, you'll spend five minutes after school."

It was almost dark when Brown and White reached home and their worried mother and exasperated father. After the boys explained why they were late coming home, and promised they hadn't meant to be late for classes, Grover and Grace acknowledged that they understood.

Finally, Grover dug the last snow from the remaining dry logs he had brought through the winter and, with his sons' help, cut them into stove wood. There were three piles of wood, each four feet high and 16 feet long, enough wood to warm the house through what was left of cold weather, and cook food until next winter.

Grover had hardly begun spring plowing when the plow point broke. Stumps and roots could be plowed out, but hidden stones sometimes broke the point. Grover had to leave his work and drive to Mancelona. He hadn't used the faithful old Ford since the first snow in autumn, so he filled the radiator, added oil, and cranked the engine to life.

Aside from the family pulling their coats more tightly around their legs, and wrapping Bryce into a blanket, the trip to town went as planned. Coming home, however, Grover heard a knock in the engine that soon grew ominous. He knew he would have to take the pan off the engine and check the rods. Grover hadn't worked on the car before, but several neighbors had tightened rods on their cars, and he had listened sympathetically to their plight.

Fortunately, Grace had bought her husband a set of socket wrenches for Christmas, so Grover had the tools he needed for the job. The car stood high enough off the ground that he could lie on his back and work on the engine.

When the oil was nearly drained, Grover tried his new wrenches for the first time. Once he took out the stud bolts the oil pan dropped and he could see the rod bearings. The three front rod bearings felt fine, but the back one had a definite slop! Grover took out two shims, put the bearing cap back on, and carefully felt for any movement. The bearing still was not tight.

Grover carefully took out two more shims, tightened the cap, and the bearing felt tight. He crawled out from under the car and engaged the crank. Pulling with all his might, Grover could not turn the engine over. Again he slid under the car and replaced one of the shims he had taken from under the bearing cap. A now very uncertain Grover engaged the crank and turned the engine over several times. Patting the radiator, Grover told his Tin Lizzy "We won!" Then, disgusted that he had said this aloud, he mumbled, "A car is faster than horses, but it has no soul."

Deciding thicker oil might prevent future problems Grover filled the crankcase with Mobil "D" and cranked the engine to life. No abnormal sound came from under the hood, just the reassuring putt-putt of the idling engine. Grover decided to stop at the Ford garage on his next trip to town to get advice.

It was three weeks before Grover had to again leave his farm work and drive the seven miles into Mancelona. He stopped at the Ford garage to see Harry Williams, from whom he had bought the "Model T." Harry repaired Ford cars. Surely he would be a good source of advice.

The news was not good. Harry listened carefully, shook his head from side to side, and said. "When the engine starts knocking, the crank's probably out of round. The engine will have to be overhauled and the crankshaft ground or the knock will keep getting worse."

Seeing the dark frown that briefly crossed the face of his customer, Harry continued. "Your car's given you a lot of good miles, Grover. Come look at this new Model "A." Ford's building a really great automobile now!"

Grover's mind had not yet left the problem with their present car. Apparently, it could be fixed, but Harry hadn't told him how expensive it would be. Distractedly he followed Harry to the shiny black sedan.

Opening the driver's door, Harry stepped back and motioned Grover to sit behind the wheel. "Your car's seven years old. I think it's time to trade it in."

Harry hoped that Grover noticed that he could open the driver's door and not have to climb over the side or get in from the passenger's door like he did with the model "T." Harry walked around and sat in the passenger seat. Putting his hand on the gear-shift lever, Harry continued to expound the merits of this new model. "This car has three speeds forward; that's really a big improvement."

"You've driven your brother-in-law's "Star" so you know second gear's a big help on long hills," Harry was making his pitch. Grover knew he would like second gear, but Grace's brother was having more trouble with his "Star" than Grover ever had with his model "T." Stepping out of the new "Model A," Grover shook his head. "I think we'll drive our old car a while longer, Harry. It's treated us pretty good."

Harry apparently read the thought. "This is a lot more car than that star! You won't have to keep putting timing gears in it."

Boots had put three timing gears in his car in one year. That argued strongly for the Ford.

Thoughts of Grace's brother Boots and his automobile flooded Grover's mind. Boots had lived with them for a short time. Young, and looking for speed, Boots had bought a "Star," primarily for that purpose. It was fast, no denying that. No denying that Boots used all the speed it had either! He kept telling Grover and Grace if you went fast enough on those rough gravel roads, the car stayed on top of the washboards and the road didn't feel rough at all.

Maybe Boots was right, but Boots' type of driving was a lot faster than Grover wanted to go, and after Grace's first ride with her brother, she wouldn't get in the car with him again.

Once more Harry's voice broke into Grover's thoughts. "This car has a self-starter. Your wife can start it anytime. The windshield wiper runs by vacuum. You have both hands to steer when you're driving in the rain."

Grover was digesting what Harry was telling him now. He either had to fix the old car or buy another. Once you have a car, it seems you just can't live without one. When he saw Grover's apparent interest, Harry lavished praise on the new model "A." "The headlights run from the battery. They're just as bright when you're driving slow as when you're on the gravel road." There was apparently no end to the advantages of the new car. Harry went on, "The car has a heater. You can ride in comfort while getting to your destination—just as if you were sitting by the fire at home."

The last point wasn't a big deal. Only state highways were plowed in the winter, and there was no way Grover could get his car to a state road in winter. The other points all seemed to be major advantages, though.

Grover climbed out of the car, looked at it admiringly, and asked. "What does it cost?"

"Grover you can drive this 1930 Model "A" out of here for $540," Harry insisted. "I could sell you that 1926 model T for half as much, but you'll be a lot happier with this new one. Your credit's good!"

Grover was definitely interested; he'd been watching those "Model A" Fords sneak past him on the road. "I'll talk to Grace and we'll think it over. We can probably get a few more trips out of our old one before I have to tighten the rods again."

After his chores were finished that evening, Grover reluctantly brought up the subject of a new car. "Ma, we have to do something about a car. I don't have time to keep working on this one. Harry says it'll keep getting worse. He thinks we'd be smart to buy a new one. He says that in the end it will be cheaper for us. Probably he's right. It's a lot of money, but we have to do something pretty soon."

Grace was nervous. "We already owe a lot, Grover. We're making our payments, but how much debt do you think we can handle without getting into trouble? What with the stock market crashing last fall and a lot of people out of work. . . I just don't know."

Grover and Grace decided they would pray and postpone the final decision for a while. Only a few days later Grover broke the frame on the spring-tooth drag and had to get it welded. They'd used Earl before, and his work was good. Not expensive either, when compared to buying a new part. Earl's one drawback was the reputation of refusing to be rushed regardless of need. Grover was bringing his broken piece into the welding shop, but stopped at the door when he heard a customer heatedly telling Earl how badly he needed the part he was waiting for.

Earl continued working until he had finished his weld, shut off his torch, lifted his goggles and answered. "You need that piece? This kid needs his bicycle, too! I'll do your weld tomorrow."

Grover waited for Earl to lift his goggles again before speaking. "I hooked a stump and broke the frame on my drag. Can you weld it for me?"

Earl looked carefully at Grover's broken piece, nodded, and gave the welcome answer. "Come back tomorrow evening. I'll have it ready for you."

Grover worked until mid-afternoon the following day, hurriedly fed his horses, and drove to Mancelona to pick up the drag frame from Earl.

Grover had just passed Catland Marsh about half way to town, when the dreaded knock in the engine began. At first, he wasn't sure. Grover drove slowly and listened carefully, hoping that what he heard was not really that rod bearing again, but before he reached Earl's welding shop, there could be no mistake. The rod was beginning to hammer pretty loudly.

The broken frame lay on the welding bench, still hot. After admiring the welding job and paying the small bill, Grover asked advice. "You do a lot of mechanic work, Earl. My car has a pretty bad knock. Harry wants to sell me a new car, but I don't know if I need to get rid of this one. See what you think."

Earl opened the hood and felt the tension on the fan belt. "Crank it up and we'll give a listen." The prognosis wasn't good. "That crank's in bad shape, Grover. It won't even get you home." Earl scratched the back of his head. "I can repair the crank, but it really isn't worth the cost. I think you'd be smart to take Harry's advice."

The decision could wait no longer. Grover slowly drove two blocks to the Ford garage, signed a note for the new car, and drove it home. He would have preferred to talk to Grace first, but had no choice.

Grace wondered what on earth was keeping Grover. He usually told her if he was going to be late for supper. Now it was an hour past suppertime and he still wasn't home. She kept his food warm on the back of the range. Suddenly she heard a car coming that didn't sound like their Ford. Maybe it was Mr. Brown, the missionary. It was nearly time for him to bring the Sunday school material.

The kitchen door opened and Grover greeted his wife with a wide grin. "Come see what I bought for you, Ma. I think you'll like it."

All three boys bounded out the back door behind their mother. A sleek, black Model "A" sat where Grover always parked. Ma was stunned. They always made decisions together, and she didn't like the thought of all that debt.

The boys were stunned, too, but in a different way. Brown climbed into the driver's seat. Three-year-old Bryce sat in the car too. White gasped, "Is this really ours, Dad?"

Grover liked to surprise his family, and he surely had succeeded this time! When the excitement subsided and the boys were reassured that it was really their car, Grover explained to his wife why he made the sudden purchase.

Grace agreed he had done the right thing, but still she was worried about their finances. She knew Grover always wanted to give the family more than he could afford. Finally, resigned to the increased debt, she told herself, "It'll turn out all right. It always has."

Grover turned to his excited sons. "You want to go for a little ride? We can go to Manistee Lake tonight. We have good headlights." There was a lot of shouting and jumping as Grover promised, "As quick as I eat a bite and get the cows milked, we'll go."

The lingering twilight of the northern Michigan spring day was ebbing, as the eager family set out in their new Model "A." "Look at this, Ma." Grover demonstrated the shiny steel button beside the clutch. "Put your foot on this button and it does its own cranking. You'll like that. When you want to go somewhere, you won't have to get me to crank the car."

The boys eventually tired of cranking the windows up and down.

Brown and White were becoming more and more help on the farm. Brown loved working with the horses and was gradually becoming an accomplished teamster. Released much of the time now from driving the horses, Grover worked with ax and shovel. Teaching boys the fine art of using an ax without chopping into the sand was frustrating! Grover always kept his ax razor-sharp. When the boys used his ax, it quickly lost its sharp edge.

The solution, Grover decided, was to get each of them an ax. "Look!" Grover was patiently trying to teach White the proper use of his axe. "When you chop off brush, chop up, not down."

"How can I chop up when I'm chopping right at the top of the ground?" White thought his dad must have been joking.

"Watch me." Patiently Grover showed his son the correct technique. "Swing the ax along the ground, then tip the edge up a little when you hit the brush. The earth holds the brush and you're chopping up."

Some of the trees they cut while clearing the field were big enough for firewood. At the end of each day's work, the poles were loaded on the wagon and hauled home to increase the pile behind the house. When haying season ended land clearing for the year, the pile of poles had grown enough to furnish a full year's firewood.

After the last load of poles was on the pile, Grover called Ot, the Southwell's prosperous neighbor and said, "Ot, we have a pile of poles behind the house big enough for a years wood. Could you bring over your tractor and buzzsaw and help us cut them up?"

Ot guessed he could take that much time. The tractor had enabled him to get his plowing and dragging finished much quicker this year.

Responding to Grover's question of cost, Ot hesitated briefly, and asked. "Do you think $2.00 an hour is fair, Grover? I don't want to hold you up, but there's some expense with the tractor."

Grover agreed the price was reasonable and Ot brought over his Fordson tractor and buzzsaw the following morning. Ot fed the saw, Grover threw the wood away, and the three boys carried poles to the saw. Since the work was by the house, the job of necessity included Bryce, who was now big enough so he could help. Bryce held a hand on the light end of every pole as his brothers carried them to the saw. Whatever his brothers did, he tried to copy.

In four hours, a pile of poles had been transformed into a year's supply of stove wood. Many, many hard hours on the crosscut saw had been replaced by four hours with a mechanical marvel.

Grover thanked his neighbor, gave him a ten-dollar bill, and said, "It's well worth the extra $2.00 Ot, to see a big job finished."

When haying season ended, the annual township roadwork began. This year Grover decided to build the road through the timber between Twin and Manistee Lakes that had been Frank Cunningham's goal.

Dozens of big stumps in the roadway would have to be blown out with dynamite. Grace's cousin, Fred, had experience using dynamite so Grover asked him to do the blasting. Planning just how to set the charge and estimating (guessing might be a better word) the number of sticks required to clean out the stump was a challenge. It was critical the charge be large enough, but too much was wasteful.

The maple and beech stumps with their mass of short roots, were blown out very efficiently. The elm stumps, which had fewer but much longer roots, proved to be more difficult. The same amount of explosive that completely removed a maple or beech stump would merely split an elm. The long roots remaining had to be dug out by hand until the horses could pull out the ends.

Fred carefully surveyed the last stump that blocked the road. He looked at the remaining dynamite and told Grover, "We have 35 sticks of powder left. What do you want to do with them?"

Grover hesitated before answering, "We don't want to store explosives. Put all of them under that last stump and we'll move the crew out of the way."

Fred packed the dynamite under the big elm stump and cut the piece of fuse a foot longer than usual to give him adequate time to move out of harm's way. After warning everyone of the danger, Fred lit the fuse and hurried back to stand with Grover.

In a few seconds a deafening roar sounded as bits of stump soared high in the air. Sand rained down on those who had stayed nearer than safety dictated.

When silence replaced the thud of falling debris, an excited Jim spoke for the group, "There's nothing left to dig out *this* time!"

"It didn't make a much deeper hole than when we used 15 sticks." Fred observed. "Not a bad way to end a job!"

Two days later the last of the holes were filled and a sand road between Twin Lake and Manistee Lake was completed.

Grover laid his final check on the supper table as he told Grace. Let's finish paying for the car now. Harry's charging us more interest than we pay at the bank."

Grace agreed. With one debt paid, she and Grover could increase payments to the bank.

Now that she felt that their debt was under control, a greatly relieved Grace looked again at the check. "Another winter in the woods, Grover, and one more summer's work on the township roads will pay all our debts."

The long struggle for independence on the family farm was becoming a reality. When the snowflakes fell the crops were harvested, the crib was half full of corn, the haymow was full, and there were 20 bushels of potatoes in the cellar. From the garden, Grace had canned peas, green and yellow beans, and sweet corn. She had carrots, beets, and cabbages filling bins in their little cellar.

Snow blanketed the fields in mid-November, and slowly it's solid white layer covered the ground where Grover and the Fuzzy Brothers were eager to begin their winters work.

Brown and White now skied to school each day while their father kept busy husking corn. Grace was making goodies in preparation for Thanksgiving. Bryce was building some architectural marvel with his blocks, and flakes of snow were falling lightly.

It was nearly Thanksgiving when "Old Tom" finally drove his cutter up the driveway. Grover walked from the barn to greet him.

"Come on in. Grace just made a new pot of coffee," Grover invited his former colleague.

After brief conversation over coffee and cookies, Tom delivered his message. The tone dropped in his voice. "Grover, Antrim Iron Company shut down their whole operation. They have not been able to sell anything. The lumberyard's full. There's no place to pile any more wood."

"Pig iron's piled the full length of the railroad siding." Tom shook his head. "They can't sell that until the steel mills start working. They don't know when they'll be able to sell any lumber, so they've laid off all the men and shut everything down." After a deep breath, Tom concluded. "Ray wanted me to tell you so you wouldn't start cutting." Tom gathered his hat, and thanked them for the coffee. After he left, Grover and Grace sat lost in thought. Grover was always an optimist. But Grace said, "I wonder what we'll do about the loan from the bank. We only have money for a few months payments."

Grover knew the banker, Mr. Mills, had always been friendly and co-operative, but he also knew that Mr. Mills hadn't been so friendly with those who didn't pay when they promised. Grover always had just worked a little harder when he needed to provide extra cash. Now there was no work available.

He was really glad that his family had food for winter. As in prior years, they had bought two barrels of flour and 100 pounds of sugar, in case the roads were blocked with snow. Sure, the bank loan was a problem, but Grover was confident there would be a solution.

"Probably Antrim Iron company won't be shut down for long," Grover thought. "If we can get by until roadwork begins next summer, we'll squeeze by."

Planning their expenditures to the penny, Grover and Grace took Bryce in the sleigh to Mancelona while Brown and White were still at school. Grace bought a few things she absolutely had to have for the kitchen as well as new coats and overshoes for the boys. Grover went to Wisler's hardware and spent sixty cents for a box of 410-gauge shotgun shells. He might as well do a little hunting.

When Brown and White came home from school, Grover walked across the road with the shotgun under his arm. The two boys followed closely behind. He hoped to find some partridges, or even a snowshoe rabbit.

Snowshoe rabbits, numerous in the ground hemlock (commonly called shin-tangle because it was troublesome to horses and their teamster skidding logs,) would also provide meat for the Southwells.

"Any kind of wild game will stretch the pork in the crock," Grover told Brown and White.

He began to take them out to teach them what he knew about hunting. He cautioned them to remain quiet and alert. It was hard for White to stay still. His vivid imagination enabled him to see an animal in every leaf that moved. "What if—?" White was such an avid reader and he had difficulty differentiating between reality and imagination.

Grover patiently knelt by his tow-headed son. "White, I know you're excited, but we have to be quiet. We can't have any more "what-if-ing." Wait 'til you are sure you see something we want to shoot."

The hunt was largely unsuccessful, but provided one exciting moment when the little group of hunters was nearly home. Grover saw what appeared to be an unusually thick clump of needles at the end of one limb on a small hemlock tree. Looking carefully, he saw a partridge nestled in the foliage. After quietly showing the clump to Brown and White, Grover pulled the little shotgun to his shoulder and fired. The partridge fell to the ground. Other partridges exploded from the tree, their wings making a thunderous roar. For Brown and White, the hunt was a great success.

The next evening when Brown and White came home from school, they wanted to go hunting again. Hurrying to the barn loft where Grover was husking corn, both boys spoke at once. "That was fun Dad! Let's go again tonight!"

Grover hated to disappoint the boys, but work was work. "Help me husk this corn," he said, "and we'll go tomorrow night."

The next day Grover had a long and hard talk with Grace about letting their sons hunt. "It'll be good for them," he told Grace. "The exercise and excitement will help them grow up. It'll teach them responsibility too. I'll go with them until I think they can handle it alone."

There was a great difference in the opinion of husband and wife as to when it would be safe! Grover remembered the responsibility that had been heaped upon his shoulders in his boyhood, and knew they were ready. Grace worried about safety in everything the boys did. Hunting worried her most of all.

When Brown and White were dismissed from school the following day, they reached home in record time. Grover wanted Brown to practice shooting the gun before they went to the woods. A tin can sitting on a fence post made an ideal target. Grover handed Brown the shotgun and watched carefully as his son inserted the shell, pulled back the hammer and calmly shot the can off the post.

Grover gave clear instructions and made sure they were understood. "Brown will walk first with the shotgun. I will follow him, and White will follow me. After we hunt this way for a while, White will take his turn carrying the gun."

It was a nice evening for hunting. A light snow had fallen, and the little group made very little noise as they walked along an old skidding trail. Brown shot two partridges on his first turn carrying the little shotgun. The three hunted together more than a week and walked many miles before Brown fired the gun again.

When Grover was confident Brown could be trusted to handle the shotgun, he gave White the same opportunity. Grover followed his tow-headed son closely, waiting for even a red squirrel to show itself. Finally White's opportunity came when a partridge jumped to a low limb, stretched its neck, and waited until White slowly cocked the gun and shot it.

Now that both boys had killed game, they carried the gun on alternate nights. Grover went with them evenings until he was confident Brown and White could hunt safely on their own. Grover's confidence was very difficult to transfer to his wife. He didn't want Grace to worry, but the boys had to grow up. He explained to her how carefully they had been instructed, and how well each one could handle the shotgun. Grace was sure that if the boys went hunting by themselves, she would have at least one dead son, maybe two. It was with great fear and after much questioning of her husband's judgment that she finally nodded, not in agreement, but acceptance.

The boys never knew about their parents' discussion, but they soon learned that if they wanted to go hunting, it was wisest to ask their father. He gave them permission any time it seemed reasonable. With their mother, however, it was never the right time to hunt.

When winter came Brown and White focused on snowshoe rabbits, which weren't very wild and left footprints in the snow. Following the tracks slowly, Brown and White became quite successful in their quest for the white rabbits. Grover remembered well that when he was a boy at the Hackney farm, he was there to help with the work and work he would! Seeing the happy faces of Brown and White as they excitedly told of the birds and rabbits they shot, and the ones that were, "so close" but still got away, gave Grover great satisfaction. Vicariously, he lived through his boys the life he had missed in his youth.

This was the first winter since Grover turned eighteen that he had not worked in his beloved timber. Grover exercised his horses as he drove through the skidding trails and picked out the very best of the dry beech trees and skidded them to the house for stove wood.

Grover sawed, split and piled enough wood to supply two years fuel and did what he could to make home improvements without purchasing anything.

Driving through section 17 where he had worked in previous winters, Grover noted the location of dead hemlock trees. He had little doubt that next winter Antrim Iron Company would again be working, and his knowledge of where those trees were located would be valuable.

In January, a modest storm provided work rolling the roads for three days. Every dollar Grover earned stretched the Southwell's meager savings. He and Grace would survive until roadwork began in summer. There was pork in the crock, plenty of canned vegetables, and the boys regularly brought home a rabbit or two.

Taxes were due in February and that took all but a smidgen of Grover and Grace's savings.

Chapter 20

The Depression

G rover and Grace's spirits lifted as they prepared for spring planting in 1932. Confident that the lumber and pig iron that plugged the railroad siding at Antrim would soon be sold and Antrim Iron Company would call back the unemployed workers, they faced the future with renewed hope. Everyone was confident life would resume as it had through the roaring 20's. But it was not to be.

On the first day of May, Grover and Grace's three boys brought home little paper boxes filled with bright spring flowers, a May Day tradition. Children could choose from yellow adder tongues, white and pink Dutchmen's breeches (more commonly called "Boys and Girls"), and trilliums (locally called a lily). Occasionally even a Lady's Slipper would adorn the basket. In addition to the boxes of flowers, the boys brought home the mail from the mailbox located at a spot where they crossed the main road half way home.

After admiring the pretty flowers and filling two vases with them, Grace opened the letters. One was a business- sized envelope from the Mancelona bank. Mr. Mills stated bluntly that the payment for April was overdue and Grover should present himself at the bank.

Grover and Grace talked a long time before bedtime. They had planned to catch up their payments when the township built a road. Now they realized there would be no roadwork this year. The Antrim Iron Company had not paid their taxes, and without that income, the township could not build roads.

There was no work available in the automobile plants in the lower part of the state. Those who worked for auto-related industries were in the same boat. Unemployed men from the city had been walking through northern Michigan seeking any kind of work, some even asking for a sandwich. The depression affected them more than a year earlier than it had the employees of Antrim Iron Company. The resources of even the most frugal were exhausted. While rural people could supply most of their food from a garden, those in the city did not even have this opportunity. Their situation was indeed desperate.

With no other possible source of income, Grover and Grace agreed to sell enough of their property to pay the bank. It was the only honorable thing they could do. The next morning Grover went to Mancelona and told Mr. Mills he would hold an auction sale in order to pay the bank what he owed. Mr. Mills did not much care what Grover sold as long as the bank got its money.

The sale was scheduled as soon as bills could be printed and distributed. Mr. Mills was the clerk. That is, he collected the money and could give a bank loan to someone making a purchase.

The larger farmers in the area still had a little money. Cap and Jack were the major attraction. The team of black percherons were known for being well trained, well fed, and strong. Selling that team was almost more than Grover could bear. He loved those horses! Still, they were the Southwell's most valuable possession. The horses would have to be sold if the bank was to be paid. They also sold all the cattle except one cow and one heifer. They even had to sell old Suz, the prize sow.

Bud wanted to buy the pigs, but Mr. Mills would not loan him the money. The auctioneer called a brief recess while Bud spoke to Grover.

"Grover, you know me," Bud said. "I'll pay the note when I sell the young pigs. If you'll just sign my note, I can borrow the money."

Grover was unsure. Neighbors certainly trusted each other, but no one had any money and no sure way of earning any. Still, the pigs had to be sold to pay the Mancelona bank and Bud appeared to be the only person who wanted them. "Probably Bud will be able to sell the pigs for as much as he's paying," Grover told himself. After a brief hesitation, he nodded and put his signature on Bud's note, guaranteeing payment.

Six months later, Bud had neither the money nor the pigs and Grover was obligated to pay for what had been his own pigs.

There'll be a good crop of hay, Grover was sure. *We can't quit now!*

When the boys left for school next morning, Grover pulled a chain across the garden making straight rows for the vegetable seeds to be planted. The first two rows across the front were for flowers. Grace loved seeing the bright blossoms from the kitchen window.

There was little conversation as husband and wife worked together, carefully preparing and planting the garden. Each with their own thoughts, and each determined to say nothing to deepen the others concern. Physical work relaxed both Grover and Grace. They went together to prepare dinner, and began to plan what to do with the little cash they had left from the sale, after the bank was paid.

They agreed the first priority was horses. Without horses, the farm work could not continue. Grover grimaced at the thought of what kind of horses he could afford. His first thought was horse dealers. Not all of them were honest. Grover was reluctant to be looking for a cheap horse, but he was thankful for the experience he had. He knew most of the equine weaknesses, and he'd heard about various tricks used to cover flaws in a horse.

Grover's first purchase was fortunate. A nearby dealer had a high strung, ill behaved, but physically sound mare that he had not been able to sell. Confidently Grover drove her home. Smiling, he told Grace, "I'll name her Ginger. She has plenty of it!"

Grover looked in vain for another cheap horse that would make a suitable mate for Ginger. He could wait no longer. They had to get the crops in. He reluctantly bought an old mare named Pearl. According to the farmer from whom he purchased her, the horse had been a real pearl for many years.

Grover, who had worked with only the best of horses, determined to work with what he had. He moved the center pin in the evener a couple inches to the left, giving Ginger more than half the load. Before the end of May, they had the crops planted. The cornfield was much smaller than Grover had planned, but at least there was a cornfield, and there was horsepower to put up the hay.

The boys were a big help with hauling hay. Bryce, now five years of age, sat on the spring seat beside his father. Pearl seemed exceptionally sleepy. She never walked faster than was absolutely necessary.

Grover picked the braided horsewhip from the corner of the hayrack and cracked it over Pearl's back. It was an effective though temporary remedy. He never hit a horse with the whip, but it made a resounding crack.

"Don't hit her Dad," Bryce exclaimed. "She'll go. She's just slow, that's all."

Bryce loved animals. Chum, the collie, was his constant companion. There was also a Rhode Island Red hen, which came to his call. Bryce often walked with the old red hen tucked under his arm and Chum at his side, or the three sat comfortably in the shade of the big maple tree in the front yard.

By mid-summer the garden furnished the complete diet for the family. Even with unlimited vegetables, they still had to buy some items. One morning Grace offered a solution. "We have more cabbage than we can eat. I think I'll take a bushel to Mancelona. Maybe we can trade them for flour."

With an eager white-haired son for company, Grace made the rare trip to Mancelona and carried the bushel of cabbage into the A&P store, which was almost devoid of customers. Grace waited until the manager finished filling an order, then asked, "Would you like to buy some cabbage, Mr. Johnson?"

Looking at the carefully cleaned heads of cabbage, Mr. Johnson made an offer. "I can give you two cents a pound for them, Mrs. Southwell."

Grace was disappointed at the low price but she desperately needed a sack of flour. The sixty-cent payment received for the bushel of cabbage was enough to buy a 25-pound sack of flour and a box of salt, too. As Grace and Rex carried out their purchase, Mr. Johnson began making an attractive mound out of the cabbages.

Just as she and Rex reached the door, they overheard the next customer asking the price of the fresh cabbage.

"We'll sell them for five cents a pound. They're fresh this morning." The low price appealed to the customer, who bought several heads.

Grace shook her head and spoke quietly to her son. "Two cents to grow them and three cents to sell them." There was no more income for the summer and the pork was gone.

Still, the family was adequately nourished.

The telephones were another casualty to the community without adequate income. One by one, the families no longer paid the monthly bill. Ot and his partners worked to keep the lines up but then their business also fell due to lack of funds. Limbs across the telephone lines or broken insulators made one line after another inoperable and the few who could pay their bill, saw no reason to continue. There was no one left to talk to. It was the end of what had been a great asset to the community. Ot never bothered to collect the inoperable telephones. Families took the telephones off the wall and stored them in the attic, hoping to use them again.

School opened on the last Monday in August. Grace patched overalls and darned socks. There would be no new overalls and shirts this year. She told the boys. "At least you're clean."

On their first day back in school, Brown and White came past their grandfather's house on their way home. Tuden, who had seemed to be fine two weeks earlier, struggled to the door. He assured the boys he was "all right," but it was obvious to them, he was not well.

On Saturday, Grover and the boys dug Tuden's potatoes and rutabagas and carried them to his cellar. Grover frowned as Tuden hobbled from the stove to the table with his meager dinner. "We'll have to watch him this winter," Grover told his sons."

When the first snow fell, Grover instructed their sons to walk past Tuden's house every night on the way home from school. They were to split and carry in wood for the next day, and check on the old man.

Only a few days later Brown told his father, "Granddad isn't moving around much. It was kind of cold in his house."

That evening Grover and Grace carried supper down to Tuden and watched him as he ate.

Tuden moved to his trusty old rocking chair and spoke slowly. "Grover, I haven't been to Saugatuck since my children were taken away. I'm not very strong, but I'd really like to make a trip back. Some of my friends may still be alive."

Grover understood.

Looking from Grace to Tuden, he replied, "I'll write to Harry Allett. He's had steady work for the county. Maybe he could come and get you." Grover added, "I'll get the horses and bring you up to our place until he comes."

When Harry arrived the following Saturday, he said he'd enjoy having Tuden spend some time with them, and would find as many of Tuden's old cronies as he could.

After supper, Harry brought in a 38–40 Colt rifle from his car. "You need this, Grover. You can kill a few deer. They'll provide some meat." Grover protested. Harry had given him more than enough. First the little shotgun, now he was here picking up Tuden and taking him to Saugatuck. The gift of a rifle was just too much.

Harry was adamant. "I have my 35 Winchester and you need a rifle. This was built before the turn of the century, but it's accurate. The magazine holds 15 cartridges." Harry grinned, "Just in case you can't hit him the first time."

Tuden was exceptionally quiet when he got in the car with Harry the next morning. He and Grover shook hands. Grover wanted to give his father a hug and tell him he would be missed, but men just didn't do that. Harry reassured Grover. "I'll take good care of your Dad."

Just before leaving, Tuden told Grover, "You better go get my fiddle and the shotgun. They're the only things of value I own."

Grover assured Tuden they would look after them.

As Harry drove away with Tuden, Grover looked at Grace. "I doubt if we'll see Dad again." Their relationship had not always been pleasant. Tuden had worked hard to reestablish any relationship at all. Still, in later years, the bond between them had been much stronger.

As soon as Tuden and Harry were gone, Grover and his three boys walked to the little house by the lake, picked up the violin and shotgun, and returned home. Tuden's treasures were stored carefully in the attic, awaiting their owner's return.

The lazy curl of smoke from Tuden's stovepipe was missing as the boys skied past their grandfather's place on the way home from school. Snow covered the little house overlooking the partly frozen lake, making a beautiful, but lonely, picture.

Grover's crop of corn was very good. Having sold most of the livestock and all the pigs, he had a surplus of corn. George Coon, meantime, had a 200-pound pig and a two-year-old steer that had pastured through the summer, but George had no corn.

George furnished the pig and steer, while Grover took care of them and fed them corn for six weeks. They butchered the animals together. George's share was two-thirds. Grover took one-third from the back half of the pig and one-third from the front of the steer. Now both families had a considerable supply of meat for the winter.

Brown and White added to the meat supply to the extent of their skill tracking and shooting snowshoe rabbits. Having been warned that there would be no more shotgun shells through the winter, both boys waited patiently for a sitting shot.

February and March passed without township income from tax money. Everyone had hoped the Antrim Iron Company would pay their taxes this year, since this paid for roadwork. Not only Antrim Iron Company but even residents deferred tax payment.

The spring of 1933 brought no hope of outside work. It was a repeat of the year before. There was no income except whatever farm produce could be sold. Grover and Grace, having sold almost all their cattle, had very little cream to sell. Fortunately, their chickens laid eggs. The occasional sale of eggs provided flour and salt for the Southwells.

Seed saved from the previous year's corn, beans, and peas were supplemented with five-cent packets of lettuce, cabbage and carrots. Since the garden would be almost the sole source of food, Grover covered it exceptionally well with horse manure and expanded it to include more corn and beans.

In early May, Tate Clayton, a nearly destitute professional fighter from Chicago came to Coldsprings Township with his wife and small son. He purchased a couple acres near the Hardy school and built a small log cabin from the trees found there. To welcome the newcomers, several neighbors helped him lay the logs and complete the roof.

When Mr. Brown brought supplies for Sunday School to Grover and Grace in the last week of May, he visited the homes in the area to announce the opening date of Sunday school and issue an invitation. Mr. and Mrs. Clayton welcomed the announcement. Two years earlier with the excitement and success of a boxing career fading, Mr. Clayton had realized God was missing from his life and accepted Christ as his Savior. He was filled with zeal and wished to tell of the difference in his life and how, with God as his companion, he could face the uncertain future with confidence. Mr. Clayton began to bring a short sermon each week after Sunday School classes ended. The talks were short but emotional. He readily acknowledged his lack of education, but vehemently spoke of the grace of God and the death of Christ on the cross.

The residents quickly accepted the Clayton family. Most had no more schooling than Tate Clayton did, and all faced an equally uncertain future. Life had become a daily struggle for existence. The peace of mind exhibited by this transplant from the city was inspiring and most local residents attended services faithfully. Only a few, however, chose to accept Christ as Savior.

Another neighbor moved to the area in June. George and Anna Nichols and their eight children moved into an old house by Croy Lake. The house leaked and part of the foundation had rotted, but it sheltered the family until they could find something better. George and Anna joined many families from the city, who were moving to the country where they could raise a big garden. Their children had not been getting proper food. Welfare was provided in the city but George and Anna, like Grover and Grace, were too proud to accept welfare.

Cherries ripen in July and George told Grover they could work picking cherries at Doc Jamison's orchard on the Old Mission Peninsula. George and his family were going and, since they had a large old tent, if Grover and his family wanted to go too, they would share the tent and the families could share expenses. Grover and Grace decided that they must go. They sold their one milking cow, butchered and canned their chickens, put the two-year-old heifer and the horses in the pasture where they could get water, and joined the Nichols family at Doc Jamison's orchard.

Doc had a good crop of cherries. The quicker the cherries were picked the less chance of a hard storm damaging them. Doc was paying twelve and a half cents a lug (a half bushel).

The picking crew arose early and ate a quick breakfast so they could be in the orchard at first light. They took a short break for a snack at noon, and again when picking ended in mid-afternoon. Then they walked down the hill for a cooling swim in Grand Traverse Bay.

After two weeks, the orchard was picked clean and many of the picking crew, including the Nichols and Southwells, moved to the Northport Peninsula where the cold wind from Lake Michigan delayed ripening and the cherry harvest was just beginning.

For two more weeks, the families labored from dawn until mid-afternoon, then walked over the hill to Leg Lake for a swim in luke-warm water. Occasionally they walked an additional half-mile to swim in Lake Michigan where the water was cold and clear. The children loved swimming in Lake Michigan, but their parents preferred the warm water of the little lake near the orchard.

Three young men who had camped under a piece of canvas near the Nichols and Southwell families during the harvest, asked Grover and George where they could go for another job.

George and Grover felt keenly the despair in the eyes of the strong young men. George reluctantly answered that this was the only work he knew of.

Grover told the men depression years were bringing the same problems that had driven young men from Ireland. He was sorry

he couldn't be of help, but their search for work reminded him of
a song Harry Allett had sung:

But our farm, it was too small. It would not support us all,
And so one of us was forced away from home.
With a teardrop in my eye, I did bid them all good-bye,
And I sailed for Castle Garden all alone.

To be sure I wandered on, thinking that I might find one
That would give an honest Irish lad a chance.
But as I went from place to place, with starvation in my face,
Everywhere they say, "We want no help today."

Grace was determined that their boys would attend high school.
Grover was not convinced of the value of another four years schooling but was determined to provide the best for their sons, regardless of the sacrifice.

Tuition was furnished but there was no provision for transportation. Grover arranged with Clyde Smith, owner of the Sunoco
gas station, to trade produce for gasoline and Brown drove to
school through September and October. When snow began to
fall another arrangement was necessary. The county plowed snow
from the Darragh road, but that was a mile and a half from the
Southwell farm.

A quarter mile from Dick William's corner (the nearest point
from the Darragh road to the Southwell home), Mac McCormick's
garage sat conveniently empty. Mr. McCormick allowed them to
use his garage nights through the winter, allowing Brown to walk
the unplowed road and drive on to school.

When the snow melted from Palmer Park in Mancelona, high
school baseball season started. Baseball had been an exciting part
of Grover's youth, and he encouraged Harold to stay in town for
practice. Brown was athletic and the many hours he and White

had spent playing catch and batting flies made him to able to compete well with boys from town. Once Brown played regularly on the team, school became much more attractive to him. A year later White joined his older brother in high school. They walked the roads that were blocked with snow in winter, and then drove the remaining five miles to Mancelona until both boys finished high school. Although he was not as athletic as his brother, White got a lot of joy from playing baseball, and joined the team later.

In September Grover and the family drove 20 miles to Elmira and picked up potatoes during "potato vacation." For this, they were paid three cents a bushel. With some cash for basic needs, life was a little easier than last year, although the Southwells still had to count every penny.

Cash Phelps, once camp boss at Gorham, had planted an apple orchard near the south end of Torch Lake. Grover took the family to see the orchard and, hopefully get some apples.

Mr. Phelps remembered the teamster and greeted Grover warmly. After brief reminiscences, Mr. Phelps told Grover. "There's a lot of good apples on the ground I can't sell, you can pick up all you want for ten cents a bushel." The Southwells sorted apples carefully. Many fell in soft grass and showed no sign of damage. They picked up five bushels of varieties that would keep through the winter, and paid Mr. Phelps 50 cents.

Mutual hardships forged bonds among neighbors, and the parents all made it to the Christmas program at the Davis school. The teacher managed to buy a small bag of candy for each student. The parents sang Christmas carols with the children and enjoyed their recitations. The few dollars from the cherry orchard earnings and the potato fields were carefully hoarded for essentials. The boys were warned not to expect Christmas gifts. Even a Christmas tree would be an empty gesture.

Not surprised, the boys thought they could do without gifts, but Christmas without a tree? Never! From the swamp on the north side of section 17, Grover dragged home a beautiful balsam. The odor of Christmas filled the living room. A neighbor had grown popcorn and gave the Southwells a few ears. Only half the kernels popped, but there was plenty for the tree. The boys joyously strung popcorn on thread and draped the strings around the tree. There were a few half-burned Christmas candles left from other years. It wasn't safe to burn the candles too low and get near the branch. A burning Christmas tree was a recipe for disaster, but at least they could be lit on Christmas Eve.

On Christmas morning, the boys were astonished to discover Grover had made a toy for Bryce. Wrapped in bright red paper was a box of 22 caliber long cartridges for Brown and White! After being told not to expect anything, it was the biggest gift of their lives. Grover didn't think they would be able to kill anything with shorts, so had bought the more expensive longs. That year the price of .22 cartridges was fifteen cents a box for shorts, 20 cents for longs and 25 cents for long rifles. With the small single-shot, .22-caliber rifle they had been given, that box of cartridges enabled the boys to hunt rabbits and squirrels all winter. Neither of them would shoot unless he was confident he would put the animal in the game bag.

Soon after Christmas, Harry wrote that Tuden had passed away and inquired what he should do with the body?

Grover and Grace were without any money. They decided it would be necessary to go the County welfare office. Grover had never before asked for anything, but to provide burial for his father, Grover would bow to the need and ask for help. The next day Grover drove to Kalkaska, the county seat, and explained he needed help to bury his father.

When the officer in charge learned the body was in southern Michigan, he refused to provide assistance. He pointed out the county just could not spare the money. "Somebody will bury him. They won't just let him rot," he told Grover, as he dismissed the request. It was the first and only plea for government help Grover ever made.

When it was clear that there would be no aid for their predicament, a very despondent Grover drove slowly home and told his wife, "Now a man can't even bury his own father."

The sorrow from the loss of Grover's father, and the further anguish caused by his inability to give Tuden a decent burial was increased by a tragedy that came to their newest neighbors.

George and Anna Nichols, with whom the Southwell family had spent a month the previous summer picking cherries, were expecting a baby in January. Anna had borne eight children without a problem. There was no reason to expect trouble with this birth.

The Southwells were eating breakfast when Mr. Nichols came to the door with his oldest son, Delbert. George had difficulty speaking. He coughed and wiped his nose. He shook his head slightly, as if still not able to take it in as he told them, "Anna died last night. She was trying to have our baby and just didn't have the strength." After another round of coughing and false starts, he continued. "Our telephone is out, and I was wondering, might I be able to use yours to call the undertaker?"

Grover stared, and tried to grasp what George was saying. As far as he'd known, Anna had been in good health. Grace dropped a spoon, then quickly picked it up. She put her hand over her mouth to stifle a cry. The boys stared at Mr. Nichols without moving a muscle. Grover said, "George. I am so sorry. Our telephone doesn't work either. Come on into the house and drink a cup of coffee while I harness the horses, then I'll take you to town."

The bond of friendship had developed quickly as the two families struggled together through the summer to meet their desperate financial needs. The loss of Anna and her baby was devastating to the Southwell family as well as the feeling of acute empathy for George and his eight children.

The shock from Anna's death was heightened the following week when the Mancelona Herald carried the headline,

Woman Dies in Sordid Condition!
Only husband there to help her
As she dies giving birth to ninth child.

Grover felt a fire burn inside him as the full impact of the article sunk in. Slowly at first, it began to flare and it was held back by nothing but a thin firebreak. He went immediately to the newspaper editor. He strode in and confronted the man. He wanted to grab him by the shirt collar, but he held himself in check.

"How do you think George feels now, Mr. Goddard? It wasn't bad enough to lose his wife! He had no money—how could he get a doctor? This article is outrageous!" He managed to gain some small control over his temper, then said vehemently, *"You need to print an apology."*

The editor answered in a voice that sounded more as if boredom had set in than that he was defending himself. "That's the way it was, Grover. There should have been a doctor at that house. And I won't apologize for printing the truth."

Grover seldom came to this level of anger, and usually, he did his best to avoid this kind of confrontation. "Well, you can cancel my subscription! We don't need a paper if you can't understand that none of us has any money. We do the best we can!"

Both men felt strongly that they were in the right, and their parting that day became permanent.

Chapter 21

Ray of Hope

The previous autumn there had been a township election. Counties were taking over the roads from the townships, so there was no longer a need for a township road commissioner. Township officers were doing their work and being paid with IOU's that were to be paid back when tax money became available. The township treasurer's only wage was the fees collected when taxes were paid. Grover had reluctantly accepted the office of township treasurer, agreeing that someone had to do it.

In early March, the manager of the Antrim Iron Company paid an unexpected visit to Grover and Grace. "We've sold some lumber and will pay our taxes, but we won't pay a four percent fee. If you collect the taxes for one percent we'll pay you, otherwise, we'll pay the county."

The deadline of February 1st required only a one per cent fee. If taxes were paid before March 15th, the collection fee was four percent. If taxes were not paid by March 15, they were considered overdue, and the delinquency was turned over to the county, where the collection fee was four percent. Antrim Iron Company owned a lot of land. The bookwork would have to be completed before the accounts went to the county on March 15, but any income at all would give the family a lift. There wasn't much they could do, so Grover agreed to collect the taxes for one percent. Grace put in long hours working on it, day after day, but by March 15th the work was done and the township treasurer received his fees. There was money for food, a few clothes and seeds for spring planting.

Unfortunately, the income was not enough to avoid one more financial crisis.

There were small mortgages on both Tuden's forty acres and Grover and Grace's eighty acres. Now there was a serious danger of foreclosure. They had to come up with enough money to pay off those mortgages. One possible source was the sale of Tuden's lake. Nobody wanted to buy a farm in this area, but someone might buy the lake. The boys loved it there. They often paddled Tuden's old boat to a submerged log and watched a school of bass swim into the deep water and out of sight. They seldom caught a fish, but loved trying just the same.

"Ma, I sure don't want to sell that lake." Grover stroked the stubble on his chin as he sat drinking coffee one day after dinner. "Tuden loved it and it's where the boys spend all their free time. But if we don't pay the mortgages, we won't have the lake or our place!"

"I know, Dad. I wish there were another way, but I surely can't think of one."

With some tax money in the treasury, township officers could now collect their back pay. It was sufficient reason to hold a rare township board meeting. At the meeting Grover told the other officers he was willing to sell his father's forty acres on the lake for $1000."

One of the men, Henry Neher, said his brother John might be interested. John was getting offers for his farm on the outskirts of Chicago almost monthly from the operator of a riding stable, and was considering retiring to northern Michigan.

Just before Memorial Day, John Neher came to look at Tuden's place. Grover paddled the double-ended wooden boat Tuden had made, taking the potential buyer around the lake. He pointed out the bubbling springs in the southeast corner of the lake, almost hidden by an overhanging cedar tree. Paddling slowly, Grover noted the water was clear and cold enough to drink. Last of all, they went to the southwest corner of the lake where John was excited by the large school of bass.

John's brother had told him that Grover would sell the place for $1000, but John knew the desperate financial straits that plagued the area and wondered if he might get it for less. Just before leaving, John made Grover an offer. "I don't know when I'll sell my farm in Illinois. I could give you $500 cash if you want to sell it now."

With mortgages overdue, Grover was in no position to bargain. He gazed out at the pristine lake with the few old cedars, and recalled good times he'd had there. His thoughts came to the boys, who thought up endless ways to enjoy the small quiet lake. He pulled on his ear slowly, then turned and gazed out toward the hill. He wished he weren't having this conversation. His heart sunk at the thought of doing what he knew he had to do. When would another buyer come along? No one had cash like that these days. John's offer would barely cover the mortgages, but it was enough to save the Southwells from foreclosure.

"I guess I don't see how I can turn it down, John."

"All right. Deal then?" John put out his hand. Grover bit his lip and somehow managed to mumble agreement. For five hundred dollars, Tuden's dream home became John Neher's retirement home.

Having sold a considerable portion of their pig iron and some of their best lumber, Antrim Iron Company began to repair and update their plant in Antrim. They planned to resume production as soon as possible. The railroad tracks, steam locomotives, and railway cars, after laying idle for years needed extensive repair.

Trucks were considerably bigger and better than when Gorham camp operated, and the managers of Antrim Iron Company decided to haul their logs and four-foot wood to Antrim by this modern method.

The steam locomotive and railway cars, while still used at the complex, no longer ran to the logging camps, and a new era was ushered in.

In a radical departure from the traditional logging camp, Russell and Acil Wood formed a partnership, which they named "Wood Brothers." They negotiated a contract with Antrim to cut and deliver the logs and four-foot wood to Antrim. Men were traveling any distance to find work. Russell and Acil were confident the help they needed would be readily available.

The newly formed partnership bought new Chevrolet trucks and semis to haul the logs. They contracted hauling the four-foot wood to local residents.

The Wood Brothers bought a D-4 caterpillar tractor fitted with a bulldozer and made trails, (which they called roads) so logs only had to be skidded a short distance.

Sawyers and woodchoppers were hired. The Wood Brothers bought good horses and wanted good teamsters.

Acil Wood stopped by the Southwell farm on Memorial Day to offer Grover a job driving horses. The $30 a month pay was in addition to room and board. Wood Brothers were building a few small shanties modeled after the old logging camps.

Acil said that enough logs were already cut so Grover could start the next day. They were working in Rapid River Township, about six miles from where the Southwell family lived. Acil spoke optimistically of the future. He and his brother expected to keep the Antrim Iron Company supplied with logs and wood. He was confident Grover would have work with them for a number of years. Grover promised to discuss the offer with Grace and get back to Acil.

Acil was impatient. "The horses are at camp and we need a teamster now."

Grover looked at Grace, trying to read her thoughts, then promised, "I'll let you know tomorrow." Grace didn't want Grover to be away from the family, but they needed money desperately!

Finally, Grover concluded, "I need to go and work for a while. Brown is capable of handling the horses here. He and White can put up the hay this summer." It was a terribly low wage but the only job available. Grover left early the next morning and began to work for Wood Brothers.

"We pay the end of the month," Acil told Grover as they walked to the barn. "The logs have to be in Antrim before we're paid." No more was said. Grover harnessed the horses, selected the tools he needed, and began skidding logs.

June was an unusually hot month. An occasional thundershower forced the crew to the barn temporarily. Grover worked through light rains but when the weather was too bad for the horses, they quit early.

When June 30, arrived, Grover was given a check for $22. He looked at the check and protested, "You told me $30 a month, Acil. You're eight dollars short."

Acil spoke sharply, "You didn't work a full month! Some days you quit early, and once it rained all day!" Grover's mouth dropped open. He had done the job he'd been hired for, but this employer chose to charge him for the bad weather. He should have known. He shoved the check into his pocket, and said, "Well, Acil, if that's the way you pay, I can do without this job." He turned on his heel and strode away.

Grover knew his decision about the job with the Wood Brothers would cost him, but he didn't like to have honest, hard work go unappreciated. He'd had enough of that at Hackney's. Somehow, he'd have to find a way to keep food on the table.

In mid-September, Grace mentioned the following two weeks were potato vacation at school. Grover said, "You know, Grace, we're living, but we aren't making any progress with the farm. It looks like we'll have to help harvest someone else's potatoes." For two weeks the family picked up potatoes near Elmira, earning 3 cents a bushel.

On Saturday morning, the first week in October, Grover told his older sons, "Let's dig our potatoes and get them in the cellar, then we'll go hunting."

Brown and White were excited for the first hunt of the year. People usually did not hunt until the leaves had fallen, but Grover wanted to provide a bit of recreation for the boys, who had worked hard all summer. He'd spent some of their scarce funds on ammunition, buying a box of cartridges for the rifle from Harry Allett, a box of 410-gauge shells, and a box of 10-gauge shells for Tuden's double barrel.

When Grace called them to dinner, the potatoes were already in the cellar and the boys were hurrying Grover to get started on the hunt. "You'll want your dinner," Grover told them, "We'll be taking a pretty good walk."

When dinner was over, Grover assigned the guns. He carried the heavy 10 gauge, double-barreled shotgun and Brown carried the rifle. White was pleased to have the trusty 410 shotgun all to himself.

Grover wanted to take the boys to an area they hadn't hunted before. When the guns were loaded, and safe handling of their guns carefully discussed, he told them. "We'll walk down around Farrer Lake and see what we can kick up. That should be a good place for birds." Walking past the mailbox on the way to Farrer Lake, they put the mail in Brown's game bag since they probably would not come back that way. The hunt was completely unsuccessful. They heard a few partridges thunder up, but since the trees were covered with leaves, they hadn't been able to see a thing

Grover offered another diversion. "It doesn't look like we'll get any meat today," he told the boys. "Let's go past the cranberry marsh."

The cranberry marsh was at the bottom of a hill on a gravel road, about a half-mile from their mailbox. They walked into the marsh holding their guns high to keep them dry, while parting the brush looking for cranberries. They found a few but not many.

Suddenly they heard a voice. "What you hunting, boys?" Charlie Hicking, the game warden, had coasted his vehicle quietly down the long hill looking for whoever might be opening the hunting season a couple weeks before the law allowed. He had observed the three guns waving above the cranberry bushes and chuckled to himself.

Grover quickly answered, "Cranberries."

Small game season wouldn't be open for another two weeks and deer season was a month and a half away. Charlie had been looking for a neighbor who had a reputation for selling deer when he coasted down the hill. There in the cranberry marsh were three men holding their guns high. It was an easy catch.

When the three reached the road, Charlie checked their guns, unloaded them, and noticed the game bag. The bulging bag obviously spelled a successful hunt.

When asked what they had killed that day, Grover replied, "Nothing."

Charlie walked casually over beside Brown, reached in the game bag, and pulled out the newspaper. A faint smile crossed his face. Charlie then noted the two shotguns without comment, but looked sharply at Grover as he unloaded the deer rifle. "Pretty early for that Grover," he commented.

Grover explained that these were the only three weapons they had. They hadn't been looking for any specific animal.

Charlie loaded the boys and guns in his back seat, with Grover seated beside him, then drove toward Kalkaska, the county seat. The route took them past Grover's mailbox, a half-mile from the Southwell's home.

Charlie stopped by the mailbox and broke the tense silence. "Grover you know it isn't worth it, any game you might kill isn't worth the chance you take."

Grover was careful in his reply. "I know it was the wrong thing to do, but we haven't been able to give the boys any kind of recreation all summer. I told them this morning that if they worked hard, when we finished digging the potatoes we would go hunting. This is the way it ended."

Charlie took a book from the glove compartment, detailed the offense, had Grover and each of the boys sign, then said, "Grover, I can let you go this time. But if I catch you again, I'll have to spank you twice."

Grover winced at the expression, but having received only a warning, the grateful father and his two sons headed toward home. There would be no more hunting. Their guns lay on Charlie's back seat and they certainly couldn't afford to replace them. Charlie drove about 20 feet before he stopped and called out. "You better take your guns."

Grover thanked Charlie for his consideration and assured him there would be no need for the double spanking.

It was a lesson they all would remember. Grover wondered if Charlie bent the law to let them off, or decided against prosecuting because the county would have to feed his family if Grover were locked up. They would never know, but were especially grateful they still had weapons with which to hunt when the season opened.

Grover got up early and was busily cutting stove wood when the timber cruiser for Antrim Iron Company, Tom, appeared with his horse and buggy one morning. Tom didn't come around as much, now that Grace's cookie jar was empty. Today he had a message to deliver. "The company wants to salvage the maple that's blown down. They don't care about the hemlocks, but they want to save the maple."

Grover knew there was more income from the hemlock than the hardwood. "We'll pick up what we can, but we'll take the hemlock as we go."

Tom didn't think that was a problem. It was what they had done before.

Grover struggled through the winter with Ginger and old Pearl. It was tough skidding logs with the team he had. Ginger was really a great mare but old Pearl's days of heavy work were over. Still, Grover and the Fuzzy Brothers had a small income through the winter.

In early spring of 1935, with very little money, Grover found a possibility to buy another horse.

A horse dealer was bringing western cow ponies through the area for sale to the farmers. They were smaller than the draft horses commonly being used but at least they were horses. Grover picked out a little bay mare he named Gyp, well broken for saddle but not for a harness. Grover worked with her and eventually Gyp became a decent partner for Ginger.

When the snow had nearly melted, Doc Jamison, the cherry orchard owner, bought a registered Percheron stallion and took him through the northern Michigan area to any farm where the owner wished to raise a colt.

Grover could see his dream coming true. Ginger was a little excitable, but a good mare. She could bear colts, Grover could raise and train them and have the team he so longed for.

The first colt, a beautiful dappled gray filly, was born the following spring. Grover loved the dapples and named his treasured colt Roxie. A full brother joined Roxie two years later. This colt, too, was a dappled gray and Grover named him Rock. His dream of raising his team of colts was slowly but surely coming true.

Chapter 22

Challenges and Hardships

With some wages, every phase of life gradually grew more bearable. The extreme poverty was behind them, but for Grover and Grace every need was still pressing. Clothing, long worn out, needed to be replaced. They had depleted everything in the pantry. Ever so slowly, the most critical needs were met and the pressure, under which they had fought to survive, began to ease.

Grover decided to run for Coldsprings Township Supervisor in the biannual election in the autumn of 1935. Supervisors from the twelve organized townships served as the governing board of the county. Grover felt Coldsprings Township needed stronger representation. Each year the supervisors met in Kalkaska for approximately two weeks while they conducted the county's business. The extra income paid to supervisors also would be welcome. He ran uncontested and was able to represent Coldsprings Township at the annual board meetings in Kalkaska.

Property assessments also fell under Grover's area of responsibility as supervisor. People were building new houses throughout the township. Manistee Lake was especially attractive to those who could afford a summer cottage. These assessments kept Grover busy through March and early April.

Brown and White did a much larger portion of the farm work in 1936. Grover no longer concerned himself at all with cutting and carrying in stove wood. The boys usually pumped and carried water for Grace. Occasionally she became impatient with Harold and Rex as they continued to disagree about which one of them had last filled the reservoir and water pail. Many times, she found it easier to pump it herself!

The very best virgin hardwood in Antrim Iron Company's vast holdings lay in section 13 in Coldsprings Township. The road to Twin Lakes curved through this timber. Driving on Twin Lake Road, which meandered between maple trees that stood like sentinels, Grover remembered the pine forest he had walked through with Tuden. The sun never penetrated the treetops. This, too, was reminiscent of the pine forest, which had sheltered the upper Manistee River not too many years earlier. Grover pointed out to his sons the various species of the huge hardwood trees, and began to think about what might be done to save them. This forest was rapidly disappearing, too. Surely there was some way to preserve this majestic tract for posterity.

Near Grayling, Colonel Hartwick's widow had bequeathed Hartwick Pines to the State of Michigan to maintain as a park.[8] The white pines that grew there would be saved for future generations to appreciate and experience. Grover envisioned a similar park on the shore of Twin Lakes where the beautiful hardwood forest might be preserved.

He discussed it with his family. "Twenty-five years ago, it seemed the virgin timber was inexhaustible, but it's now it's almost gone. When I first came here, it was everywhere. If we don't do something, there won't be a single big tree left."

---

[8] At this time, Hartwick's pines were estimated too small to cut.

When the board of supervisors convened for their annual meeting Grover introduced a petition. It called on the state of Michigan to buy a quarter section (160 acres) of the best hardwood forest on the shore of Big Twin Lake. He explained the urgency.

"The forests in Rapid River Township are nearly gone. Coldsprings Township holds the only large area of virgin hardwood that remains in the Lower Peninsula, as far as I know. There is no doubt that Antrim Iron Company will begin cutting there—and soon. I urge you men to seriously consider this purchase so our children won't be deprived of the sight of the forest."

A local schoolteacher and writer, Cecil Bailey, also took an interest in preserving the remnant of forest. He wrote articles about it in the local paper. He wrote to University of Michigan Departments of Botany, Zoology, Forestry and Conservation. He engendered their support and tentative approval of the Department of Conservation, who came and inspected the tract, and told Cecil of their approval. They made a favorable report to the Lansing office. The only thing remaining was to obtain legislative support.

One year later, when the annual meeting of the county board of supervisors met, Grover immediately questioned what action the state had taken on the petition to purchase the land by Big Twin Lake.

John Gillette, the supervisor from Clearwater Township who was chairman of the board, admitted, "Nothing's been done."

The legislators knew all about Hartwick Pines State Park. They also knew Major Hartwick's widow, Karen, had donated the park to the State. They agreed that Hartwick Pines State Park was nice, but that it had been a gift. The county supervisors were not offering the land as a gift; they were asking the state to buy it. Their request had been discussed and while the majority of legislators agreed that saving a portion of the hardwood forest was important, the State did not have money for non-essential projects. Pos-

Giant Elms with over 4000 board feet in two bottom logs

sibly, Antrim Iron Company could be prevailed upon to donate the quarter section in question.

Antrim Iron Company's response was swift and unsentimental. They renewed the Wood Brothers contract with instructions to cut the timber on section 13 as soon as possible. Any thought of donating the land containing the best of their timber for a park was completely rejected. With State legislators moving so slowly, the timber would be removed before any action could be taken to preserve it.

In the spring of 1937 Brown graduated from High school and found temporary employment helping a plumber in Grand Rapids, some 150 miles to the south. Things were changing.

Grover and Grace marveled that almost no one seemed to understand that the timber, which had played such a major role in the development of the area, would soon be nothing more than a memory. The fate of the last tract of virgin timber was looked upon only as a progression of the changing landscape.

Before summer ended, the beautiful forest near Twin Lake that Grover and others had tried so hard to save was transformed into a wasteland of broken saplings and remnants of fallen trees. When section 13 had been harvested, the lumberjacks moved to section 21, northwest of Manistee Lake. The largest log ever felled in the area was an elm. This giant elm was cut into 16-foot logs. The bottom log scaled almost 2,100 board feet and the second log almost 2,000. The two logs combined contained more than 4,000 board feet. Word of the unusual tree quickly spread, and many people came to take pictures before the logs were moved.

Grover and the Fuzzy Brothers continued to salvage logs and four-foot wood from section 17 but all of them knew their years of winter employment were just about over.

In the spring of 1938, Roxie was three years old. Grover happily placed the harness on the colt he had wanted for so many years, and hitched her beside her mother. Ginger no longer was required to pull more than half the load. Roxie was easily able to do her fair share.

Gyp, the cow pony, a valuable addition when she was needed, could be sold as a well trained little draft horse.

In May White graduated from high school and worked through the summer on a dairy farm near home.

When both older boys had graduated from high school, Grace sought medical attention for a goiter, which had bothered her for several years and now interfered with her breathing. Dr. Sargent diagnosed the ailment and advised that her goiter could not be treated medically; it would have to be removed surgically. The surgery was completed successfully in the hospital in Petoskey, and Grace returned home to care for the family. The operation, however, weakened her severely.

The family's income continued to inch up and make up for the effects of years with virtually none. Almost all the level land on their farm was cleared of stumps and brush. With Roxie in the harness, Grover had a good team of horses. He would be able to farm more land if he had it.

Louie Engmark, the owner of the farm Grover and Grace rented when they were first married, had died. His wife, Beatrice, had no source of income and their land was about to be sold to pay for back taxes.

The Engmark's eighty acres would be valuable to the Southwells. It included two large cleared fields available for planting crops. The swamp provided cedar for fence posts. Rapid River, though small, flowed through the swamp providing drinking water for cattle in the pasture. The buildings were of no value. The house had burned and the barn roof collapsed under the weight of snow. Grover and Grace paid Mrs. Engmark one hundred dollars for a quit claim deed, then paid her back taxes and acquired clear title to the property.

Food spoilage was always a problem, even with the swing shelf in the cellar. Grace suggested Grover use some of the old boards from the Engmark barn to build an icehouse. An icebox (refrigerator) would save food and enable her to provide a variety of specialties she could not otherwise prepare in summer.

Whenever he could spare a day from the farm-work, Grover tore down what was left of the Engmark barn, salvaged the lumber, and built an icehouse. The sides were boarded inside and out over two by four studs, and the gap filled with sawdust gathered from an abandoned sawmill. An extra load of sawdust would cover the ice once the icehouse was filled.

By Christmas, Croy Lake, which was less than a mile from the Southwell's, was covered with 12 inches of clear blue ice. Brown and White, who were unemployed, helped Grover cut ice from Croy Lake and fill the icehouse. Cracks between the ice cakes were

Bryce with Chum and pet Rhode Island hen

packed with sawdust and a thin layer of sawdust covered each layer of ice so the cakes would not freeze together.

Grover was able to buy a used icebox in Mancelona since most town people had upgraded to electric refrigerators. The icebox was a great help to Grace, and was a pleasure for the family. The cold milk tasted wonderful! The icebox also meant that Grace had to go down the cellar stairs to the swing shelf far less often.

Young Bryce was always accompanied on his walk to the Davis school by their collie, Chum. Wherever Bryce was, Chum was never far away. Chum, like Mary's lamb, was not allowed at school. Each morning Chum walked a half-mile with Bryce before Bryce sent him home. Then each afternoon around 3:30 Chum left the house. When Bryce entered the mountain road on his return from school, Chum lay waiting for him. No one ever knew how the dog could tell when it was time to meet Bryce, but it was apparently as natural to him as it is for geese to know when to fly south.

Grace was still not strong when Bryce became ill in November 1939.

Usually Bryce ate numerous pancakes and as much sausage as he was allowed but on this Friday morning he said he "just wasn't hungry."

Grace felt his forehead and noted it was unusually warm. Bryce insisted he was not sick and that he was able to attend school as usual, but Grace was still concerned. She decided he should stay home.

The following morning, Bryce was much worse, so Grover drove to Kalkaska and asked Dr. Sargent to come check their son.

When Dr. Sargent arrived late that afternoon, Bryce's temperature was 106 degrees. The doctor examined Bryce carefully, and then told the anxious parents. "The boy has a serious case of pneumonia. There is very little chance that he will live but there's a new drug available at hospitals, which might help him. I'll give you a prescription for Sulfa, but the nearest place it's available is the hospital in Grayling."

Grace Humerickhouse, Bryce's teacher, who had stopped by after school that evening to check on the health of her student, was waiting also for the doctor's diagnosis. She had recently purchased a new Ford V8 coupe and offered, "Take my car, it will be quicker."

Harold drove to the hospital in Grayling, and was back in what was probably record time. However, either the drug was administered too late or it was not effective.

Dr. Sargent and his associate, Dr. Inman, stopped the next morning to check Bryce's condition. They could offer no hope. Bryce died that afternoon, only 36 hours after the doctor was first called.

The grieving parents were numb as they went through the next hours and days, struggling to cope with the devastation that losing their young boy brought to their hearts. The shock on Grace's already weakened body delayed her recovery for a long time. The months dragged on heavily for Grover, just as they did for his wife.

Rex found work with a large farmer and farm equipment dealer in the winter of 1939–40 and later moved on to Detroit where he completed his radio schooling and obtained his commercial radio license.

The nation still was plagued with a very high unemployment rate, but Harold found work in Lansing driving a delivery truck in the spring of 1940.

It was gratifying for Grover and Grace that their two older sons now had work, but they had lost their three sons in less than a year. That year and the next were years of constant readjustments and adaptations. They coped as well as they were able. They had each other and Jesus.

Chapter 23

. . . .

Adjustment

The farm income was now sufficient to meet Grover and Grace's needs after years of struggle to make ends meet. They both missed the boys, yet enjoyed the quiet evenings together. Once again Grover took his mandolin from its case, bought a new set of strings, and sang with Grace in the evenings.

Just before sunset one evening, Grace looked across the road where virgin maple trees still stood, and noted the brilliant red, yellow and gold leaves of autumn. "We've enjoyed that scene for many years, Grover. We'll miss the panorama of colors in autumn and the light green shades of newly opening leaves in the spring." After a pause, she added, "In early dawn, the silhouettes of those trees enabled me to imagine many things!"

Soon the colors faded, and clean white snow again blanketed field and forest. Grover was happy to have electricity to pump water for the growing herd of cattle and safe, bright lights in the barn. He no longer needed to carry the dim kerosene lantern from place to place while he fed the livestock and milked the cows.

Both Grace and Grover appreciated lights in the house, thanks to electric lines installed in 1941. Even though an Alladin lamp with it's mantle had replaced the dim yellow glow of the kerosene lamp, electric lights were brighter yet and far more convenient and safe.

Grace had time now to prepare special treats for her husband. He never tired of her sugar cookies. She served meat every day and marveled that the family had lived for years when the only meat available was the occasional rabbit or partridge Harold and Rex had brought from the woods.

When Thanksgiving came, Grace prepared a traditional Thanksgiving dinner. Harold and his wife Marie came and shared the meal with his parents. Marie brought the chocolate-fudge cake that was her specialty. Less than two weeks later, the nation went into shock when the Japanese bombed Honolulu.

Barely two decades had passed since the end of World War I. Grover and Grace's generation had shared the early patriotic fervor and later the sorrow, as friends and neighbors died in Europe.

The current war in Europe had been raging for two years and the Japanese had conquered much of East Asia. Tension had arisen between Japan and the United States because of the United States' presence in the Philippine Islands. But the attack on Hawaii shocked the entire nation.

Patriotic fervor again swept the United States. Franklin Roosevelt called December 7, a day of "Infamy." Congress declared war on Japan. For Grover and Grace and their entire generation, it was a time of sorrow, knowing many of their children would die in the service of their country.

Germany and Italy joined Japan in war against the United States and its allies. Citizens of the United States were galvanized into action as the completely unprepared nation mounted its defense. Newly conscripted soldiers trained with wooden rifles because there were insufficient real weapons. Japanese submarines made minor attacks on the coast of California, and a German submarine made a similar attack on the Atlantic Coast. Enemy submarines were sinking many United States merchant ships. Cities on both coasts turned off their outside lights at night to prevent merchant ships from being so easily seen.

The nation turned its entire production capacity to the war effort. Factories that once produced automobiles built jeeps, trucks, tanks, and airplanes for the military.

The entire population began saving anything that could be recycled to supply needed raw materials. Nylon stockings, which had only recently entered the market, were no longer available as nylon was used to make parachutes. Meat and butter were rationed, as were gasoline and shoes.

Grover and Grace were thankful they had recently received electricity to provide lights and pump their water, but any other electric convenience would not be available until the war was won.

The Antrim Iron Company suddenly had a market for everything they could produce. The pig iron, which had once clogged the railroad siding, was shipped as soon as it was cast. Alcohol and acetate from the chemical plant were equally in demand. Lumber could be sold before it even had time to dry.

Wood Brothers and the locals who had purchased old trucks were forced to make repairs to keep the equipment operating. Grover and the Fuzzy Brothers were encouraged by the Company to cut and skid as much timber as possible in what would be their last year working in section 17.

When the snow was nearly gone in the spring of 1942, Leon Keil, who drove the caterpillar tractor for Wood Brothers, began bulldozing roads through the section which had for so long been the private domain of Grover and his little crew of lumberjacks.

Grace grew increasingly restive, unable to relax. During winter she cleaned house and re-cleaned it. She had made special meals for Grover and attempted to be pleasant company, but now was impatient to begin planting the garden.

She busied herself with every task imaginable. The garden was kept completely clean from any weed. She walked to the field to help Grover work in the hay. In spite of her husband's protests, Grace could not rest. Grover had no idea what he could do to help the wife he loved to relax. It was obvious her body was incapable of the obsessive strain that she was putting herself under. Finally, he persuaded her to go with him to the doctor.

Dr. Sargent found no physical problem, but Grace's unrest was readily apparent. The doctor finally told Grover, "You'll have to get her off the farm. She'll work herself to death!" Grover drove home slowly. "Ma, see if you can't slow down a little. You can come to the field, but you just can't continue to do the heavy work."

Grover watched as his wife grew more and more haggard. He realized he must heed the doctor's advice. He sent a letter to their oldest son, now living in the city. "Brown," he wrote, "We have to leave the farm. Your mother is working herself into her grave. If you want to take over the farm, come on home. We'll work something out."

Brown, now married, was not happy in the city and welcomed the opportunity to return to the farm. He and his wife drove to Mancelona to be sure Grover's offer was real. They learned the change was necessary for his mother, and promised to return the next weekend to take over his parents' farm.

Grover started working in the Kalkaska County Garage and bought a small house within the village limits of Kalkaska. The change in occupation was not what he would have chosen, but Grover refused to look over his shoulder. He would try to appreciate his new job, which enabled him to provide a more relaxed life for Grace. That surely made the change worthwhile.

The wrench of leaving the farm they had worked so many years to develop was less severe because it was in the hands of their son. Brown loved horses. That satisfied Grover's greatest concern. Rock and Roxie deserved the best. Brown would give them both love and care. The horses would return the favor.

They lived only ten miles from the farm and could visit often. The garden was always larger than they really needed. Now the two families could share its bounty.

What had appeared to be the solution to Grace's problem only aggravated her unrest. While the strain on her body was alleviated and she regained her strength, she remained extremely unhappy. The enforced idleness through the war years was almost more than Grace could bear.

Grover's work of greasing, changing oil, and making minor repairs to the county's aging trucks kept him busy, but at least once a week they drove to the farm where Grace almost immediately headed for the garden. She had always loved tending the garden, and now it gave her an outlet for emotional stress. Moreover, the plants flourished under her care.

Gradually the tides of war turned in favor of the United States and her allies. As people grew confident that the war would eventually be won, relief was tempered by ever-increasing casualty lists. The generation that had fought World War I, "The war to end all wars," again grieved at the loss of so many of their children. In the last year of the war, production finally began to equal the needs of the citizens and rationing gradually ceased.

When the struggle with Japan finally came to an end with the signing of that nation's surrender on the battleship U.S.S. Missouri, families looked eagerly to the return of their sons and began to plan for the future.

Antrim Iron Company closed the entire complex and sold all their land for a reasonable price, but retained the mineral rights. They had arranged to have some test wells drilled for oil and the results were promising. By selling the land and retaining mineral rights, they eliminated their property taxes.

Harold purchased 80 acres from Bruce Williams (Uncle Charlie's son) and Rex, who returned from service in the spring of 1946, purchased another 80 acres from Bruce's brother, Fred. Additionally Harold and Rex purchased 480 acres of land on section 17 and began to farm together. Harold and Rex intended to clear stumps and brush from the land on section 17 and add it to the Southwell farm. Farmers were prospering now that the war was over. Harold and Rex had plans for a much larger operation.

Two years later, Harold and Rex urged their parents to return to the farm. Grover's knowledge of building would be helpful to them. Their sons were confident the income would be sufficient for the three families.

In January of 1949 Cecil Bailey, who had been teaching the Barnhart School about six miles from the Southwell farm, died suddenly of a heart attack. There was no one to teach for the remainder of the school year. A school board member asked Grace, "You taught school a number of years ago, Grace. Could you come and finish the school year for us?"

Grace eagerly agreed. The thought of teaching children again after the years of enforced idleness gave her new purpose, although Grover was reluctant to see his wife return to work. However, Grover also loved children and their need for a teacher took precedence. Grace could finish the year if she wished.

She enjoyed the work and her contact with the children immensely. When one poor family of children was being ridiculed by some of the others, she became their champion.

When the warmth of summer finished her commitment, Grace was offered a contract for the following year. Grover was not happy about the suggestion and Grace, not wanting to offend her husband who had cared for her so long, declined.

In the winter of 1949–50, Grover began to experience severe shortages of breath on cold mornings. Although he shielded his mouth with a mitten, it was difficult to walk to the barn in sub-zero weather. Warm April days alleviated Grover's problem temporarily, but then he experienced chest pains while doing heavy physical labor. He was not willing to stop work when there was so much to do. Brown and White needed adequate buildings for their livestock.

Finally, in midsummer, Grover told Grace about his physical problems and Grace insisted they see a doctor immediately. The diagnosis was not encouraging. "It's angina, Grover." Dr. Sargent said. "I can give you some nitroglycerine tablets to help, but the pain's a warning to you to quit the heavy work or Grace will be a widow!"

It was a long slow drive home from Dr. Sargent's office in Kalkaska. Grover knew the farm was not ready to support three families. Everything the couple owned was wrapped up in the farm. The young team of horses was valuable, but Brown used them every day. For the first time since the worst of the depression, Grover saw no hope for the future. He had always worked through any problem but now he was not able to work.

Grace was lost in thought also. She would not wound her husband's pride, but she had a plan. "Grover, my health is good now. Teaching school was always a pleasure for me. Country schools are begging for teachers. Let me apply for a job this winter."

Could a man sit at home while his wife worked? Such a thought was foreign to Grover. He reached for his wife's hand, which was resting on his shoulder. "I don't know, Ma," Grover spoke slowly. "I haven't thought of anything else, but I really don't want you to have to support me."

No more was said as Grace prepared supper. A good evening meal, complete with a cup of coffee (unusual in the evening) and a couple sugar cookies with "bugs" (raisins), enlivened Grover's spirit somewhat.

He picked up his old mandolin, carefully tuned a string, and played "Daisies Won't Tell," as they sang the old song together.

Grace again put her hand on her husband's shoulder. "I'd really like to teach this winter, Grover. I'd have to get my teaching certificate renewed to teach a full year, but there is time if I apply now. Maybe next year you'll be stronger."

When Grover woke up with severe pain in his chest and took a second nitroglycerine tablet, he looked at his wife dejectedly. "It looks like you might have to teach, Ma."

Grace's request for a teaching certificate was granted. It was a temporary certificate with the added requirement of six hours of college credits each year—or until she had a degree—for continued certification. She signed a contract to teach the Birgy School. The school was located twenty miles south of the couple's home, but there was a small cottage beside the school that they could rent.

Grace was pleased both for the opportunity to take care of finances, and to work with children again. She would deal with the issue of college credits next summer.

Grover, who was convinced now that he had to avoid heavy work, slowly loaded stove wood into a two-wheel trailer. Together he and Grace drove to the Birgy School and piled the wood near the little house where they would live during the winter.

Each Friday when school was dismissed, Grover and Grace returned to their farm, filled their trailer with more stove wood, and drove it back to the little cottage beside the Birgy School on Monday morning. Grover enjoyed handling the wood, but he had to take more and more nitroglycerine pills.

He turned to cooking and housework. What had been Grace's domain was strange to him, but Grover resolved to learn. Working slowly around the house never seemed to cause him a problem. He could even carry in the next day's wood without needing nitroglycerine pills, if the weather was not too cold. Dr. Sargent had warned him not to go outside in extreme cold, so when the temperature moderated in the afternoon Grover filled the wood box for the following day.

Soon Grover developed one recipe that he and his wife especially enjoyed. Grover called it Vegetable Soup. (Vegetable it was—but whether or not soup was a proper term was questionable. No crackers were needed to absorb the liquid.) The recipe contained a variety of vegetables and seasonings.

The school year passed quickly for Grace and she signed a contract for the following year, promising to attend college in the summer to obtain the required six hours of credit.

In the summer of 1951, though Grace was nearly 60 years of age, she attended Central Michigan University in Mt. Pleasant as a student, and earned the required six hours of credit. In school with mostly teen-age peers, Grace thought wryly of the similarity of the time when she attended high school. Then she had felt somewhat embarrassed, studying with younger students. Here Grace was not alone. There may not have been another classmate who was sixty years of age, but there were many adults. Grace kept very busy and finished the term with a "B" in each subject.

Grover, at home alone while his wife taught school, thoroughly enjoyed Brown and White's children. He found countless ways to amuse them, one of which was making little parachutes and fastening small weights to the cords. The children could wrap the strings around the shroud and throw the parachute into the air. Invariably, the weight straightened the cords as the little parachute slowly drifted back to earth. Grover made pistols for the children from pieces of wood and rubber bands cut from an old inner tube he found.

His most elaborate toy was a little wooden man, hinged at every joint. He placed a board on his knee and stood the little man on the board. When Grover rubbed the board, the little man danced. The children never tired of Grover's companionship.

During the summer, he was able to cut enough stove wood for his and Grace's use the following winter. The pain in his chest seemed to be less and less troublesome. Grover was becoming hopeful he could resume a normal workload.

Chapter 24

Completion

In June of 1952, Grover began drawing Social Security. He said, "There are only two birthdays that mean anything, when you're 21, and when you're 62."

Though his Social Security check was small, it was an increase in the family income. He and Grace carefully laid aside payments to be able to buy a better car. Both had always wanted to travel. With a good automobile and the extra income, they'd be able to satisfy this desire.

Brown and White were at the point where a decision had to be made about the farm. They were not earning enough to continue as they were. They decided to figuratively put all their eggs in one basket, so they borrowed heavily to buy expensive "Foundation Certified Seed" potatoes. They expected an exceptional income at harvest time. However, nature had other plans. They were caught with a hard freeze in August 1952. It was enough to push their farm operation over the edge.

With no way to meet their obligations, let alone support their families, Harold and Rex were forced to sell the 480 acres they had purchased on section 17. They paid their creditors and began to work in a Mancelona factory. The farm which Grover and Grace worked a lifetime to establish would never operate as a farm again.

Though Grover's angina became less of a problem, he began to have trouble with his hip. It became apparent to him that he would never again be able to support his wife financially. After several visits to the doctor, (who could find no reason for the pain in his hip), Grover decided it must be his age and struggled with increasing pain. It got to the point that he was no longer able to cut and handle stove wood. He had a propane furnace installed in their home.

Grace continued to teach at Birgy School for three more years, and returned to Central Michigan University each summer to renew her teaching certificate. She was grateful for her ability to bring in an income.

Finally in the spring of 1956, Grover's hip became so painful that he returned to the doctor. "We have to do something. This pain is getting to be more than I can take."

The doctor still puzzled over Grover's case and sent him for X-rays, which revealed his underlying problem to be prostrate cancer. The cancer had obviously existed for a long time. The pain he had suffered was caused by the cancer, which had now spread to his hip. There was no cure available. The doctor prescribed painkillers.

In 1956 Grace began teaching in the Crawford school, 8 miles from their home and was able to drive to work.

In spite of Grover's health, he and Grace still wanted to do at least some limited traveling. So they bought a used 1956 Ford in autumn of 1957, realizing that if Grover's hip continued to be more troublesome, he would soon not be able to ride.

Last photo of Grover (with Grace)

Even though he was in great pain, Grover continued to care for the house and make meals for Grace. They tried to plan for a trip while she continued teaching at the Crawford school in 1957–58. When the school year ended, they discussed what each had come to know—that they would not be able to travel and they just had to accept it.

Grover's only request was that he remain in his own home for the duration of his life. With a heavy heart, Grace cared for her failing husband throughout the summer. The pain he endured caused extreme grief to her. She could not ease his physical pain, but resolved that she would support her husband in every way that she could.

Grover grasped that his lifetime was nearly ended. One bright September morning when autumn leaves showed their brilliant colors in the sunlight, Grover called Grace to his bedside. With a faint smile and in a soft voice, Grover spoke words that would be indelibly written in the mind of his wife.

"Ma, I'm like an autumn leaf, barely hanging by the stem in the ancient tree. Some of the leaves are a golden yellow, and others a brilliant red. Some have already dropped from the tree and are being raked up and burned. I know that my stem will break soon and I'll join the ones who've already fallen. But I see someone waiting for me."

Grace felt the tears well up in her eyes, then spill over and travel down her cheeks. She looked into his eyes, once so appealing and bright. The color had faded, but she thought she saw something new in them. Gone was the restlessness, and in it's place, what was it? A peaceful look, a serenity that comforted her somehow, and brought ease to her heart.

Grover seemed to be in a philosophical state of mind. "You know, while I hang here, wavering back and forth, I think of how short the time has been since I was just a "bud" breaking out in the spring—when I was eager to see the sunshine and feel the cool raindrops. I absorbed some of the sun and rain, grew, and returned something to the tree that bore me. But you know, the nourishment was always more than I needed."

Grace didn't want to think about these things, but she knew her husband needed to express his feelings. She took his right hand in hers, and held it gently. She wiped a tear that had lingered on her chin with her other hand.

"Through the summer of my life I felt the cooling dew . . . the warm sun . . . the gentle breeze. There were times when I was whipped back and forth by strong winds; but the tree was sturdy and my stem held firmly. Occasionally a beautiful butterfly visited me. Other times, worms tried to destroy me. Even though the worms made holes and caused me to become unsightly, the tree held me fast until I was healed by the sun and cooling rain." His shoulders relaxed then.

"I know the stem is going to break free soon. I can't tell if I'll float gently to earth, or be buffeted as I fall, but I can see the One who is waiting for me. He has my name in a book, and is waiting to enfold me into the page he has prepared." He squeezed Grace's hand. "You know, Gracie, other leaves are falling into the blazing hot fire. I am so glad my name is in His book!"

The exertion of speaking such heartfelt expressions tired him, but still he went on. "And Grace, you've been there for me all this time." His feelings for his wife of so many years were so intense that he rarely spoke this way. Words were simply inadequate to portray his deep gratitude for her companionship. "Where would I have been without you?"

Grace smiled through her tears, and as she put her hand lovingly on the side of his head and pressed his cheek against hers, she whispered, "Grover, we've been blessed by the Lord. He brought us together, and he's sustained us all these years."

Clean white snow blanketed everything in mid-November. By Thanksgiving, Grover was no longer able to walk. The doctor prescribed effective painkillers to be administered by the family. With the relief this gave him, Grover was granted his desire to live out his remaining days in his own home.

Rex and his wife Evelyn lived right across the road from Grover and Grace's, and they cared for Grover through the night and helped on weekends. May Armstrong, a lifelong friend who was now widowed, helped Grace during the week. The long winter was a struggle for her as she cared for her husband and tried to keep him comfortable. Throughout his final year, friends often remarked that they received more encouragement from Grover Southwell than they felt they gave to him. As long as he was able to communicate, he refused to complain.

In mid-April 1959, at the age of 68, Grover met his Maker, and went to his real home—a beautiful home that would never be taken from him, one that he would never have to struggle to keep.

He was buried in the Coldsprings Township cemetery, next to his son and baby daughter. Late March storms had provided a thick white blanket, which still covered the ground as they laid him to rest.

Epilogue

Grace had endured the death of a baby daughter, a strong son almost 13 years of age, and now her husband. It took a heavy toll and she grieved privately and deeply. Nevertheless, in June, she roused herself from her grief. She began to focus on what she might yet do with her life, and determined that she needed to keep busy. Unfortunately, as always, she faced financial need. Of course, she never dreamed that she would live thirty years longer than her husband.

Once again she attended Central Michigan University through the summer, received a renewal of her teaching certificate, and taught at the Darragh School, which was only five and a half miles from her home. She no longer felt at ease driving in the winter storms, so she rented a small cottage near the school to live in through the winter. Though the cottage was not well heated and Grace was very uncomfortable, she attended college and returned to teach one more year. Finally at the age of 70, Grace said, "It's enough."

While teaching at the Darragh School, she had the chance to interact a great deal with Rex's children, Kay, Dave, Don, and Del.

Phil came later. They developed rich memories of Grace from their daily encounters. She appreciated Harold's six children, too, but they lived further away.

Grace thought it a serious flaw that Mancelona schools (where Rex's children attended) did not have a Christmas program. She remedied that oversight for her own grandchildren by giving them small parts so they could participate in the Christmas program at Darragh School.

She continued to live in her own home. She drew a small pension and health insurance from her teacher's retirement, plus a small social security pension. Her lifetime of frugal ways due to necessity served her well later in life and allowed her to be financially independent.

In the summer of 1962, Grace went with Rex and Evelyn's family on a vacation. They went around Lake Superior and on to Iowa to visit Evelyn's mother and stepfather. Returning home they came through Chicago and visited other friends. Grace would have preferred to take the trip with Grover, nevertheless she enjoyed the opportunity to experience new sights and sounds.

She did her own work around the house. Like her husband, she didn't complain, though she did occasionally say that she was lonely and longed to be reunited with Grover.

One day in midsummer 1963, Grace saw smoke rising from an old gravel pit where household castoffs, including a mattress, had been dumped. It was nearly a quarter mile from her house but she walked down with a shovel and extinguished the fire. She was always terribly afraid of fire, but the effort that day was almost too much. Granddaughter Kay remembers that they weren't allowed to ring the dinner bell at her parent's home across the road, because Grandma would likely consider it a fire alarm.

Grace's love for children never diminished and she taught the elementary Sunday school class in her church until she was well past 80 years of age. She knitted an afghan for every new baby in church. As long as she was in her own home she tended her garden, and once took the little 410-gauge shotgun and killed a woodchuck that had the audacity to eat her vegetables.

In 1978 Grace gave Rex the Ford that she and Grover had hoped to travel with. She became more dependent upon Rex and Evelyn, but their relationship remained strong and Grace contributed much to their mutual welfare and contentment.

In 1980 Harold, who lived in Flint, took Grace on a leisurely trip to Smith Creek and Bad Axe in the thumb area of Michigan, where she lived as a child. Grace was able to find their old home at Smith Creek and had a wonderful time traveling with Harold.

After three winters of staying with Rex and Evelyn in their Florida winter home, Grace preferred to stay in her own place alone, while Rex's son, Del, attended to her needs. She was exceptionally strong until the summer of 1987, when at the age of 94, she fell and broke her hip. Though the hip was successfully replaced, Grace never regained her strength and lived her last months in an assisted living facility in Kalkaska. She was a joy to those around her to the last.

In January of 1989 her wish to be reunited with Grover was granted when she quietly passed away. She was buried beside her husband and the two children who had gone before her in the pretty little Coldsprings Cemetery on the hill. The view overlooks the portion of Coldsprings Township in which she and Grover had spent most of their lives.

In one of those small twists of irony, Rex's son, Don, who resides in Chicago, purchased Tuden's acreage with Southwell Lake in the summer of 2003. Tuden's beautiful jewel on a green pillow is back in the family. Southwell children can play there once again.

Appendix |

The Model T Ford

I t was Henry Ford's goal to build an automobile affordable to most of the populace. For that reason, the car he designed would lack some refinements found on other automobiles:

    a. For starting the engine, a crank hung from under the radiator. (Only the most expensive cars had a self-starter).

    b. The car had no accelerator. A gas lever on the steering column under the right side of the steering wheel took its place.

A spark lever was under the steering wheel on the left. The timing of the spark must be slower (the piston would be further past the top of the stroke) when the engine is cranked to ensure the piston goes forward, not backward, when the gasoline is ignited. Firing too quickly caused the engine to (kick) spin the crank backward, which could, and occasionally did, cause broken arms. The spark lever was placed all the way to the top when cranking the engine.

As the speed of the engine increased, the spark lever was pulled down accordingly. The driver adjusted the location of the spark lever to balance the speed he was driving. His decision was made by the sound of the engine.

A battery was used to get spark to start the engine, as with a modern automobile. To start the car the ignition switch was turned left to connect to the battery. After the engine started running the driver turned the switch to the right and the car ran on the magneto. When the ignition switch pointed up the car was stopped.

On the fly-wheel of the engine was a row of horseshoe-shaped magnets. (The magneto) As the fly-wheel spun, these magnets provided the electricity to run the engine and also the headlights.

A small generator recharged the battery but did not provide power for other needs.

There were three pedals between the feet of the driver. The left pedal was low gear, the center pedal was reverse and the right pedal was the brake.

To the left of the driver was a lever. When the lever was pulled all the way back, the parking brake, (called the emergency brake) was on. As the lever was moved slightly ahead the car was in neutral. This is where the lever was put when the driver was using low or reverse gears. When the car was moving ahead about ten miles per hour the driver released the low gear pedal and pushed the lever on his left all the way forward, putting the car into high-gear. There was no intermediate speed.

Because of the location of this lever (emergency brake) there was no door on the driver's side of the front seat.

A handle inside the windshield matched the windshield wiper in front of the driver. The driver pushed this handle from side to side to wipe the windshield. There was no wiper on the right side of the car.

Until the late 1920's all Model T's were touring cars. Similar to today's convertible, there was plenty of fresh air. The top could be pulled up and fastened to the windshield and side curtains were available to snap on the sides of the car. There was no heater but this was not a problem in the north because snow prevented the use of the car in winter.

The gasoline tank was under the front seat. There was no fuel pump. The fuel flowed by gravity to the carburetor. If the driver wished to go up a very steep hill it was necessary to have the tank nearly full, so the level of gasoline would be higher than the carburetor.

Tire sizes at the time were indicated by the outside diameter and the tire width, viz. 30 x 3. The narrow width and high pressure (60 psi) let the tires cut deeply into soft roads.

The steering ratio (turns of steering wheel to turn of the front wheels) was very low, making it hard to hold the wheel straight when driving in rutted roads.

There was no water pump. The car depended on wind blowing through the radiator for cooling. In normal driving this was satisfactory but any extended driving at low speed caused the engine to overheat. A boiling radiator was common. This was acceptable but one must keep the radiator quite full to prevent the engine from overheating.

Appendix **II**

Antrim Iron Company

The Antrim Iron Company complex consisted of five separate, but interconnected, operations. (1) The *furnace*, which may have been modern at the turn of the century, was by 1940 what a visitor from Chicago referred to as "The year One." (2) The *retort*, which was an oven to convert wood into charcoal and pyroligneous acid. (3) The *chemical plant*, which used the acid to make alcohol, lime and other minor substances. (4) The *farm*, primarily to keep horses for use at the plant. Finally, most interesting was (5) the *sawmill* powered by a steam engine, which will be described first.

All this description is from my memory. It will be approximately correct. More than that I cannot promise.

The railroad bringing logs from the woods ran along a sizable pond (called the hot pond) possibly 30 feet wide and 200 feet long. This pond was heated by waste steam from the engine powering the mill.

All logs were dumped from the railway cars into this pond, which washed any dirt from them. The pond was kept quite full of logs and two men with hobnail boots (somewhat similar to foot-

347

ball shoes) walked on the logs carrying a long pole with both a point and hook at its end. With these they moved the logs to the end of the pond and directed them to a conveyor. The conveyor took each log up approximately 15 feet to the slanted deck from which the logs rolled to the saw.

Steam powered arms were raised and lowered by the head sawyer to allow a log to roll onto the saw carriage and keep others from coming near enough to interfere. Steam powered arms on the carriage rolled the logs as desired to prepare them to saw.

The carriage, mounted on a large steam cylinder, took the logs past the band saw as it cut off each board. The head sawyer moved the carriage ahead sawing off the board as fast as needed, and returned the carriage very quickly.

Three men rode the carriage. One man at each end of the log dogged it (fastened it to the block) to hold it in place as it went past the saw. The third man (the setter) activated another steam cylinder to push the log out the proper distance to cut off the next board. After the board fell from the saw they were carried sideways down a conveyor where saws could be raised at the discretion of the trimmer (another man) to cut off any undesirable part. Men took the boards from the end of the conveyor to where they were piled.

Any thick hardwood slab was sent to a resaw where this choice, knot-free, wood was cut into handle squares. All waste slabs and pieces went to the hog (a grinder which chewed them into small pieces) and were burned in the boiler furnishing power for the mill.

The retort was a series of ovens where the four-foot wood was cooked into charcoal and the vapors were condensed into acid.

Small steel railroad cars holding a cord of wood were pushed into the ovens with the locomotive. Heavy steel doors on the ovens were held shut with wedges driven into slots.

At the opposite end of the ovens was a passageway some 12 feet wide with similar steel doors, and across this passageway were cooling ovens with the same type doors.

When the wood was cooked (12 hours I think) men went into the passageway, knocked the pins out of the doors with sledges and the locomotive pushed the cars containing charcoal (which took fire as soon as there was oxygen) across the passageway into the cooling ovens.

Several cars of wood separated the charcoal from the locomotive. When the charcoal was in the cooling ovens a man disconnected the charcoal cars from the wood cars, and the locomotive pulled the wood cars back to be left in the cooking ovens.

Men then closed the doors on both the cooking ovens and cooling ovens and drove the retaining wedges back to seal the ovens. This did not take long but it was unbearably hot and the men referred to the job as "20 minutes of hell."

When it was nearly time to "pull retort" the other end of the cooling ovens were opened and the cars of charcoal were pulled out of the ovens by horses. This required the very best of horses. It was a severe strain to start the cars moving. Sometimes the wheels slid after being in so much heat. Because of the severe strain on the horses, after a few days of pulling retort the teams were sent to the farm to do farm work and fresh horses brought to the plant.

The furnace was called an "Open hearth furnace" and all material was carried up an elevator and dumped in the open top.

Iron ore came by rail from Iron Mountain in Michigan's Upper Peninsula and charcoal to remove oxygen from the ore was provided by the retort. Lime was also added.

A sand mold was formed for each new batch of pig iron (the name given the resulting iron). A clay ball was placed at the outlet to hold the iron until it was ready to pour. A man then broke the clay ball with a sledge and iron flowed into the mold.

A slag (glass-like substance) formed on top of the iron and when this began to flow it was diverted into a separate mold. This slag was a waste substance until someone found a use for it in the 1940's and it was all sold.

As soon as the iron was solidified, though still white hot, men with wooden shoes walked on the mold and broke the iron into pigs weighing approximately 75 pounds each. The men worked in pairs. One pried up the soft iron with a long bar and the other broke it with a sledge. Meanwhile someone with a fire hose kept sufficient water on the men's shoes to allow them to keep working.

When the iron was broken into pigs more water was used to cool them sufficiently to handle, and the pigs were taken to the railroad track to be loaded and shipped later. The sand was then reformed into a mold and the process repeated.

Retrospect

A vine covered house by the side of the road,
No children, no laughter, to grace that abode.

Weeds cover the fields where oxen once lowed,
The place was deserted, the lawn was not mowed.

I cried, "What a waste of a pioneer life
Where, for years they had struggled, a man and his wife."

"Oh no," said my friend, "Your thinking's not right.
This house, now deserted, once rang rich with life."

"The children who played on this manicured lawn
Are bonded by love, even though they've moved on."

"Then I saw an old man so feeble and frail
His fingers now tremble to open his mail."

"A body once sturdy and straight as a rail,
Now bent and distorted, the face deathly pale."

I cried, "What an end, after working long years!"
The state of that soul nearly brought me to tears.

That feeble old man then bade me come near
And spoke of the memories of those he held dear.

The family, now grown, are all happy and strong,
They are bonded by love, even though they've moved on.

—Rex Southwell

To order additional copies of

TALL TREES TALL PEOPLE

Have your credit card ready and call:

1-877-421-READ (7323)

or please visit our web site at
www.pleasantword.com

Also available at:
www.amazon.com
and
www.barnesandnoble.com.

Printed in the United States
19248LVS00003B/43-102